Belizean Sextet

Belizean Sextet

Six Tales of Adventure

Brian Babineau

Copyright © 2012 by Brian Babineau.

Library of Congress Control Number:		2012920949
ISBN:	Hardcover	978-1-4797-4638-5
	Softcover	978-1-4797-4637-8
	Ebook	978-1-4797-4639-2

All rights reserved. No part of this book may be reproduced or transmitted in any form or by any means, electronic or mechanical, including photocopying, recording, or by any information storage and retrieval system, without permission in writing from the copyright owner.

This is a work of fiction. Names, characters, places and incidents either are the product of the author's imagination or are used fictitiously, and any resemblance to any actual persons, living or dead, events, or locales is entirely coincidental.

This book was printed in the United States of America.

To order additional copies of this book, contact:
Xlibris Corporation
1-888-795-4274
www.Xlibris.com
Orders@Xlibris.com

Contents

A Letter From Grumpa 9

Shakedown In Belize 54

Encounter On King Street 103

Showdown In Belize A Sequel To Encounter On King Street 122

Armed And Dangerous 193

Paradise 224

Dedication

To Evelyn: the love of my life. Thank You

A Letter From Grumpa

Sheryl was bemused not amused when she received a brown envelope from her Grumpa postmarked Belize, Central America, with a note saying, 'here's a letter for you, kiddo,' where the return address should be. 'What's he up to now', she wondered as she slit open the envelope with her Swiss Army knife. She hadn't heard from him for months but that was so typical of their relationship which was oddly very close considering that her own father wouldn't even speak to him. He'd pop in and out of her life, sometime with a quick visit when her dad wasn't home, or a clandestine phone call or a coded email, or sometime with a postcard from a city he was visiting, and now this, an envelope containing a rather long letter judging from its bulk.

Sitting at the kitchen table, she shook and pulled the letter from the envelope until it spilled out, almost knocking the salt off the edge. 1, 2, 3, 4, 5, 6, 7 sheets of 8 ½ x11" on lined paper, front and back. Wow. Hand-written with a black ballpoint pen, pretty legible, too, she thought, for an old man, almost blushing at her irreverence because, of course, her Grumpa was old, had been as long as she had known him but he was very, very young at heart.

He had dated the letter a few days before she received it. That seemed a long time, she thought, but wasn't that what people referred to as 'snail-mail'? She smiled when she read the salutation, "Hey kiddo, whassup?" That was how her Grumpa always began his emails and postcards and that was how he began his conversation when he phoned her. "Hey kiddo, whassup?" he'd rasp, and then he'd launch into a comical and more often than not fascinating monologue about where he was and what he was doing, then abruptly stop and say, "Enough about me, what about you, what about that old man of yours, you're on the clock, ready set go!"

Just as she began to read the first sentence, she heard a car in the driveway. She got up and peeked out the kitchen window and was a little surprised to see her father getting out of their new bright-white Chevy Malibu LT v6 sports model car. She was always glad when her father came home in time for supper with her but without any hesitation she grabbed up the letter and the envelope, headed quickly upstairs to her bedroom, dropped her contraband on her computer desk, grabbed a book from the floor and flopped on her bed as if she'd been reading.

"Hey, baby, I'm home!" her father called out.

"I'm in my room, Daddy."

She listened to him mount the stairs. The door poked open and her Daddy stuck his head into her bedroom. "Everything okay?"

"Yep."

"Just reading?"

"Yep."

"Any mail?"

"There's some magazines and letters in the living room."

"O.K. I'm going to grab a beer." He started to close the door, then opened it again and half-stepped inside. "It's my turn for supper, right?"

"Yes, Daddy . . ."

"Feel like going out somewhere . . ."

"There's leftovers in the fridge. Remember the fabulous meal I cooked last night? We can make it stretch."

"You sure?"

Sheryl looked up from her book. Her Dad looked tired. His hair seemed to have turned grey overnight and there were lines on his face and bags beneath his eyes. Still, she thought, he's still cute in a goofy kind of way. She could understand why her Mom had been attracted to him. She couldn't quite understand what her Mom saw in the woman she had left him for.

"Of course I'm sure. You grab a beer and I'll be down in a little bit and fix us something to eat. Okay?"

"Yeah, sure. That's great. Thanks."

She waited a few moments till she heard the fridge being opened downstairs, the squish as the door closed, the snap of the beer cap, and then she rolled off her bed and retrieved the letter from her Grumpa. Lying belly down on her comforter, she began to read.

"Hey kid, whassup? Its Grumpa here, up to my neck in trouble as usual but this time maybe I've bit off more than I can chew. Only time will tell how this one's going to turn out.

Haven't been in touch with you for quite a while, sorry, so I'll try to catch you up to date. Let's see, the last time I saw you we were at somebody's birthday party, your dad was there, not speaking as usual, and you had a boy in tow, I remember teasing both of you, and I left shortly after that. Thought you looked real cute, by the way, but then you always do. You may be my only granddaughter, even my only grandchild, but you are far and away my favourite and always will be. Stick that in your pipe and smoke it!

Anyway I'm sure you know I've been retired for a few years and what with my pension from work and money from the government to thank me for getting so old so fast (and a bit tucked away for a rainy day) I fancied a little trip abroad and took off for Belize. Did I ever tell you about Belize? It's where I am now. It's where your Gramma and me went years ago for our much belated honeymoon and after she died I went back a few times for some fun in the sun and then I got thinking what the hell, I'm not getting any younger and just took off. Can't say I let anyone know but then who but you would care? I really should have let you know but I'm doing that now so please forgive me.

Well, the truth is I've been here a couple months and was having a ball. Met some good folks, reconnected with some Belizeans I'd met on earlier vacations, got tied up with an American drifter named Harvey Abscombe about my age. Like me he's got a limited income but you know what kiddo live within your means and you can live well in Belize.

We drifted around a bit. Stayed at the Hotel Mopan when we were in Belize City but Belize City's a place you go to to go somewhere else. Ended up on Caye Caulker, that's an island off the coast of Belize, small but cozy and prices to suit any budget. We rented a place by the month just off the beach and close to all the action and that's where what happened happened.

Ask any Belizean what the 'sea lottery' is and he'll tell you straight out. Belize fronts on the Caribbean Sea and it's only a mile or two from one of the most active drug smuggling rings anywhere in the world. Boats full of cocaine, pot, any drug you can think of pass by Belize from Mexico or to Mexico, from South America, anywhere in the Caribbean and Central America and they are hunted down by the so-called good guys and even the downright bad guys who are like pirates so what happens is if they're about to get caught they dump their load overboard, taking careful note of where they let it go. That's for future reference.

In the meantime, on certain nights of the month, fishermen all along the Caribbean corridor go out to sea and wait to win the lottery. If it happens, and it happens often enough to make it worthwhile, the fishermen haul the bundles into their boats and make for shore. Once there, they hide their loot, knowing that sooner more than later someone's going to come around asking if anyone's found something that doesn't belong to them. Somehow the two parties get together and settle on a price, American cash for the drugs, and everybody's happy. Except when the parties can't agree on a price or a third party butts in which was the case when I happened along.

Kiddo, I'd had a good day that day. Bicycled around the caye in the morning, swam at the 'split', had a good lunch with a few beers, met up with some friends, drank a little rum till the sun went down and then crashed in Harvey's and my cabana. Woke up around 4 in the morning, Harvey was snoring his head off, and went for a walk to clear my head. Nowhere in particular, just along the seashore and then up and down a few streets until I passed behind an up-scale hotel and I heard a window open, looked up and saw a backpack fly out the window, then the window closed and a few seconds later I heard gun shots, quite a few of them, and I ran over and grabbed that backpack and took off. Did I know what was in it? No not with a certainty but there'd been talk around town that someone had won the sea lottery a couple weeks back. I just grabbed it without thinking and took off back to the cabana and woke up Harvey and we dumped out the contents of that backpack and counted out about 250,000 laundered u.s. dollars. Oh boy.

Well, I soon found out I'd bumped into a hornets nest and them hornets were mad as hell. Seems like a couple Chinamen on the island, rich business men, fronted the two hundred and fifty grand and hired some thugs from Belize City to pose as the bad guys. They set up a meet with the fishermen, negotiated the price and arranged to exchange commodities at a certain time and place. I guess the Chinamen intended to sell the dope back to the dope smugglers or put it out on the market and make a quick $100,000 profit. Trouble is the real-deal bad guys got wind of the meet and busted it up, really busted it up, but not before the Chinamen (or someone) tipped off their henchmen and one of them pitched the backpack full of cash out the window and nearly into my outstretched arms.

Now the bad guys had their bundles of dope back but like the greedy macho bastards they were they wanted the cash payment too. Not surprisingly the Chinamen wanted their front money back and both parties undertook to find who had purloined the backpack. Which meant that both parties were looking for me but at that time didn't know it was me they were looking for, if you take my drift.

Kiddo, those were a few bad days, believe you me. I wish now I hadn't picked that backpack up but I did and couldn't turn back the clock. We both knew the worst thing we could do was make a run for it. The only way off the island was by water taxi which started at dawn with a boat to Belize City and at 7 with a boat to San Pedro in the other direction and you could bet dollars to donuts the passengers on those excursions would be scrutinized very thoroughly.

The second worse thing or plain stupidest thing was to submarine in our cabana and not come up until the storm above settled because that's exactly what our pursuers were looking for. Any unusual behaviour. Like a local saying, 'Haven't seen them two white guys in a while. They're in there but they don't come out'. So at about our usual time Harvey and me strolled into town and had a few beers and a full Belizean breakfast of huevos rancheros, fried beans, fry jacks and sausages. Everybody was talking about the big shoot-out at the hotel. Rumours were flying but all in all it seemed like one fisherman was dead and one badly wounded and helicoptered to Belize City, one local goon dead and the other in shock, and blood stains down the corridor and the exit stairs indicated at least one of the original bad guys had been hit.

That's when the talk started about the Chinese intervention in what should have been a routine business deal. There was no talk then about the money not being recovered. Only the Chinamen and the bad-guys knew for sure there was a backpack with $250,000 bucks in it and they wanted to find whoever had it.

Back in our cabana Harvey and me had a heart-to-heart. He said take the money to the police, end of story. I said are you crazy? Maybe I shouldn't of took it in the first place but taking it to the police was suicide. Harvey said how so? I said because the cops would probably kill me, kill us both, and keep the money. He said yeah you're probably right and I said well maybe they wouldn't kill us but somehow they'd confiscate the money and kick us out of the country. He said isn't there anyone on the island you can trust and I said no and he said yeah you're probably right, neither do I. So right then and there I offered Harvey 50,000 bucks if he'd just keep his mouth shut and not rat me out, at least not until I figured out what I wanted to do. He said okay and then we did what we did best. After a little siesta we went out and got very, very drunk.

Look, I'm exhausted. This writing thing has worn me out."

Sheryl stopped reading and rolled over on her back. Her Grumpa's letter was not at all what she had expected from him. He was always joking, full of mischief and fun. This was something different. He said it himself. This time he might have bit off more than he could chew and he was reaching out to her. She squinched her face and squeezed shut her dark-brown eyes. Obviously, this was something she would have to take up with her Daddy, and it was equally obvious that it would be a very unpleasant undertaking. Her Daddy and Grumpa had been estranged for years, maybe even before her Gramma had died, though maybe 'estranged' was the wrong word because her Grumpa was always asking after her Daddy. It was Daddy who wouldn't speak to Grumpa, wouldn't even speak about his own father. That was just the way it had been for as long as she could remember and although she had tried to get both or either of them to explain what had happened the response from her Daddy was always, 'Never mind. It's all water under the bridge now', and from Grumpa, 'Tell you what, kiddo, when I find out you'll be the first to know'.

She glanced at the clock on her bedside table. Daddy would be getting hungry, she knew, but maybe if she read a little more of Grumpa's story, and that is what it was, a story more than a letter, she would better be able to know how to broach the matter with her Daddy. She flipped over on her belly again and, rubbing her feet together above her, began to read:

"Hi I'm back again. Getting a little nervous. Went into San Ignacio this morning with my artist pal, Marcos Madeiros. He's got a little pick-up truck and I was crunched down on the passenger side with a straw hat pulled down on my head, just watching the ebb and flow of humanity when I spotted the Mexican bad guy I'd got to know on Caye Caulker. He was slouched outside of Emma's, a well-known tourist hangout. Marcos couldn't understand why I didn't want to drop in at Emma's for a beer . . . But I'm getting ahead of myself, aren't I. Let me back up a little.

Back in Caye Caulker, after the 'incident', and after I decided to take the money and run, I realized I had to get the money off the island asap and that was easier said then done. What I did I taped ½ the money to my chest and back with duct tape. Canadian, eh? It was all in 100 dollar bills, so I taped 5 packs of 100 x $100 across my chest and 5 packs of 100 x $100 down my back to a little above my waist. Neat, eh? Put on an ordinary dark-coloured short—sleeve shirt and nothing showed. Next morning I want to get the 10 o'clock water-taxi to Belize City so I show up a little after nine because everybody's saying it's crazy at the terminal with the cops checking passengers before they're allowed to board. I'm wearing running shoes without socks and boxer style swimsuit with my short-sleeve shirt. I'm also carrying my backpack with an expensive radio I bought a few weeks back stuffed inside. When it's my turn one of the tourist cops asks me where I'm going. I tell him Belize City. He asks me when I'm coming back and I say on the five o'clock and show him my return ticket, as if that should mean anything. Then I thrust the unzipped backpack at him and tell him I'm taking my radio back because it's not working and I'm totally pissed off. He looks in and pulls it out. Looks inside the backpack and shakes it upside down. "Get out of here, Pops" was all he said. So I stroll up the walkway to the dock and kind of hang back with the crowd waiting for the taxi to arrive from San Pedro and this tall, tough-looking guy reaches out from nowhere and asks me what I've got in the backpack and I tell him the cops already checked it out and he said he wasn't a cop and told me to give him the backpack. I looked at him and I thought holy shit this guy's not kidding, he had a look that said don't mess with me and I wished I wasn't standing there with 100,000 dollars that belonged to him wrapped round my body. I said, 'Hey, no problemo', which made me feel stupid, and I handed him the backpack and he took the radio out and looked at it and shook it and looked into the backpack and shook it and said 'Que pasa, viejo?' and I explained it was a radio I'm taking it back because it's not working and I'm pissed off about it. He had long black hair, very dark complexion and the cruelest eyes I've ever seen, like black coal, and he x-rayed me with them and then he said, 'Vaya con Dios, old man', and I nearly s..t myself.

First thing I did when we arrived in Belize City 45 minutes later was walk over to the cooler at Arrivals and buy two Belican beers which I chugged before I walked out of the terminal. I'm telling you. Whew. That guy really scared me.

Next I walk over to the Hotel Mopan where I am a guest in good standing. Jenny was in her office and I tell her I want to put something in her office safe and she says that's alright and leaves me alone while I rip the packets off my body and put them in a plastic shopping bag that I knot with the handles and leave on her desk. I also left the radio, figuring Jenny could keep it or would know who to give it to when I had a chance to talk to her. There was nothing wrong with it. Jenny's okay. If I can't trust Jenny I can't trust anyone. Or, to be more honest, I had to trust her because I didn't know anyone else.

Next morning I'm at the terminal again with more packs duct-taped to my body. Same time, same place, same cops checking things out and same bad guy motioning me over with a wiggling finger but this time he called me amigo as he checked out my empty backpack and said, Vaya con Dios again as I shuffled into the line to board the water taxi. Only problem is before I can board another guy steps in front of me and says, 'What's goin' on, man?' and I look up and see this real big black guy standing in front of me, he's wearing black slacks and a white shirt and he's got those blue sunglasses that you see in commercials, and black tightly-curled hair, and

I'm thinking, 'Holy Crap what now? And he says, 'You go to Belize City yesterday, man?' and I nod and he says, 'And you come back yesterday?', and I say 'Yeah, that's right' and he says, 'And you're going back again today? What's up, man?' 'Nothing's up, man,' I say

'Yesterday I took a radio back to get fixed and today I'm going to pick it up' and he says, 'Must be a goddamned good radio, man, going back and forth like that' and I say, 'Yeah, really good goddamned radio, that's why I'm going back to get it,' and he says, 'Okay, man, see you when you get back,' and I almost s..t my pants again. Second day in a row.

Back at the Hotel Mopan in Belize City I tell Jenny I want to put something else in her safe and she says that's okay and we go through the same routine but this time I tell her I need a room for a few days (because I'm not going back there ever again). What I plan to do is leave the money at Jenny's, minus a couple thousand, come back home to Canada, wait things out and move back in when the going's good. Only problem is Jenny hunts me down next morning at breakfast and looking over her shoulders asks me if there is anything I know that she doesn't and I say no and she says well there's something I know that you don't then and I say oh what's that and she says the word is out that the police are looking for a certain Canadian tourist for questioning in connection with that mess in Caye Caulker. But not to worry, you haven't been identified publicly, yet, but if I know anything the press can't be far behind. So if you have dreams of flying out of Belize forget about them, they'll have the airport covered like a blanket. And if you're putting me in jeopardy get the eff out of here, please Barry. Nothing personal, you know that, but I've got you registered staying here and they'll sure as shooting check hotel records and if you're still here when that happens I'm going to be up shit creek without a paddle. I start to say something and she says Barry be gone, please, but before you go, go to the desk and tell Matrice you want to book the room for two more weeks, pay in advance please, and then get out of here. That way they may hang around a little longer waiting for you to come back to your room. That's the best I can do, Barry. Now take the bag you left in the vault and go with God. Everyone seemed to be telling me to go with God which is a funny thing to be telling an atheist.

But I did what she told me, then I walked downtown and bought all the stuff I'd need to replace what I left behind in Caye Caulker, socks and underwear and a couple shirts etcetera and stuffed them on top of the money packs I hid at the bottom of my backpack. I had 200,000 u.s. dollars and didn't know where I was going to spend the night. Crazy, eh?

Break time break time. Marcos just drove in and he's suggesting we share a monster splif and talk about the meaning of life. That sounds pretty good to me right now. The splif part anyway. Don't think I'm ready for the meaning of life part. Maybe when I get older. If I get older.

"Baby, are you all right?" Sheryl was startled by her Daddy's voice.

"Okay, Daddy, I'll be right down."

"Don't rush. I just wondered . . ."

"I'm coming. Crack another beer. And crack one for me, too, please."

Sheryl looked in the mirror before she went downstairs. She thought she was pretty enough but her nose was like a little ski-jump and her nostrils were too big and she wished her hair had more bounce to it. But as her Grumpa would say, "You get what you're born with, kiddo, and if you're not satisfied with that you're shit out of luck."

Brant Buchanan sat at the kitchen table with an empty and a full bottle of beer in front of him. He was reaching for the full bottle when Sheryl skipped down the stairs and entered the kitchen. He marveled at her good-looks, her beauty, not quite the spitting-image of her mother but close enough to assure him that his daughter had inherited more of her mother's features than his, except of course the little ski-slope nose which he had inherited from his mother.

"Glass?" he asked, pointing at the capped beer on the table.

"No, Daddy. You know that."

"Just asking. Everyone drinks out of the bottle these days and I don't know why . . ."

"Daddy, I know the story. Drinking out of the bottle gives you gas. Right?"

"Right. Don't you get gas?"

"Do you mind if we don't talk about what does or does not give me gas?"

"Sure," Brant said as he snapped the cap off her beer and passed it to her, then picked up his open bottle and poured it into a frosted beer mug, looking with satisfaction as the foam frothed exactly to the rim. "But you don't know what you're missing."

Sheryl glanced at her father as she heated up last night's supper. He looked tired, but that was nothing unusual. He worked hard as a criminal lawyer in Toronto and for his age was very successful but she wondered if he didn't still grieve the loss of his mother when he was eighteen, her age now, and, she couldn't help but think, the loss of his father, figuratively speaking, at the same time. Not to mention the fact that his wife of sixteen years had left him for another woman and divorced him two years later when Sheryl was 16 years old. That was a body blow to both father and daughter. Sheryl wanted to be a writer and she knew that her own family history was a gold mine if she could find out how to excavate it.

Sheryl set the table and scooped out cold potato salad for both of them and bowls of re-heated rice and seafood gumbo.

"Looks good," Brant said.

"Cheers, Daddy," Sheryl said as she tipped her bottle of beer and took a few gulps.

"Hey, whoa," Brant said. "What's the rush?"

"Nothing. You're ahead of me, that's all. Trying to catch up . . ."

"This is a race?"

"No it's not a race, Daddy, but you know what?"
"No. What?"
"We've got to talk."
"We're talking . . ."
"No, I mean about something else . . ."
"What something else . . ."
"Your Daddy . . ."
"Don't call my Daddy Daddy . . ."
"You're father . . ."
"That's not much better . . ."
"Grumpa . . ."
"That's better. Much better. That's what you call him and I'm okay with that. What about him?"
"He wrote me a letter . . ."
"A letter? Is that what you want talk to me about?"
"Yes."
"What's he want now?"
"Daddy, he's never wanted anything, ever. He's never ever wanted any thing."
"Well, what's he wanted . . ."
"He's only wanted . . . he's only wanted . . . to be my friend . . . he's only wanted to love me . . . Daddy, he's my grandfather!"
"Okay, okay, okay. I'm sorry, baby. I really am. It's not fair to you." Brant picked up his mug of beer and chugged it down. "Look at me," he laughed. "Let's have another one, okay? Let's have another one and relax and talk about your Grumpa."
"Are you being sarcastic?"
"Not a scintilla, my precious."
"Well, hang on and I'll go and get the letter."

While Brant waited for his daughter, he felt the beer buzz through him. He liked a beer when he got home, maybe two during the course of the evening, but now he was on his third and he had just finished supper. Damn that man, he thought. Damn him, damn him. Hadn't he done enough damage? Hadn't he broken the heart of his mother, broken the heart of his son, and now wanted to break the heart of his son's daughter? Brant knew he had to play this one very carefully. He didn't know for sure what the old man was up to but he knew his father was closer to Sheryl than he wanted him to be. He figured he had already lost his father. He'd lost his wife. He couldn't afford to lose his daughter.

"Well, here it is," Sheryl said, plunking the large brown envelope on the table. "Check it out."

Brant emptied the sheets of paper out of the envelope. "I see what you mean. This far surpasses a letter. A story to be sure, a history of the world, part two or even . . .

"Daddy?

"Yes?"

"Are we going to be serious? Or not?"

"Of course we are."

"Then cut out the sarcasm, okay?"

"Okay."

"Let's see," Sheryl said. "I've read about six pages . . ."

"Then why don't you start on the dishes . . ."

"Because you read a lot faster than me . . ."

"What is this, a race?"

"No, but . . ."

"I'll tell you what. You pick up where you left off and I'll ready the dishes . . ." He glanced across the table at his daughter's raised eyebrows and said, "Okay. You're right. I'll do the dishes. Deal?"

"Deal."

"And when we've both read it, we'll talk. Deal?"

"Deal."

As Brant began to clear the table, Sheryl reorganized the numbered pages and began to read.

"Well, here I am again, back at work, pen in hand, lined sheets of paper waiting to receive the word according to Barry while my pal Marcos stands before his easel creating another masterpiece of visual art. What a pair we are.

Marcos is working on a big canvas and I don't think he even knows I'm in the room. He's been working on the painting for days and it's getting close to being finished. It shows the upper part, chest, head and arms of a very attractive white woman with strands of bright blonde hair and out of her out stretched hand all kinds of life flows, butterflies and dragonflies, fishes and snails and flowers of every description in shades of gold and blue and green, it's beautiful and it's obvious to me that the woman in his painting is his wife and she's the creator of the universe but when I said that to him last night he became angry and told me not to talk so crazy no matter how high I was. I backed off, didn't want to upset him but truth to tell it is a portrait of his wife Christine La Fleur who left him 8 months ago and took their two children back home to Quebec to raise and educate them. (Where else would I get a spiral binder with lots of pens and a treasure trove of envelopes of different sizes?) I know it's her because it looks like her and I know what she looks like because I've known the both of them for quite a few years.

I am living in Marcos' (empty except for him) family house on the banks of an un-named river about 15 miles out of San Ignacio and very close to the border with Guatemala. We're a couple miles away from a tiny town called Rocky River, population approximately less than a 100. There's no electricity in Rocky River and there sure as hell isn't any in the house of Marcos. When the sun goes down, the lamps go on and the fire glows in the cooking pit. We eat supper and smoke a joint or two and pass a bottle of rum back and forth. He likes his rum with fruit juice and I like mine with water. It's not a bad life but I know it isn't a happy life for Marcos right now and I can't say it's a life I would have chosen for myself, there being no companionship except for Marcos.

Marcos is a little man in stature, mostly Mayan I think but with some other ancestral blood in him as well. I'm sure he's told me of his origins before as I'm sure I told him about my mixed ancestry but sometime you wake up in the morning forgetting some of the unquenchable truths that were disclosed the night before. His skin is light brown. His jet black hair curls and falls over his shoulders, and his eyes are the colour of coal. He's also incredibly fast on his feet and very, very strong for such a little man.

Marcos doesn't have a clue why or how I ended up at his doorstep. I just did. He may have his suspicions, I suppose, like I'm on the lam from cops in my own country or I'm running away from my wife, whatever, it doesn't matter to him, that's not part of the equation. All the matters to him is that for the past years we met about once a year, I dug his art and bought at least one painting every time and we got stoned or drunk or both, and then out of the blue I show up at his doorstep in the rain-forest, his sanctuary, driven by a guy he knows and trusts, Bob Usher, and Bob says take care of this guy and that's all there is to it.

Now, since you don't know how I ended up at the house of Marcos, I'll tell you. I took a bus from Belize City to a little town tucked in the rain forest of Belize called San Ignacio. I've done this before. I always tell the driver's mate to drop me off the main highway at the ChinaLife Super Store, otherwise I'd have to go downtown and take a taxi back. I'd walk about a mile down a side street and arrive at the Aguada Hotel, my favourite hotel in the Cayo District of Belize. But this time I thought better of it. It was like blazing a trail. If they checked the bus station, and they would, they'd soon find out a guy who looked like me took a bus to San Ignacio. Let's face it. Old, white, overweight, grizzly beard. Oh, yeah, that guy. Yeah he got off at the ChinaLife, said he was going to walk to the Aguada. So I rode into town, mingled with the crowd and flagged down a taxi to take me back to the Aguada. I sat in the back and didn't talk, which is unusual for me and gave the driver 10 belizean bucks for a 7 buck ride, thinking that wouldn't stick in anyone's memory.

The gal at the desk was new to me and she looked at me like I was some weirdo so I asked her to call the owner of the hotel, Mr. Bob Usher. He comes out from his office at the back and it's all Barry, Barry and Bob, Bob and I signal that I want to talk to him in private and he nods and we adjourn to his backroom office.

He comes right to the point before I have a chance to say anything. What are you doing here, Barry? He said he didn't know what was going on but I was definitely a hot tamale and I asked him what that meant and he said that meant I couldn't be registered as a guest because the cops were dropping by on a regular basis to see who was staying at the hotel but he could put me up in a private room reserved for friends and members of the family. I say that's cool and he says where else can you stay? And I say well, how about Marcos Madeiros, you know him? And he says do I know him? We go way back, Marcos and me. I'll take you there tomorrow. In the meantime, Barry my friend, shave your beard and cut your hair. I'll send Zeno with some scissors and then he hauls out a big circle of keys, pulls one off and points to a little cabana just off the swimming pool and tells me to freshen up and enjoy myself at the restaurant, just chit the booze and food on him. Nice guy. But nice didn't amount to much under the circumstances. The only question that mattered was could I trust him with my life?

If waking me up before dawn the next morning was any indication of how much he wanted me to leave (as opposed to, let's say, killing me), I was relieved. In fact the first thing I did when he shook me awake was step into the bathroom and relieve myself and the second thing I did was accept the cold bottle of beer he thrust into my outstretched hand and I'm thinking that maybe I was a little bit groggy, but what did he think would happen if he chitted my food and booze for a night? And what did he think would happen if he didn't?

Anyway, it was still dark when we got to Marcos' place. Bob pulled his Jeep close to the shanty where Marcos lived and turned off the lights but didn't shut down the engine. I saw Marcos approach the Jeep through the darkness. 'What's he know?' I whispered.

"All he knows is I said you needed a place to stay without any questions asked and he said, 'Okay', okay?"

"Hey, my amigo," Marcos said as he opened up his arms to embrace me. "You are welcome here. Mi casa es su casa."

As we hugged one another, I saw Bob approach Marcos. As they shook hands, Bob passed Marcos a fist full of dollars. Well, let's face it. There were going to be some expenses. Bob probably knew it but Marcos sure as hell didn't know that I had a lotta moola stashed away in my backpack. I'm not saying it would have made any difference but . . .

So that's how we spent the next couple days. Marcos took care of his vegetable garden, painted, cooked a couple meals, smoked some pot and went to bed. I did the same thing except I didn't garden, paint or cook but I wandered around, went down to the river, tried to fish and did what I'm doing now, write, write, write.

I'm writing to let you know what happened to me because I've got a bad vibe this isn't going to turn out so good. I'm not exactly trying to set the record straight, it is what it is, but I am trying to explain where things went wrong, and why, and how I didn't have the strength to do the right thing when it counted most.

You see, after your Gramma died, before you were even born, I fell apart. I pretended to be like the man I wanted to be but in truth I was made of glass and when she died it was like an anvil fell on me and left me shattered. That woman was everything to me, from day one, from the moment I met her, and there she was dying from cancer and what could I do? What could I do? So I brought her tea and

I wiped her brow and I held her hand and I listened to her cry out in pain and I cleaned her up when I had to and what was that all about? What did that add up to? She was dying and we both knew it, it wasn't a matter of if it was a matter of when and I thought Brant knew it too but maybe he didn't so I just went on as best I could. It's not that these things are neat and tidy.

Dying isn't exactly a package delivered by postal express. The fact is that life goes on in the midst of death and truth be told I clung to my day job like a sailor clings to a life raft when he's adrift at sea. I longed for time out of my house, out of my home, because I didn't know what to do there, it was all upside down, but I knew what to do when I went to work. I knew how to weld. I knew how to teach others to weld. I knew how to walk away from a day's work and go out with the boys. I got to know better than I had ever known before how good that first frosted beer tasted and how much better each one after that felt as it went down my throat. Don't get me wrong. I was home whenever I had to be home but not a day more, not a moment more. I'm sorry about that and you can tell your dad how sorry I am about that but when I was at home, especially toward the end, all I saw was my wife, the love of my life, Beatrice, your grandmother, dying in front of me and whenever I got the chance I ran away. I ran away from her, from her death, and I ran away from him because I didn't know who he was and I didn't care to find out. That ain't nice but it's the truth.

And I've got to say, kind of in self-defense, where was Brant in all this? Christ Almighty he was a grown young man, 18 years old. When I was his age I was working on the pipeline up in northern Alberta, freezing my b . . . s off but making good money. It didn't occur to me I had to take care of him too. No one took care of me back in the day. And why didn't he take more care of his mother? Didn't he have a part to play? Maybe I messed up a lot but I don't remember him washing her when she shit herself or cleaning up her puke when she heaved off the side of the bed. And come to think of it, what the hell, why didn't he take a little care of me? At least offer a word or two of sympathy instead of steadfastly avoiding me or looking at me as if I'd caused her cancer.

Hey, kiddo, I'm looking over what I wrote and it's not very pretty is it but I've got to get this out of me, I want to get this on the record, I don't want this to remain unspoken and forever unwritten. Don't you agree? Anyway, after your Gramma died, after she was cremated, as she wished, her ashes were interred in a vault in the cemetery and I remember thinking one night of something from the bible, something about ashes to ashes and dust to dust and I realized that she was the ashes and I was the dust and unlike the ashes that were collected and preserved in an urn I was the dust that was blown on the wind and I went wherever the wind blew me. Do you know that after your Gramma died my company sent me to China for three weeks, I went to Russia for I can't remember how many weeks, and to half the states in the U.S.A. and yes to Belize on an assignment and of course across Canada and it was like huff and puff and you're somewhere doing something and then you're somewhere else being huffed and puffed and blown away cause you are nothing but dust, there's nothing left of you but dust.

As I write this, it's all I can do not to weep. That was the time Brant needed me most, and I was not there for him. I was the father he thought he never had, though I always loved him in my way. He was the son who never loved me, at least not that I ever noticed. Maybe I needed a father, not a son. Ain't life a bitch.

Anyways I may as well tell you, 'cause if I don't your Daddy sure as hell will, after she died I started boozing pretty good and did some dope and it hurts me to tell you but I didn't behave myself in other ways. I started to bring women back home with me, not always but now and then, and I think Brant hated that more than anything, he thought I was betraying his mother, my wife, but Jesus Christ it wasn't that at all. I was just so lonely, I needed someone to touch, I needed someone to smell, I needed someone beside me when I woke up in the middle of the night . . . I tried it without any companionship and it just wasn't working out. It was like I had a paper bag over my head with duct-tape wrapped around my neck and every breath I took was like my last, I was like asfixiating and I didn't want to die.

The only golden moment happened when you were born. I visited the hospital a couple days after. Your mom was so welcoming. Your dad bristled at my presence. I told Felice how beautiful she was, and she was, and she is, and how beautiful you were and you were and still are, and I touched your tiny hand and I swear you grasped my finger and I thought okay, this is my little kiddo. Her daddy may not care for me but I adore her. And we've have fun over the years, haven't we? We've had our stolen moments, you and me. I've watched you grow up but let's face it, if Beatrice had grown old with me I'd have been a Grampa not a Grumpa and you would have had a Gramma unlike any other.

Time out. Marcos just drove in back from town. He wants to talk to me.

Okay, what Marcos just told me was all hell broke loose last night in San Ignacio. Remember the guy I told you about, the Mexican guy at the terminal in Caye Caulker, the guy I spotted in town a few days ago. Well, him I have figured for the front man for the drug guys, the guys who wanted the Chinamen's $250,000 and the drugs the fishermen scooped from the sea, but there was the other guy, the black guy that braced me at the terminal, asking me where I'd been and why I was going back to the city. I figured him for the Chinamen's bounty hunter. His job was to find me and get their money back so they wouldn't look totally stupid, so they wouldn't lose 'face'.

Anyway, he must have sniffed his way to San Ignacio in pursuit of me and my Mexican amigo. Seems their paths crossed. From what Marcos told me they met in a local bar and probably got suspicious of one another when they heard each other asking the same questions about my whereabouts. Can you imagine anything crazier than that? Anyway after a night of drinking they went their separate ways and when the sun came up in the morning a kid fell over the body of the black guy with his legs stretched out in an alley behind his hotel and his throat slashed. Marcos said that the only reason his head was still on was 'cause it was held up against the wall behind him, at least that's what people were saying.

Everybody must've known it was the Mexican that killed him but nobody saw it and the Mexican had an air-tight alibi, said he was up all night playing poker with his friends and didn't leave but once to take a leak in a buddy's back yard. So my Mexican friend has first dibs on me again and you can bet he won't be leaving till he kills me and recovers the money. Bob Usher told Marcos to tell me I'd better go deeper into the rain forest and that's what we're going to do right now.

Here I am again, deep in the rain forest, in a little shanty in a clearing with a half dozen other shanties. Marcos says we're not far from the Guatemala border but I don't know how he knows that. Anyways, there's hardly anybody here, a couple old women (who am I to talk about age, eh?) and some little kids who need caring. Marcos says the men are either hunting or fishing the nearby streams and the younger boys and girls and the women have all been taken to places where there are tourists they sell their crafts to. Guess I'll see them all when they get back.

Believe it or not, I'm comfortable here. It's the quietest place I've ever stayed at in my life. Oh there are sounds all right, but quiet sounds like the wind whispering through the trees and the trees, man, you have to lay on your back and look up to see the tops of them. The place smells clean too, clean with a little sniff of decay from rotting tree trunks, that kind of thing. My room has a straw mat where I'll sleep, a couple blankets for when it gets cold at night, a clay jug with fresh cold water. Right now I'm sitting on a stool out front, bent over a bamboo table scribbling in my notebook. They must think I'm a crazy old coot.

We took the truck for the first part of our trip into the rain forest, driving over hard rock roads for about half an hour and then we left the truck and walked the rest of the way on a windy path that brought us to the village, or hamlet or whatever it is. Marcos introduced me to the old ladies who laughed and giggled the whole time. I couldn't understand a word they said. Marcos says it was some kind of Mayan dialect. Doesn't matter. The plan is to stay here till the coast is clear and then try to make a run for it though I still don't know where I'll be running to, most probably Guatemala since it's nearby. I'm sending this letter with Marcos when he comes back later today. I'll send it first class so it gets to you fast.

Sorry to dump all this on you, kiddo. I've got some good people here trying to help me and everything might work out for the best, I just don't know, but if things don't work out for me I guess I really do want to try to set the record straight about where I've been and what I've been up to and all the rest of it. Think well of your old Grumpa, kiddo, lots of love, say hello to my son. You might even tell him I love him."

Sheryl set the pages of the letter down and pushed them across the kitchen to her father.

"Are you all right," he asked, looking at her closely.

"Been better. Where are you?"

"At the painting part . . ."

"What's that all about?"

"That's all about your grandfather getting stoned in the morning in a shack by the banks of a river on the edge of a rain forest watching his artist buddy paint a picture . . ."

"Daddy, don't get all bent out . . ."

"I'm not getting bent out of shape, Sheryl, I'm just telling you what it's all about."

"Well, finish the letter, Daddy," Sheryl said. "Then we've got to talk."

Brant scooped up the pages from the table and stacked them with his own. Sheryl sat quietly at the table, looking around the kitchen, the same kitchen she had sat in since she was born. She thought of her mother, her wonderful, loving mother, and imagined her stepping from the stove with a bowl of porridge or a plate of carved chicken, and then sitting down with her daughter and her Daddy and laughing and talking as they ate their meal. And now her mom was living across town with her lady lover while her Daddy read a letter from his father to his daughter . . . what a wacky, wacky world.

"Well?" Sheryl asked. "What do you think?"

"What do I . . ."

"Do you think he's all right . . ."

"Well, I'm not sure what you mean by . . ."

"Oh, cut the crap, Daddy. Is Grumpa in danger?"

"Yes. He wouldn't say what he's saying if he wasn't in danger . . ."

"So, Daddy, what are we going to do about it?"

"Well, let's see. We said we'd read the letter and then talk. Right?"

"Right."

"So let's talk."

"Okay. Where do we start?" Sheryl looked across at her dad slouched in his chair across from her. "How about where your father talks about your mother dying? Is that a good starting point?"

Brant waved his hand dismissively.

"How about where your father talks about how he behaved after your mother died? Can we start there?"

Brant waved his hand dismissively again, looking around as if there was someone else to talk to.

"Daddy, it's you and me," Sheryl said, "and we're going to talk because you promised me. Now, you were home when your mother was dying, right? And . . ."

"I was 17 years old then."

"All right, and . . ."

"I was 18 when she died."

"Your father said you were 18 . . ."

"Yeah but he makes it sound as if I was always 18. All I'm saying is I was 17 when it started . . ."

"What started??"

"Mom's dying started, that's what started. Sheryl, where's this going?"

"I'm just trying to figure out what went wrong between you and your father, that's all."

"There was always something wrong between me and my father, as far back as I can remember."

"Any idea why?"

"Not the faintest. Maybe I didn't measure up to what he wanted as a son, I don't know. I do know that he didn't measure up to what I wanted as a father . . ."

"What did you want, Daddy?"

"Nothing special. Just a dad who cared for me. Played ball with me. Talked to me. He wasn't at home that much and when he was he spent most of his time with my Mom."

"But, Daddy, didn't you read what your father said in the letter? He was trying to make a living. He was good at what he did but it took him away from home."

"Yeah. I read that but did you read the part where he says he was, this sounds silly but I don't know how else to say it, 'fooling' around'?"

"Daddy, he says that happened after your Mom died . . ."

"Oh, that makes a difference?"

"Yes, Daddy. I think that makes a huge difference."

"Why?"

"Well, for one thing, it means he wasn't unfaithful to your mother when she was alive, not like Mommy was unfaithful to you . . ."

"That's totally unfair, Sheryl . . ."

"Is it? I'm wondering why you hold your father to a higher standard than you hold your wife?"

"Couldn't we talk about this some other time? Couldn't we just focus on your grandfather right now?"

"Sure, Daddy. I mean, I'm just glad we're talking . . ."

"You said 'for one thing'. What's another thing?"

"Well, after your mom died he admits he fell to pieces and found comfort where he could find it. I can't find any fault with that. He was . . ."

"A grown man. Unattached. Foot loose and fancy free. Yeah, I've heard that before. In fact, that was always your grandfather's line. That's how he sold it to the world, but I didn't buy it. Sure, he was here, there and everywhere after my mother died, and before, too, when you come to think of it. There's no doubt he provided for us, the two of us, yes, yes, before you point it out, he paid for my university education, but wasn't it blood money? Or guilt money? Or whatever the hell it was.

But in the meantime, pardon me, baby, I'm getting a bit worked up. If he was all stressed out and lonely, what was I?"

"You tell me."

"What was I?" Brant reached over to the jug of water he had placed on the kitchen table, picked it up and poured himself another glass. "Well, in a way, I was just a kid . . ."

"He says at 18 he was out west working in the oil fields . . ."

"Well, I wasn't, baby, okay?"

"Why not, Daddy?"

"Because . . . oh I get it. I didn't have to work in the oil fields because my father was out there working his ass off paving the way for me, right?"

"Sure, what's wrong with that? Isn't that what he did? Isn't that what you're doing for me? Isn't that what all parents should do for their children?"

"Wait a minute, baby . . ."

"Why, Daddy? Isn't it true?"

"Well, sure, in a way . . ."

"Well, in what way is it different?"

"It's just that times change, that's all. That was then this is now . . ."

"And this now becomes that then. Do you know how dumb that sounds, Daddy? It's like a recipe for nothing to happen. Do you know how old I am?"

"Of course. You're 17."

"Well, I used to be, but I had a birthday a few months back, which you forgot, and surprise, surprise, now I'm 18."

"I'm sorry. Happy Birthday, baby, and please spare me your sarcasm, but doesn't that prove my point. You're too young to understand what it was like . . ."

"When you were 18?"

"Yes. Exactly . . ."

"When you were going through the agony of your mother's death and your father's indifference . . ."

"Exactly right."

"And I haven't been dying a death by a thousand cuts?"

"What do you mean?"

"Do you think it's been easy losing my mother, watching her pack and walk out the door with her lover, leaving me behind with you?"

"I never heard you complain . . ."

"I'm not a complainer, Daddy, and besides, what was the use? The question never came up; she basically said she was still my mother and she loved me but she had to live with Mary Lou. End of story."

"So what if she had asked you to leave with her and live with them?"

"I'd have told her to go to hell . . ."

"So what's the problem . . ."

"There's no problem, Daddy. I love you and I'm glad we're still together. And I love Mommy, too. She's doing what she has to do and I wish her nothing but happiness, but that's not exactly what I'm talking about . . ."

"What are . . ."

"I'm talking about loneliness . . ."

"Loneliness? How could you be lonely?"

"Well, you aren't home very much, are you?"

"Not as much as I'd like to be, that's for sure. But I've got to make a living, you know . . ."

"Where have I read that recently?"

"Touché. But what about your friends?"

"I've been having some trouble with my friends, or I should say with some of my friends."

"What kind of trouble?"

"Do you remember Jimmy?"

"Yeah, I remember him. Never liked him much but you dropped him, didn't you?"

"Yes, I did, Daddy, I dropped him like a hot potato because he was getting weird, he wasn't at all like the Jimmy I thought I loved . . ."

"So what caused the trouble?"

"Jimmy did. He didn't like being dropped so he started telling his friends what a bitch I am, told them I made fun of them, how stupid they were and all that, which was just crap because I didn't and then he . . ."

"What?"

"Daddy, he posted some nasty stuff on Facebook, some pictures . . . he posted some pictures, not porn or anything, I mean, no beaver shots or anything like that, but private pictures, pictures that weren't meant to be shared . . . it's so embarrassing . . . and somebody ran off copies and brought them to school . . . oh Daddy . . ."

"Why didn't you tell me?" Brant reached across the table and put his hands on hers.

"Well, it's hard to talk about things like that, isn't it? Isn't that why you never talked to your father about your mother? Isn't that why you never told your father how lonely you were? Isn't that why he never talked to you about it, because sometimes it's too hard, sometimes it's easier to let really important thoughts remain unsaid . . ."

"Sure, I guess but . . ."

"Can't you let bygone be bygones, Daddy?" Sheryl squeezed her Daddy's hands. "Please? I look at you and your father, and I look at you and me and I'm thinking this is stupid, this has got to end. Don't you see?"

Brant looked in his daughter's eyes and saw all the love he used to see when his mother looked at him. He smiled. "I'm beginning to see the light."

"So. What are we going to do?"

"We're going to find your Grumpa in Belize."

"Oh, Daddy, only I can find my Grumpa in Belize. Who are you going to find?"

Brant looked at her and smiled again, thinking, 'who is this remarkable young woman sitting across from me. I better get to know her a lot better than I know her now'. "I guess I'll be looking for my father," he said, a little sheepishly.

"So what's the plan?"

"The plan is to make arrangements immediately, fly out of here tomorrow morning and get to Belize sometime tomorrow afternoon. Make sure you have your passport and pack light, no checked luggage, okay? This is a search and rescue mission. Get in, find him, get out, the three of us."

"I get the 'get in', it's the 'get out' I don't get."

"Well you shouldn't worry. I've been thinking about this since I read the letter. I haven't played my ace in the hole yet, baby . . ."

"Your ace in the . . ."

"Right. And soon as I book our flight I'm going to phone him . . ."

"Phone who?"

"Phone my buddy Francis Aloyious Bennet-Pryce, best damned lawyer I've ever met . . ."

"And he's practicing . . ."

"Criminal and corporate law . . . in Belize City. Let's get ready to rumble!"

The San Ignacio police released Alfred Miguel Sanchez from jail later the same day they took him into custody on suspicion of murder. He had steel proof alibis for his whereabouts the night before. He had a passport attesting that he was a citizen of Mexico. And he had the support of persons unknown high-up in the police hierarchy, one of whom had made a phone call to the Chief of Police in San Ignacio commanding him to release the prisoner immediately.

"You know he did it, Chief," Sergeant Ramsey protested.

"No, I don't know. I suspect. But suspicion without evidence is worthless. You know that."

"I could break those eye-witnesses."

"But you won't."

"C'mon, Chief. What about his passport? That's as bogus as a 3 dollar bill."

"But that would entail another investigation and there's not going to be another investigation . . ."

"But why?"

"Because, unlike you, I obey the orders of my superior officers. Now get that murdering Mexican son of a bitch out of here muy pronto or your dumb ass is gonna find itself behind bars marinating in its own juices. Do I make myself clear?"

As the Sergeant marched off to carry out the Captain's orders, the Captain looked out the window at the blue sky and shrugged as if to say to God in Heaven,

What else could I do? It was lamentable but true that here on Earth the Commander of the Belizean Police had more authority than God Himself and matters of right and wrong would have to be settled at another time in a different court room.

Alfredo Miguel Sanchez walked down the steps from the police station savouring the warmth of the setting sun, rejoicing in the sights and sounds of the little town, his nostrils assailed by a mixture of smells as he strolled down Burns Avenue checking out the action. At a corner bar catering to young tourists seeking adventure and young Belizeans offering their services, he spotted a couple, he Indian brown with long black hair, she American white with cropped blonde hair, embracing on the front porch. Their lips touched as they talked and the sight aroused him. Alfred had no gender bias. Each gender had openings that could fulfill his desires, and, of the two genders, male or female, he slightly favoured the male of the species. The male seemed more ready to accept the pain he inflicted on him, thus prolonging the pleasure of the coupling. Alfredo shook his head and snorted so loudly the couple stepped apart. 'Do not worry, my little children,' he thought as he passed by, 'I have my work to do first'.

Alfredo was deeply disappointed with himself. It was unlike him to wander off the path of duty. He should have solved this matter days ago, not let it slide while he got drunk and had to kill a man. He would find the old white man he had encountered on Caye Caulker, the man who had stolen the money of those who employed him, the man who had tricked him and escaped from him. He knew what his prey looked like. He knew what the old fool wanted to do in San Ignacio, so tantalizingly close to the Guatemalan border. Find him, kill him, take the money. That was his mission. Then, and only then, would he unleash himself on those innocent others.

At the only car-rental agency in San Ignacio, the clerk tried to explain to his dark-skinned customer that he had to provide photo-proof of identity and a valid credit card before he could rent a vehicle. Alfredo rummaged through the shoulder bag he had retrieved from its hidey-hole in his hotel room. He knew that as soon as he left the premises with his car the clerk would run to the police whether or not he provided him with everything he asked.

"I'll tell you what, amigo," he said, pulling a deadly-black 45 Colt automatic out of the bag. The clerk gasped with fear. "I'm not going to kill you. Not yet. Maybe not ever, who knows. But first I'm going to be nice. Comprende?"

The clerk broke into a sweat.

"You know who I am, don't you?"

"Si, si, I know, I know. Please don't hurt me, por favor. Take the car, any car you want, senor. I won't tell anyone, believe me. No one, senor, I promise."

"And I believe you," Alfredo rummaged in his bag again, pulling out a cell phone and conversing with someone in Spanish. He snapped the cell phone shut and continued talking to the clerk. "You heard your name mentioned?" he asked, pointing at the clerk's identity badge.

"Si, si. Yo comprendo espanol."

"Bueno, hombre. Then you heard me tell them to kill you if the police arrest me. Kill you and your family, but kill you last, after the others have been butchered and then slaughtered. But enough rough stuff. Let's do this right, mi amigo. Take this credit card and this passport," he said, pulling out different documents and handing them to the clerk. "Now fill in all the forms the way it should be done, give me a copy as my receipt and we'll shake hands on the deal. But first," the clerk twitched as Alfredo reached into his back pocket and pulled out his wallet. Counting out 10 one hundred dollar American bills, he folded them in two and stuffed them in the clerk's shirt pocket. "I am generous, am I not? But betray me, amigo, and you are sure to die."

Alfredo drove his rented car out of San Ignacio on the Western Highway toward Belmopan, the capital of Belize. 10 miles out he u-turned and parked in front of Caesar's, a popular hotel with a casino that had been mentioned more than once when he was questioning the locals. He approached the desk clerk, a Spanish-looking young man talking on his cell phone. Alfredo had to clear his throat to get the clerk's attention.

"Hey, amigo, what's chances of getting a room for the night?"

"Pretty good," the clerk replied, whispering something on the phone.

"Is that a yes or is that a no?"

The clerk raised his head and looked into the face of a man who looked back at him as if he could reach over the counter and slit his throat as easily as he would swat a fly. "Oh, that's a yes, sir. Yes, sir."

"Business slow?"

"No. Yes. Up and down, sir."

"This your regular shift?"

"Yes, sir."

"3 to 12?"

"Yes, sir."

"I'm looking for a friend. We got separated. Old white man, white hair, white beard, not fat, not small, maybe 6', speaks English, seen anyone like him in the past, oh, let's say, 4 or 5 days?"

"No, sir."

"You sure about that?"

"As Christ is my Saviour, sir."

"Then I'll keep looking for him. Here," Alfredo said, pulling a 50 dollar bill from his wallet, slapping it on the counter top. "Keep your mouth shut."

Alfredo turned the car back to San Ignacio. According to the bus driver on the Belize City to San Ignacio run, a passenger fitting the old man's description had taken his bus and exited at the end of the run downtown. That's why Alfredo had concluded that the old man was in a downtown hotel room. That's why he hadn't questioned the taxi drivers on duty that night. The old man might have taken a taxi to a hotel on the periphery of San Ignacio. He might have taken a taxi to a friend's house, though Alfredo's outside contacts made no mention of any such friends. Alfredo himself had arrived by bus at night, two days after the old man got there. Maybe in the night, he had missed something.

As he cruised back into San Ignacio through San Ignacio's twin town Santa Elena, he noticed a large bill-board ad for a hotel called the Aguada, less than a mile off the Western Highway to the right. He made a right turn, cruised to the hotel, parked his car and walked toward the entrance. It looked good, he thought. Well kept up. He glimpsed the hotel pool through the bougainvilleas as he approached the door. Very nice. He caught a good vibe from the place. This was somewhere the old man could hole up.

He stepped through the entrance door and was surprised to find himself in a full-fledged restaurant. He observed the bar across from him with the credit-card signs and the cash registers and concluded in the absence of any other signage that the bar also served as the front desk for the hotel.

He decided right then and there that he was hungry and would have something to eat. "Senorita," he called, pointing to a booth by the window. "Aqui?"

"Sure," she replied. "I'll be right there."

As she approached he noticed how plain she was, unadorned and overweight. "Como esta?" he said, flashing a smile replete with gold fillings. "Habla espanol?"

"No, senor."

"But you understand?"

"A little, senor. Poquito."

"You are muy hermosa, senorita."

"Gracias, senor."

"I need a room for the night, senorita, but first I must eat . . ."

"Here is the menu, senor . . ."

"No, no. I know what I want. Huevos rancheros, refried beans and corn tortillas, double order of breakfast sausage, double order of bacon, very crisp. Comprende?"

"Sir, I understand, but we don't serve breakfast after mid-day."

Alfredo reached back to pull out his wallet and pulled out a 50 dollar bill. "This is for you, my beauty. It's not part of the bill, it's for you. Now see what the gal in the kitchen can do for me, okay. And before you go, could you tell me, por favor, if you were on duty, late afternoon, a few days ago? And if you were did you happen to check in my buddy? I'm looking for him, old white guy, white hair, white beard, not too short, not too tall, English speaking?"

"Yes, I remember him."

Alfredo gave her his full attention. Such a quick response. Did she remember the old man because she had checked him in? Or had she heard about Alfredo and the money he was throwing around town and was playing a high-stakes poker game with him. "That's very, very good. You must have noticed that his arm was in a sling," he said, testing her.

"No sir. I didn't notice that."

"That's strange. But you must have noticed the scar across his face, a very ugly scar."

"No, sir. I did not notice that, sir."

"But you said you checked him in, woman."

"No, sir, I said that I remembered him. That's what I want to tell you." She looked at his wallet. He pulled out another 50 and placed it on the table. "I didn't check him in. Mr. Bob came out from his office and they were hugging and laughing."

"Mr. Bob? Your boss?"

"Yes sir. Mr. Bob Usher, the owner. Some call him Robert, his formal name, but I call him Mr. Bob. Mr. Bob said he'd take care of him and he put him in the guest room out back, it's reserved for family, sir."

"I see. And, is that it? Did he stay? Did he leave? What else is there you want to tell me?"

"There's something else, sir. I couldn't sleep well that night so I took a blanket and walked out by the pool. It's pretty at night, and really early in the morning, before light, I saw Mr. Bob knock at the guest-room door and . . ."

"And?"

She looked down at the 50's on the table. Alfredo added another 50 to the pile.

"And that old white man had been shaved, sir. His hair was still white but much shorter and his beard was gone. Mr. Bob handed him a beer and off they went but, sir, I don't know where. I honest to God do not know where they went."

Alfredo looked at her. He appraised her. He thought the greedy bitch has squeezed me for every dollar she can get and she is smart enough not to make me pay for something she does not know. "Go get my breakfast supper, my little one. I won't be staying for the night as I had planned. My friend is playing a joke on me. It's a good one. And here's a little something extra to make you forget we ever had this conversation," he concluded, placing another 50 on the table.

As she reached for the money, he enveloped her forearm in his hand and squeezed, hard. She winced with pain. "I have been generous, have I not?" She nodded and tried to pull away. He pulled her back with one hand and reached the other under her skirt, pinching her thigh till she cried out. "Now go," he said, pushing her away. "I am very, very hungry." As she walked away, he grabbed her skirt and hauled her back. "And, my lovely senorita, if you learn anything, anything at all, that might assist me in my endeavor to find this friend of mine, leave a message with the night clerk at the Hi-Et Hotel. You will be well rewarded . . ." She tried to walk away, "but if you are a bad girl, I will have to punish you. Do you understand?"

Alfredo drove back to the Hi-Et Hotel and approached the desk clerk, a debauched middle-aged American who had found a new home in Belize. "Hola, amigo, Como esta?"

"Ah, Senor Sanchez. I am well, thank you. And how are you this night, sir."

"Muy bueno. I want to assure that my room still awaits me should I need it."

"But of course, senor. You have paid for another week. There is nothing to worry about."

"You are aware of the difficulty I faced this morning with the police?"

"Of course, senor, this is a small town, how could one not hear . . ."

"But this is no concern of yours?"

"None whatsoever, sir. You know what the Americans say, 'Innocent until proved guilty.'"

"Beyond a reasonable doubt."

"Exactly, sir."

"I'll be in and out for the next few days. Would you have someone do my laundry? It's in a bag in my room. And one other thing," Alfredo said, leaning over the desk, "just keep an eye open, will you. Let me know if anything unusual comes to your attention. And if anyone comes in wanting to contact me, make sure that I know." As he stepped back, he left a 100 bill on the top of the desk and a blank business card with his cell phone number.

"Your wish is my command, Senor Sanchez," the desk clerk replied, already deciding what he would do with the windfall.

The flight from Toronto to Miami was uneventful, after the x-raying and searching and the unavoidable wait while the plane was de-iced before take-off. Sheryl and her father were not able to sit next to one another but sat two rows apart on the same aisle side.

At the Miami International Airport they detected their way to the departure lounge for the next step of their journey. "Daddy, I've got to pee," Sheryl confided when they found a place to sit down and drop off their backpacks.

"Go for it, baby," Brant said. "Something to eat? Nothing but pretzels on the next flight."

"Sure, Daddy," Sheryl replied, squirming. "Turkey sandwich with mustard and tomato."

As they sat eating their sandwiches, waiting for their flight to be called, Sheryl said, "Well, Daddy? Tell me about your friend?"

"Oh, sure. Francis. Your mother knows him well. In fact, when I met him he was dating your mother."

"Guess that was going nowhere."

"Sheryl. C'mon . . . Your mother wasn't always the way she is now. Or maybe she was but wasn't letting on. She sure fooled me. But anyway, he was a year ahead of me at law school at U. of T. I'd seen him around. Heard he was a real sharp dude from Belize. Had to look Belize up on the internet to find out where it was. Then I had to do a little research to find out what it was. Anyway, we met, hung out a little bit, and then in the course of time found that we had become good friends."

"What was the attraction?"

"Bright. Personable. A lot of fun."

"Physically?'

"Physically? Good looking guy. Tight-curled black African hair. Dark mahogany complexion. White teeth. Sparkling brown eyes . . ."

"Whoa down there, Daddy. Sounds like you were fucking him."

"Sheryl! Give me a break. You asked me to describe him and I did. I wish I had me on the witness stand when I was cross-examining a witness. Detail, detail, detail. But what's with the language . . . fucking him. What's all that about?"

"It's about language, Daddy, and my choice of a word describing sexual intercourse, in this case between you and your new best friend, who I've never even heard of and you haven't answered my question."

"No, baby, I wasn't."

"Good. What a relief. Where would I go if another parent left me for a same-sex lover?"

The flight attendant interrupted all conversations by announcing that Flight 4143 was ready to board passengers from Miami to Belize City.

"I'll tell you one thing, my lovely daughter," Brant whispered as they crossed the gang way into plane.

"What's that, Daddy?"

"Once you meet Francis, you'll never forget him . . . and you won't have to fuck him to find that out."

The 737 touched down at the Goldson International Airport ten miles northeast of Belize City. Brant and Sheryl jammed into the aisle and pulled their backpacks from the overhead bins, struggling to put them on and then resigning themselves to carrying them out by hand.

A hot wind wafted them as they descended from the plane and walked across the tarmac to the airport. It was a bright, sunny day, nothing out of the ordinary for the Belizeans unloading the luggage from the plane or the airport employees directing them to Customs, but for Canadians leaving a snow-struck Toronto with temperatures well below freezing, it was a sudden and much welcomed change. Sheryl had done some traveling to the southern states and once to New York City. She had certainly never walked across a tarmac before. That was something new. She looked around her. The airport wasn't anything to brag about. The buildings looked worse for wear but she realized she was in an impoverished country and it didn't matter anyway. She was here to track down her Grumpa and get him back home where he belonged. She would reflect on impressions of Belize when the deal was done.

She stuck close to her father, clutching his backpack. The Customs room they had been herded into was packed; two airplanes had landed within minutes of one another, and though most passengers had to wait to pick up their luggage at the carousels, the line-up at Customs was still intimidating. "Oh, Daddy," Sheryl said, pulling his head down so she could speak to him in a whisper, "I'm sorry I've been so nasty. I didn't sleep much and I'm cranky, okay?" She hopped from foot to foot.

"Of course it's okay. It was a good question. I'm cranky too or I would've kept my mouth shut. Now," he said, putting his arm around her, "it looks as if we are in for a long wait, so hang on . . ."

"Excuse me, sir." Brant and Sheryl swung around to see who was speaking. "Mr. and Mrs. Buchanan?"

The Customs Inspector was a large man with sweat beaded on his forehead and plastered on his white shirt. "No, not really," Brant replied. "I mean we are both Buchanans. I'm her father and she's my daughter."

"Of course. My mistake. Would you follow me?"

"Wait a minute, wait a minute, where are you taking us?" Brant demanded, his lawyerly instinct for fair play and due process mingling with his natural suspicion of authority.

The Inspector turned and looked at them and smiled. "I see you haven't been notified. Forgive me. Mr. Bennett-Pryce has asked me to intercede on your behalf and we are going to by-pass customs. Follow me, please."

Father and daughter exchanged looks as they wheeled about and followed the Customs Inspector against the flow of passengers lining up for inspection. The Inspector arrived at a door marked Private-Customs Officials Only, rapped on the door and pushed his way in, waving for the Buchanans to enter.

"Brant!" a voice cried out. A man stepped out from behind a desk and approached them. He crossed the floor arms outstretched and took Brant in his arms, hugging him. Brant responded as enthusiastically, pounding his friend on the back. They placed their hands on each other's shoulders and grinned at one another. "So good to see you, man," Brant exclaimed, "Thank you so much for . . ."

"Shush, shush, shush, enough of that. Now, please, introduce me to your daughter."

Brant waved Sheryl over to his side. "Sheryl, I want you to meet my friend Francis." Sheryl looked up and saw Francis looking back at her with a bigger-than-life smile on his face and an outstretched hand and said, "I've got to pee real bad."

"George," Francis barked at the Customs Inspector, "direct Ms. Buchanan to the nearest facility. Please hurry."

Fifteen minutes later, they arrived at the Princess Hotel in downtown Belize City. The chauffeur drove into a No Parking zone and parked the car, opened Sheryl's door, picked up both backpacks, and waited while Brant and Sheryl followed Francis into the lobby. "Thank you, Michael," Francis said, "We'll be down shortly."

Francis motioned for the Buchanans to follow him as he headed for the elevators. "Don't we have . . ." Brant started. "You're already checked in, my friend," Francis replied. "Let's get down to cases."

In the suite, which Francis was accustomed to, Brant noted with approval and Sheryl marveled at, Francis invited them to sit down. "I regret being so peremptory, but I've take the liberty to order some food for you. This might be your last chance for a while to have a bite to eat." He picked up the phone and said "Please send someone up with the turkey sandwiches. Thank you." He noticed the look his guests exchanged and as he hung up the phone said apologetically, "Sorry" and then said, "Well, Brant and Sheryl, here we are. Please understand how honoured I was by your call last night, Brant. You more than anyone will appreciate that we have to move with haste.

Your Grumpa, Sheryl, is indeed in great peril. I have contacts who have informed me there are at least two men after your grandfather, representatives of two conflicting groups of people. Your Grumpa was well advised that one of them was murdered a few days ago. But that's not the end of the treachery you face. Everyone in the underground knows what went down in Caye Caulker and what's at stake. Let's put it this way, there's 2 to 3 hundred thousand dollars of free money somewhere out there and if you get it, you keep it. The cops know it, every desk clerk in Belize knows it by now, the politicians know it and every government apparatchik knows it, including the diplomatic core."

"Jesus Christ, Francis, then what are we doing here?"

"You're here, Brant, because you want to get your father out of Belize alive, with or without any money he may still have. Am I right?"

"Of course you're right. I just . . ."

"You know how I work, Brant. Let me make it clear. After we visit the Canadian Consulate which we are scheduled to do in about 45 minutes, you guys aren't going to see me again until we get together in Toronto a few months from now."

Sheryl looked at Francis unable to believe how fast he talked and how much sense he made. Her father had described him to a T, charming, bright and drop-dead handsome. She regretted how flippant she had been. Francis sat across from her wearing dark slacks and a very expensive short-sleeved shirt, casual yet dressy but she realized instantly that it wasn't about good looks and good clothes at all. What overwhelmed her was his decisiveness, his boldness, which she suspected and hoped was wrapped in caution, a realization that for every plan there had to be a fall-back position.

"Okay, buddy, what's the plan?" Brant enquired.

"First of all, the Canadian Consular-General. His name's Andrew Smith. I know the guy, he's likeable enough, but he's the same as all the rest of them. He won't cheat but he will lie. Lying is just a diplomatic nuance to that crowd. He won't be after the money per se, but if he can direct the money this way or that way somewhere down the road he'll be paid in full for ratting out your father. So what I propose is that we present ourselves to him as if we don't have a clue what's going on. You haven't heard from him for a long time, which is unusual. . You are concerned, that's all. Maybe it's no big deal, but where's my father, where's my Grumpa? He hasn't been well lately. Maybe he's fallen ill.

Brant, you tell him about our connection back in Toronto. He won't know that yet but in a few days he'll have a complete dossier on our relationship. I'll tell him, look, I have no interest in this except Brant's my friend and if you can help him I'll be much obliged. He'll know what that means, even though he may wonder why I don't know what's going on, but if I did know he'd figure I would be going for a slice of the pie, which I'm not."

"Wow," Sheryl exclaimed. "I can't believe this."

"Well, believe it, Sheryl, because this is how it's going to work out. You have your part and I have mine. I'll tell the Consulate you've checked into the Princess Hotel under your name but on my tab for two weeks which he will already know and that you are going to visit Caye Caulker tomorrow which is the last place you know your father stayed. You are concerned that he's sick. You are concerned that he's befuddled. You only want to find out what's wrong with him and if necessary bring him back with you. You may need his help. That's why you're taking the time to meet with him. Okay?"

"Okay so far," Brant said. "What next?"

"Next we come back here to the Princess Hotel. I wave at the desk clerk as we walk through the lobby. We go to your room where you attend to your immediate needs, and I suggest everyone have a pee," Francis paused, winking at Sheryl, who blushed, "and as soon as possible you slip out the back entrance where you will be picked up by an employee of mine, a tough guy with a security background. He'll be driving a limo with diplomatic plates and he will have documents, legal, I can assure you, that confirm his diplomatic status. He'll take you directly to the Aguada Hotel in Santa Elena outside of San Ignacio where you'll meet Robert Usher, owner and proprietor."

"Okay, okay, I'm with you so far. This is fantastic, Francis. Sheryl, are you okay?"

"Yeah, I'm like, holy shit, we're moving fast."

"And we're going to move even faster. You're dropped off at the Aguada where my fellow Rotarian Robert Usher is waiting for you. He'll go with you up to Marcos' place and drop you off. I expect he'll go inside with you. It's a good idea for Robert and Marcos to compare notes, make sure they understand what each of them is doing. Then my man will return Mr. Usher to his hotel where he will resume business as usual. Marcos will leave you at his place while he takes his pickup truck to your Grumpa's Mayan hide-away and brings him back to his place. There you will be re-united. Marcos will phone Robert Usher at the Aguada and tell him to tell my driver to pick you up. Then Marcos will park his truck by the side of the house with the lights on. That's the all-clear sign. You'll be taken across the border and driven non-stop to the international airport and will fly out of Guatemala first thing in the morning. You should be back in Toronto sometime in the afternoon."

"What about the money my father has, or says he has?" Brant asked.

"I don't care about the money, but let me make this clear: it is my legal opinion that your father has broken no law and would not face prosecution if he were apprehended by the police. In fact I can assure you that he would be deported sans money of course and flown out of the country before the next commercial airplane left the airport. Nor do I have any moral or ethical concerns. If bad guys in a shoot-out kill one another and in the ensuing confusion lose track of a bag full of money, it's of no interest to me. In this regard, though, I would be prepared to hold the money here if that was something your father wanted. He might not want to run the risk of taking the money through Customs in Canada. But that's far and away the least important matter facing us right now."

"No doubt about that. Money's not the root of my father's troubles."

"Excuse me, sir," Sheryl ventured.

"Please call me Francis."

"All right, Sir Francis . . ."

"Sheryl."

"I'm just kidding, Daddy. But I do have some questions, Francis."

"Shoot."

"Maybe I'm just not picking up on things as quickly as you two guys, but, first, why doesn't your man take us directly to Marcos' place? Why the hotel first? Why Robert Usher? Why not straight to Marcos? Next, let's say everything goes as we hope and we arrive at the airport in Guatemala, aren't we going to have problems at Customs? I mean we don't have visas and they are required in Guatemala, right? And if someone checks Grumpa's luggage and finds bundles of undeclared money, won't red lights start flashing?"

"Good questions, Sheryl, and genuine concerns. You're going to the Aguada to pick up Robert Usher for two reasons. First, he knows where Marcos lives and my man doesn't. And it will be night and Marcos as far as I can tell lives in the middle of nowhere. Secondly, to be honest with you, I don't know Marcos. I've never even heard of him until now. He's an artist and I dig that but does that mean he would risk his life for someone he hardly knows? Bob Usher knows Marcos and says he's okay. That's all I know. And Bob and your grandfather are friends. Or so I've been told. But if it's all true, and I'm counting on it, that's why I want them to have a few minutes together. It's one last chance for Bob Usher to sniff out this guy Marcos the artist to make sure he's a true friend not an imposter.

With reference to your concerns about what happens at the international airport in Guatemala, maybe I didn't make myself clear earlier. After I talked to your father last night, I swung into action . . ."

"No kidding," Brant blurted.

"I devised this plan by reaching out to friends in high places, calling in some markers and cashing in a few pro bono chips. That's why the limo you'll be riding in has diplomatic license plates and the driver driving you has papers that give him and by extension you diplomatic immunity. You'll get across the border, be waved through any roadblocks, skip customs and be boarded on the plane that will fly you back to Toronto, but it is just a plan. It's been well orchestrated but it has yet to be implemented. I learned in school here in Belize that there's many a slip 'twixt the cup and the lip. It's my estimation that we have a 24 hour window of opportunity and when that time's up the window slams shut."

"One more question, if I may?" Sheryl asked.

"Yep."

"It's about the money, the drug money. I can see why the Chinese businessmen took the chance to make a quick profit. Then they lost everything and would naturally want to at least get their 'investment' back, but the drug guys? They've recovered the drugs and have probably sold them by now plus they effectively stole a ¼ million dollars or more from the Chinese even though they never got their hands on it. I'd call that even up. Why not take the dope and get out of town?"

"That's getting right to the heart of this situation, Sheryl. It's not about the money, at all. It's all about power. It's all about the mystique of invincibility. It's all about respect. These guys quite literally have money to burn. By analogy, imagine a native in the rain forest cooking with fire wood. He cuts and stacks a cord of wood, lights his fires from day to day, eventually runs out of wood. So what does he do? He walks back into the forest, cuts down another tree and hauls out another cord of fire wood. These drug dealers are like that, except they stack bundles of drugs, and when they run out they, so to speak, go back into the forest and harvest more bundles, whether it's poppies, or pot or pharmaceuticals, or whatever. So if it isn't money, what is it? The Chinese businessmen showed great disrespect and they will have to pay. In my view, if they don't get out of Belize soon and go back to the States or Taiwan, they'll be found dead in the garbage dump on Caye Caulker and there will be a few dead Belizean thugs found floating in the backwater canals in Belize City. Then the drug dealers will be gone and the drug lords will erase Belize from their memories."

"What about my father," Brant interrupted. "Will they track him down and kill him, too?"

"I don't think so, Brant, and here's why. The Chinese challenged this group of drug dealers, this drug lord. They dared to compete and the punishment for that will be death. Your father, on the other hand, poses no such threat. As Sheryl pointed out, he took the money from the Chinese, not the Mexicans. They'll probably keep a man on his track till the wet work regarding the Chinese and the Belizean goons is completed. If their man catches him before we catch up to him, he'll kill him, have no doubt, but there will be no standing order to follow him to the ends of the earth. Right now we seem to have a little time on our side, very little, so we have to move fast."

"Will you be in peril, sir? I mean, Francis."

"Let's just say I'd much rather we implemented our plan without a hitch, but it's a daring plan and there is a substantial risk attached to it, a risk I must say that is primarily borne by you, Brant, and your daughter here, Sheryl, and your father. You dared to be here. I dare to support you. Who knows for sure what will happen. But enough of this. Let's go see Mr. Smith, your Consular-General. You know your parts. Let the play begin."

After the meeting with the Consular-General, Francis Aloysious Bennett-Pryce backed his BMW out of the Canadian Consulate's parking lot and headed back to the Princess Hotel. Consular-General Andrew Smith watched covertly from an upstairs window. He reached for his cell phone and punched some numbers. "He just left," he spoke. There was a pause. "I think they're okay, don't seem to have a clue what's really happened. They're going to CC tomorrow. What they find there might upset them but we'll deal with that then." There was another pause. "Bennett-Pryce? Everybody raves about him. I think he's got his head so far up his ass all he sees is his own shit, but don't quote me," he giggled. There was another pause. "No, stay on him. He's headed for the Princess right now with the Buchanans. Stay there till he leaves, just to be sure. We'll have our people in place on CC when the Buchanans get there tomorrow."

Alfredo Miguel Sanchez sat in the little shit-box that passed as a car in this little shit-hole country of Belize. He was disgruntled. It was the third night he had staked out the Aguada and he was nearing the end of his patience. He had phoned and asked for back-up and was told to get the job done on his own and get back to headquarters in Mexico pronto. Mucho gracias, he thought, I wish a croc would crawl up your ass and chew your balls off from the inside. He decided to give it one more night and then he was moving in on the owner of the Aguada Hotel, Mr. Robert Usher.

He fondled the stiletto in his pocket, imagined pushing the button on the shaft of the knife that triggered the razor-sharp blade to shoot out. Robert Usher would tell him what he wanted to know or Robert Usher would be short a few digits on each hand and then Robert Usher, Bob, would be dead of a multiplicity of stab wounds.

The problem was that time was passing by and inaction made him crazy. He was parked alongside a cantina directly across from the Aguada Hotel. It gave him a bird's eye view of the entrance to the hotel and to the side-entrance where Mr. Usher and his family and his friends came and went. It also gave him a bird's eye view of the daughter of the owner of the cantina, a nubile, very sexy teenager who exuded sexuality. He had taken the time to meet the owner, Isabella Mendoza, and explain why he was parked alongside her cantina. "I'm working undercover," he explained to her, "and I may be here for a few days." He handed her 50 dollars for some consideration in allowing him to remain there. Isabella knew full well who he was and didn't give a rat's ass. She thought of telling Mr. Usher that someone was spying on him but then thought, "Why should I? What's he done for me since he moved here 15 years ago and took away half my business?"

Isabella Mendoza knew that her biggest problem was that her 15 year old daughter, Carmen, was ripe and ready to be seduced as she, Isabella, had been many years ago. What chance does a little woman have, she sighed to herself, when her own body betrays her and her brain drowns in the very juices she herself has created? She knew that in the end she could do nothing to stop her daughter from destroying herself but now the real, the visible, enemy was the man parked off to the side of her cantina. Working undercover! The only cover he wanted to work under was the cover that would cover him and her daughter when he had his way with her. She would keep her eyes on both of them.

"Buenas noches, senora," Alfredo said as he walked into the cantina. "Agua, por favor, and what do you have that might quench my appetite?"

"Nothing that you would savour, senor, but look," she exclaimed, "isn't that a vehicle driving into Mr. Usher's private entrance!"

Alfredo swung around and caught the headlights of a large car parked in front of the private entrance. He left the cantina and ran to his car. All he could see was the emergence of people, the driver and two others. Then Mr. Usher appeared at his door and beckoned them to come in. Alfredo exited his car and slipped into the darkness, emerging at the side of the Usher residence. Extending himself, he could see through the window. Usher was shaking hands with two white people, a woman and a man. They were not the old man he was looking for, but he thought they looked like the old man. Not exactly, but the man who looked to be about his own age bore a resemblance to the old man as did the woman who could have been the daughter of the man. Son and granddaughter! It was the break he had been waiting for.

It made sense. They had come to save him. Come to whisk him away with his ill-gotten gains. Well, he would have to show them that that's not how it happened in the world he inhabited.

He returned to his car to wait and see what would happen. The old lady from the cantina approached the car and leaned on the open window.

"Senor?" she said. She would try anything to save her daughter who she believed was in great danger. "What do you want with my daughter that I can't give you?"

He looked up at her and laughed. "Youth and beauty, you old hag. Now go away."

"But I have experience, senor. I can do things to you that it will take years for her to learn."

"Do not embarrass yourself any more, you old whore, but take this," he rifled in his wallet and pulled out a hundred dollar bill. "I would have given you ten times this amount for a little sniff of her vagina. Now get out of here. I have work to do tonight."

Isabella Mendoza snatched the bill he offered her and yelled at her daughter, "Get inside, you bitch-in-heat, or I'll lock you in the storeroom!"

Alfredo returned his full attention to the hotel across from him. Finally, he was rewarded. Mr. Usher and his two white friends emerged from the private doorway and clambered into the limousine. Alfredo gave them a moment and then without turning on his lights followed them, feeling certain he knew who they were going to meet. Where they were going to meet him was an open question, one that would soon be answered.

Alfredo followed the car from a distance, confident in his ability to see by a sliver of moonlight. Off the main highway, the roads deteriorated. Clay gave way to rock and at times it was as if he was driving on a pathway unfit for any vehicles, especially unfit for the car he had rented which should have been junked years ago. He followed from a distance. 10, 15, 20 minutes and more passed. The brake lights on the limo ignited the darkness. He watched as it swung sharp left in a u-turn, headlights glaring, and stopped in front of an old shack. He guided his car into a copse of trees on the other side of the road and found some camouflage behind the slender trunks and branches.

He watched as people emerged from the limousine. There was Mr. Robert Usher, 'Bob', followed by the middle-aged white man and his luscious daughter. The driver of the limousine remained seated behind the wheel. Alfredo observed a small pick-up truck by the side of the shack, pulled up snug in its shadows. He was excited but calm. It was not a situation he was unfamiliar with but it always felt good just the same. Something was going to happen. There would be action, most likely violent, and he would be rewarded, not only back home with his bosses, but right here, tonight, probably with the sweet young thing who had come to rescue her grandfather. The anticipation was exquisite.

Inside the cabana, Bob Usher was expansive in his introductions, gesturing as he spoke. "Marcos, you will be pleased to greet the son and daughter of your friend, Barry. And this, Mr. and Ms. Buchanan, is Marcos, a Mayan by birth, a fabulous artist by inclination and talent, and a good friend of mine and of course a good friend of your father's."

Brant stepped up and offered his hand to Marcos who gripped it as he looked into the eyes of his friend's son. Sheryl stepped toward them, arms outstretched but stopped as Bob Usher cleared his throat.

"I wish we had more time to spend together but I have to get back to the hotel. That's not my idea. That's part of the plan. The other part was to give you guys a chance to check out Marcos before you commit. Everything check out all right?"

Marcos and Brant and Sheryl exchanged glances and nodded.

"Okay, Marcos will go and fetch Barry. When they get back, Marcos will contact me and the limo will come and get you. With any luck this little adventure will soon be over and you'll be back home in Canada. How long are they going to have to wait?"

"40, tops 50 minutes," Marcos advised.

"Don't worry, folks," Bob Usher continued, "believe me, there's no one lurking outside waiting for you to arrive at Marcos's place. Nobody knows you are here. And on a more pleasant note, I hope someday you will pay me a visit where we'll have the chance to get to know one another better. Until then, have a safe journey."

"Thank you, Mr. Usher," Brant and Sheryl chorused. Brant stepped forward and grasped Usher's hand. "We'll never forget your kindness."

Sheryl touched Marcos as he walked toward the door. "Marcos?" He turned and opened his arms to her. As they hugged, she felt the strength in his arms. She snuggled her face in the long, black hair flowing over his shoulder. He smelled of smoke from a wood fire. "How is my grandfather, my Grumpa?" she asked. "He is well enough, but he will be much better when I tell him you have come to take him home," Marcos replied.

"Thank you, thank you, thank you for caring for him."

"C'mon, man. We've got to make tracks," Robert Usher said and they slipped out the front door.

Outside in the darkness, Alfredo had been calculating possibilities, visualizing what might occur. If the old man was in there now, he would be coming out momentarily. If that was the case, he would want to kill the driver of the car first, then set his sights on the one unknown in the equation and that was whoever owned the little pick-up truck and lived in that shack. The grandfather would pose no threat, nor the son, nor the daughter. The woman he would save for last.

Mr. Robert Usher would be a threat. He'd lived in the area for years. He would know enough not to go out at night without packing a handgun. Alfredo would have to zero in on him after he shot the driver and the shack guy. He visualized them coming out of the shack approaching the limousine. He saw himself flow out of the shadows and race toward the limo. Bang, driver, sitting behind the wheel. Bang, shack guy, startled, no time to react. Look for Robert Usher going for his pistol. Bang, Robert Usher, dropping down dead. Motion others into the shack, shooting driver, shack guy and Robert in the head, just to be sure. Then the fun would begin.

He waited. He watched. The door to the shack opened and Robert stepped outside, followed by a little guy, who looked Mayan. That's the shack guy, Alfredo reasoned. Robert and the shack guy waved and headed in different directions. Alfredo tensed. Were they trying to outflank him? Robert walked over to the car and got in the front passenger side. The shack guy walked to his little truck in the shadow of his shack and got inside. Headlights from both vehicles glared and pulled out onto the road going in different directions.

Alfredo restrained himself from rushing into the shack and wreaking havoc. He assumed the shack guy was driving his pick-up truck to pick up the grandfather and bring him back for a glorious reconciliation. It was the grandfather he wanted, or, more precisely, the money the old man had stolen. But what if the shack guy came back with the grandfather without the money? He would have to wait and see, but he knew that whatever happened, no matter how hard he had to work, he would succeed. He would get the money and he would get his pleasure, too. He sat back in the darkness, eyes wide-alert, and waited.

Barry was a little buzzed on local rum mixed with coconut juice when Marcos barged into the communal gathering deep in the rain forest. Barry wondered why Marcos was hollering about getting out of there. He looked at his Mayan friends who sat on stools in front of his cabana drinking and laughing. "Marcos, my friend," he cried expansively, "come join us for a drink, or, if you have brought us something more civilized, let us pass around a joint and enjoy the pleasures of the evening."

"Barry, Barry, I'm not joking. Your son and granddaughter have come to get you out of here. We have to leave. Get your stuff together; let's move. Now!"

"Are you kidding me?" He looked at Marcos. He had never seen him more agitated. "Did you say my granddaughter and my son?"

Yes, man, your son. Your son and your granddaughter. They are waiting for you at my place."

"My friends," Barry shouted, realizing that if he spoke in Spanish or English his friends would not understand a word he said. They never did. They dug his intonation, his gestures and his rum, but not his language. "My friends, mi amigos, I have to go. There is rum inside. One Barrel Rum, help yourself."

"Barry, come on!"

"Okay, okay. Let me get my stuff together." Barry went inside and grabbed his backpack full of money and his few belongings. "But Marcos, I've got to give these people something . . ."

"Yes, you should. Give them a hundred dollars. They'll be happy."

"A hundred? I've got so much, man . . ."

"Right, man, and if you dump it all on them now, what's going to happen? Think about it as you get your ass out of here. You want to do something good, you got to have a plan, man. Are you okay for our walk out of here?"

"I'm good. I'm good. My granddaughter and my son! Let's move."

Barry walked behind Marcos, catching glimpses of his white blouse as he twisted through the forest. The night air invigorated him. Adrenaline clicked in. Sheryl must have received his letter, his opus. He was almost embarrassed because he never thought when he scribbled it that he was going to get out of this alive. Now his son was waiting for him, waiting to take him home. And kiddo, his wonderful, beautiful kiddo. Would wonders never cease?

"Come on, my friend," Marcos called. "We are almost at the road. We have to hurry." Marcos himself was panting. "They told me that time was of the essence. I think it means we have to hurry."

In the pick-up truck, Barry slowly got his breath back. Marcos drove like a crazy man with his hair on fire. "Slow down, bro. You haven't told me where we're going?"

"To my adobe, man."

"Yeah? What then?"

"What then, man? I don't know."

'You don't know where I'm going after we get to your adobe? Man, I need a drink right now."

"No, you do not need a drink. What you need to do, man, is sober up 'cause I think you've got a long night ahead of you."

"Like what?"

"Like flying out of Guatemala tomorrow, back to your own country."

"You said you didn't know where I'm going?"

"Barry, Barry, I have ears. I listen. I don't know anything, believe me, hombre."

"I'm sorry, man. I wouldn't be anywhere if it hadn't been for you . . ."

"Forget about it, man. We're almost there. Get ready to meet your family."

Marcos was about to park his pick-up in the shadows alongside his shanty but at the last second pulled in front. "Look, Barry, I forgot I've got to pick something up in town. You go in and greet your family. Me, I'll be back in 15 or twenty minutes." He slipped the gear into neutral. "Go, man. I'll be right back."

Barry pulled on Marcos' sleeve. "How do I look, man?" Marcos turned and looked at his friend. He had heard Barry talk with friends from Canada. They liked to twist words around to make a joke. "You never looked very good, Barry, and you don't look any better." "Thanks, man" Barry said as he opened his door. "Now don't you be gone too long."

As Barry left the car and approached the front door, Marcos glanced to his left, pulled out and headed into the hamlet of River Rock.

Under cover of darkness across the road in the copse, Alfredo watched the arrival of the old man and the departure of the Mayan. He could not know where the Mayan was going but it was a break in his favour. He would do what he had to do in record time and then enjoy the rewards that came with success.

Barry approached the door and slowly opened it, peeking inside. There was kiddo, beautiful as always and grown up, a woman now, and there was his son, Brant, somewhat rumpled but the good-looking, tough, manly guy Barry had always envisioned.

"Grumpa!" Sheryl cried as Barry stepped into the shanty. "Oh my Grumpa," she ran toward him, arms outstretched, "Oh my Grumpa, my Grumpa, my Grumpa, I got your letter and here we are. Daddy and me and we are going to take you home with us. We are going home, tonight, Grumpa. It's all set up. We are going home."

Barry held his granddaughter, tears welling in his eyes. "Hey, kiddo, surprise, surprise. But who's this? Who did you bring with you? It can't be my son, can it? It can't be Brant, can it?

"It's me, Dad," Brant said, walking toward his father. "It's your son, Brant, and I want you to come home with us. We've talked, Sheryl and me, and we want . . . '

"I wish I had a camera to take a picture," Alfredo said, walking into the room. "But who would I send it to? You'll all be dead pretty soon, but, look, I'll keep you in my memory-bank, is that okay? When I retire from this business, I'll remember how utterly pleasant it was to kill each one of you. But for now, everybody stand still and listen up."

Grumpa, Brant and Sheryl stood transfixed, shocked into nwith deep, dark eyes and bloodless lips standing in front of them. He was dressed in black: black hat, black shirt, black jeans, black boots. Barry recognized him in a split-second. Brant and Sheryl took two seconds to realize who he was. They all knew that they were in big, big trouble. Sheryl recalled Francis saying, 'There's many a slip 'twixt the cup and the lip".

"You want the money?" Barry asked.

"Of course I want the money, you old fool. You tricked me once, you tricked me twice, now you'll give me the money."

"I'll give you the money. It's not mine anyway. Take it. It's dirty. I never should have picked it up."

"I agree," said Brant, taking a step forward. "The money is yours. You don't have to hurt us . . ."

"Well, this is more fun than I thought it would be. Let me explain, mi amigos, you were all dead when I walked into this room," Alfredo said. He pulled his automatic from the waist band under his shirt. "I wish I had more time, but the little guy could be back at any moment. Where's the money, old man?"

"What do you mean 'the little guy could be back any moment'? You mean you aren't in cahoots with him?" Brant challenged.

"Don't talk crazy," Alfredo replied, betraying some anger. "I'm not in cahoots with anybody. What the hell are cahoots? I saw the little Mayan bastard drive away . . ."

"It's okay, son," Barry spoke out. "When he dropped me off he said he had to go into town for something. I was surprised, too, but he said he'd be back soon."

"Then let's get going, old one. You're starting to annoy me. Where's the money?"

Barry pointed to the backpack a few feet away from him.

"Get it and bring it over to me."

Barry scooped up the backpack and dropped it at Alfredo's feet.

"Empty it."

Barry emptied the backpack. Bundles of 100 dollar bills spilled out. Alfredo poked one of the bundles, separating it from the rest. "Now pull out a bill from the middle of this bundle and hand it to me," he ordered. Barry did as he was told pulling out a 100 dollar bill and handing it over to Alfredo who crumpled it up with his left hand, lifted it up to his face and smelled it.

"Okay. That's good. That's what I came after . . ."

"Then let us go, man," Barry cried out.

"Take the money, mister," Brant said. "There are two of us to one of you . . ."

"Well, to be accurate, it's 3 of you against 1 of me," Alfredo chuckled, nodding toward Sheryl. "Unless you count this." He waved the pistol at them. "I'd say that makes it 3 to 2 in your favour and this," reaching down he pulled a knife from his boot, "this stiletto which just about makes us even at 3 each, wouldn't you agree, except that I have all the armament and you're just useless white folk from Canada who wouldn't shoot a rat if it was gnawing on your testicles." He pushed a button on the handle of the stiletto. "This is what it looks like when it is excited" The blade flashed out. "That's what I look like when I'm excited."

"Oh, you have a 4 inch dick," Barry said.

"You know, old man, killing you is going to be such a pleasure, but I'm going to have to kill your son first, because he's younger and faster, and then you, and then eventually your granddaughter. She's so hot it might take me hours to quench her fire." He swung the pistol toward Brant. "Nothing personal, hombre, it's just something that has to . . ."

Marcos raised the 4 inch well-whetted wood-cutting hatchet high above his right shoulder and put all his strength into the swing. The hatchet struck Alfredo's head cutting 3 inches through his skull, spewing blood and brain all over the room when Marco pulled out the hatchet. The body collapsed on its knees. Marcos reached for the stiletto that had dropped on the floor, grasped it in his hand, grabbed Alfredo by his hair, jerked his head back, stuck the sharp point of the blade through the skin of the neck, pushed the blade down, moved it across the skin and slit the throat of Alfredo Sanchez. "Just to be sure," he explained to the others as the corpse toppled over, blood pooling like a halo around Alfredo's head.

The others stood stock-still, dumb-struck. "You," Marcos shouted, pointing at Brant. "Help me get this thing out of here."

Brant stumbled out of his trance and bent over the body. "Grab his arm," Marcos ordered, grabbing the other arm. "We'll take him out the back door to the latrine." They lifted him up, head lolling, and dragged him out the back door, leaving a swath of blood behind them.

"Oh, Grumpa," Sheryl cried, folding herself into her grandfather's outstretched arms. "Oh, Grumpa, I had no idea anything like this would happen, no idea . . ."

"Okay, kiddo, it's going to be okay." He held her close in his arms. She smelled young and fresh and he wondered why he had done this to her . . . why had he written that letter? Why had he mailed it? Why was he surprised that she came to Belize to save him, old fool that he was? Was this another pile of crap he left on the trail behind him as he staggered through life, leaving others to clean up his mess?

"I'm so sorry, kiddo," he said. "I'm so sorry you had to see this. I've never seen the likes of it in my entire life, but look," he said, holding her back so he could see her "look on the bright side, if that wasn't him it would have been me." He grabbed her, hugging her till she hurt. "I've been so lost, so lost for so long, I'm so, so sorry, kiddo. I'm so sorry."

Sheryl held him and guided him to the table in the centre of the room and sat him down. She looked at him and saw an old man, ashen faced, tears streaming down his cheeks. "It's okay, Grumpa," she soothed. "It's going to be okay. We're going home. We're going to be okay. Believe me. We are going to be okay."

"Okay, my friends, we have to sit down and talk," Marcos announced as he and Brant barged back into the room. "But first, I must make this call." He reached into a pocket in his shirt, pulled out a cell phone and flipped it open. "Robert", he said when the call went through, "everything's cool. But there's been a slight complication. Tell the driver to get here fast." He sat and looked at the others and suddenly exclaimed. "Aiyyaiyai, my friends, please excuse me," and scooted out of the shanty. He remembered that he had to park the pick-up truck along the side of the shanty with the lights on or the mission would be aborted. "I will be right back."

"Daddy, are you all right?" Sheryl asked, tugging on her father's sleeve.

"Yeah. I'm all right. It's just that I've never, you know, I've never . . . baby, baby, how are you?"

"I'm going to be all right. I'm not sure about Grumpa."

"I'll be all right, kiddo," Barry said, trying to compose himself. "No way I'm going to break down after what we've gone through." He struggled to his feet and opened his arms. "Come here, son. Give your old man a big hug." As they hugged, Barry whispered, "Can you ever forgive me"? "Nothing to forgive, Dad. I've been the fool . . ."

"Okay, break it up guys. Help's on the way." Marcos said. "If everything goes as planned you should be out of here in half and hour."

"Goes as planned? Who the hell planned this, anyway?" Barry asked.

"I'll bring you up to date on the way to Guatemala, Dad. Long story short, a friend of mine, Francis Bennett-Smith, planned all of this. He's a Belizean lawyer practicing in Belize City. You'll get to meet him in a few months. He told me to tell you he'll take care of the money for you if you're worried about getting it through customs."

"You trust him?"

"With your life."

"Well, I like that idea," Barry said, searching through his backpack. "I'm going to stick a few thousand in my wallet and leave the rest back here and, like Marcos said, make a plan to turn bad money into something good. Except for this, Marcos," Barry extended his hand with a stack of bills in it. "Here's 5 grand, my friend. It's yours to do anything you want."

"Five grand?"

"Five thousand. Dollars. U.S. Comprende?"

"Thank you, my friend," Marcos said, taking the money. "Maybe I'll visit my kids in Quebec. That'll be cool. But wait a minute. I've got something for you." He walked over to a table in the corner of the room and came back unrolling a canvas. "This is for you, man," he said, holding it up, "and it's not my wife, man."

Sheryl and Brant recognized the painting from Barry's description of it. It was stunningly beautiful, the long blonde hair flowing, the face exquisite, eyes dark and shining, nose aquiline, arm extended, hand releasing butterflies and flowers, ocean spray and fishes, a panoply of creation, a chain of being.

"No argument from me, Marcos. I was wrong and admit it. I know who it really is. I always have."

"Who is it, man?"

"It's Beatrice, my wife, the love of my life. And you brought her back to me. Thank you, Marcos. Thanks for your friendship. Thank you for saving our lives."

Brant and Sheryl hugged the little man. "We'll never forget you, Marcos," Sheryl said with tears in eyes, "and we're coming back to visit you as soon as we can."

"I've got a question, Marcos. Something I can't figure out. Why didn't you come in with me when you brought me back?"

"Yeah, that's what I wanted to ask, too," Barry said. "What happened there?"

"Nothing really," Marcos replied. "I got a glimpse of something in the trees across the road and saw a figure standing by a car, so I off-loaded you, went up the road and when I figured he couldn't see my tail-lights I did a U and came back. Good thing I did, too. That bastard was about to kill all of you."

"Marcos," Sheryl asked, "you were so brave, you didn't hesitate for a moment, have you . . . ?"

"No, it is my first time. But I have killed many animals in the forest, some for food, some to protect my family, and that's all he was to me, an animal, a dangerous animal that had to be destroyed."

"Are you coming with us, man," Barry asked. "We can't leave you with all this." He gestured with his arms at the blood-streaked floor and at the door beyond which a dead body lay by the latrine in the back yard.

"I'll be okay, man. First I will dispose of the Mexican's car in Guatemala and bring the money to my people in the village. They'll take care of the blood and the body while I'm away. Then I will go deep into the forest and restore my soul, and when I return everything will be forgotten . . ."

"What about your people?" Barry asked. "Won't they be in danger? Won't the police . . ."

"Yes, the police will be looking for you and for the Mexican. The Mexican's friends will want to find out if he's dead or run off with the money. But do not be concerned, my friends. My people, it's hard to explain, but my people do not hate the outside world, they just don't accept it. When you visit them, they will treat you with kindness and respect, but when you are gone, you will be forgotten. When the police come to question them, or when the Mexican banditos bully them, they won't lie. They will tell the truth as they know it. 'There were no such men' and they will mean it. If the strangers threaten too much, or hurt one of my people, those strangers will not walk out of the forest. But you, my little sister, will you survive this adventure?"

Sheryl stepped forward between her Daddy and her Grumpa, clasping their hands. She had learned so much in such a short time. She knew now as she had never known before that life was fraught with pain and peril and only death waited at the end of the journey, but she had responded to a challenge, her father had joined forces with her, and together with the help of some incredible people they had saved her Grumpa's life. "Yes," she said, raising their hands, "with these guys on either side of me, I will survive. We'll all survive."

A horn blasted outside.

"They're here," Marcos exclaimed. "Hasta la vista, mi amigos."

THE END

Biographical Stats And Postscript Notes

Grumpa aka Barry Buchanan was born 1945 in Brantford, Ontario, Canada; married Beatrice Broadbear in a civil ceremony in 1969; father of Brant Buchanan; grandfather of Sheryl Lisel Buchanan.

Barry Buchanan returned to Belize 8 months after he had escaped from it. There was no problem with Customs. With the assistance of Francis A. Bennett-Pryce, he has set up a trust-fund to assist Mayan-Belizeans to pursue post-elementary school education. He has hired Marcos Madeiros as a consultant. He plans to spend at least 4 months a year in Belize.

Beatrice Buchanan (nee Bradshaw) born 1945 in Hamilton, Ontario, Canada; married Barry Buchanan in a civil ceremony in 1969; died of pancreatic cancer in 1988 at age 43.

Brant Buchanan only child of Barry and Beatrice Buchanan, born in Mississauga, Ontario, Canada in 1970; married Felice Boudreau in a roman-catholic ceremony in Toronto in 1990; father of Sheryl Lisel Buchanan.

Brant Buchanan continues to successfully practice criminal law in Toronto. He has partnered up with Francis Bennett-Pryce and opened an international law consultancy firm in New York City, USA. He looks forward to the day that his daughter will join the firm. He remains reconciled with his father, Barry Buchanan, but there are moments . . .

Felice Buchanan (nee Boudreau) born in Toronto in 1972; married Brant Buchanan in a roman-catholic ceremony in Toronto in 1990; mother of Sheryl Lisel Buchanan; divorced from Brant Buchanan in 1998.

She remains a loving mother of her daughter and a good friend of her ex-husband. Deeply disappointed in the roman-catholic church in which she was raised and educated, she has left the church, and she and her partner have become active members of an organization promoting equal rights for homosexuals around the world.

Sheryl Lisel Buchanan only child of Barry and Felice Buchanan, born in Toronto, Ontario, Canada in 1992; granddaughter of Grumpa aka Barry Buchanan.

Sheryl Buchanan received a scholarship to attend the University of Toronto where she will obtain a degree in English Literature after which she will study law. She looks forward to the day she can practice law with her Daddy and her Daddy's best friend, Francis Bennett-Pryce. She was wounded but not scarred by her experience in Belize and intends to visit Belize with her Grumpa whenever the opportunity arises. Her affection for her Grumpa continues unabated.

Francis A. Bennett-Pryce, law-school friend of Brant Buchanan, citizen of Belize from a prominent family, successful corporate and criminal lawyer with an international reputation.

Francis Bennett-Pryce continues to succeed in his practice of law in Belize and in the international community, allowing him to partner up with his good friend,

Brant Buchanan, and open an international law firm in New York City in the USA. He has developed a deep fondness for Brant's father, Barry Buchanan, and for Barry's friend, Marcos Madeiros, and has helped them set up a trust-fund for deserving Mayan-Belizean children.

Marcos Madeiros disappeared for a few months only to re-appear in his home-village with a couple thousand dollars US as a gift for them, proceeds from the car Alfredo Sanchez had rented in San Ignacio. Marcos also brought with him a number of paintings he painted while in seclusion, one of which came second in a juried art show in Belize City won by the internationally-acclaimed Belize artist, Pen Cayetano. He enjoyed a reunion with Barry Buchanan and began work with him and the lawyer, Francis Bennett-Pryce, as a consultant for a trust-fund set up with Barry's winnings from the sea-lottery.

Alfredo Sanchez, almost certainly an alias, was never heard from nor seen again. He was not missed in any meaningful way. Two drug-thugs were dispatched by a notorious drug lord in Mexico. They were instructed to determine if Alfredo had betrayed his masters and if so to kill him and return the money where it belonged. Frustrated by the Mayan's reluctance to admit anything whatsoever of the very existence of Alfredo Sanchez or the old man he pursued, the thugs overstepped the bounds of acceptable Mayan social behaviour and themselves permanently disappeared into the rain forest.

The hoteliers Jenny, owner/manager of the Hotel Mopan, Belize City, and Robert Usher, owner/manager of the Aguada, Santa Elena in the Cayo District, continue to offer guests whether from home or abroad clean, comfortable, secure and affordable lodgings. Robert Usher became President of the Belize International Rotarians at the last national convention.

Harry Abscombe, Barry Buchanan's American friend and room-mate on Caye Caulker, may have eluded pursuit and escaped with the $50,000 Barry gave him to keep his mouth shut long enough for Barry to reach the mainland. Rumours persist, however, that he took the water-taxi to San Pedro on the Ambergris Caye and slipped across to Orange Town where he was seen living the high life in a manner not commensurate with his modest income. Others say that he didn't get further than the same dump the Chinese businessmen were found except the crocs were hungrier on the day he was dispatched. The jury is out.

True to Bennett-Pryce's prognosis regarding the Chinese business men who dared challenge a notorious Mexican drug lord, the remains of the bodies of two Taiwanese—Chinese nationals, Yan te Sung, 'Sunny', and Moo Tran Sang, 'Moonie', were recovered from the garbage dump on Caye Caulker. What body parts that were not recovered had been devoured by crocodiles which fed nightly on the food left them by the citizens of the island. Coincidently, police in Belize City recovered two bodies found floating in the back-water canals of the city slums. They were both well-known to the police and were easily identified.

The Canadian Consular-General to Belize, Andrew Smith, was rewarded for the magnitude of his incompetence by being appointed Ambassador to the West African country of Togo, formerly a French colony. He quickly distinguished himself as the only unilingual (English) ambassador from a bi-lingual (English/French) country (Canada), who refused to meet with anyone who could not speak with the King's tongue and spent most of his time in neighbouring Ghana where the natives there had the good sense to be educated in English. Mistaking notoriety for popularity, the Reform-Conservative Government of Canada awarded him the Badge of Canada for service beyond and below the call of duty.

SHAKEDOWN IN BELIZE

The sun dipped quickly into the Caribbean Sea, sending a golden sheen across the waves that lapped ashore on San Pedro, a burgeoning town on Ambergris Caye off the coast of Belize, Central America. On shore, except for new-comers who marveled at nature's beauty, the beat went on in San Pedro.

San Pedro was the most popular tourist spot in Belize. A once quiet town on a largely uninhabited Ambergris Caye it was almost equidistant from Mexico and Belize but within the boundaries of Belize, the smallest and only English speaking country in Central America. The fathers of San Pedro opened their arms to the Caribbean Tourist Industry and in less than twenty five years the town had been transformed from 'quaint' to 'hot', from hut to high-rise hotel, from foot to bicycle to motorcycle to car to truck, from SUV's to quads, from travelling back-packers and north-americans looking to get away from it all to locusts of college students from the U.S.A. and Canada and avaricious land developers who recognized a good deal when they saw it and rushed to cash in.

"That's how it went down." said Bob the bartender at 'Bob's Bar and Barbeque'.

He was chatting with a couple of tourists who sat attentively on bar stools in front of him. It was a Sunday, early evening, usually a quiet time. "But, hey, wait a minute. Here's the man himself. Johnny! Johnny Lomas! Over here, mate!"

Johnny Lomas knew what Bob the bartender wanted. A few months earlier he had an experience on one of the cayes off Belize. He'd spent a few nights in jail on a trumped up charge of willful damage to a hotel window, a matter that should have been resolved at the police station and certainly shouldn't have resulted in being marched to a police lock-up. But then the Belizean media got wind of the incident, the Canadian consulate in Belize City dropped the ball, and the whole thing turned into an international affair.

Wearing Ecco sandals, non-descript knee-length khaki shorts and a short-sleeve bright red rayon shirt emblazoned with sun-sets and palm trees, he walked across the dance floor toward Bob and the bar thinking that all he wanted was a quiet drink or two. It was getting close to 6:30 p.m., the sun was setting and the bar was nearly empty. Angelina was in their room writing letters to friends who never wrote back, preferring to telephone or email, and if everything worked out he would have an early night and get the first water taxi to Belize City in the morning. And then he thought, 'Oh what the hell, a little company won't hurt' and, truth to tell, he'd always liked telling a tale, even a tall one at times.

"Hey Bob. Give me my regular. Double One Barrel in a tall glass with bottled water, in case you've forgotten since last night. Hi folks, what's Bob been bull dozing over you?"

He looked at the couple at the bar, mid to late forties if his own kids were anything to go by, well-tanned, well-kept, well-off, likely American though affluent Canadian tourists had the same look. Wearing an emerald green v-neck sundress, she was a pretty brunette with tired eyes. He was dressed for success in his Dockers, knee-length khaki Tommy Hilfiger shorts, a blue loose-fitting Victorinox short-sleeved shirt, and, as if made to order, a deep tan and thinning dark hair brushed straight back. For all the pretence to the contrary, Johnny thought the man look flushed, probably over-refreshed, and flabby.

"Hasn't had a chance to bull doze anything over us yet," said the brunette. "We was just asking him about the guy that got busted for breaking some windows in a hotel, or something like that . . . was that you?"

"Yes, it was. Indeed it was," Johnny replied, reaching for his rum, anticipating the warmth it would spread through him. "But, if you don't mind me asking, who are you? I mean, you have me at a disadvantage, don't you. Bob, would you do the introductions?"

Bob was pleased to be asked to make introductions. He dispensed pleasure from his post behind the bar as he once dispensed pleasure as a server in restaurants and bars around the world. He was a good-looking, well-conditioned man with dark-brown curly hair and a smile that made his eyes light up. Now in his early thirties, he'd left New Zealand, his home and native land, when he was eighteen and never returned. When asked why not, he would reply that he hadn't the foggiest. When asked if he would ever return, he would reply that he had no immediate plans to do so. He seemed quite content where he was in San Pedro, owner and bartender of the establishment he had bought from the previous owner for whom he once worked. Rumour had it amongst San Pedro's full-time inhabitants that he must have won the sea-lottery, a term used to describe the recovery of large packets of drugs dumped overboard when smugglers were pursued by the navy police. On that matter, he had nothing whatever to say.

Bob did some mental calculations. He knew Johnny pretty well. It didn't take long in his line of work to size people up and he knew Johnny well enough to know that he could be a handful with a few doubles in him. On the other hand, Johnny was having or had just had his 15 minutes of fame, so why not ride the wave? The folks at the bar had brought up the subject, why not let them meet the man who had made all the news and, if the conversation pleased them, why not take the tip that might accrue?

"Sure, Johnny. This here's Brad and Brenda, nice folks from Canada, same as you. Got a time-share in Cancun and thought they'd check out San Pedro for a few days. That right, folks? Don't want to misrepresent you."

"Hi. I'mma Johnny, as an Italian friend of mine used to say when he answered the phone. I told him drop the 'ma' but he couldn't do it. Anyway, has Bob misrepresented you in any way?"

"No," Brad replied, "not really, except maybe the 'nice' part. There's more to us than that but it's a starting point, isn't it? And yes, our passports say that we're Canadian."

"Yes," Brenda interjected, "so many people take us for Americans. I mean, that's not bad or anything but what is it, the way we act, the way we dress?"

"Maybe you don't say 'eh?' enough", said Johnny.

"Good one, mate," Bob exclaimed. "If I had a tenner for every time I heard a Canadian say 'eh?' I'd be a rich man and if I had a drink before me I'd raise my glass and say, 'Cheers!'"

"Even though you are rich, or so they tell me, put one on my tab, you Kiwi rascal," Johnny said, leaning across the bar, "and bring my new Canadian friends whatever they're drinking."

"Oh no, no," Brenda exclaimed, "You don't have to!"

"Of course I don't have to. But I want to. And you don't have to accept if you don't want to, but why on earth wouldn't you?"

As Bob fixed the drinks, Brenda looked at Johnny and said, "That's very kind of you, isn't it Brad, and we are pleased to accept . . ."

"As long as we can return the favour . . ."

"Yes, of course," Brenda continued, "but to get back to where we began, we only just mentioned to Bob that we'd heard there was someone staying at the hotel back of Bob's who'd had a little problem with the Belizean authorities and we wanted to be brought up to speed when in you walked . . ."

"And hey-presto!"

"And here you are . . ."

"And would you like to hear my story?"

"Love to," Brenda replied enthusiastically.

"Whatever," Brad said.

"Okay, let's see." Johnny paused and sipped his drink. "It's not that I haven't told the tale over and over again, but I always wonder where to begin . . ."

"At the beginning," Brad spoke, hands folded in front of his mouth to form a megaphone. "Start at the beginning."

"Brad, be quiet."

"Quite right. Hush up, mate." Bob said as he placed the drinks on the table.

"Okay," Johnny said, "let's begin when we arrived on Caye Hermoso[1] a few months ago . . ."

---

[1] Caye Hermoso is an imaginary island off the coast of Belize in the Caribbean Sea

"Johnny, time out," Brenda interrupted. "I'm sorry. I'm serious. Who's 'we' when you say 'we'?"

"That's a good question. 'We' is me and my partner, my significant other as they say."

"So you're not married," Brad said.

"Depends what you mean by 'married'."

"Well, is your partner a 'she' or a 'he'?"

"Brad, shut up."

"I concur. Shut your gob, mate" Bob said, holding a wine glass up to the light to make sure there were no stains on it.

"You can't talk to me that way, you're only a . . ."

"Bartender?" Bob said.

"Whoa, whoa down there. Brad, is that your name? Brad, don't be such an asshole."

"You can't call me an asshole . . ."

"C'mon, Brad, you're way out of line. What's with the questions about my partner? What's with Bob's 'only' a bartender? Not that it matters but he does happen to own this place. I'm starting to think maybe you are an American."

"Never mind about my nationality. You called me an asshole . . ."

"So what, Brad? What are you going to do about it?"

"Brad, Brad honey, you ain't going to do anything about it. This gentleman said he was going to tell us a story and you are not respecting him. Now, are you going to start respecting him or not, because if the answer is 'or not' we are out of here right now."

Brad sulked before answering. "Okay, I'm sorry, Brenda. Maybe I was out of line, but he shouldn't've called me an asshole."

"Don't apologize to me, honey. Tell Johnny you're sorry."

"I'm sorry, Johnny," Brad mumbled.

"I'm sorry, too," Johnny said. "Perhaps I overreacted to your question. But I never said that you were an asshole. All I said was that you were acting like one."

"Oh, there's a difference?"

"Yes there is. A fine line, I grant you, but there is a difference."

"Okay, okay, tell us your story . . . Bob, I'm sorry, okay?" Brad turned to address Bob the Bartender. "Guess I started too early. Cut me off the hard stuff, okay? Give me a pint of draft, and I don't care what it is as long as it isn't under 5%."

"Got you, boss-man."

"That's my sweetheart." Brenda stroked Brad's crossed legs. "Let's listen to the guy and talk after."

"Okay? Okay, without preamble, my partner, Angelina, and I take the last water-taxi out of Belize City and get to Caye Hermoso about an hour before sunset a few months ago . . . Anyone want dates and times?"

"Unless it's important," Brad replied, sullenly and sheepishly at the same time.

"Okay then. We arrive at the caye. We spot Jesus in his golf-cart taxi and give him thumbs up. He loads our luggage and takes us . . ."

"Whoa. It's my time to say 'Whoa'" Brenda sputtered. "You mean you went from the water terminal to your hotel on a golf-cart?"

"That's right, miss." Bob interceded. "There's no motorized vehicles on Caye Hermoso, with a few prominent exceptions such as the police and the construction people. Only battery-driven golf-carts and bicycles. It's not like San Pedro with cars and trucks and motorcycles and quads. It's like San Pedro used to be like 20 years, so I've been told. Go on, Johnny, go on."

"May I?" said Johnny, looking at the couple beside him at the bar. He hadn't finished his drink but he was feeling a little feisty already. He wondered who they were and why they wanted to hear his story. Nevertheless, he was still prepared to tell his tale if they would be prepared to listen.

"So, as I was saying, there we were on Caye Hermosa, luggage stowed on the taxi, no problem, on our way to the hotel where we had reservations, a lovely 3-room cabana 30 feet from the Caribbean Sea fully equipped with a full kitchen. We'd checked it out the year before and it was something we'd come to want more than when we first travelled to Belize. The full kitchen, I mean. So it was a little more expensive than we used to pay but worth every penny.

'I'm sorry, sir,' the desk clerk says, 'your cabana is not available at this time.' And I'm looking at her and she's not hard to look at, maybe twenty years old, carmel—coloured skin, pretty eyes, and I'm trying real hard not to get upset so I say, 'And when will it be available?' And she says, 'Probably tomorrow'. 'You know we have reservations, don't you?' 'Yes sir'. 'Then what do you propose we do from now till we can move into the cabana we thought we had reservations for?' 'My boss said to offer you another accommodation'. 'And what would that be?' 'They's a nice new cabana at the back, brand new'. 'And?' 'My boss said you can have it.' 'Full kitchen?' 'No, but nice, nice and new'. 'How much?' 'My boss says regular 100usd a night, for you 50. 'A hundred usd! That's more than we're paying for our cabana by the sea.' I looked over at Angelina and she's shrugging her shoulders as if to say c'mon let's move on so I say, 'Okay, all right, 50 usd for tonight and what we'd agreed on for the next 9 days. Here's my credit card, run it through now so we don't have to go through this again.'

So she runs it through, I sign. A guy comes out of nowhere and helps us with the luggage. It's getting dark fast but we're able to follow him down a path, it's like we are walking away from the hotel to some dumpster in the back, but then we see it, a new-looking cabana, isolated but okay, hell, it's only for one night. The guy opens the door and lets us in, and it's like, okay, it's new all right, has that new smell, like fresh paint, but we're both thinking let's just get inside, open the windows, turn on the fans and just settle down. The guy flips us the keys, doesn't say a word, just flips us the keys and disappears.

Only problem is, once we're inside with the lights on, we realize there is only one stand-up fan in the whole cabana, no air-conditioning, which we don't like, anyway, but in these conditions it would've been a good idea, even as a back-up unit, and the windows are all stuck shut. We turn the fan on to max but it's just circulating musty air. We check out the windows but they all seem to be nailed shut, except, we discover, one. It's the biggest window in the cabana. Trouble is, we can't get it to open. Try as we might, and I mean I'm on one side and Angelina's on the other, and we can't get that sucker to budge. Then, one or another of us gives a yank, out of frustration, and the window moves forward and slides into a groove and we haul it down and by god we've got some fresh air. We just carry the window over to a side wall, prop it up, and flop back on the bed laughing. It's not great, but with the stand-up fan and some live air coming through the window screen of our one open window, it feels like a victory. We pop a warm bottle of red wine and toast ourselves with plastic glasses We're bone tired but I think I've got to let them know about the window removal and tell them to get the other windows opened for future clients so I get my flashlight and walk up to the office. It's closed. What the hell, I say to Angelina when I get back. It's only one night. We're paid up. Let's get out of here and find someplace to eat."

"Wow," Brad said, pushing his empty draft glass across the bar to Bob. "This is a regular Steven King horror story. Fill 'er up there, Bob, please and thank you, and one for the lady and the same again for the gentleman, if I may be so bold."

"Oh, Brad, can the sarcasm, he's just getting started, aren't you . . . ?"

"Johnny," said Johnny

"Of course, Johnny. Aren't you, Johnny? Just getting started, I mean."

"Of course. And I won't accept Brad's kind offer of a drink right now. For I have many miles to go before I sleep, and a big day awaits me in the morning. Why don't I just pick up where I left off if that's all right with everybody?"

"Yeah, yeah, get on with it," Brad muttered as Bob brought his drink. "For Christ's sake, get on with it."

"So we slept all right. A bit stuffy. Air circulation not what it should be, but you learn to make do when you travel, right? Check out time's 11 but we can't check into our new cabana till 3 so we pack our bags and lug them up to the office and arrange to have them brought to our cabana along with the keys at 3 p.m. We kick around the caye, do a bit of shopping, have lunch etc. etc., get to our cabana around 3—there's no one there. Sit on the front porch, it's a nice view. white caps on the blue water, coconut trees, white beach, but it's getting pretty hot and we want to be in our bathing suits not our shorts and shirts, we want to be splashing in the salt-sea water not sitting on a hot porch when the same guy who moved our luggage the night before shows up in a golf cart and unloads our luggage and flips us our keys. Doesn't say a word the whole time. I feel like flipping him the bird but restrain myself. Anyone that ignorant could be dangerous.

We open the cabana and step inside and it's just like we saw it last year. We open the windows, turn on the fans, Angelina runs over to the kitchen and checks everything out, we unload our groceries, start to unpack and there's a knock on the screen door. I go to the door and I see the shape of a cop through the screen and there's another figure behind him, I can't make him out very well. I open the screen door a foot or two and ask, 'Yes? May I help you?' and this cop in khaki says, 'Good evening, sir. I'm Officer Blah Blah Blah,' I don't get his name, 'with the Tourist Police. Are you Johnathon Lomas?'

'Yes, I'mma Johnny.'

'Beg pardon, sir?'

'Yes, I am Jonathan Lomas. Please call me Johnny.'

'Very well. I have with me here Mr. Sanchez, the owner of this hotel. May we come in, Mr. Lomas?'

'Uh, no,' I said without any hesitation. 'Let me step out on the porch with you.'

There are two guys out there, one dressed up in the uniform of the Tourist Police, black boots, black beret, lanky, clean shaven, and the other much shorter, older, greasy black hair, sweat-stained cotton long-sleeved shirt, pock-mocked face pumping sweat.

'Is everything all right, honey,' Angelina called from the kitchen.

'As far as I know,' I replied, and stepped out on the front porch where I met what would be the nemesis of my life.

'Sir,' Officer Blah Blah said, 'Mr. Sanchez here, the owner of this hotel, informs me that you were a guest at his hotel last night. Is that so?'

'Yes it is.'

'You rented cabana 37 at the rear of Mr. Sanchez's property?'

'Yes I did but . . .'

'Let me do the talking for now, Mr. Lomas, or Johnny as you prefer to be called.'

'All right. Ask me anything you . . .'

'I'm asking you if you left the cabana this morning as you found it?'

'Yes, yes we did. We . . .'

'Nothing changed? Nothing broken?'

'Nothing I know of.'

'What does that mean, nothing you know of? Are there things you don't know of or things you don't want to tell me?'

'Hey, hey, what's this all about?'

'It's all about Mr. Sanchez here, the owner of the hotel, who informs me that when he checked your cabana shortly after you checked out he found a window, a large window, on the floor, smashed and broken. Is that it, Mr. Sanchez? Smashed and broken?'

Mr. Sanchez took a step toward me. "Yes, that is correct,' he sneered. 'That is very, very correct. And I demand restitution.'

'Say what?'

'You heard,' Blah Blah said. 'Mr. Sanchez is a reasonable man but he is concerned that you vandalized his cabana and left without any notification . . . '

'What? What? Wait a minute.' I turned to the screen door and shouted, 'Angie, come out here, please. There's something I want you to listen to.'

Blah Blah stepped toward me. 'Why not leave her out of this. Let's settle this like men.'

'Like men? What do you mean by that? Why don't you want my wife hearing what you have to say? We're travelers in your country, pal. As a tourist policeman aren't you interested in protecting us?'

'You don't seem to understand, Johnny.' Senor Sanchez spoke without moving. 'In my country, the tourist police are responsible for the well-being of tourists in Belize, but equally, I repeat, as an equal responsibility, they must protect Belizeans from the tourist.'

'What the hell are . . . '

'Johnny,' Angelina burst out on the porch, 'what are these guys doing? What's going on?'

'Come here, honey.' I put my arm around her shoulder. 'I want you hear what these guys have to say . . . '

'But Johnny we . . . '

'Take my advice, sir, leave her . . . '

'But she's in it. And she's a witness to it. So go on, get on with it. Whole lot of shake-down going on here, Angie, whole lot of shake-down going on.'

'Johnny, what do you mean?"

'You'll know in a second or two, honey. But believe me I know now. Ever smelled a skunk on the side of the road?"

'Sure I have . . . '

'Well, it's like that. And you never forget it, right? Well, we just ran over a skunk on the road and it stinks to high-heaven."

'I resent these remarks, Mr. Low-mass,' Senor Sanchez said. 'Officer, please remind this gentleman I am prepared to make an offer that will not make it necessary to press formal charges, though I must say that I am having second thoughts about it.'

'Yes sir.' Blah Blah turned to me again. 'Mr. Sanchez informs me that he is prepared to drop charges against you if you will pay for the cost of the window.'

'What are the charges?'

The officer and Senor Sanchez confer. The officer steps forward to report. 'The charges are willful destruction of property, vandalism and misrepresentation as a person in good-standing.'

'Say what? What's that last one . . . '

'Never mind the last one. These are serious charges, sir. If convicted, you face a big fine and time in jail and if you have heard anything about Belizean prisons, sir, you wouldn't want to do time in Hattyville.'

'I don't want to do time anywhere . . . What's he want for the window?'

'Mr. Sanchez is prepared to let you pay for the cost of the window at $800usd.'

'800 dollars? 800 dollars to replace one lousy window.'

'800 dollars to replace the window and for installation of the window. Much damage to the infra-structure. Big job. I saw it myself. You must have been real angry. Mr. Sanchez says he does you a favour at 800.'

'Let me talk to my partner.'

'All right then, sir. I'll confer with Mr. Sanchez.'

I pulled Angie off to one side of the porch while Officer Blah Blah conferred with Senor Sanchez. 'Don't worry, honey, I just want to see how low they'll go . . . '

'How low they'll go? Why not just pay up?' Angie was agitated at that point. 'We have the money . . . '

'Angie, you know I can't do that. We didn't do anything wrong. This is a classic shake-down, honey, and there's no way I'm going to let them get away with it. C'mon, honey, you know I can't be shook down, not and live with myself after, and least ways not by these guys, but don't worry, I'll listen to what they have to say . . . '

'What they have to say? Johnny, what's going on?'

'We're negotiating, honey, but there will be no deal. Just watch the numbers fall, all right?'

'Excuse me, sir. Don't want to interrupt but Mr. Sanchez informs me that to make this matter go away he will accept 1200 dollars, usd of course, if that will make it easier for you.'

'Well, you know what, to make this matter go away, I would have been willing to reimburse Senor Sanchez for something I never did by paying out maybe $50, and maybe even, because I don't need the grief, I'd suck it up and pay out $100, that's Belizean currency, of course, which is two Belizean dollars to every American dollar, but you guys have pushed it too far. You're getting nothing from me. Nada. Comprende? Nada. Get my drift, senor. End of story.'

'Then I'll have to take you to the police station.' Blah Blah said.

'Do what you have to do.'

'You'll have to spend the weekend in jail before we can deal with this matter.'

'Let's see. This is Friday. You're telling me you can't deal with this matter till Monday?'

'At the earliest, sir. You know how it is on a weekend. And when the week begins again on Monday there's usually a back-log, isn't there? But excuse me, sir, Senor Sanchez would like a word with me.'

Blah Blah stepped over to the corner of the porch and briefly conferred. He stepped back and reported again. 'Sir, Mr. Sanchez says that although you are in the wrong, he admires your spirit, and he is prepared to accept 700usd as restitution for the broken window and moreover will give you 10% discount on the rest of the week. What do you think of that? Is that okay?'

Trying to look defeated, I said, 'Let me talk to my wife in private, okay?'

'Of course, okay. But please, Mr. Lomas, it's very hot out here. Let's get this matter finished and done with.'

Angie and me stepped back inside and pulled the screen door closed. We heard Sanchez remonstrate outside on the porch. I put both my hands on Angie's shoulders and said quietly, "Angie, this is bull-shit and you know it.' She nodded her head and looked me in the eyes. 'They're going to take me to the station. They're thinking as soon as they get me out of here I'm going to break and make a deal.'

'But you're not, are you?' Angie said.

'No, I'm not. So, honey, we gotta play this smart, gotta play it on the safe side, okay. As soon as they leave, get the hell out of here.' She nodded. 'Where do you think you'll go?' I asked.

'I'm thinking Val's. They won't think I'll seek help from a Belizean and she's got the internet connection at her guest-house.'

'Right. They'll probably hold me overnight, maybe over the weekend at the very worst, so lay low. Okay.'

'Don't worry. I'll get in touch with the Canadian consulate in Belize City and with Jaguar in San Ignacio. Anyone else you can think of?'

'Get in touch with Barry. Tell him to check out the station and if I'm not there track me down at the lock-up. Barry will be our go-between.' Barry was an American/Belizean from Seattle who stayed 6 months a year in his cabana on Caye Hermoso and six months back in the U.S. We'd met him years ago and he had become a good friend.

'What about Janet?' Angie asked.

'Oh yeah. Right. Almost forgot. Janet at the Hotel Mopan. For sure, Janet. She's got good contacts with the Belize Tourist Association, hasn't she? So, as soon as they take me away, clear out, okay? Take as little as you can. I'll wait to hear from Barry. He'll make sure you know what's going on. Okay?'

'Okay . . . '

'Sorry to interrupt you two love birds . . .' Blah Blah interrupted, knocking lightly on the screen door.

We held each other's hands and lightly kissed. Her eyes shone with love as we parted. I hoped mine did, too.

"What happened then?" Brenda asked.

"What happened then was that I learned the true meaning of the word 'shakedown'" Angelina Antoniolli said as she slipped up behind Johnny and hopped on the bar stool beside him. She was tall and slender and looked much younger than Johnny. From her complexion, darkened no doubt by the Belizean sun, her roots were in southern not northern Italy. In her bright yellow sundress with lustrous black hair caressing her shoulders she would be considered by anybody's estimation a very attractive woman. "I'd like a glass of pinot grigio, Bob, please.' Then she turned her attention to Brad and Brenda. 'Hi, my name's Angelina. I'm Johnny's co-conspirator and I was wondering why Johnny was taking forever having a drink at the bar with Bob."

Bob placed a glass of pinot grigio in front of Angelina. "Folks, this here, as they say, is Johnny's Angelina. Angelina, this is Brenda and Brad from Canada . . ."

"More accurately, Alberta . . ." Brad sputtered.

"Oh, now I get it," Johnny said.

"Get what?"

"Get why you and I might not be getting along."

"Whoa, whoa there boys," Brenda interrupted. "We're in the middle of a good story, let's not screw it up." She reached across the bar, hand extended. "Hi, Angelina, my name's Brenda. Sorry to steal your man away from you but I've got know what happened next."

"Hey, baby," Johnny said. "Just got talking, you know me."

"Sure do."

"You been listening a little bit?"

"Uh huh."

"Want to pick it up from here?"

"Sure, Johnny. Get yourself another drink."

Angelina straightened herself out and leaned a little toward the bar. She realized instantly why Johnny didn't much care for Brad. He looked soft and self-indulgent, two attributes Johnny despised. Being from Alberta didn't help much, either. Johnny was from Windsor, Ontario, a union town and Johnny was a union man through and through. The crew that Brad rowed with in Alberta was likely anything but union.

Angelina herself was a union woman, though by career not conviction. She left her home town of Niagara Falls after she finished grade twelve and migrated to the city of Toronto where she worked at several entry-level jobs as a secretary before being hired by the Canadian Auto Workers union starting at category 2. She was bright and conscientious and though not particularly ambitious caught the attention of others and was promoted on a regular basis until at an early age she became the executive assistant to the President of the CAW, a very prestigious position. Along the way, she met Johnny who was then working out of Head Office as an organizer. She had a live-in at that time and Johnny was married with a wife and three children. She was thirty years to his forty-five. They had liked each other the moment they met but it was all business-related until her partner of more than ten years walked out on her and Johnny's teen-age bride of more than 30 years died within a few months after being diagnosed with inoperable pancreatic cancer. Angelina watched Johnny, a vibrant life-loving man, slowly degenerate into depression, and one day, on a whim, said to him, 'Johnny, let's have a drink after work'. They did and it worked out and he moved in and she rationalized their age difference by thinking, 'When I was twenty he was thirty-five. That's huge. When I was thirty, he was forty-five. Okay. And when we fell in love it was, like, this is a nice fit, why should a few years here or there make any difference'.

"Okay," Angelina cleared her throat. "First off, the cop, the guy Johnny keeps referring to as Officer Blah Blah, whose real name we find out in the course of time is Officer Petano King Wright, locally just called P.K., so this P.K. guy steps right into Johnny's face, and I'm thinking oh no, because I know Johnny and he's not one to push around, and P.K. says, 'Johnny, you are making a big mistake. We're not here to cause any trouble; we're here to keep you out of trouble. Isn't that right, Mr. Sanchez? We're here to keep Mr. Lomas out of trouble?' 'That is certainly correct, Officer,' Sanchez replies, 'but I don't think the gentleman is listening. Perhaps you best take him to the station where I'll make a formal complaint'.

The cop steps back but he and Johnny keep staring at each other. 'You hear that? It's your call.' Johnny says something like, 'No it's not. You got all the power here. All I've got is what I told you. We didn't break the window and we aren't going to pay you a penny. If that means you take me to the station, let's get on with it.'

The cop was getting antsy, you could see it. He kept looking over to Mr. Sanchez. 'You don't seem to get it, Johnny. Our little trip to the station is just the beginning.' Johnny starts to say something but the cop cuts him off. 'It's just the beginning, man. Mr. Sanchez here's going to lodge a formal complaint, we're going to file formal charges and you're going to go to jail.' Then Mr. Sanchez butts in and says, 'Think of your wife, Mr. Lomas.' And Johnny says, 'I always do.' And Mr. Sanchez says, 'Well, I guess if you can't take care of her, we'll have to, right Officer?' and P.K. says, 'Oh yes, sir. We'll take real good care of the lady, we always do.' And they both laugh and I can tell that Johnny wants to hurt them both so much but he sucks it up because he knows that one false move and they'll have him in jail for assault.

'I'll tell you something, amigos,' Johnny says. 'I've got a real good memory.' 'Well, if it's that good, how come you can't remember that you broke my goddamn window!' Sanchez says. And Sanchez and the cop both laugh again but it's the first time anyone's used any language like that and I'm thinking Johnny's getting to them, probably no one's stood up to them before."

"Wow!" Brenda exclaimed. "This is getting hot. 'We'll take care of the lady if you don't'. Oh me, oh my."

"I still say pay the sons of bitches and move on,' Brad snapped. "What the hell. What're we talking about here? 700,800 bucks? Keep negotiating, get him down to something like 500,600 and get out of town."

"Because we didn't break the window. We were set up for a shake down," Johnny replied. "What else could I do? Pay up? Sell myself out?"

"Sell out, my ass! You said it yourself. They've got the power. Make a deal and get the next plane outta Belize. When you're safe and sound back home, that's when you start to make noises."

"And who's going to listen then? Listen, pal, sometime, not often but sometime you have to take a stand. You shouldn't run from that opportunity, you should embrace it."

"But Brad's got a point, Johnny," Brenda said. "You've got your pride and all that but you've also got Angie to think of . . ."

"Think I didn't think of that? What's wrong with you folks? I've got my pride, make no doubt about that, but I'm going to sell myself short because Angie's a woman? Is that what you're saying? Bullshit. I did what I did because I knew that Angie was there for me, she's strong, she doesn't want to see me brought down by a couple of two-bit shake-down con men, and I knew she'd get me out of whatever trouble I'd got myself into. That's why I love her."

"Oh, is that why you love me? I thought it was because I read so many books."

"That, too."

Bob quit polishing the brass railing around the bar, "You know, folks. I've heard this tale before and I must admit that's a sticking point with me, too. Brenda and Brad have a point. But so do you Johnny and Angie. I'm just saying there's two ways to look at the same thing. As the illustrious Shakespeare might have said, though he didn't, not to my knowledge, 'When is strong being stupid and weak being smart?'"

"Oh my god," Brad moaned. He leaned forward, elbows on the bar. "How dare you blaspheme the Bard? I think for that remark you owe us one on the house."

"I'll drink to that," Johnny responded.

"You would," Angie replied, "But I would too."

"Me, too," Brenda added, "But I'd like a Slow Screw Against the Wall."

"Wouldn't we all, darlin', wouldn't we all," Bob smiled, "but it would be my pleasure to serve you all whatever you wish, whenever you wish it and wherever you want it."

As Bob bartendered the drinks, Angie spoke up. "I hear what you're both saying, but check this out: they get hold of Johnny, one on each side! Talk about collusion! You'd think Sanchez was a cop too, and they marched him off the porch, down the stairs, over to the road where Blah Blah had his motorcycle parked under a palm tree . . ."

"Thought someone said there were no motorized vehicles on Caye Hermoso" Brad exclaimed. "C'mon . . ."

"The police have a motorcycle . . ." Bob began.

"Two motorcycles," Johnny interrupted. "Two 125 c.c. Hondas. Not a bad bike, and a . . ."

"But Johnny," Angie laughed, "you looked so silly when he got on his bike, and it's not a big bike you have to admit, and you jumped on behind him and held on to his shirt as he took off."

"Comic relief, my love. And what did you do after Sanchez walked down the stairs and up the path where he had his personal golf-cart waiting to take him to the police station? Nothing very funny, I trust."

"You kidding me? I ran back into the cabana like I'm a track star, stuffed a back pack with things I'd need for a few days, opened the floor safe and grabbed our passports, our American money, our travelers cheques and my pearls, and got the hell out of there. I left my bike tied up with yours on the front porch and took off on foot. The sun's behind a cloud so it was kind of shadowy and I took a back way to Val's Back Pack Emporium, nearly scared Val to death when I burst into her private apartment at the rear of the Emporium hissing, 'Val, Val, lock the door, we've got to talk!'"

"She must have been scared silly," Brenda said.

"Oh yeah, she was pretty upset all right, but Val doesn't scare that easily. She's a tough girl who's led a tough life, but when she found out her husband had betrayed her she applied the rule she lived by: one strike and you are out. She ditched him, sold the little restaurant she owned and operated, left her two sons with her mother and moved from Hopkins Village to Caye Hermoso and started the Emporium for backpackers, complete with cheap lodging, access to the internet and laundry service. It was an instant success.

So, sure she was startled, but when she saw it was me she locked the door and we huddled in the corner of the room on a couple cushions and I told her my story."

"And?" Brenda asked.

"She was real cool. Offered to do whatever she could to get Johnny out of jail and then confided to me that she'd been hearing about shady dealings by the Tourist Police ever since the new Corporal came to the caye more than a year ago."

"Shady, like how?" Bob asked.

"Like things from her guests, the back packers, about being rousted late at night and forced to hand over money or face the consequences or having the cops pull a joint from a kid's backpack that wasn't there before and demanding money to make the problem go away . . ."

"Didn't they report it?" Brad demanded, again drawn into the story. He begrudgingly admired Johnny's stand on principle while at the same time thinking it was absolutely stupid. He knew he would have ponied up and not reported it back home because it would make him look foolish and weak which he knew he often was. Being born into a rich family—his grandfather discovered gas and oil on his cattle farm in Alberta, and his father parlayed that into an empire—wasn't as great as it was cracked up to be. Kind of took the need to compete or even try hard out of the equation, he thought at times, though he was not by nature introspective. His father ordered him home after 5 years at the University of Toronto without even obtaining a pass degree, and, as ordered, he went, but his bad habits were deeply ingrained and his relationship with his papa worsened as the years went by. Oddly enough, the only good thing that happened after his return to Alberta was his meeting of, at one of his favourite watering-holes and marriage to, at another of his favourite watering holes, Brenda, a young and vivacious waitress with no social credentials whatsoever but very little pretension either. Their marriage, much to the wonderment of many, had endured and had even had a somewhat salubrious effect on both of them

"Well," Angie countered, "when you're being hassled by the police who do you report it to?"

"That's a good point," Brad replied. "It's a kid's word against a cop's. Cop wins."

"You got that right," Johnny cut in, "and while all that's going on, I'm sitting on a bench in the police station being interrogated by the ranking officer of the Tourist Police Unit of the Belize Police Force, BPF, Caye Hermoso detachment. By the way, I learned all the niceties of rank and jurisdiction afterwards."

"What's the ranking officer look like?" Brad asked

"Well, he was standing behind the counter on the visitors' side of the station, looking in to the office section, dressed in civvies, which surprised me. White sports shirt, ball cap. Middle-aged. Jet black hair, kind of long for a cop, I thought. I wasn't sure of his ethnicity, not that it matters. Maybe Mayan. Maybe a mix. Anyway he had an air of authority about him when he swaggered into the station. There was no doubt that he was in charge of the Tourist unit on beautiful Caye Hermoso, that's for sure.

The interrogation went something like this: 'So I've been called in on my off-day to deal with this matter, Mr. Lomas. I'm in a rather foul mood, as you can appreciate, so can we proceed with some dispatch?'

'Just as fast as you wish, sir. But I'd be privileged to know your full name and rank and jurisdiction in this matter.'

'My, you are a lively one, aren't you?'

'I don't know what you mean by that, sir, but I am a Canadian citizen in Belize and I know my rights and right now I am demanding that I be allowed to contact the Canadian Consulate in Belize City.'

'My, my, you are a stranger in a strange country and you are demanding. P.K., send someone around to advise my assistant that I may have to avail myself of his services later tonight.'

'Yes, sir.'

'And now, Mr. Lomas, if I may ask you a few questions . . .'

'Only after you have answered a few of mine, sir. What is your full name, rank and jurisdiction?'

'Oh let's get past this, please. I am Corporal Montezuma of the Tourist Police attached to the Belize Police Force on Caye Hermoso and believe you me you are well within my jurisdiction. Now, may I proceed?'

'Under protest.'

'Oh, duly noted. Under protest. P.K. please make note of that. Now, a few questions if you don't mind?

Will you admit you stayed in the room the night in question?'

'I don't admit anything. We accepted alternative lodging because our cabana wasn't ready and we paid for that night and 9 other nights, in full, in advance.'

'I'm not asking you if you paid the bill. I'm asking if you stayed in the room that night, the night in question.'

'Yes.'

'And while you were in that room, did you have occasion to remove a window?'

'Yes.'

'Why did you remove the window from the frame?'

'Because there was no air conditioning, there was one floor fan operating, the other windows seemed to have been nailed shut and the window in question wouldn't open, it would only, we discovered, slip out, like if you wanted to clean it, so we slipped it out and propped it up against one of the walls. And we got a little breeze as a result.'

'So you admit to removing the window from the frame?'

'I don't admit anything. I'm explaining what happened.'

'You sound like a lawyer. Are you a lawyer?'

'No I'm not.'

'Were you angry at the time?'

'What?'

'Were you angry? Were you frustrated? Were you mad that the window wouldn't open, only slip down?'

'No'

'Are you angry now?'

'I'm getting there . . . '

'So there is anger. Officer P.K. please note that the accused admitted that there was anger . . ."

'I didn't admit any such . . . '

'Excuse me, sir, but I'm conducting this examination and I'd thank you to quit interrupting . . . '

'I'm not interrupting; I'm trying to clarify . . . '

'P.K., please also note that the accused became belligerent during the interview. Now can we all settle down and address ourselves to the facts of this case. Mr. Lomas, is it your position that when you and your wife, by the way, where is your wife?'

'I assume she's in our cabana waiting for me.'

'Good, good. Yes, she should be at home waiting for you. P.K., dispatch an officer to check in on Mrs. Lomas to be sure she is okay, and, P.K., tell the officer to inform Mrs. Lomas that Mr. Lomas may not, in fact, will likely not be back tonight, and assure her that we will take good care of her in her husband's absence.'

Now by this time, I'm going effing crazy. I want to leap from the bench, pile-drive that s.o.b. to the floor and start doing some serious damage to his body but of course I can't do that, it would be very counter-productive, so the interview, examination, interrogation call it what you want continued . . .

'So your position is that when you left the cabana the window was propped up against the wall unbroken?'

'That's correct.'

'Mr. Sanchez, what do you think about that?'

'There's nothing to think about, Corporal. I was informed that Mr. Lomas had vacated the premises and from what my staff tells me, I arrived at the cabana not five minutes after Mr. Lomas left it.'

'And why were you visiting the cabana?'

'It is my practice, sir, to inspect every one of my cabanas after it has been vacated to make sure that everything is in order. In this case, everything wasn't.'

'And what did you find?'

'I found that a window had been removed from its frame and was lying in a corner of the room.'

'And in what condition did you find it?'

'The window frame was bent out of shape and the window panes were smashed. There was glass all over the floor.'

'What did you do then?'

'I immediately attended the police station, this police station, and reported the incident to Officer P.K. Wright.'

'Is that correct, P.K.?'

'Yes sir.'

'And what did you do then, P.K.?'

'I accompanied the complainant, Mr. Sanchez here, to the cabana in question and upon entry discovered a window, broken and smashed as Mr. Sanchez has described.'

'Was there glass all over the floor?'

'Yes, there was, sir.'

'And where is the evidence to that effect?'

'Excuse me, sir, but it's just back here.'

And good old P.K, walks behind a counter in the police station, disappears for a moment and re-appears with a window that has been broken and smashed and a small cardboard box which, when he shakes it, sounds a lot like shards of glass.

The charade continues: 'Mr. Lomas, do you still maintain in the face of this most incriminating evidence that when you left your cabana this morning the window your removed from its frame was not broken!'

'Yes I do.'

'Then how do you account for this?'

'I can't.'

'Why not?'

'Because that's not the same window I removed from the frame in the cabana. It's not the same size, for one thing, it's not quite the same colour, and the window that I removed didn't have so many little window panes.'

'Jesus effing Christ,' the Corporal exclaimed.

'P.K.' I inserted, 'Please take note. Inappropriate language by the Corporal.'

'You think this is all a big joke, don't you, Lomas!' the Corporal snapped. 'Please be advised for the last time that this is a serious matter and you are in serious trouble.'

'Oh, I'm well aware of that . . . '

'Then give it up, man. Make restitution to Mr. Sanchez here and this all disappears. Don't you understand?'

'I fully understand.'

'Then what's the problem?'

'I didn't break the window"

'Sanchez!'

'Corporal?' Sanchez replied, startled by the Corporal's tone.

'What's the very least you'll settle for?'

'500usd and we all go home for supper.'

'Lomas!'

'No way, Corporal. This is a shakedown and I'm not buying into it . . . '

'A shakedown!' the Corporal was apoplectic. 'Are you saying I'm part of a shakedown!'

'I'm telling you what it is. You decide whether you're complicit.'

The Corporal turned to Officer P.K. and sputtered, 'Get this piece of shit out of here. Take him to the lock-up. We'll see how tough he is in the morning. And P.K.?"

"Yes sir?"

"Don't write this up. Understand?"

"Yes sir."

"We've got Mr. Lomas for twenty four hours. Let's make the most of it."

"Yes sir."

"And?" Brenda interrupted, turning to look at Brad as if to say 'what would you have done under the same circumstances?' "They were giving you another chance . . ."

"And? And Officer P.K. hauled me off the bench and grabbed me by the arm. Sanchez hustled over and grabbed me by the other arm just the way they did at the cabana and they goose-stepped me out of the station, down the stairs, across the street and up the road to the police lock-up. Everybody knew where it was and it was rumoured to be a nasty place to spend the night. I was about to learn that the rumours were very, very true . . ."

"How'd you feel then?" Brad spoke up. In spite of his reluctance, he had been listening closely to the story. "Bet you were crapping your pants as they took you away."

"I didn't know for sure where Angelina was or what might be happening to her. I didn't know for sure what was going to happen to me. Does that make you feel better?"

"Yes, it does." Brad said, raising a glass of beer in the direction of Johnny Lomas. "You're not as big an ass-hole as I thought you were when I met you." He laughed triumphantly. "Got you, didn't I?" When no one responded, he went on. "But seriously, folks, Johnny actually had doubts. He actually thought about Angelina. When did you realize you were in trouble, Johnny, big, big trouble?"

"Well, pal," Johnny said, pulling on the last of his rum and water, "I guess I realized the moment they shoved me ahead of them to my cell that they were calling my bluff and . . ."

"Your bluff!" Brad snorted. "You mean to tell me . . ."

"Yeah, my bluff. I bet everything on a bluff and it looked like I lost the bet. What other strategy did I have?"

"Pay the man! I keep telling you. Your pride's not worth it. You know what, I believe your story, I really do, and I have no doubt that these guys are in cahoots, including the Corporal, but it's their turf, not yours, I bet they've done this more times than this once. Pony up, man," Brad's voice quavered, "make the best deal you can and get out of Dodge."

"That was never an option. I told you that. I had to stand up to them and hope they'd drop the whole thing but, I don't know, maybe they couldn't lose face or maybe they lived in a very small world and thought they had complete control over it."

"Sounds to me they did." Brenda ventured.

"Well, at that time, they did, sure enough." Johnny looked at Brad and Brenda. "Really want to know how I felt? Sick. How's that? Okay, Brad? And things were about to get a whole lot worse."

"What happened?" Brenda asked.

Johnny took a sip of his drink and continued. "My cell was roughly 6' by 8' . . ."

"What's that in meters," Brad asked.

"Roughly 2 by 2 1/2," Angelina translated. "But do you really have to know? It was small, okay?"

Brenda kicked Brad in the ankle.

Johnny continued. "There were three or four roughly 3" by 12" slits across the outside wall, about a foot from the ceiling. That's the only air that got in. There was a bucket in one corner . . ."

"Yuchh," Brenda exclaimed.

"Quiet," Brad hissed, waving his hand dismissively as the others turned and looked at him. "I mean, let's get on with it, okay?"

"And there was a chair in the middle of the cell."

"And that was it?" Brenda asked. "No bed. No bedding."

"That was it. I learned later there could be upwards of six or eight men in there at one time."

"But this time there was only one, right? And that one was you." Angie said softly.

"Yeah, that one was me, until I got company" Johnny took another sip of his drink and continued. "Now let me say, before we go any further with this tale that I've been in some scraps before in my line of work. Some scraps and scrapes, sometime involving the law. Sometime not. Let me put it this way: I got hired by Chrysler in Windsor when I was eighteen years old. I got interested in the union after a couple years, got involved, got trained and educated, and when I was thirty got hired on full time as a local organizer for the Canadian Auto Workers, the CAW."

"CAW. Goddammit!' Brad exploded, throwing his hands in the air. 'I should've known it. Effing union goon . . .'"

"Brad. Brad." Johnny repeated. "You talk about goons as if you knew what you were talking about. Do you think management hired-guns don't intimidate workers with threats of violence? Do you think when we were organizing new members the hired-guns didn't follow women home and warn them that they'd better not vote for the union? Do you think local leaders weren't roughed up, organizers weren't beaten up, do you think I didn't witness a management goon slap a woman in the face in front of twenty of her fellow-workers and would have done more if I hadn't stepped in and splattered his nose all over his face?"

"I don't know anything about that and I don't care. All I know is unions are getting too big for their britches . . . ?

"Brad," Johnny's voice was soft but his eyes were hard. "Listen up and listen real good. I've done some things that you may not approve of but things that had to be done. But I never did anything like what was done to me that night in a lock-up on Caye Hermoso. Now are you going to shut up and listen or do I have to spank your little butt and send you off to bed?"

"Don't you, don't you," Brad fulminated, nearly speechless. He was not used to being spoken to the way Johnny spoke to him. "I won't . . . I'll . . ." He looked around but there was not a sympathetic face looking back at him, not even Brenda. "Never mind." He paused and sputtered, "I spoke, I spoke out of turn. Never mind, never mind. Bob," he gestured for another beer, "and another one all round, on me."

"I'm cool, Bob," Johnny said. "Big day tomorrow."

"Me, too, Bob," Angelina echoed. "I've got to get us both to bed. Early morning water-taxi to Belize City. Can't miss that boat."

"Not right now," Brenda said. "I'll catch up to you later, babe."

Brad wanted to remonstrate, feeling slighted that they wouldn't join him in a drink. He was feeling good himself, the alcohol he had consumed before still bubbled through him but he wasn't drunk, not yet, and he was actually listening to the story that Johnny and Angie were telling him.

"Oh, Brad," Brenda cooed, patting him on the head. "That's a good Brad. Let Johnny tell his story his own way, okay? Now, sorry, Johnny, you were saying?"

"I was saying that things started getting rough. It must have been around midnight when I heard a commotion outside of my lock-up. Voices, muffled. The rattle of a key in the lock. Then the squeaking hinges as the door was pushed inward. Light from the outside flooding in, blinding me. Someone silhouetted in the doorway. I recognized a voice. The Corporal's voice. Something like. 'Don't go too far. Don't go all the way.' The door's pulled shut with a clang. 'Don't worry, Corporal,' the stranger in my cell says, 'I won't go all the way,' he chuckled, 'but I'll go as far as I can.'"

"Who was it?" Brad asked.

"I think I know," Brenda whispered.

"You're right, Brenda," Johnny said. "It was the guy who took our luggage from the office to the first cabana and the same guy who transferred it to our cabana by the sea. We now know who he is but at the time I didn't have a clue. All I knew there was a guy in my lock-up, an intruder, if that makes any sense. I took a step toward him and as my eyes adjusted again to the darkness, a glimmer of light shone through the slats and that's when I recognized him.

'Hello,' he said. 'We meet again.' And those were the last words he spoke to me. He was a big man, looked real strong, and was very fast. Before I had a chance to say a word in reply, he blasted his fist into my solar-plexus and I went down on my knees, numb, sparkles in front of my eyes. I noticed without feeling anything how methodical he was. The first thing he did after he brought me down was take a sap out of his pocket and rap me hard on each elbow, just to make sure I was numb enough. Then he took a handkerchief and put it over my lips, tying it at the back of my head. I watched as he took out a roll of duct tape, how Canadian I thought, pulled a long strip off and wrapped it around my face over the handkerchief so my lips were sealed.

Did any of you see the movie 'Reservoir Dogs'? Quentin Tarantino? There's a scene in it where a sociopath crook is torturing a cop. The cop's duct-taped in a chair. The sociopath's shuffling around the cop, humming a song, flashing a switch-blade at him, finally cutting off one of the cop's ears. Well, it was like that, but my guy didn't have a knife. The last thing he wanted to do was disfigure me. He just wanted to hurt me real bad so I'd be a good boy in the morning when the Corporal returned, and, as I regained my senses from the first blows, the pain began. He hit me everywhere he could with that sap so long as it wouldn't show. He slapped my kneecaps so hard I almost went crazy with the pain but I couldn't make a sound except maybe through my nose. I don't know. He slumped me belly—down on the chair and gave my buttocks a good going over. He threw me back down on the chair and gave me a good shot you-know-where and the pain was so bad I thought I was going to die. The only reason he didn't do it again was I started to convulse like I was going to vomit and the last thing he wanted was a corpse labeled Death by Asphyxiation. Then he went to work on the soles of . . ."

"Johnny, stop it!' Angie cried. "Stop it, stop it, stop it! I've never heard any of this before, not this torture stuff, you just told me he beat you up pretty bad, you never told me about this!"

"I'm sorry, Angie."

"Is it true? Is everything you said just now true?"

"Yes, it's true. Every word of it is true. I've wanted to tell you but I couldn't . . . then tonight, I don't know why, it all spilled out . . ."

"Oh baby, baby." Angelina stood behind him as he sat on the bar stool. She wrapped her arms around him, nuzzling his ear. "You should have told me, baby."

"I know. I know. But it's out in the open now. Let's finish the story, grab a bite to eat and hit the sack early. We've got a big day tomorrow."

"Okay, Johnny, but you take a little break. I'll fill these folks in on what was going on in my life at that time."

Angelina resumed her place on the bar-stool. Wiping her eyes and looking pensive, she said, "Let's see. The last time you guys heard of me I was holed up with Val in her apartment hearing some very interesting things about the Corporal and Sanchez. I told Val I had to contact some people right away: the Canadian consulate in Belize City, Jaguar aka Albert Mackenzie in San Ignacio, Janet at the Hotel Mopan in Belize City and Barry Oleney on the caye.

Val said she'd track down Barry immediately and she got up and disappeared into the night. Her message to Barry would be to contact Johnny asap, check in at the police station and if Jonny wasn't there, check out the police lock-up. We didn't know then that the next day would be a day too late, Barry could have shown up and told to come back the next day so who knows if it would have made any difference.

Anyway, as soon as Val was gone, I was on the phone to the Consulate of Canada in Belize City. I had two phone numbers and an email address. I know it was after office hours but hell their hours were from 9 to 1, so I figured one of the numbers was for emergency situations. I identified myself and left a message on both lines. Contact me at Val's number, Urgent. You know, to this day I haven't received an answer, and I phoned at least twice after that and emailed I don't know how many times."

"Christ Almighty," Brad grumbled, "and we pay these people? Did you say 9 to 1? In the morning? What happens in the afternoon? Champagne and cocktails?"

"Yeah, I did," Angelina replied, "but hang on. "I also got an email response but it was after all hell had broken loose and even then it was like a form-letter, you know, 'regret to inform you' . . . blah blah blah . . . 'Canadians abroad are subject to the laws of the countries they travel to . . .' blah blah blah . . . 'please advise as your husband's case works its ways through the Belizean judicial process."

"It's like what Sanchez said about the Belizean Tourist Police" Johnny interjected. "Half their job is to protect Belizeans from window-smashing Canadians. It's like our

Consular General's saying, 'Tell Johnny to quit causing so much trouble. If he can't behave himself, tell him to stay home.'"

"Okay, okay," Brenda urged," but you still had other phone calls to make, didn't you, Angie?"

"Right. I still had to call Janet and Jaguar . . ."

"Jaguar," Brad interpolated. "What kind of name is 'Jaguar'?"

"Why, that's Jaguar's name. Didn't you ever read Catch 22?" Johnny asked. "That was required reading in my union education. How about Animal Farm? Did you read that? Or The Jungle? Or the Grapes of Wrath?"

"No, not really."

"Well, if you ever get a chance, read them."

"Okay, I'll add them to the books I'll never read. Who wrote them?"

"You'll never believe this but they were all written by 10,000 monkeys on key-boards typing randomly. The staff picked up all the outpourings every day, fed them into a computer, cross-referenced them and in the space of 25 years produced all of the above plus the complete works of Shakespeare and the Bible, old and new testaments."

"Wow, that's fantastic. But I still won't read them. Now, who's Jaguar, and, oh yeah, what kind of name is that?"

"Well, about the name, I could tell you that the jaguar, the Belizean Jaguar, is the king of the rain forest, lithe and powerful, but the fact is Jaguar, our Jaguar, got his name because he's so black."

"So black?"

"So black."

"So what?"

"So it is not common for a Creole kid with a Creole mommy and a Creole daddy from Belize City to be so black. Most Creoles are a mix of many ethnic colours plus white English or white Spanish. Jaguar is dark, dark like ebony. He looks like the black Jaguar of Belize and that's how he got his name."

"And what's your connection?" Angie asked, knowing the answer.

"I was in Belize a long time ago. Not much after Belizean independence in 1983. CAW assigned me to an international union work-group to assist unions in the third world. And don't even ask what the acronym was. Anyway, there I was, in a pokey little office in San Ignacio in the Cayo District looking into allegations that the owners and management of a unionized plantation were mistreating its workers and threatening them with dismissal or worse if they complained.

There was a knock on the door. No wait, there was no knock. A guy just pushed the door open, walked across the office floor, sat down across from me and said, 'How much do you want to bring Reyes down?' And I say, 'A lot. What have you got?' And he says, 'A lot.' 'How much do you want?' And I'm expecting him to say.' 'A lot.' And he says, 'Nothing, Mr. Lomas. Just bring him down.' And then he stands up, flips a file folder on my desk and walks out of my office. That's my introduction to Jaguar.

Turns out he was working on an assignment for a national newspaper on corporate corruption and he'd dug up some hard-core facts including incriminating evidence that would destroy Mr. Reyes, the owner and general manager of the plantation we were investigating. But when he filed his report he was told it wouldn't be printed.

Jaguar wasn't very happy about this. He realized the editor of the newspaper had been convinced it wasn't in the paper's best interests to publish the report he'd written. The report he'd flipped on my desk. The report I had in my hands.

I read it chapter and verse. I asked my colleagues to check it out and asked local guys to verify certain facts. After that I visited Mr. Reyes. He was very hospitable, as most of the most corrupt of them are, and after a couple Johnny Walker Blue scotch on the rocks and a cigar or two, he asked me to draw up a ten year collective agreement, being reasonable, of course, and I did and in time, after I was well out of the picture, the agreement was signed by both parties, union and management. It's a model collective agreement and it's still in effect, updated and improved from time to time by mutual agreement. And I, of course, still have the file."

"So he used to be a hot-shot journalist. What's he still doing in San Ignacio? Isn't that the hubcap of Belize?" Bob questioned.

'Well, some say that Dangriga is the exhaust system of Belize, if you take my meaning. I guess every car part has its function. As for what he's doing there, you gotta go where the job takes you, right, and for Jaguar, right now, it's San Ignacio. And it's a pretty nice town in many ways. A little wild west up there in the rain forest on the border of Guatemala but its home to 9,000 Belizeans.'

Brad muttered something and quaffed some more beer.

Johnny said, "Angie, you gonna pick it up now?"

"Yeah, sure Johnny. I got in touch with Jaguar. Told him what happened. He said, 'See you in the morning. Early. I know where Val lives.' And hangs up. He's at Val's before 7.

He walks in the front door without knocking. 'Got a ride to Belize City over night. Caught the first water-taxi to Caye Hermosa. Hope I'm not too late for breakfast. Missed supper.' I brief him while Val fixes him a plate of fry-jacks, scrambled eggs, sausage and re-fried beans, plus watermelon and a banana. He packs it back, looks up, says, 'Thanks for the briefing. Somebody better get in touch with Johnny, like right now if no one's contacted him yet. These are bad boys. I got a whiff of them in San Ignacio but they were transferred before I could follow their tracks. I'll be back later this afternoon.' And he's out the door. I've met him before, with Johnny, several times over the years and he's never changed. He's like a whirlwind.

But let me continue. He leaves and Val's right after him, hops on her bike to tell Barry he'd better get over to see Johnny at the lockup but he's gone already. Barry's no slouch either. He just didn't know how fast things would move. None of us did.

We find out later he gets at the lockup just before 8 and just as the Corporal of the Tourist Police marches up to the lockup with his entourage, including Officer P.K. and his trusted companion Senor Sanchez.

This is kind of what Barry told us when we met up later in the morning. I'll try to tell it in his words, all right, as best as I can remember. I guess the Corporal wasn't too pleased to see him. 'What are you doing here,' the Corporal screams. 'You have no right . . .'

'I have every right, sir, and you know that and all these present are my witnesses. I wish to see Mr. Lomas and I will see him.'

'You will not, you will not be allowed to see him. Guard, see that this man is not admitted into this building.' And then the Corporal and his entourage turn around and march up the stairs to the lockup with Barry right behind them.

As the others pass through the main door, Barry approaches the guard. 'How are you today, Louis?' Barry asks. 'Very well, sir' 'Not going to be any trouble is there?' 'None that I can think of.' 'Thank you, Louis.' 'Thank you, sir.' And Barry passes through the door and into the lockup.

'What I saw then, you wouldn't believe, Angie,' Barry told us. 'I've known Johnny for quite a few years and the guy I saw shambling out of his cell into the lockup office wasn't Johnny Lomas. I don't even know if 'shambling' is a word but if it isn't it should be. He walked as if he had chains wrapped around his ankles but he didn't. And he was grey. And he was kind of shaking, kind of spasms shooting through him, but he was standing as tall as he could, though you could tell he was in pain.

And then the Corporal looks at Johnny and laughs and says, 'You're looking rather spry this morning, Lomas. Have a nice rest, then?' And Johnny nods, kind of head bowed, you know? And get this. The Corporal and his boys don't know I'm standing in the door way, everyone's attention is riveted on Johnny and the Corporal. 'Anything you want to tell me?' And Johnny nods, yes. And the Corporal exchanges smirks with his boys. 'And what is it you want to tell me?' Johnny mumbles something. I can't hear what he's saying. 'Speak up, man. What do you want to tell me!' And Johnny straightens up as best he can, he's trembling, something's making him tremble, and he shouts, no, that's not even close, he bellows, 'This is a shakedown and I won't pay you a penny!'

Well, the Corporal is furious. His face is beet red and his eyes are so bulged it looks like he's going to pop his pupils. He whirls around and sees me and says, 'What the hell?' He turns to one of the guards and says, 'Guard, accompany Mr. Lomas back to his cell. My assistant will be here shortly to attend to his needs. And that man,' he points to me, 'if he is still here when I get back I'll throw him into the lock-up. I know some things he doesn't know I know. And no one, I repeat, no one, except my assistant, is to visit Mr. Johnny Lomas. Is that clear?' The guard nods assent.

After the Corporal and company leave, I call one of the guards over to me. You gotta remember I've spent close to 25 years on and off on Caye Hermoso and I've made a lot of friends. Kofi, the guard I called over, cleaned the beach for me when he was a kid. I give him 20 usd and tell him to fetch some food, some for Johnny and some for his buddies. I ask him what foods Johnny can eat. He says, 'Oh, he can eat most anything if he's an appetite for it.' Can he chew? 'Oh yes, sir, he can eat most anything he wants.' How do you know this? 'I seen it all before, sir. I seen it over and over again. That man who comes in to do it, he won't hurt the face, no sir. That man won't hurt the face.'

After he left to get the food, I went to visit Johnny. He's in the cell, on the chair kind of bent over, the fist of one hand under his chin, like The Thinker, you know? And he's trembling, I'm thinking the pain's come back and taken hold of him again or he's got a fever or something, and he looks up at me and my god the hate in those eyes could kill a man. He's trembling to control the hate in him and he looks up at me and says, 'Barry, you're my go-between. Go tell Angie the worst is over but I might have to stay here for a few more days. I've got to get better, man, before she sees me. But the worst is over, you can tell her that. You're here, others will come and it's got to get better. Tell her I got it real good, they thumped me real good, but it's nothing new. Nothing I can't handle. And let me know what's going on outside, okay? Who's she heard back from? What's going on? Okay? Barry, man, I need a couple days to get my shit together, no big deal. Tell her to come and see me tomorrow, later in the day, early evening.' I said, 'Okay.' And as I walked out of his cell I've got tears streaming down my cheeks.'

Angie paused, sniffling, eyes shining. "And if I knew then what I know now I'd have been over there so fast they'd think they'd been hit by a hurricane . . ."

"C'mon, Angie . . ." Johnny remonstrated.

"I mean it, Johnny. I know you've been in some scraps, you've told me about them, but most of that happened a long time ago. And this wasn't a scrap, Johnny. This was torture, plain and simple . . ."

"They'll pay for it . . ."

"Pay for it, like hell. Johnny they haven't even come to trial yet and the son-of-a-bitch who tortured you has disappeared, never mind been arrested and charged with anything."

"Angie," Johnny said. "Want to stop now? We're under no obligation . . ."

"No, Johnny. No. Let's finish it. Might be good practice anyway. Okay, folks, sorry about that. Where was I?"

"You were being Barry, Johnny's friend, and he'd just been visiting Johnny," Brenda offered."

"Right. Barry told me he walked out of the lockup, waved to the officer at the desk, left the building and started to walk down the stairs when it hit him. 'The Corporal's assistant? Who's that?' And in a flash he knew.

'Guards, guards,' he shouted, 'c'mon down here. I want to talk to you.' So they came down the stairs and gathered round him. 'They're not the cream of the crop, for sure', Barry told me. 'They aren't even real cops. They're paid dirt wages but it's hard times in Belize and they're just trying to make a living. 'Guys', he said he said, 'there's some bad shit going down. You know?' They all nod. 'Now, the Corporal said when he left that his assistant was coming back to take care of Mr. Lomas, is that what you heard?' They all nod again. 'And is that assistant the man I think he is?' They nod. 'And is that assistant going to do what I think he's going to do?' Yes, sir, they all say. That's what he's going to do.

'Well, we're not going to let him do that, are we?'

And just then, according to Barry, the local gendarmes stormed up to the lock-up, slammed on the brakes of a black 1996 ford sedan, and in a cloud of dust four heavily armed policemen exited the vehicle, followed by their superior officer, Commissioner Ray Gallant . . ."

"Whoa, whoa there. What's this? Another vehicle in Paradise?" Brad exclaimed. "Next thing you'll know there'll be tanks rumbling down the road. What the . . . but never mind. Never mind. Commissioner Gallant of the Belize Police Force . . . Corporal Montezuma of the Tourist Police? What's going on here?"

"What's going on," Johnny answered, "is that there are different police forces in Belize. Kind of like the local police and the OPP, or the OPP and the RCMP. In Belize, the Police Force and the Tourist Police often inhabit the same turf, with different duties but with the same chain of command. Oh, there's a rivalry between them, make no doubt about it, just like at home."

"Let me tell you what Barry told me," Angie offered. "Barry said he was astounded when the Commissioner showed up, especially with such a show of force. The Commissioner walked over to where Barry was standing and led him over to a spot where they could talk without being overheard. 'What's going on, Ray?' Barry said. They'd known each other for years apparently, even played poker together from time to time.

Barry said the Commissioner said, 'You all right, man?' 'Yeah, I'm cool man. What's up?' 'What's up is there's a shit-storm brewing in Belize City and it's blowing our way. I got a call early this morning, I mean early in the morning from a high-ranking officer of the BPF who doesn't have to get up early in the morning under normal circumstances, you understand, and I've was ordered to take command of this building and anyone in it. What're you doing here?' 'The only guy in the building is my friend Johnny Lomas.' 'So? What's your part in it?' 'So? He was thrown in the lockup by the Tourist Police on trumped up charges brought against him by Senor Sanchez . . .' 'Oh,' the Commissioner said, 'that ass-hole.' 'Assisted by Officer P.K. Wright.' 'Oh, that ass-hole.' 'Under the command of Corporal Montezuma of the Tourist Police.' 'The mother of all ass-holes!' 'Johnny's been in there since 8 last night. Around midnight the Corporal's assistant visited him.'

'Jesus effing Christ!' the Commissioner shouted. 'What kind of shape is your friend in? Take me to him right away.'

'Wait a minute, wait a minute, Ray' Barry gripped the Commissioner's arm, stopping him. 'I've just seen him. He's going to be okay.'

'He's going to be okay is he?'

'Well you're here now and you're . . . '

'I'm here now, to be sure. And before I arrived here I relieved Corporal Montezuma of his command and placed the Corporal and his men under house arrest. But I was also ordered to arrest and confine in whatever way and using whatever force necessary the assistant you refer to . . .' the Commissioner paused to get his breath, 'who is likely a member of the secret Belize Secret Police, a total bad-ass guy named Morton Usher and I can't find him on Caye Hermoso!'

'Well, Ray,' Barry said he was almost pleading. 'Ray, he was here just hours ago . . .'

'Barry, believe me, if I say he isn't here, he isn't here. It's an island, Barry. Maybe there are no roads in and out but there are other ways to leave an island. Do you understand me?'

'Of course.'

'And from what I've been told and what I know first-hand until Morton Usher is in chains locked in an escape proof jail cell your friend is in clear and present danger. Am I getting through?'

'Okay, okay, Ray. I hear you, I hear you. But what did you say about the Corporal and his pals?'

'I told you, the Corporal and his pals are in custody waiting for your pal to leave his digs so they can move in. Until then they are quite happy at the station.'

'What about Sanchez? Have you arrested him?'

'Barry, Sanchez is none of my business right now, but be assured if it becomes my business I'll know where to find him.'

'One more thing, Commissioner . . . '

'What's that?'

'I ordered my friend some food.'

'I'll see that he gets it.'

So that was Barry's take on things at that point in time but before he got back with his news, the phone rings in Val's apartment, it's about 9, and it's Janet phoning from Belize City . . ."

"And who is Janet?" Brad asked, without his usual sarcasm.

"Janet's the owner of the Hotel Mopan in Belize City. Great place, by the way, if you ever have to stay in the city. Her mom founded the Belize Tourist Association years ago and its members are the movers and shakers of Belize society. So Janet's very well connected. She's excited when she talks to me. 'This is going to get political,' she says, and I say, 'What do you mean?' and she says, 'I talked to the leader of the opposition last night . . .' and I'm thinking oh, that's nice, that's very, very nice . . . 'and he contacted the Minister of Tourism in his shadow cabinet and then phoned back with a couple new contacts and told me to get all the information I could to them asap and they'd go after the Government during Question Period when Parliament sits on Monday. He said they'd target the Minister of Tourism, the Minister of Home Land Security and by connecting the dots the Prime Minister himself."

"Oh, wow," Brenda exclaimed, "I'm starting to feel better and better after what those creeps did to Johnny but," she put the palms of her hands together to form a T and said, "time out, time out. I've got to whiz right about now. Way overdue. Wish me luck." And she swiveled off the bar stool and began to walk slowly toward the Washrooms. "Me, too," said Angelina. "Don't anybody leave."

"Hey, where's everybody going?" Brad swung around to watch the women walk away. "Are they coming back?" He turned to face Johnny.

"Yeah, they're coming back. Want another drink?"

Brad looked back at Johnny, bewildered. Was the guy making a joke? Sure, he wanted a drink. One more drink would tip him over to a full-fledge piss-up and that was a very exciting possibility. On the other hand, if he said 'No' now, he could probably have something to eat for supper and cruise his way back to semi-sobriety, which would likely please Brenda.

"Uh, how about you? Are you having another one?"

"You know, Brad," Johnny said, meaning every word, "I'd love to, but I have to get up early in the morning and catch the first water taxi back to Belize City."

"No. Me either. Neither. I guess I could do without."

You hungry?"

"To be honest? No, not really. Food is not what comes to mind. But, yes, I'd like to eat something. Sure."

"Well, then, let's order supper for us while the girls are gone. 2 barbeque ½ chicken and 2 grilled barracuda steaks. What do you think?"

"Well, Brenda might . . ."

"I don't mean to be insensitive, Brad, but I really don't want to wait around while every one makes his mind up. If we get two chicken, two fish, two coleslaw and two garden salads, how can we go wrong? We can mix and match, okay?"

"Yeah, sure," Brad replied, not at all sure. "Sure, let's do that."

"Bob," Johnny called when he caught Bob's attention. Bob's Bar and Barbeque was filling up and Bob had been spending time at the servers' bar station, dispensing drinks to 3 servers who supplied booze and food to nearly forty people, and the night was young.

"Hey, guys, what's up?" Bob said as he approached the bar. "Where'd the girls disappear to?"

"The girls went to the loo", Johnny confided. "And what's up with you? Busy?"

"Yeah, mate, it's pretty good, I must say. For a Sunday. We've got tourists, and travelers and locals hanging together, looks like a good night."

"Okay, we'd like to order some food . . ."

"Wait a minute, Bob," interjected Brad, "Okay. I mean, yes, we want food, but first, Bob, before we order I've decided to go cold-turkey for the rest of the night so, please, get me a double tequila in a shooter, no salt, no lemon, just a double tequila, straight up."

"That's cool," Johnny said. "Do it your way."

"Join me?"

"Why not? But make it quick, Bob."

Bob smacked the shooters on the bar and stepped back. Johnny and Brad lifted their shooters, touched glass and downed the tequila.

"Very good," said Bob. "Well done. Now who's picking up the tab? I don't think you'll want this on your food tab."

"I am," both men replied.

"Tell you what, gentlemen, the ladies will soon be back. They won't want to hear you guys arguing over drinks you don't want them to know you had. Capeche? Give me $10usd each right now, that does not include a tip, and quickly, gentlemen, and the drinks will not appear on your bill. Now, do you want to place your food order before they get back?"

"Well, maybe we should wait . . ." Brad hedged.

"No. No. We said what we said and we're going to . . . oh, oh."

"What?" Brad exclaimed.

"The ladies are rapidly approaching," Johnny and Bob said in unison, smiling as Angelina and Brenda walked toward them.

"What are we going to do now?"

"Don't worry, Brad. I'll think of something."

"Hi guys," Angelina said as she sat on her bar stool. "Everything okay?"

"Yeah, for sure. Everything's cool. But in your absence, we ordered something to eat." Johnny said.

"What did you order?" Brenda asked. She was accustomed to do the ordering and she didn't even know she was going to eat.

"Well", Johnny answered, "we ordered 2 barbequed ½ chicken, 2 grilled 'cuda, 2 coleslaw and 2 garden salad. We can mix and match. Oh, and baked potato all round with sour cream and butter. Is that all right?"

"Well, you might at least have asked us . . ." Brenda said.

"Well, it's mix and match," Brad said wryly, as if that explained everything. "And now I've got to go."

"And," Johnny added, "Bob said we'd better order now or else we'd be at the end of the line . . ."

"Too true, mate," Bob slipped in. "The shite's about to hit the proverbial fan, if you take my meaning and pardon the expression, and besides the order has already been placed, but I could cancel it, of course, if that's your . . ."

"But Johnny, I agree with Brenda, you should have at least asked . . ."

"Angie, I'm sorry. We had to make an executive decision. I can't speak for Brad, but I've had a little bit too much to drink. If I don't eat now I'm going to have a hard time getting up in the morning, and you, too. We've got to catch the 6 o'clock to Belize City. Let's have a bite to eat, finish our story and get a good night's sleep. We're going to need it."

"Excuse me," Brenda interrupted, "did you say that you guys made an executive decision?"

"Yes."

"Like, both of you agreeing?"

"That's right."

"And what exactly did you agree on?"

"On the food we ordered," Johnny said wearily, "and, well, we also agreed we'd cut back on the booze."

"You did?" Brenda exclaimed.

"We did."

"Brad made an executive decision? With you?"

"He did."

"Boy, am I ever liking this. Brad made an executive decision . . ."

"Well, it was a shared executive decision . . ."

"But he was a part of it, right . . ."

Johnny nodded and said, "And it was absolutely his decision to cut back on the booze."

"Good heavens, will wonders never cease?"

"Excuse me, folks," Bob interjected, throwing a wink in Johnny's direction. "I'll just go and fast-track that order before we get really busy."

As Bob hurried away, Johnny spotted Brad emerge from the Washroom area and start walking in the wrong direction. Brenda spotted him, too, and stood up, waving.

"Brad! Woo hoo! Honey! Over here!"

Brad swung around and weaving slightly followed the sound of his wife's voice.

"Where were you going, honey?" Brenda asked as Brad sat down on his bar stool.

"Thought I saw someone I recognized," Brad replied.

"But honey we just got here. We don't know anybody . . ."

"I'm sure Brad knows somebody everywhere he goes, don't you, Brad?" Angelina said.

"Sure."

Johnny cut in. "So let me bring you up to date, Brad. The ladies were delighted we took the initiative and ordered supper for all of us."

"We were?" Angelina and Brenda chorused.

"Sure you were. If you hadn't been you would have cancelled the order."

Brenda and Angelina looked at one another and shrugged.

"I was in the lockup, having just seen Barry," Johnny quickly resumed telling his tale. "It's Saturday morning. Barry leaves to report to Angelina at Val's. It's very quiet and then I hear a car screech up to the lock-up. I can't see what's happening so I call out but there's no one there. I'm getting a little nervous, you know? I mean, where's Barry? Where are the guards? I never had trouble with the guards, except they let that bastard into my cell.

I hear voices and then the sound of feet stamping toward my cell. Then someone calls out. 'Mr. Johnny Lomas?'

'Yes,' I reply

'My name is Commissioner Gallant of the Belize Police Force, Caye Hermoso detachment. I am here to secure your safety. Do you hear?'

My safety? I want to say. Well you're a little bit late, but I clear my throat and say, 'I hear you'.

'I'm going to open the cell door, Mr. Lomas. Don't be alarmed. I think I know what you've been through. I mean you no harm.'

I say, 'Okay, Commissioner. Come on in.'

And this guy walks in, this Commissioner Gallant, in fact I've seen him before on the Caye, he makes his presence felt. He's tall, dark-complexioned, khaki uniform clean and starched. He waves his hand at me, motioning me.

'You need a break. C'mon into the office, Mr. Lomas."

'I'mma Johnny.'

'What? Oh, okay. I get it. You're Johnny. Come on out, Johnny.' And as he ushered me out into the office, he's barking orders to his staff. 'Tell the guards to clean this pig-sty, right now. I want a cot brought in with a new sleeping bag. I want a couch, a table and another chair. Make sure he's well fed, do you hear? And has all the water he wants to drink. And, oh yes, bring him a basin with soap and water and towels and when I return if there's a drop of anything in his privy bucket I'll make those responsible lick it clean. Questions? Good. Get on with it.'

Then I follow him into the office or guard room, which isn't really an office but a space with a desk, a couple chairs and some filing cabinets, and he proceeds to tell me what I guess he told Barry, what Angelina said Barry said. I was to be confined to the lock-up till Monday when a Magistrate would arrive from the mainland and order me released. Everything had to be done by the book, he said. He didn't know it but that's exactly the way I wanted it to play out, too.

And so we sat there, passing the time of day while the guards scoured the cell, brought in everything they'd been told to bring and reported back to the Commissioner who dismissed them with a wave of his hand.

'There's one other thing,' the Commissioner said as he rose to take his leave.

'Yes?'

'Maybe I shouldn't even ask, but I'm asking anyway: Do you need a doctor?'

'No.'

'Sure?'

'Commissioner, you know the man we're talking about. I know him, too. He doesn't break bones. He breaks people.'

'You're a brave man, Johnny.'

'Sure,' I said."

"Well, hello, hello. What have we here?" Bob sang out, approaching the bar with two servers behind him. "Something for din-din, then? Just put the plates etcetera on the bar," Bob instructed the servers, one resembling a Hawaiian hulu dancer and the other amply endowed server with a rich-chocolate complexion and prominent booty most certainly a Garifuna from southern Belize. "They're going to mix and match."

After making choices, the gentlemen deferring to the ladies' preferences, they all tucked in, admitting between bites that they had indeed been hungry, even ravenous. And Brad, confiding that he rarely ate supper before 10 p.m., if at all, had to acknowledge that eating supper earlier might have some merit.

Finished sucking on a grilled chicken wing, Johnny continued with his story. "The Commissioner repeated that I was not under arrest but that he had been ordered to remand me into protective custody until the Magistrate arrived on Monday. That being the case, I requested visitors be allowed and he concurred, asking me to draw up a guest-list which included Jaguar and Barry and Val and several others but not Angelina. The Commissioner obviously knew of our relationship and asked, 'Is there some reason you haven't included your partner?' and I replied, "Put her down for Sunday, p.m., please. I would like to see her, but I'm pretty stiff and sore and some parts of my body are swollen, if you take my meaning?' 'I do indeed' he replied. He stuck around for another half hour or so and then took his leave.

Jaguar showed up about an hour later and interviewed me. He was all business. He told me he had put his editor on notice of a Stop Press column for the front page of the Sunday edition and was advised that the request had been noted and he would have to have the column in as early as possible on Saturday, no later than 9 p.m.

'You know, Johnny, this story is virtually writing itself. All the pieces were waiting to be picked up and yours is the culminating incident.'

I asked him to tell me what was going on but he said he didn't have time just then. 'Let me do my job, Johnny,' he said, 'then I'll fill you in and we'll celebrate'. Then he was gone, just as Angie described, like a whirl-wind.

Barry showed up later, and Val, and they brought me up to speed on events. I had a couple of questions myself. First of all, I wanted to know how the Tourist Police had commandeered the Police Station. Barry said he'd wondered about that and asked the Commissioner. Commissioner Gallant told him that was easy. The Tourist Police detachment was under his command, they had their special duties to perform, but they were on the duty roster and on the week end in question they were in charge of the police station.

'Wow,' I said to Barry, 'So, that's when they'd set their trap for Sanchez' prey. They'd know well in advance when they were on duty at the station, tip off Sanchez, he'd look over the bookings and identify some poor schmuck and the next day they'd swing into action. Son of a bitch. They picked me 'cause they thought I'd be easy. That's embarrassing.'

'Okay, what's your second question?' Barry asked.

I said it was about the Commissioner himself. He'd made a good impression on me but c'mon this all happened on his watch. So my second question to Barry was what's going to happen to Commissioner Gallant?

Barry said, 'You know what? He's a good friend of mine, and I mean a good friend of mine. We go back. But you're right. It was on his watch and he's going to have to pay. He's definitely out of here. Probably a lateral transfer to some back-water village in the rain forest, same rank, same wage, but nothing to do till he slides into retirement.'

Barry had some beers and a large bottle of One Barrel brought in and real glass glasses. The guards kept the food coming, at our expense, of course, and joined in the party. 'Nothing like a little rum to ease the pain,' I said

"I'll drink to that," Brad joked, holding up a glass of water.

"Yeah, well, glad you were enjoying yourself, party-man' Angelina cut in, waving a fork with a piece of grilled barracuda on it, 'because my life was nothing short of hectic. On top of worrying about you, which I'd been doing non—stop since they took you away, I was getting phone calls from all over. Janet phoned a couple more times to advise me of the ever-increasing interest in Johnny's plight on Caye Hermoso. I got a call from a reporter from the Toronto Star, an old buddy of Jaguar's it turns out, but I brushed him off. When Jaguar told me what his friend wanted and why I agreed to do a phone interview later in the day.

Jaguar kept popping in and out. So did Barry and so did Val, come to think of it, even though it was her pad, not mine, and I was the intruder, not her. Not to mention that I was a little hurt that I wasn't on Johnny's A-list. Sure, sure, rationally I understood his rationale, but emotionally I felt left out and abandoned. And, oh yes, lest I forget, people I knew and people I'd never ever met before started knocking on the door asking if I was all right.'

"Ahh, honey, I'm . . ."

"Shut up, baby," Angie interrupted good-naturedly, 'I'm telling the story now and I'm telling it my way. We can make up later.' She swiveled her hips to make the bar stool closer to Johnny and put an arm around his shoulder.

"What I'm saying is, as the sun set over the caye, only 24 hours have passed and it's like my life has changed. My lover-man was in jail, had been beaten up, I didn't know anything about the torture thing, and I'm embroiled in a national maybe even an international scandal. And all I want is to curl up in bed, get a good night's sleep, wake up at dawn and get outside before it gets too hot.

Is that too much to ask, I asked, and it was, so I settled down and waited for Barry and Jaguar to return. Val was taking care of business: she still had to make a living but she would join us later. Then the guys returned, Barry much the worse for wear, if you know what I mean. Now I know why. Jaguar's still bouncing off walls like Tigger in Pooh Bear and we sit down and try to sort things out.

Jaguar says he's filed his report. It'll be in the Sunday edition of the San Ignacio Star but he's already leaked the story to Channel 7, Belize News, a T.V. station known to favour the opposition party and, as I already knew, to the Toronto Star, also known to favour the opposition Liberal party.

He tells us the four man Tourist Police unit was made up of known misfits. 'It's like the Catholic priests,' he explained, 'when they got caught bumming little boys they just got shuttled down the road to another parish where they could bum again. Hallelujah.'

They were small time scammers, Jaguar explained, but when they got together on Caye Hermoso they decided to pool their talents for shake downs, extortion and fraud and put something aside for the time they would be sacked. They all seemed to realize the end of their career was coming on fast. They were in effect planning for the future without a cop's pension to prop them up in old age.

'So what'd they do?' I asked.

'Just what happened to Johnny, with variations on the theme. Like what Val told you. Real drug busts late at night: 'Oh my, what have we here? Mary Jane? Cocaine? Daddy's gonna be real pissed at you, boy. Think he'll post bail if you land in jail? Or do you want to pay the fine now?'

Bogus drug busts on the beach at night: 'Pay the fine or do the time'.

Kids screwing on a blanket on the sand. Flash. Flash. 'Oh that's a nice pic. Isn't that you? What's she doing? Wanna pay the fine now or take your case to court and let the Judge decide?'

Homo shake downs: 'Hey, queers, you can't do that shit here. It's a criminal offence in Belize. You can pay me now or pay me later' and if they didn't pay up they'd be escorted to the lockup and after a little visit from guess who before sunrise they'd give the cops anything they wanted and get out of Belize on the next plane.

And then Sanchez horned in and set up the broken window scam. He re-painted the cabana at the back from time to time to make it smell like new and entrap the victims. After the paint and a few renovations, it was all profit'.

I said, "That's pathetic. It's really, really ugly, but it's like so small time".

'It was. It is,' Jaguar replied. 'But it pays well as long as you don't get too greedy. You can chip away. A score here. A score there. Don't push it. Take the money and run. Double your salary. Double your fun.'

'So what went wrong?'

'They got greedy.'

'Why?'

'Don't get me wrong. They would have screwed up anyhow, we're not talking about the best and brightest here, but it all went sour when our real villain in this story showed up and took over.'

'And that would be?' Angelina asked.

'I think you know. The guy who beat your husband . . .'

'Who is he?'

'I've been on his track for a long time but he's elusive as quick-silver. His official name is Morton Usher but I'd bet dollars to donuts that's not the name he was born with.'

'What was it?'

'I don't know yet, but I think he comes from Guatemala. I think as a kid he fought for the rebels against the government. I think when the rebels surrendered he disappeared into the rain-forest. I think like so many others he emerged from the rain-forest as a renegade turned robber turned killer turned sociopath. And finally, in this case, turned Morton Usher.'

Barry wanted to know how someone from Guatemala could cross the border into Belize and change his identity.

'It's easy as hell and very commonplace,' Jaguar explained. 'There are thousands of Ushers in Belize. You do a simple name search and find a deceased Usher roughly matching your gender and age. You apply for a birth certificate and after you get it you're off to the races.'

'So what happened then?' I wanted to know.

'He applies to the Belize Police Force. Gets accepted. Passes. Gets assigned, and after that things get a bit murky, like where he was stationed, stuff like that, but whatever happened at some point he applies for and gets accepted by the Belize Secret Police. And then he virtually disappears. He becomes a will-o'-the-wisp, a shadowy underground figure, and it's about that time the rumours started. What rumours? Well, rumours about a killer cop, a cop who did the wet-work for the Secret Police'.

'Wet-work?' I didn't know what that meant, at the time, but I sure found out. I remember looking over at Barry and he was nodding his head . . ."

"I don't know what either," Brenda said. "But I can guess. Do you know, Brad?"

Brad nodded and motioned for Angelina to continue.

"Well, Jaguar told us he met a guy in San Ignacio who knew Morton Usher. This guy said he remembered one time during a night of hard-drinking with Morton and some of his cronies when Morton told them there were three kinds of men: those who could not kill a man, those who could kill a man but only if he had to, and those who wanted to kill. He said that Morton looked at them as he guzzled a bottle of beer and his eyes said, 'You know what kind of man I am. What kind of man are you?'

Anyway, Jaguar continued his biography of Morton Usher. He didn't know how Morton Usher ended up on Caye Hermoso, whether he was on assignment or on the run from the Secret Police, that would all come out in due course, he supposed, but he added that the reason Morton had been drawn to his attention as a reporter was because of the rumours that Morton was out of control, had become a rogue cop.

'And then he arrived on Caye Hermoso,' Jaguar said, 'and it was like the last element needed for the perfect storm. He pushed the guys to be more active. He insisted they raise their demands. From what I have learned just today, he took over the leadership of the gang, and who would stand up to him? Sanchez? No way. Maybe the Corporal, but could he kill because he wanted to?'

Val had come in during Jaguar's explanation. She said that Morton Usher's appearance and behaviour matched the stories some of her guests had told her. From what she had heard from others, including a young couple who had paid up and left Belize on the next plane, there was one guy that stood out in their minds. One guy who struck fear in their hearts. One guy no one was going to mess with and that one guy must be Morton Usher . . ."

"Jesus Christ" Brad sputtered, spitting water.

"Brad, are you okay" Brenda asked.

"Yeah, no, I mean this guy, Mortimer or whatever his name is, c'mon he's . . . I mean, Bob, I need a drink . . ."

"Honey," Brenda entreated, "you said . . ."

'I said I'd slow down, not go cold-turkey. Step at a time, Brenda, let's not overdo it. Bob, por favor, a pint of your best," he paused, looking at the others, "light beer."

"Coming right up, mate. One pint of bud light."

"Make me another rum, will you, Bob? Better make it a single", Johnny jumped in. "Anything else, ladies? One for the road?"

"Sure, give me a glass of pinot grigio," Angelina replied, "then we'll wrap this story up and head for bed."

"Okay," Brenda said, "me too. Same as her."

"Okay, tell you what," Johnny said, "I'll pick up the pace and Angie and me will play tag-team for the rest of the tale. How's that? Okay with you, honey?"

"Okay with me, baby."

"Okay, let's see, it's Saturday night, right. Jaguar's filed his story. Everybody crashes. I wake up on Sunday with a huge hang-over. One of the guards comes back with up-right fans and I get one in my cell and the guards have one in the guard room. There's a new set of guards and one of them asks me if I'd please go into the guard room so they could clean my cell. I walk to the screen door at the entrance to the lock-up and notice five or six people standing around. One of them notices me and shouts, 'Way to go, Johnny!' pointing me out to the others. I'm thinking, 'What the hell?'

Well, guess what? The Sunday edition of the San Ignacio Star arrives on Caye Hermoso sometime after noon hour and that's when, as Bob would say, the shite really hit the fan. There were two hundred papers on the water taxi from Belize City and they were snapped up before the vendors got to the beach. By mid-afternoon there were dozens of people demonstrating outside the lockup, some carrying signs saying things like 'Let Johnny Go' and 'Free Johnny'. As far as I could tell, the crowd was made up of local Belizeans including ex-pats like Barry and curious tourists and travelers and it was getting bigger and bigger as the day went on.

Barry and Jaguar came over at some point and we ordered more beer and rum. Jaguar brought me a copy of the paper. I think the page one headline was, 'Corrupt Cops on Caye Hermoso? Rumours of corruption appear to have turned into reality after four Tourist Police stationed on Caye Hermoso have been suspended and remanded into custody and arrest warrants have been issued for a local hotel owner and a shadowy member of the Belize Secret Police'.

'Wow,' Bob exclaimed. He hadn't heard this part of the story and was as interested as Brad and Brenda.

"Let me jump in here,' Angelina said. She had their undivided attention. "Val googled the Sunday Star in Toronto and sure enough there was a short article, not on the front page to be sure but in the first section. It went something like this: Canadian Consulate Ignores Pleas of Citizen in Belize. The writer then pointed out that there had been several incidents recently where the Conservative Government failed to support citizens abroad who had found themselves in trouble. It was like, you broke their law, deal with it yourself."

"As opposed to what?" Brad interrupted. "Do you think the government should intervene every time a crack-head or child-molester gets busted in a foreign country?

"No," Johnny said, "but don't you think that every Canadian citizen travelling abroad should be entitled to a response, and absolutely entitled to the government assuring that one of its citizens receives due process in a foreign land?"

"Spoken like a good union man," Brad said.

"You're not as stupid as you pretend to be, are you?' Johnny replied.

"Gentlemen, gentlemen," Bob refereed, "go to a neutral corner. Let's agree to disagree and move on. Angelina, you were saying?"

"What I was saying was that there's been a lot of concern recently over reports that the Government seems to want to cozy up to the foreign country more than it wants to protect Canadians abroad, and maybe that's just a perception but the fact is once the story broke in the Toronto Star Val was getting peppered with calls and emails from the Canadian media."

"So bad that when I was released from 'protective custody' on Monday, we moved in with Barry so Val could divert calls to Barry's place and let her get on with her life."

"Right," Angelina said. "And let's face it, we were pretty crowded in Val's little place. Anyway, the next few days were crazy, what with interviews and such, but we got through it okay and then we just sat back and watched the story unfold on T.V. Channel 7 picked the story up for the evening news. Channel 5, kind of the government's channel, picked it up on Monday. Back at home the major newspapers carried it somewhere in the 1st section of the paper. Opposition parties had a field-day with it in Belize and Canada but the Governments of the day in both countries reflected the criticism by taking 'decisive' action . . ."

". . . which meant arresting the bad guys in Belize and recalling the Consular-General in Belize back to Canada, giving him a good scolding, and re-assigning him after things settled down . . ."

"Hey, I didn't tag you," Angelina joked.

"Wait a minute, wait a minute," Brad intervened. "I'm remembering something about this now. Yeah, I remember thinking what a pile of crap it all was, wait a minute, Johnny, put a lid on it, I mean that's what I thought then, like more liberal press attacking the Government, but now, now I'm getting a different slant on it, for sure. Do you remember it, sweetheart?"

Brenda looked around her as if unsure who he was addressing: 'Sweetheart?' "No, Brad, I don't. I don't much follow the news of the day, you know?"

"Anyway," Angelina continued, "everything started to settle down over the next four or five days."

"But just to back up a little," Johnny spoke up, "Angie visited me late Sunday afternoon, we went into my cell, which I hadn't been using very much that day, and closed the door and just held each other . . ."

"I couldn't believe it," Angelina said, "I'm hugging Johnny and I'm crying and I'm looking around at the cell they put him in and I'm thinking 'what in the hell is this all about, is this all about a broken window? And I didn't know the half of it I find out today'"

"So the next day they come over to the lockup and pick me up and take me to the police station, the same station where all this shit started, which doubles as a court room, and the Magistrate from Belize City is there dressed in black robes with red trim and a white wig that must have weighed a couple pounds. He doesn't waste much time, calls me up to the bench, on behalf of the Government of Belize apologizes profusely and informs me that I will be summoned to appear in court in Belize City at a time specific and on a date as yet unspecified to provide evidence against the accused. He added that he hoped I bore no ill-will to the country of Belize wherein these malfeasances took place, I didn't have a clue what he was talking about at the time, only afterwards with the help of a dictionary have I been able to piece it together, but I caught the gist and asked 'leave to address the court' . . ."

"You would," Brad laughed in admiration.

"I did, and I informed the court of my fondness for the beautiful country of Belize, often referred to as the Jewel of Central America, and I gave him the old apples in a barrel speech and asked him to get rid of the rotten apples for the sake of all of us."

"Oh good for you," Brenda applauded.

"Well, what happened to them?" Brad asked.

"Nothing."

"Nothing!"

"Well, nothing of consequence," Johnny said. "You gotta know that when these matters get thrown to the court Time as we know it is suspended and we exist at the leisure of the system . . ."

"What does that mean?" Brenda pleaded. "I'm getting all mixed up!"

"Well," Johnny said, "it basically means that we all sit back and watch what I call Court-Sport: lawyers for the prosecution make their points and lawyers for the accused make their points; then the Judge interrupts and makes his points and then the lawyers for the accused object and the lawyers for the prosecution object to the objection and whenever all that's sorted out either the lawyers for the prosecution or the lawyers for the accused appeal the decision of the Judge."

"Jesus Christ," Brad snapped. "So where are we now? Is this thing going to court or to hell in a hand basket?"

"Court."

"When?"

"Tomorrow morning. 10 a.m. Supreme Court of Belize in Belize City. We will be in attendance but I doubt that we'll be called for a few days or even more. So that's why we're here tonight. We'll stay at the Hotel Mopan during the week when court's in session and come back here to San Pedro on the weekends, just to get away from it all. We got here a couple weeks ago, retirement you know . . ."

"Vacation time for me," Angelina chimed in . . .

"Wanted to settle in and acclimatize ourselves again. But anyway, it's getting late and we have to be up early so . . ."

"Right" Brad mumbled. "No, wait a minute, okay? Can I ask you a few questions before you go?"

"Angie?" Johnny asked.

"Sure, why not. Why don't you settle up with Bob and then you can field a few questions before we hit the hay."

Johnny took out his wallet and removed his Visa credit card. Handing it over to Bob he said, "Just tack on 20% to the total and bring me the receipt, okay?"

"It'll be my pleasure, sir" said Bob, meaning every word. It was indeed a pleasure to deal with a man who valued the work done by others.

"Okay, who's first? Brad?"

"Yeah, thanks Johnny. Don't want to keep you but there's a few things I need to clear up. Like, what happened to Sanchez, the hotel owner that set you up? You haven't mentioned him for a while."

"Yeah, you're right. He kind of slipped my mind. Going back to the shakedown, guess he felt a little nervous when they put me in the lock up. Locals saw him catch the first water-taxi to Belize City early Saturday morning. Funny thing is everybody, including the cops, knew where he was hiding. So when the cops went to serve the warrant for his arrest they went straight to his dad's place in Belize City and senior Senor Sanchez who thought his son was a complete fool directed them to his son's hideaway in Burrel Boom, a ritzy little town north of Belize City and they arrested him without any resistance. He'll be tried separately from the others and we'll probably have to testify at his trial, too."

"What'll happen to him, do you think?"

"Not much. His dad's pretty rich and well-connected. Sanchez junior will probably pay a fine and walk away free but he's finished on Caye Hermoso, that much is certain, and probably finished in Belize, too. Probably end up in L.A. with all the other Belizean emigrants."

"What about the tourist police?"

"Well, that's a different story. They've been charged with more than just extortion. People have stepped forward, locals and tourists. I think the charges include assault, sexual assault, extortion, of course, maybe even attempted murder. I've kind of focused on my case. But they're in deep doo-doo, believe me and will probably be sent to the Hattyville penitentiary where there'll be some guys waiting for some serious get-back."

"And what . . ."

"About our friend Morton Usher? Well, he's the mystery man, isn't he? Vanished from the caye. Didn't take the water-taxi in either direction. Police searched every house and shack and hotel room on the caye and came up empty. Jaguar thinks he's made his way to Guatemala but can't figure out how he got there. Who knows? Jaguar also thinks that if the police ever track him down he'll be killed before he goes to trial."

"Secret Police?"

Johnny nodded. "Isn't that ironic? He's got too many secrets even for the Secret Police and they'd never let him take the stand. On the one hand, I don't ever want to see that s.o.b. again and on the other I'd love to face him down in court."

Bob approached the bar with Johnny's credit card and receipt. As Johnny signed, Bob said, "Thank you very much, sir. It's been a pleasure and we all look forward to seeing you and Angelina next week. Good luck in court!"

"Oh Johnny and Angelina, thanks for sharing that story with us. I'm so proud of you, Johnny, and I'm proud of you, too, Angelina. You're a great couple and I'm more than pleased to have made your acquaintance."

"Thank you, too," Angelina and Johnny spoke at the same time, "for listening to our story."

"Good practice," Angelina added.

"And I'd like to say what Brenda said," Brad faltered and continued, "I mean about being proud and all that. I mean I'm not . . . well, you know, and we don't have a lot in common . . . but, I'd like to shake your hand, Johnny."

"Thank you, Brad. Much appreciated. Now, goodnight, folks. See you again sometime. Let's go, honey."

"Bye, bye, everybody. Wish us luck!"

Johnny escorted Angelina across the dance floor. They zig-zagged around tables laden with drinks and food and chairs supporting men and women of all different ages, races and backgrounds. It was quintessentially Belize and Johnny and Angelina loved it.

They waved to the woman at the desk in the hotel and took the stairs to the second floor. Johnny was talking to Angelina as he unlocked the hotel room door, pushed it open, stepped inside and reached for the light, saying, "I've got to piss so bad . . ."

The light flashed on as the words assailed his ears. "Hello. We meet again." Morton Usher stood a few feet away with a black revolver clutched in one hand. Johnny instantly voided, urine staining his knee-length shorts and running down his legs.

"Well, you seem pleased to see me," Morton smiled.

"Get the hell out . . ."

"Tesh, tesh, calm down, Johnny. Ma'am, don't say a word and step away from the door." He motioned to Angelina with the gun. "Come on in and everyone stay calm. We have business to attend to."

"We have nothing to attend to . . ."

"Johnny. Johnny. Johnny. You never seem to know when to shut up. Maybe this will help you." Morton pointed the gun at Johnny's chest. He spoke very quietly. "You know why I'm here. I can do it right now in front of your little lady, and then I'd have to do her, too, but I'd rather not, not here and now, too noisy, too much risk, so I'd rather we went for a little ride together."

"What kind of ride?" Johnny was stalling for time. Somehow he had to separate himself from Angie. For the first time, he wished he had not stood up to Officer P.K. and Sanchez, hadn't challenged the authority of the Tourist Police, hadn't withstood the vicious beating at the hands of the man who now stood in front of him with a gun in his hand and murder in his mind. For the first time, it occurred to him that maybe Brad, the fellow-traveler he had just met, the man for whom he felt such a disconnect, was right: shut-up, pay up and get out of town.

"A little boat ride, Johnny. Get off this island. Me, I have a little hideaway in the cayes. We'll wait things out. Who knows, you may be worth more to me alive than dead. When you don't show up in Belize City tomorrow, they'll come looking, but what will they find? Nothing. Nada. Nobody home. So they'll search for you. And they'll wonder: Where are they? Are they in trouble or did they run away? And they'll postpone the trial and we'll just wait and see, won't we?"

"Please leave Angelina out of this."

"Oh Johnny, you know I can't do that. But she'll stay alive as long as you do, take some comfort from that. But, please, I am embarrassed for you, go and towel yourself and get dry clothes. Don't think I'm getting soft, Johnny. I've tossed your room and there's nothing to be found, no guns, no knives, no weapons of mass destruction," Morton chuckled, "but then, again, you are a Canadian, aren't you?"

Johnny turned, looking at Angelina. She looked back, wild-eyed.

"Go on. Go on," Mortimer said. "You have my permission. But first of all give your Swiss—army knife to the lovely lady and she'll pass it over to me. Comprende?"

Johnny did as he was told. "I'll have to go to the bedroom first, okay?"

"As you wish. The knife, lovely lady," Morton commanded, waving her ahead of him as he took the knife from her and followed her into the sitting room. She was very attractive and he was stimulated by the thoughts that ran through his mind. He planned to be very creative with them both and when he was finished the fishes in the sea could have what was left.

"Knock, knock," Johnny said, stepping out of the bathroom. He had the same bright red rayon short-sleeved shirt but was wearing clean dark blue shorts.

Morton was seated in a large leather chair by the window, his revolver resting on his lap, still clutched in his hand. "Over here, Johnny," Morton invited, "come and sit down and we'll resume our little chat. There are plans that have to be made."

"Sit over there," Morton nodded his head in the direction where Angelina was seated and at precisely that moment Johnny whipped out a small container of dog repellent and sprayed Morton in the face. Morton collapsed in pain, screaming. Johnny got closer and sprayed him again, full in the face. "Aiyee, aiyee, aiyee" Morton screamed. The gun fell from his grasp. Johnny lunged and came up with it.

"Run, Angie! Get help!"

"Johnny!"

"Now, Angie! Go now!"

Morton, still screaming, charged at the sound of Johnny's voice. Johnny side-stepped and Morton surged past him, toppling over the sofa.

"Oh, Johnny, Johnny, don't you understand?' Morton's words rasped as he struggled to get up. 'You've got to kill me, man, and you can't do it. Can you?" Morton was on his feet, shuffling across the floor, still sightless. "I can't see you, Johnny, and you've got the gun. Why aren't you killing me?"

"I don't have to kill you, Morton. Angie and the police will be here any minute."

"I know why you're not killing me, Johnny."

"Why's that?" Johnny circled away from the shuffling Morton.

"Because you're a fighter, not a killer. I'm a killer, Johnny. Pull the trigger. Pull the trigger, Johnny. Kill me, if you can. Kill me, Johnny. Kill me or I'll kill you."

"You don't have time, Morton."

"Oh, Johnny, it doesn't take much time to kill somebody," Morton said softly, and once again charged hitting Johnny's knees, knocking him over. Johnny's head crashed on a side table but he held on to the gun. Morton crawled toward Johnny, flailing his arms until they made contact with Johnny's torso, sending his hands up and down the body in search of the revolver, finding it, wrapping his fingers around the barrel, trying to turn the barrel back to Johnny's body.

In his last moment of consciousness, Johnny looked into the face of the man who wanted to kill him. Although sightless, Morton's eyes burned like red-hot coals, the veins on his forehead writhed and bulged, his nostrils were distended and blew out a spray-like vapour of phlegm, his teeth were bared like fangs and mucous ran from the corner of his lips and Johnny knew with a dead-certainty that Morton's power was going to overcome and kill him. Morton shook his head in an animal frenzy and his sweat-soaked hair lashed Johnny's face, almost blinding him. Morton grunted with effort and clawed at the gun, trying now to rip it out of Johnny's hands. Johnny summoned whatever strength he had left and muscled the pistol toward Morton's chest. In a final moment of clarity, Johnny knew what had to be done and he felt an almost orgiastic pleasure as he squeezed the trigger. The last thing he saw before he passed out was Morton Usher's body stretched out on the floor, bright red blood staining his white starched shirt.

Two months later, Johnny and Angelina took the water-taxi from Belize City to San Pedro on the Ambergris Caye. It was a déjà vu experience for them both. They checked into the same hotel as they had checked into before and, after unpacking and freshening up, crossed over to Bob's Barbecue and Bar.

Bob the bartender was behind the bar polishing glasses when he looked up and saw Johnny Lomas and Angelina Antoniolli strolling across the dance floor toward him. It was a Friday evening at the tail-end of the Season and the joint was not jumping. Bob thought Johnny looked good, maybe a little lighter and a little paler. He was wearing a robin's-egg blue sports shirt and dark slacks. Angelina looked so fantastic he barely noticed what she was wearing. Something yellow, he thought. Tanned and glowing. Remarkable eyes. Curly jet black hair. 'Settle down, boy,' he said to himself. 'She's too old and she's already taken. But if Johnny ever dumps her, I'm making the first call'.

"Well, well, well, what have we here? I was hoping you would return. Been reading about you. You're national heroes, you know. When did you get back?"

Johnny and Angelina hopped up on bar stools and rested their elbows on the counter.

"Oh, we've been back in Belize for a few weeks, hanging out along the coast in Hopkins Village and Placencia, but this is where we want to be when the fun begins... again. This is still our sanctuary, isn't it?" Johnny said, looking at Angelina.

"Well, yes," Angelina replied, "though I must say it has lost some of its lustre as a sanctuary."

"Well it better not have," Johnny countered, "'cause we are coming back here every day until the whole damn thing is over."

"Good oh, mates," Bob said. "It'll be my pleasure to take care of you. So, welcome back and the first and only the first drink's on me. What'll it be?"

"Usual for me," Johnny said. "Angie?"

"Me too."

"That's a double One Barrel rum, no ice with a side of water and a pinot grigio for the lady," Bob exclaimed, proud of himself for remembering, but not surprised, since the last time he had served them had turned into a momentous and very memorable evening.

Bob prepared the drinks and placed them on the bar counter. "All the papers and T.V. have been panting for this trial. How'd the first day go?"

"Well, it was an experience," Johnny said, picking up his drink and clinking glasses with Angelina. "A pretty good experience, I'd say, all in all, wouldn't you, Angie?"

"Yeah, all in all it was pretty cool."

"Were you called to testify?"

"No, we didn't expect to be. Just wanted to get a feel for the place, you know. We're pretty sure that we'll be called to testify sometime next week," Johnny answered, "Of course, we couldn't go into the trial itself. Spent most of our time with lawyers for the prosecution."

"It's just like our system . . ." Angie started to say.

"'Ello, 'ello, what's this I see schlepping across the dance floor," Bob interrupted, looking across the dance floor at another couple crossing toward them. They were wearing different styles of clothing, different colours, but to Bob they looked exactly the way they did the first time they met. "Unless my eyes deceive, it's that lovely couple from Canada we met the night of the, ahem, shall we say 'incident'? Brad and Brenda, I presume?"

"Hoped we could track you down," Brad exclaimed as they approached the bar.

Brenda walked quickly toward Angie and embraced her as she slipped off the bar stool. "Oh, Angie, we're so, so sorry. What an ordeal! Are you okay?"

Angie put her hands on Brenda's shoulders to give herself a little space. "Sure, sure, I'm fine," she said, eyes filming with tears. "So nice to see you again. Join us for a drink?"

"Oh yes, we'd love to, wouldn't we Brad? So much to talk about . . ."

"Yes, thank you very much," Brad said.

"What'll you folks like to drink?" Bob asked.

"A couple cold drafts of bud light," Brad replied.

"And the lady?" Bob asked without missing a beat.

"The lady? Oh, ha, ha, I get it . . . one for me and one for the lady, por favor."

"So, what brings you here again? Johnny asked. "Thought your base was in Cancun?"

"It was; it was . . ."

"But it's not anymore," Brenda finished.

"No, we're moving our base to Belize . . ."

"Brad's going to start an import/export business . . ."

"Great opportunities, really, coffee, chocolate, exotic flowers and fruits, I've been doing a lot of research, and English as the official language, that's a big bonus . . ."

"But we're not here to talk about us," Brenda interrupted. "Maybe another time, right Brad? Right now, it's all about you guys. What a horrible thing to have happen and now you're right back where you were when we first met, testifying at the trial of those criminal cops."

"That's true, right back we started from . . ."

"Oh, I didn't mean it like that . . ."

"That's okay. That's the way it is. We testify next week, and after that we take on Sanchez, and then we get on with our lives."

"We followed the story in the papers and on T.V. Religiously. Day after day."

"Yeah," Brad piped in, "we went to bed just after you that night, didn't know a thing till the morning when everyone was talking about it . . ."

"Yeah, you were in the hospital then, in Belize City, being treated for a concussion I think . . ."

"And being investigated by the Police," Angie added. "Funny thing though, they didn't know what they were investigating. Not for sure they didn't. When we got back to the room all the police saw was a man with a gun in his hand unconscious on the floor, blood splatters on the floor next to him, and later, when they followed the trail of blood, blood streaked on the wall leading down from the second floor and blood on the push-bar of the emergency exit leading to the back of the hotel."

"Good God Almighty," Bob exclaimed, "that must have been quite a struggle, mate, quite a struggle, but you obviously got the upper hand, and, I'm only saying what I read in the papers, what you had in your hand was a container of dog repellant, am I right? Dog repellant! What's that all about?"

"Well, finally, I guess it's about saving our lives. You might know from reports that he let me go into the bathroom. You probably don't know why and you probably never will. We still can't figure it out. All I was doing was buying time and he gave me a couple minutes. I had no plan. Angie was in the other room with a certifiable maniac and I had no idea what to do next, I'm literally whirling around in the bathroom, looking for something, anything to help me overpower him before he killed the two of us and then my eyes fell on my kit on the counter and I thought, 'Wait a minute'. Mr. Death said he'd tossed the apartment for weapons but had he tossed my kit? Probably looked in it but all he'd see was bathroom stuff, toothpaste, pills, vitamins, shaving-cream, that kind of thing and the repellant was only a 3" cylinder that didn't stand out in any way. I looked and there it was and I knew it was the only chance I had, we had."

"Where'd it come from, mate?"

"What, the repellant? Where'd it come from? I bought it for my grown-up daughter when she visited a couple years back. I bought it as an anti-rape repellant and she opened the package, took it out, tossed it to me and said, 'Here, daddy, you may get more use of it than me.' Later, I stuck it in my kit and forgot about it."

"Serendipitous," Bob remarked.

"Oh, yes," Brenda said, "and really lucky, too."

"The police found his truck somewhere on the beach, didn't they?" Brad said.

"Yes," Angie chimed in. "And they never found an unclaimed boat anywhere . . ."

"So they are still looking for Morton Usher, armed and dangerous." Johnny finished.

"And what do you think?" Bob and Brad spoke at the same time.

"I think he's dead. Had enough life in him to get to his motor-boat, we know he had a hide-away on one of the cayes, that's where he was taking Angie and me, and I think he got there and bled to death. That's what I think."

"What about his boat? Wouldn't it be spotted and investigated?" Brad said

"Oh, it would have been spotted all right. And investigated, too, but probably by fishermen who fish the area. They'd spot it and watch it and after a time, they'd go and investigate."

"Wouldn't they report it to the police?" Brenda asked.

"Sure, they could. You might even say they should. But maybe they didn't. Maybe they chose another option—deep-six the body, clean out the cabin with all its gear and provisions, and steal the boat. The motor would probably bring in a small fortune by their standards. What would you do if you lived a hand to mouth existence and had a large family to support?"

"What would I do, indeed," Bob spoke up. "but really, folks, I'm sure there's much more to talk about, so what thinks you about a little din-din? A little mix and match?"

After they ate dinner, Johnny and Angelina said goodnight to all and took their leave, wending their way through the throngs of vacationers who crowded the verandah, back to the hotel. It was a beautiful night, a languid breeze brushed the sea and the sand, and the moon was luminous.

At the hotel, they approached the desk and the desk clerk, a young Mayan woman with glistening black hair, motioned them over to the counter. "Just one moment, please," she said lifting up the phone. Two large, uniformed men with Security insignias on their grey shirts emerged from an adjacent room. "Mr. Lomas? Miss Antoniolli?" They nodded. "Follow us, please."

They climbed the stairs to the second floor and Johnny and Angelina waited until they checked the hallway. As they approached their room, the security guards took their positions, one on either side of the door, guns drawn. Johnny inserted the key in the lock and pushed open the door. The guards pushed past him, easing their way on either side of the corridor walls to the sitting room, guns held high.

Angelina leaned over and whispered to Johnny, "Don't tell me you have to have a gigantic leak."

"Okay, I won't."

"Won't have a gigantic leak?"

"Won't tell you."

"Oh, you," Angelina laughed, pushing Johnny inside as the door locked behind them.

Two shots rang out, louder than cannons.

THE END

Postscript by the Author

"Two shots rang out, louder than cannons." Where did that come from? I said, astonished. The story was supposed to end with Angelina pushing Johnny inside the hotel room behind the security guys, the door locking behind them. Readers could draw their own conclusions about what they found inside. All the evidence pointed to the likelihood that Morton Usher was dead and Johnny and Angelina could get on with their lives. Then the two shots rang out and everything changed.

Who fired the shots? Was Morton in there, waiting? And if he was, who did he shoot? The security guards? Johnny and/or Angelina? One of each pair? Or did Morton shoot one of the security guards and the other one shot Morton? Or did the security guards spot Morton in some dark corner and each shot him dead before he had a chance to kill Johnny and Angelina. Or were the security guards spooked by a shift in the shadows in the lightless room and shot at a lampshade or a mirror? Or were the security guards hired killers paid to kill Johnny and Angelina? Bang! Johnny. Bang! Angelina. Or were the shots fired in the corridor of the hotel before the door clicked shut or in the alley below with the window open in a totally unrelated incident?

I don't know. My imagination took me to the doorway but it would not let me go inside.

Encounter On King Street

Eddy Dupuis and his partner Jan Reddick enjoyed their meal at Macy's on King Street in downtown Belize City. It wasn't anything special, not like a night out on the town. It was just good solid food Belizean-style, red snapper whole or filleted, grilled or deep-fried, and chicken any way you wanted with rice and beans or beans with rice, accompanied by coleslaw and bread pudding for dessert. They were finishing off their drinks, a Belican beer for her and a Belican stout for him, when their waitress, Darlene, approached the table and pointed out a man with his face pressed against the window and something in his hand waving at them.

"That's Leon," she said. "He lives around here. Kinda simple, you know, but he's a good artist. He's been sketching you while you ate."

"Okay," Eddy said. "So, what's up?"

"Well, he wants to come in and show you what he sketched."

"And?"

"Well," Darlene explained, "I can't let him in unless you say it's okay. There's no one else here but that's the rule. It's up to you."

"What about it, Jan? Okay?"

"Sure," Jan said. "Where's the harm. Let him in."

They watched Darlene walk toward the door. She was a statuesque woman in her late twenties, a good waitress whom they had known from visits to Macy's during their visit to Belize, smart and personable and worthy of their trust.

Darlene led the artist Leon through the front door to the table where Jan and Eddy were seated. "This here's Leon," she said. "Leon's an artist. Leon, this here's Eddy and Jan, from Canada. They're cool. Show them what you drew out there."

Leon stepped up to the table with a sketch in his hands. He was of indeterminate years, somewhere in his thirties, scruffily dressed with a green toque pulled over his head. When he pushed the sketch at them, they noticed his shaking hands and his dirty fingernails but when they looked up into his face they saw gentle features and kind brown eyes.

"I was lookin' in the window and this is what I seen."

They looked at his sketch of them, pencil on paper. Eddy had his beer held up as if he were toasting Jan, and she was looking back at him as if she had seen this a thousand times before, but it was a good likeness of both of them and they were impressed.

"What do you think?" Eddy asked Jan, uncertain what his response should be.
"Oh, it's nice, Eddy." Jan replied. "Let's get it as a souvenir."
"Hey, Leon, we like this very much. How much?"
"Give him 10 bze and he'll be very, very happy." Darlene interjected.
"Okay," Eddy said, reaching for his wallet and pulling out his last cash. "Here's 10 bze. Thanks, Leon. And for you, Darlene, here's our credit card for supper."

Robert Alwyn-Smith awoke with a jolt at 6 p.m. He hoped he was on Plues Street but he had only vague recollections of the night or the day before. It was not quite dark. A quick glance here and there confirmed he was at home in the house his mother had bequeathed him. The shadows were familiar, the pane-less windows approximately where they should be. He struggled up from his cardboard mattress and, turning away, took out his penis and urinated on the floor boards, hearing more than seeing his urine pour between the cracks to the floor below. He found the ladder that had replaced the staircase and descended very carefully. Once at ground level he stood still and gave himself a shake, much like a dog shaking off water. He checked his pant pockets for drugs or cash but found neither. Time to go to work. He needed a fix. Bad.

Robert Alwyn-Smith had not had an easy life. His father, a Cockney from England, had been a sergeant in the British Army stationed in Belize after Belizean Independence in 1983. Robert's mother was a Creole whose mother and father had both served at Governor House on Regent Street as servants and therefore had preferred status in the under-class of Belizean society. His mother finished her A—levels at St. John's Anglican High School and after teacher—training began teaching school at the primary level. Robert didn't know when, where or how his parents met. He didn't know how long after they married he had been born. He was pretty sure he had no brothers and sisters. He had no recollection of his mother's father and mother. What he did know was that his father, whose Christian name Robert did not know or could not remember, had been ordered back or had served his time and returned to England sometime after Robert's birth.

After that, so he had been told, there had been a succession of fathers, none of whom stood out as loving or protective and all of whom had used him in one way or another. He left school at age 12, not because he wanted to but because the Catholic Church officials of the Belize City Diocese of Jesus Christ of Eternal Love expelled him because his mother could not pay tuition. His mother could not pay tuition because she had developed a major drug addiction and having some years before lost her job as a teacher lost her job cleaning rooms at the Radisson Hotel. Robert understood the logic and set about to help his mother as best he could and before very long became an addict himself. It seemed to run in the family. By the time she died, her house had been robbed of any utensil, appliance or piece of furniture.

The toilet and sinks had been removed. Robert had a vague recollection of being involved in some of the transactions. He was 17.

Robert stood unsteadily in the yard, taking deep breaths, getting his bearings. He knew what he had to do but he had to have some money to do it. It was too early for break and entry and too early to lean on his druggie friends to chip him out until he made a score but it was about time to get downtown and see if he could beg or muscle enough to get himself right again.

He cut across Canal Road and headed down King Street to Albert. He figured he might make a hit somewhere along the way but if not he would turn left on Albert and make his way to the swing bridge. If that did not work out he would cross the swing bridge and turn right toward the Tourist Village. He knew the bulk of the tourists had been transported back to their cruise ships but sometime there were stragglers who would be easy prey.

As he walked east on King Street, he saw a couple step out of Macy's. White folks. He was older, heavy, dressed like a fool in a bright red short-sleeved shirt, khaki shorts down to his knees and flip-flops on his feet. She looked younger, pretty, with long brown hair falling over her shoulders. She wore a pale-blue dress that fit her nice and reminded him a little of his mother when she was clean and healthy. He would have to draw the old man ahead of her and make his pitch. He didn't want her to hear some of the things he had to say.

He began to calculate how much he would ask for. $US20.00 would do the trick. The closest crack house was five minutes away. $US10.00 would be okay but he would need another $10.00 real fast. If the fat fuck wouldn't give him any juice, he would have to ratchet up his demands to cover the risk-factor. His right hand dipped into his jean pocket and touched the pearl handle of his stiletto. If he was caught using a stiletto in the commission of a crime, he was going to be living in Hattyville, the notorious penitentiary in Belize, for a long, long time. If he had to pull out his baby, he would settle for nothing less than $US50.00 and demand much more.

He brushed past the white guy, not touching but making the bodies aware of one another. He turned back and speaking softly said, "Hey, man, I wanna talk to you," and motioned for Eddy to quicken his step.

Eddy quick-checked the guy and said to Jan, "He's hustling something, most likely dope, don't worry, I'll brush him off. Just drop back and let me take care of this."

"Okay, baby, but be careful." Jan slowed down her step and dropped back a little as Eddy walked up to the drug dealer.

Eddy Dupuis' mom and dad brought him to Smooth Rock Falls in Northern Ontario when he was three years old. The town was humming at that time, the pulp and paper industry paying good wages to anyone who would put in a good day's work. Eddy's dad, Gaston Dupuis, had no trouble getting a job, in no small part because he had a French-Canadian name and Smooth Rock Falls was a predominantly

French-Canadian community in an Anglo-Canadian province. When his employers found out he could not read, write, understand or speak the French language, their first impulse was to kick his ass out of town, but when they learned that he was by his own admission the toughest and hardest-working son of a bitch in the mill, they agreed he could stay on until he was no longer an asset which meant as long as he took his orders from them and kept other Anglos in line.

Eddy had a good life for a short period of time. He didn't see much of his dad who spent most of the time he wasn't working drinking. But he saw a lot of his mother who was a stay-at-home mom and paid him a lot of attention while she took care of the house, cleaning and dusting and laundering, and cooking three meals a day, seven days a week, for her husband and her only child.

Robert Alwyn-Smith often wondered if he might have had a better life if everything had not started out so badly. He wondered if he had gone to school, worn one of those school uniforms that some kids wore, things would have turned out differently. Those uniforms made him go almost crazy, like the kids wearing them were bigging-up, feeling superior to those around them. The way those kids paraded down the street, laughing and playing games, stopping at the ice-cream bar and ordering butter-scotch ice cream or orange slush, then going on their way as if it was nothing special, just kids on the way home eating ice-cream. And he wondered what kind of home they were headed for, probably with doors and windows and furniture inside and electric lights that turned on and off and toilets where you could do your business and flush it down.

Then he thought of his last dad, who should not have been called dad because he came after his mother was dead but he told him to call him Dad and so he did because he knew if he didn't something bad would happen and something bad had happened last night or a night or two ago and it involved Dad and it was bad but he could not remember what had happened.

He was getting very jumpy as he walked down the street with this dumb white fuck who did not have the faintest idea what was in store for him. He thinks I'm peddling dope, Robert thought. What an asshole.

When Eddy Dupuis had to go to school, his world began to collapse around him. Although English was the language of instruction in the classroom, it was clear to Eddy, especially after he looked back on it, that it was not the preferred language. 85% of the citizens on Smooth Rock Falls were French speaking at birth. Of the 15% who were not born speaking French at birth, 8% were born speaking English and the others a polyglot of languages. From the beginning, the divide was clear: the teachers, most of whom were French-Canadian forced to teach in their second language, favoured the French speaking students, often speaking to them in French in the classroom and almost always outside. Next, no doubt, was the preference given to the Anglo kids, whose language skills were often useful. The polyglot kids were entirely left out.

The work place and the town reflected the schools. French worked with French, English with English and other-than French or English with other-than French or English workers, though there were divisions within the other-than groups, Ukrainians finding it difficult to rub shoulders with Russians and Irish finding it difficult to rub shoulders with anyone, including other Irish. In town, there were French bars, Anglo bars and bars for other-thans. Sometimes there would be inter-mingling and then there would be fights, somewhat good-natured in a brutish way but bloody none the less. Robert's father often came back on a Friday night bruised and bloody, demanding another drink before he went up to bed.

At school, outside of the classroom, at recess or the playing fields, even before school began and the kids jostled at the entrance door to be rung in by school bells, it was a constant, relentless war waged in one-on-ones or more intense encounters away from the school where groups of ten or more threw stones at one another and then charged and engaged in furious combat.

Eddy loathed school where he felt betrayed and cheated. The French-Canadians reviled him because he would not speak the language God had given him and the other-thans despised him because he had a French name. The only comfort he ever felt was amongst the English kids but many of them were suspicious of him because he had a French name but could not speak French.

He learned early to swallow his fear and fight anyone who stood in his way, embracing violence as a means of survival.

"Hey, man," Robert sang out as he walked alongside Eddie and quickened his pace, trying to increase the separation between the guy and his wife or girl-friend.

"Hey," Eddy replied.

"I need some money, man," Robert said.

"Yeah, so do I."

"I'm not kidding, man."

"Didn't think you were."

"Give me some money, man. I need it bad."

"I'm tapped out, man."

"Don't fuck with me. You got money and I need some money real bad."

"Don't fuck with me, brother. I told you I'm tapped out. End of story."

"Don't call me 'brother', mother fucker, and don't tell me you're tapped out and don't tell me this is the end of the story."

"This is the end of the story and I don't want you as my brother and I never fucked your mother."

They walked side by side for a moment silent, hearts pounding, eyes blinded by the blood of their anger. Eddy heard Jan calling to him from a distance though she was only feet behind him. "Eddy, stop it, stop it!" But he did not turn. It was as if she were far away and he was here, hot in the moment, and his entire life was wrapped up with this presence beside him, this kid, this punk, and he knew that everything between them would have to be settled right here and right now.

Jan Reddick ran after Eddy and the guy he was talking to. It was obviously not a drug deal. She didn't know what it was but whatever it was it wasn't good. Eddie had a temper, though she had never been the brunt of it. He had lived a tough life and had confided in her early in their relationship that he had played the part of the union goon in the constant fight with management's hired hacks. 'It was like hockey,' he told her. 'Each side has their enforcers. Sometimes things get ugly but you can't let them steamroller over you. Management's got the money. We've got the moxie.' When they first met, he was an organizer with the Canadian Workers Union, a break-away union from the American Workers International Union, with a growing reputation for organizing members in plants across Canada no matter what they worked at, manufacturing, mining, milling, lumbering, drilling, it didn't matter. She was a social activist in Hamilton, Ontario, just out of university and eager to save the world. Now she was running after the love of her life and the world would have to wait until she saved him first.

Robert's eyes bulged as he heard the words of the fat white man standing in front of him, words that made him wonder if the man was insane using such language about his mother, saying he wasn't his brother when of course he wasn't. He had never had a brother. He might have wished he had a brother but like his mother told him wishing don't make it true. And what was this shit about being tapped out? Everybody knew the white tourists carried cash on them. All he wanted was his rightful share. He fingered his baby in his jean pocket, the pocket was hot but his baby was steel-cold and he figured it was time for a little show-and-tell.

On the corner of King and Albert, the Indian merchants had slammed down and locked and bolted the steel doors that protected their wares from thievery. Those who worked in the stores but did not live in the neighborhood had gone home. Those who lived in the neighborhood but did not work in the stores stepped out to enjoy a few moments of quiet from the blaring music broadcast from every shop and a few moments of respite from the heat of the day. Old folk and young folk and in-between folk mixed and mingled, children playing games amongst and around them.

Thadeaus Wright occupied his usual position on the south east corner of King and Albert. He eked out a living, augmented by a small army pension from the Belizean Armed Forces, by escorting tourists on walking-tours of downtown Belize City, astonishing them with his encyclopedic knowledge of every city in every country in the world. Many years before, he had served in Her Majesty's Army and after Independence in the Belizean Army. He had always been eccentric and both armies were relieved to see him pensioned off. He retired to the neighborhood where he had been nurtured as a boy and as a retired military man with a pension was welcomed home and soon dubbed the King of King Street.

Thadeaus was always watchful and ever protective of his cross-corner domain, switching his gaze from King Street to Albert Street and back again as he conversed with friends. As he looked west on King Street, he noticed something somewhat unusual, a white man and a coloured Belizean marching rapidly toward Albert Street. He hushed his companions, pointing down the street. They all stood stock-still, looked and listened. Thadeaus detected voices rising well above the normal level of conversation. His companions all nodded when Thadeaus murmered, "Hear that?" They shook their heads from side to say when he said, "That ain't the sound of friends talking." He motioned for his followers to fall in behind him as he checked for traffic, then, slowly, they walked across the road. "That's the sound of two guys fighting, that's what that is."

As the economy in Smooth Rock Falls slumped, so did Eddy's Dad's stock decline and the boss of the pulp and paper mill told his underlings to get rid of the Anglo hothead, which is why Eddy ended up in Brantford, Ontario, just about the same time the two giant farm implements factories were pulling out of town. Eddy's Dad got a job with a unionized international coach and body firm out of Cleveland, Ohio, but after 3 months was rejected by the union because he hated the union as much as he hated management. After that, he picked up odd jobs wherever he could find them but never surrendered the belief that he was the toughest, hardest s.o.b. wherever it was he found himself working.

Eddy had to drop out of school at age 16 and make a living for himself. He bounced from job to job for a couple years then found himself a job in a unionized meat-packing plant. He passed his probation and became a member of the union. Like his Dad, he didn't have much use for unions, all they did for him, he figured, was take a part of his wage packet in union dues, and in the plant he worked the union didn't have much clout anyway.

Time after time, he saw management abuse; foremen ordering the men to undertake un-safe work, work over-time against their will and contrary to the collective agreement, perform work for which they did not have the qualifications.

He was shocked to see the floor-chairman of the union turn a blind eye on these transgressions, even going as far as walking out of the plant with his arm around the foreman, laughing as they left the building and, so rumour had it, meeting up later in a down-town bar.

The section foreman where Eddie worked was a big man, a strong man and a bully. Eddie had watched him from day one and could not believe what he got away with. One time he watched as a worker on the assembly line signaled he had to visit the washroom, which was his right. A reliever was directly behind him. The foreman shook his head 'no'. The worker gestured with his arms as if to say, 'What do you mean?' The foreman strode forward, grabbed the worker by the neck, lifted him up and threw him down on the cement floor. "You'll piss when I tell you to piss!" he roared. "Now get your sorry ass back on the line."

Some of the workers stepped away from the line and walked toward the foreman. "Get back to work you useless bastards or you'll all be collecting pogey for a long, long time!" he roared again. Intimidated, they started to back off.

Eddy pushed the stop button on his line and brushed past his fellow-workers. Without a word he walked up to the foreman, drew back his right arm and crunched the foreman's nose with his clenched fist. Blood sprayed. The foreman stumbled backwards. Eddy followed him, sending two left jabs to the foreman's heart and a chopping right to his neck that left him sprawled on the floor, unable to get up.

"Okay, guys," Eddy said. "Get back to work. This piece of shit isn't going to bother you anymore. And you," he said, pointing at the worker who had to relieve himself, "go have your piss, if you haven't had it already."

Eddy was arrested and jailed. When the union stated it would wild-cat if Eddy wasn't re-instated, management relented and launched an investigation. When the investigation was completed, Eddy went back to work and the foreman was fired. Eddy began his career as a union man.

Robert and Eddy stepped into the brighter light of King and Albert Street still yelling at one another. Robert noticed the crowd that had gathered. He checked it out. They were his people. They would support him.

"Yo, bro," Robert called out, grabbing Eddy by the shoulders and pushing him back to halt his forward progress. "We can't just keep walking, mother fucker, or we going to walk ourselves right into the sea. Let's settle this right here."

"I told you I wasn't your brother."

"You're not my brother. You my bitch."

Eddy stood still, panting, surprised at the gathering around him. He heard Jan running up behind him crying out for him to stop. He felt her arms surround him as she tried to pull him back. "Let go, babe," he said. "This isn't over yet." She let go and stepped back.

Thadeaus assessed the two antagonists. The white guy was definitely older and out of shape. Maybe 5'10" tall. Maybe 230 lbs. But he had muscle beneath the fat and fists that looked like they packed dynamite and eyes that were focused and intense.

The Belizean kid was more than 6' and a lean, mean 150 lbs. but he looked frazzled, probably a crack-head looking for a fix; in fact he looked familiar, looked like the kid over on Plues he had seen around before.

"Okay, people, listen up," Ronald cried out, adrenaline pumping, "this here's the white devil in our midst. This here's what's killing Belize!"

"No, it's not," Eddy said, calmly as he could. "It's punks like you are killing Belize. You demand money from me, threaten me? What'd I do to you? What makes you think my money is yours for the asking? I earned every cent I ever made. Why don't you get a job and make your own money, then you won't have to hassle people who come here to have a good time. I don't need that shit, man."

"Then get the hell out of here. Get out of our country. It's you and your people that come here and parade around as if it was your country and we were just slaves. It's you . . ."

"No, it's not," said an elderly Belizean woman with gray hair and tired eyes. She stepped toward Robert. "It's not about him. It's about you. Why don't you get your own shit together and make something of you self 'stead of trying to put the blame on them that come over here and do us some good."

"No, mama . . ."

"I'm not your mama, but I knowed your mama and she was a good woman till she turned bad . . ."

"No," Robert screamed. "It's not me, it's him. It's not us, it's them. You bastard," he looked across at Eddy. "You bastard, you turned my own people against me. You gonna die!"

Robert reached into his pocket and pulled out the ivory-handled stiletto, pushing the button that un-sheathed 6" of razor-sharp, double-edged steel. As he raised it up and lunged toward the devil in front of him, Eddy bent his knees, swiveled right and struck the kid with all his might, his fist cracking a rib, but it was not enough. The knife arced down on a trajectory that would have pierced Eddy's neck, severing the jugular, had not Thadeaus moved in and judo-chopped Ronald's wrist, breaking it and sending the stiletto clattering to the pavement.

Robert screamed in pain. Thadeaus stepped over, picked up the knife, walked over to a telephone pole, drove the blade into the wood, wrenched back his hand and snapped the blade 1" from the hilt. He walked back to the kid, grabbed him by the back of the neck and thrust him in front of the white guy. "This any business of the police?" he asked Eddy.

"No," Eddie replied, "our business is done. If that's all right with you."

"Fine by me," Thadeaus said. He slipped the pearl handle of the stiletto with its one inch stub of blade into the kid's pocket. "This here's yours, not mine. Now get out of here," he said, pushing Robert through the crowd and shoving him on his way. "Ain't no business of the cops, anyway," he said, walking back to the white guy. "We taking care of business right here."

Robert stumbled down an alley, full of pain and anguish, wondering why his own people hadn't supported him against the white devil. His last daddy had schooled him. He said, 'Belize was Paradise until the white devils came and turned our women into whores and our men into servants.' That was why Robert had demanded the money. It was his country. It was his money.

The alley teed at a stone wall with glass shards and barbwire on top of it. Ronald turned right and almost fell over an object in front of him. In spite of all the pain and anguish that clouded his eyes, Ronald recognized the object as a man and, upon close and then even closer inspection, recognized the man as a well-dressed Belizean with his arms cradling a bottle of rum bitters.

His fingers found the man's wallet and even in the darkness Robert knew he had struck it rich. He pulled the bills from the wallet, lifted the bottle carefully from its cradle and chugged half of it before he walked quickly away.

On the corner of King and Albert, Thadeaus met Eddy and Jan, shaking their hands. "We are so glad everything turned out right. We are very sorry you had this experience."

"Sir," Eddy said, "I know what happened here. You saved my life, no doubt about it."

"And I know what happened, too," Jan said, "and Eddy's exactly right. What can we ever do to repay you?"

"Repay me? Nothing I can think of. This is my country. This is my turf. I try to take care of both of them. These here are my friends, my family," he spread both hands to include the men and women and children who surrounded him.

"Could I offer to buy you a drink, at least," Jan said opening her purse and pulling out a little leather wallet.

"You've got money?" Eddy exclaimed.

"Yes, why not," Jan replied. "You know I always carry my own money."

"But I told him I was tapped out, and I thought I was. Christ, I would have given him 10 bucks just to be rid of him."

"Excuse me, ma'am," Thadeaus interjected. "It occurs to me that I must not let my personal pride stand in the way of my friends and neighbours without whose assistance we might all of us have been endangered." He stepped toward Jan eying the wallet she opened in front of him and plucked out a $50.00usd bill. He waved the $50 bill in front of him and cried out, "Tomy, Tomy, come here quick."

Tomy, a middle-aged man with a twisted leg but bright eyes and white teeth crowned by gold, stepped forward and grabbed the money with both hands.

"Tomy, I want you to go to the Chinaman's and fetch a large bottle of 1 Barrel rum . . ."

Some of the men in the crowd, Thadeaus's soldiers, began grumbling.

"Make that 2 bottles of 1 Barrel rum, two large." Thadeaus corrected himself, "and ice-cream for the children and sodas all round. And Tomy, if there is any money left over, bring me the change."

Back in their room on the third floor of the Hotel Mopan on Regent Street, Eddy poured himself a double Canadian Club whiskey and touched it with a little bottled water. Jan cracked a Belican beer. They sat on the mattress of the two double beds, across from each other, knees almost touching.

"Cheers," Eddy said.

"Chimo," Jan replied.

They touched glass and drank, Eddy deeply.

Eddy cleared his throat and sighed. "Well," he said, "I guess I made an ass-hole of myself."

"Don't punish yourself, Eddy. He was pretty wired."

"Not my proudest moment, though."

"No, probably not your proudest moment."

"He was just a kid."

"Yes."

"I'm supposed to be a grown man. I let him get to me."

"Yes, you let him get to you."

"But I shouldn't have, should I?"

"I guess not, but he did get to you and that's that, okay? And why do you have to be a paragon of virtue and self-control? He went after you. From the time he spotted us coming out of Macy's, you were the one he was going to shake down."

"Yeah, but I should have handled it differently . . ."

"How?"

"I don't know. Give him the money, I guess . . ."

"But you didn't have the money and you didn't know I had any money. Do you think he would have settled for no money?"

"No, for sure. No, he was going to get some money from me, by hook or by crook. He thought he was entitled to it. Poor kid, where did he get that idea?"

"I have no idea. Well, I do, but let's not get into socio-economics right now. You weren't exactly brought up with a silver spoon in your mouth either, Eddy. And let's face it, love-of-my-life, if you'd given in, he'd do it again, maybe not to you but to some other unsuspecting tourist. That's the whole problem. If you give in you encourage him. If you resist, your life's at risk."

"And yours, too. That's what makes me sick. My stupid pride . . ."

"Eddy, you wouldn't let anyone hurt me any more than I'd let anyone hurt you. You know that, in your heart of hearts, you know that's true."

"You're something else, Jan. Where did I catch you?"

"You didn't catch me, Eddy. I jumped into your boat when you were fishing."

Jan settled into her double bed after fluffing up the pillows. She wore a sleep mask and had inserted plugs in her ears. Eddy wasn't a chronic snorer but he did snore when he had been drinking too much. Before she pulled the mask over her eyes, she looked across the room to where he sat at a desk by the window. The room was illuminated only by a night-light. She watched him pour another drink, then pulled down the sleep mask and closed her eyes.

She remembered when they met at a steering-committee meeting in Hamilton, Ontario. He had been seconded from the CWU to help organize protest marches across Ontario and she had been assigned by the Social Action First Group to assist the organizing team for two weeks prior to the Day of Action.

He would have been in his mid-thirties then, older than her but, looking back, still so very young. His hair was blacker, his eyes were brighter, his laughter was contagious and they spent almost every night for the next two weeks with their fellow workers talking and planning over pitchers of beer and bottles of wine as they feasted on take-out pizza and hot Buffalo-style wings. The days zoomed by. The community activists marched arm in arm with their union brothers and sisters, joined by union workers and social activists who arrived in bus loads from across the province. It was a great success and then it was done. Eddy moved on help organize the next town and she went back to her job as a social worker.

She thought of him often, for a while. He was her favourite by far, but it wasn't in her nature to flirt, not when there was work to be done, and he seemed to be of the same persuasion. Back at work, she became more and more frustrated by a city council that seemed to pander to big business and neglect those without political clout, the working poor, the unemployed and un-employable, and the welfare families. Even worse was her disenchantment with her own social action group whose members often spent more time fighting amongst themselves and back-biting rather than reserving all their energy for the struggle to help others less fortunate than they were.

She dated different guys but there was no spark in their relationships. It was during this time that she resolved to make a major change in her life and left her job, applied and was accepted into the nursing school at McMaster University in Hamilton, emerging two years later a Registered Nurse. She accepted a position in the Emergency Ward at St. Joseph's Hospital in Hamilton and discovered her life's work.

It was there, five years ago, she met Eddy again. He walked into Emerg early one morning with a deep cut over his left eye, so deep that his eyebrow hung down in a flap.

"You," he exclaimed, "Jan isn't it? What's a nice girl like you doing in a place like this? I thought you were going to save the world and all the children in it."

"And I never thought for a moment I'd meet you again, especially not in the emergency ward of a hospital."

"Well, one goes where one has to, doesn't one?"

"At least it's not the morgue," Jan replied.

"No, that's where they took the guy that done this to me," Eddie winked, wincing.

"C'mon, let's get you fixed up."

"Lead and I'll follow."

And so it had begun, this time in earnest.

Jan smiled to herself as she drifted asleep.

Robert ran all the way to the crack-house, pumping his fist in the air, ecstatic. His luck had changed. He was rich, fucking big time rich. He'd scored beyond his wildest expectations. Maybe that white devil was an angel in disguise.

He ran deep into the wood-shack jungle whose paths and alley-ways he knew so well until he arrived at his crack-house of choice. Benji would take him in, give him want he needed. Benji was like a father to him. Robert had relied on Benji to fix him up from the time he had turned on to crack.

He twisted down one alley into another and slipped through a break in the fence that led to the back-door of the crack-house. The inside was lighted by kerosene lamps. You could see the light through the cracks in the wall. You could see pieces of the men and women inside. He wanted so much to be with his friends, with Benji.

"What the fuck you doing here, man," Benji asked him as Robert pushed his way through the back door.

"Hey, Benji, my man," Robert said, "It's all cool. Fix me up, Daddy, and let me crash till I come down."

"Are you shitting me, man?"

"I'm not shitting you man, I'm cool. Take me in and, "Robert reached into his back pocket and pulled out $50 US, handing it to Benji, "turn me on."

Benji stepped aside and let Robert in the back door. The kid looked wrecked, eyes wild, cold sweat popping from his pores. Benji felt bad, he'd always liked the kid and felt sorry for him but after last night there was no doubt what he had to do.

"Sit here, I'll fix you up."

"But . . ."

"No buts. Sit." Benji kicked a broken chair across the floor. "And shut up."

"Shut up!" Robert yelped. "I'm coming to your house to do business and you're telling me to shut up. What the fuck, man?"

Benji turned and stepped back in, blocking the yellow glow of the kerosene lamps. "What did you say, mother fucker?"

"Hey, Benji, Benji, its okay. Okay? I'm like frying, man, I need a fix real bad, man, so come on, man, fix me up and I be gone."

"You don't even know what happened last night, do you?" Benji leaned over Robert straddled on the chair. Benji was not a big man but he was mean and muscled, dark black, with plaited hair and flashy bling.

"What happened last night?" Robert stammered.

"Your Daddy dragged you in and fixed you up, fixed you up real good. Told me to make sure you got back to your place on Plues, and I did that, I did that, and now I'm wishin' I hadn't been so co-operative."

"Why not?" Robert was getting shaky. "What are you talking about?"

"You don't know you killed a man last night, the man they call Gibnut, your Daddy's used-to-be best-friend? Stabbed him to death and slit his throat? You don't remember that?"

"I don't know nothin' 'bout that, man, C'mon, I'm bakin' and shakin'. Fix me up, Benji, please, fix me up."

"The cops are looking for you, man. Don't you understand? Everybody knows you done it. It was your Daddy what ratted you out, man. It's just a matter of time but I don't want it to happen on my time or in my place so I'm going to fix you up and you're going to get your ass out of here, okay? I'm going to fix you fine, don't worry about that, and then you're out of here, and that's that."

Benji fixed up Robert real good, as he said he would. Robert sat on the broken chair in the back room savoring the synaptic jet propulsion of his brain as millions of bright images exploded and his eyes shifted and changed watching colours like a kaleidoscope.

He didn't feel Benji pat him down, pulling the bills from his pocket. Robert didn't feel Benji grab him from behind, one meaty hand on the scruff of his neck, the other on the backside of his belt. He didn't know that Benji slammed him out the back door, his toes barely touching the ground till Benji reached the hole in the fence. 'Gotta fix this fence one a these days,' Benji thought as he pushed Robert into the back-alley darkness.

Eddy sat in the near darkness drinking his CC neat, looking out the hotel window where a streetlight shone illuminating the medical centre across the road.

He remembered the time he was called into the office of the union's president, a short time after he had been hired on national staff as an organizer. The guy who hired him was there, Paul Duval, and another guy he didn't know, and the president who everybody knew and respected, even revered.

He had broken away from the American domination of the auto workers in Canada and almost single-handedly negotiated deals with the Big Three auto makers that catapulted him into national stardom.

"Sit down, Eddy," the president said, motioning to a chair in front of the president's desk. "Eddy, I want to talk to you about something I don't ever want repeated, ever. Is that clear?"

"Yes, sir."

The president sat down in his chair. "On that basis, then, I am going to proceed. Eddy, you have been hired by this union to be an organizer, and that is what you will be, but there is something else I want to discuss with you today. Paul here, and Henri, in accounting, and I have been thinking for some time of a need to address certain problems that beguile us from time to time in our efforts to protect the rights of our members. Do you know what I'm talking about?"

"No, sir, I don't."

"Well, then I'll be blunt. I'm talking about management's use of thugs in certain circumstances. Do you see where I'm going?"

"I think so, sir."

"Oh, we can pull off a good strike, you know that, but when it gets down and dirty we don't really have a counter-force to fight back. Our rank-and-file are good solid men and women but they don't have the disposition to fight it out in the back alleys, if you take my drift, and they are sometimes intimidated by brute force and forced to make concessions that aren't really in their best interests."

The president leaned forward, staring into Eddy's eyes. He was a small man, Eddy realized, much smaller than he had expected person-to-person, but the power in his eyes more than made up for his size.

"Eddy, we want you to lead a group of men, tough men like yourself, who can be called in when circumstances dictate and take on these thug sons-of-bitches. Ten, maybe twelve men at the most. Dedicated union men. In military terms, special operations, 'special ops' for short. The whole enterprise has to be covert and very, very secret.

It's going to cost money, too, I'm well aware of that. There will be obvious expenses related to travel, training, per diems, legal costs, and, of course, wages. We don't expect you to do two jobs for the price of one, Eddy. That's why Henri's here. He's devised some ways to finance the whole operation without anyone being any the wiser. Right, Henri. Creative book-keeping, eh? So, Eddy, what do you say?"

Eddy was breathless He could hardly believe what he was hearing.

"Oh I know this must come as a shock to you, Eddy, but you know what I'm talking about and we know you are the man for job. How old are you, Eddy?"

"30, sir."

"You've risen through the ranks fast, Eddy. Any you can rise even higher." The president leaned forward again and continued. "Eddy, you have a well-deserved reputation, a reputation that's preceded you to this very office. You are already a legend. We've had our eyes on you from the time you flattened that asshole foreman in the meat-packing plant in Brantford, did you know that?"

Eddie shook his head no.

"Would you think about it, Eddy?"

Eddy again shook his head no.

"What?"

Paul Duval leapt from his chair. "Eddy, don't let me down. At least think about it!"

"There's nothing to think about, sir," Eddy said, swiveling to address his boss. "I'll do it."

"What?"

"I'll do it, sir," Eddy spoke directly to the president. "And I appreciate your confidence in me. It's like you say in your book, sir, we're at war and wars are fought by armies, no matter how small that army may be, and every army needs a 'special ops'."

The president pushed himself back from his desk and stood up, motioning Eddy to do the same. He proffered his hand and Eddy took it. Both men had grips of steel.

"You'll take orders from Paul. Be assured that Paul has my blessing for anything he orders you to do. And one more thing . . ."

"Yes, sir?"

"This meeting never happened."

"Yes, sir."

Eddy smiled wryly at the recollection as he poured himself another drink. He thought of all the ways he had tried to justify his behaviour, rationalize his position as chief union goon.

Dog eat dog. Survival of the fittest. War has no morality. All his cherished shibboleths, self-righteous, delusional bull-shit. When all was said and done, the rock-bottom truth was that in his world it had been brute force against brute force and he had become an alpha-A brute.

He recalled in particular a moment in his special operations career when he went mano a mano against a management thug with an international reputation.

The thug had been called into an organizing campaign being waged by the Union in Vancouver. His job was to intimidate the workers so much that they would be afraid to sign union cards. It was a big plant, close to a thousand non-union workers. The thug brought in a team of men and immediately went to work. They phoned workers at home and threatened them. They followed women into the parking lot after work and verbally abused them. They followed the local worker promoting the union cause to his house and beat him up on the front porch, then rang the doorbell for his wife and children to see what they had done. Eddy tapped three of his squad to accompany him to Vancouver.

After several days of surveillance, Eddy and his men accosted the head-thug as he approached his hotel. It took all four of them to get him into the car and drive to a safe house.

Inside, things got bloody. The thug wasn't especially big but he was brutal and very, very strong. Eddy's men had a hard time holding him upright so Eddie could put a beating on him. One of his men made the mistake of letting his hand get close to the thug's mouth and he snapped his teeth and bit off the end of his finger. "Jesus H Christ," Eddy's man cried out.

"Don't let go of him," Eddy warned. "Get a good hold of him."

Eddy stepped closer to the thug who continued to struggle. "Watch his feet, Eddy," one of them cried out.

"You think you're tough," Eddy said.

"I know I'm tough. Not sure about you."

"You the toughest?"

"Try me."

"Okay." Eddy stepped closer, on an angle to avoid the thug's feet kicking him. He lashed out with his fist and smacked the thug in the eye.

"Oh, ouch," the thug said, "please don't hurt me."

Eddy snaked a hard left that hit the thug in the mouth, splitting his lips.

"I've got a dental plan," the thug said, still struggling.

Eddy saw that his men were getting winded. "Break his arm," Eddy instructed, indicating the thug's elbow.

"He don't have the balls," the thug grunted

"Eddy, he's right, I just can't do it."

"That's okay, Jules, that's okay," Eddy said, suddenly leaping forward, pushing his man out of the way, grabbing the thug above his elbow. In one fluid motion, Eddy wrenched the thug's arm high over his head and popped the shoulder bone out of its socket.

"Let him go," Eddy ordered.

The thug slumped to the floor, howling with pain, holding himself up with his good arm. Eddie walked around him. He lashed his steel-toed work boot into the man's face, crushing his teeth. "Hope your dental plan's better than mine," he said. He walked around the thug again stopping to stomp on the fingers spread out on the floor. The thug toppled over, screaming. Eddy indicated to one of his men to hold up the thug's other hand. "Got a knife?" The man nodded. "Cut off his little finger."

"Eddy, maybe that's enough," one of his men said, watching the knife cut through the skin and sever the sinew between the joints.

"Yeah, I don't want him to go into shock. Listen to me, tough guy, you tell your boss the same thing happens to him if he doesn't withdraw his opposition to the union. You got that? You hear me?"

The thug nodded his head, sobbing with pain. "Marcel," Eddy said, "you stay here. We're going to drop this piece of shit off at his boss' mansion. Be back in about forty minutes to pick you up."

The cops found Robert where Benji said he would be.

"Man, this mother's wired. Gonna be real hard getting' him back to the station."

"Who said anything bout getting him back to the station?" his senior partner said.

"Ain't we takin him back to the station?"

Manfred looked at his junior partner with quiet contempt. "Nope," he said.

"Then what we gonna do?"

"Boss-man said we should take care a business."

"What's that mean?"

"That means boss-man don't want this mother-fucker anywhere near the station."

"Why not?"

"Listen up, man and listen real good. This ain't no quiz show. This here's a hard-core reality show and you is in it, same as me, and we better get good ratings or our ass is grass . . ."

"But I thought we'd arrest him and put him in jail . . ."

"Well you thought wrong, man, and I'm gonna tell you why, one time only, and then you're in or you're out. It's that simple. This is the day you really join the police force. Or you don't. Here's the deal," Manfred paused then continued. "This guy's dead, understand? He's livin' and breathin' but he's dead. His own Daddy reported him to the police. There's no doubt he done it. So what are we gonna do, take him down to the station, read him his rights, process him, let him sit in jail for a year or two, put him on trial, find him guilty, send his sorry ass to Hattie Ville where I guarantee his ass will be more than sorry, it'll be half tore out, young good-look kid like that, and then let him rot in penitentiary till he dies? That don't make no sense."

"Then what . . ."

"We already know the outcome. Boss-man just wants us to ass-sell-orate the process. You know what I'm saying? We the ass-sell-orators. That's what Boss-man means when he says 'take care a business'. He means ass-sell-orate. And that's what we gonna do. Now you grab hold a that shoulder and I'll get a hold of this one and we'll go for a little walk down here aways to the canal."

At the canal, a little light from the sliver of moon reflected back at them. "Hold him tight," Manfred ordered his junior partner, pleased his partner seemed to understand what was going on. Manfred rifled through Robert's trousers. In one pocket he found a $50 dollar bill that Benji had missed. In another he found Robert's pearl-handled stiletto, Robert's little baby. "How'd this get broke," Manfred said. "Shit, this baby be worth something if it don't be broke."

"But ain't that evidence . . ."

Manfred gave his junior partner a withering look. "Give me your sap."

"What?"

"You heard me. Give me." He took the sap from his partner's hand. "Hold him up, tight. That's right." Without another word, Manfred swung the sap and whacked Robert behind his ear with all his might. "Let him go," he ordered and, as Robert began to slump down, Manfred kicked him in the back, propelling him forward into the canal.

Robert didn't know that he flew through the air with the greatest of ease, didn't know that he splashed face first into the dirty canal water, his lungs rapidly filling up, his arms stretched out like a fallen angel, didn't know that his mother had loved him to the day she died.

"C'mon, partner," Manfred said, putting his arm around his partner's shoulder. "We goin' back to the station and tell Boss-man we take good care of business, real good care."

Eddy sighed, an audible sigh, almost a cry. Jan stirred and rolled over. Eddy turned and looked at her, a little bundle in bed.

He recalled the first time he met her when they organized together in Hamilton, Ontario. What a fire-ball she was. She lit up the room with her wit and sparkle. She was indefatigable. Last to say good-night, first at work in the morning. He marveled at her, but she was beyond approach at the time. He was tied up in a relationship and Jan was someone you didn't want to string along, definitely not the one-night-stand kind of woman that he had become accustomed to. And, he had to admit, even then, the weight of his covert union job was starting to drag him down. He had been drinking heavily for the year before his Action Day gig, had been having mood swings that shocked and frightened him and he shuddered at the thought that if she got to know who he truly was she would look at him and laugh or even worse turn away in disgust.

How ironic that they would meet again in a hospital in Hamilton after she had reported for duty in the emergency ward and he had checked himself into the same ward after getting skull-ripped by a crow-bar in an early altercation between management thugs and union goons on the roof-top of a plant in Burlington.

It was love at first (or second) sight. She was like a tonic or a balm to him. She soothed him. He shared with her some of the horrors of his life. She held him and calmed him.

Yet he had endangered the love-of-his-life because he could not contain his anger when confronted by a street kid in Belize City. He had let his anger rise. He let his blood bubble and blind him. He could have taken that kid and broken him into little pieces but he misjudged the knife and the knife would have killed him if Thadeaus had not intervened.

And the kid, the kid on the street who accosted him, who was he? Why was he so strung-out? Why was he so angry? Where were his mommy and his daddy? What was he doing with a pearl-handled stiletto? Why was he willing to kill? Eddy turned scarlet with shame as he pictured the kid running away, spurned by his own people. He wished he could meet the kid somewhere and make amends but he doubted he would ever see the kid again.

The whiskey bottle was empty when Eddy, fully clothed, crawled into his double bed and sprawled on his back on top of the sheets. He lay there, drunk, listening to the echoes of past violence, watching in colour a documentary in his mind of his many violent misdemeanors; eyes wide open, staring into the darkness.

THE END

Showdown In Belize
A Sequel To Encounter
On King Street

EDDY & JAN: Arrival in Belize

Eddy Dupuis and his partner Jan Reddick flew into the Belize international airport a week before Emile O'Neal, their soon-to-be nemesis, arrived in Belize.

The flight from Toronto was uneventful, no trouble with baggage, the usual check at customs, a two-hour lay-over in Miami, and touch-down in Belize at 2:20p.m. Central time. They were met by a driver they had hired on a friend's recommendation and were to be driven directly to the village of Placencia at the tip of the Placencia peninsula on the south/east shore of the Caribbean Sea, 75 miles or so south/east of Belize City as the frigate bird flies. The trip would cost them $300usd but would be worth every penny if they could by-pass Belize City, a city they wanted to avoid after having had a very unpleasant experience there several years before.

"Why go back to Belize?" Eddy challenged Jan early in the autumn when they decided they needed a break. "There are so many other places to choose from, I mean Caribbean places, Jamaica, Antigua, the Dominican . . ."

"We discussed that before we decided on Belize, Eddy," was Jan's response. "Do we have to re-visit the whole thing again? We decided we didn't want a Rastafarian one-love experience in Jamaica. Sure we like Bob Marley but that's what iPods are all about. C'mon, Eddy. An all-inclusive resort in the Caribbean? That's not us, baby. I know, I know, the other central-American countries are supposed to be cheaper but they are also poorer and more violent and they are Spanish-speaking outside of the resort and unless you've been taking Spanish lessons without telling me about it we don't speak Spanish . . ."

"Yeah, but, c'mon, Jan, I lost my cool in Belize City. I lost my cool and ended up almost getting killed by a strung-out punk kid. What's that all about?"

"That's all about you losing your cool, Eddy. That's not about Belize. And the kid got away, so what's the worry? We won't go back to Belize City if you don't want to, I'm down with that, by why eliminate the country because you didn't act like

Mahatma Ghandi? Eddy, my love, I'm not sure you have a passive bone in your body. Never have; likely never will. As for me, all I want is for everything to work out for everybody all the time and it never does. It likely never will. All I'm saying is there's more than one place in Belize we can visit. So let's go back to Belize, kick back and try to forget what we left behind for a week or two. Me, I loved Caye Caulker. It's a great little island. I loved the Oasi and that fantastic couple that run the place, but if you associate it with your experience in Belize City, let's check out a new place. Okay?"

Eddy had no response to that. He looked at her and saw the woman he had met years ago, older to be sure, but still as bright, feisty and beautiful.

She was right, of course. It wasn't the country of Belize that marred their last vacation. It was a confluence of circumstances that brought a strung-out Belizean punk kid in contact with Eddy Dupuis, a man struggling with his hair-triggered temper and his tendency, at times a requirement in his line of work, to meet force with force.

The confrontation on the corner of Albert and King Streets in downtown Belize City could have been a lot uglier than it was but for the intervention of an ex-soldier in the British Army stationed in Belize before Independence and a sergeant-major in the newly created Belize army after Independence. Lionel King, a Belizean by birth, disposition and inclination, after many distinguished years of service to Crown and Country, returned in retirement to the neighbourhood in the core of Belize City where he was born and raised and where soon after he was dubbed the King of King Street by his small army of kids, single-moms, old-timers and rag-tag hangers-on who held he and his pension in the highest regard.

As it was, on that fateful evening, the King watched in slow-motion as the kid pulled out a stiletto knife and under-handed it toward the white guy's belly. Reflexively, the King brought down the thick mahogany cane he carried. The kid ran away with cracked wrist-bones and Eddy went back to his hotel and drank himself to sleep, cursing the nature that had provided him with a very comfortable living while at the same time breaking his heart that he couldn't be a better man than he had become.

Janet had seen the decency in Eddy from the day she met him and had tried to draw it out but time and time again he had let her down as he let his anger rise and his temper take control. She had stood by him through all these times but there was no way he was going to tell her where she could or could not take her vacation. And, besides, she recollected, she was right. They had had a great time on Caye Caulker, too bad it had been overshadowed by the confrontation on King Street but she knew that no matter where you go, you bring yourself with you . . . Mexico, Cuba, Jamaica, the Dominican Republic or anywhere in the entire world. It didn't matter. Eddy would be there with all of his baggage, suitcase and back-pack full of contradictions, inexplicable angers, violent outbursts, heart-breaking regrets, breath-taking moments of love and kindness. She would be there with her baggage, too, which, she laughed to herself, consisted mainly of Eddy. But why not return to Belize? Why not check out a new location that had all the sun and sea and sand they desired at a cost they could afford?

It had been several years since the encounter on King Street. Eddy returned to work as an organizer for a major Canadian union where he doubled as the sergeant-at-arms of a special operations unit (Special Ops) whose job it was to meet force with force when dealing with anti-union thugs hired by management organizations determined to stop before it started or break before it got its first collective agreement the Union that had been infiltrating its employees.

During that time, Janet continued to work in the emergency ward in a hospital in Hamilton, while at the same time working on Eddy to ease himself out of his special ops position and settle into organizing full time. Eddy's boss, Jim Douglas, the revered president of the union, himself about to step aside, in a private conversation with Janet at an Xmas party in Toronto, conceded that it was time for Eddy to move up, and in the New Year made him the head of the organizing wing of the union, ostensibly removing him from the rank of union goon. Janet was delighted. Eddy knew better but he didn't have the heart to tell her that the promotion was conditional on him accepting the covert position of captain of the goons, not knuckle-busting anymore but approving and coordinating the knuckle-busting, taking direction from and answering only to the president himself.

EMILE: Arrival in Belize/Vengeance Is Mine

Emile Frederic de Quinzio O'Neal literally tingled as he stepped down the steps from the 737 that had flown him from Miami to the Goldson International Airport in Belize, Central America. Before Miami, he had flown from Toronto, Ontario, Canada, leaving behind him temperatures only an Inuit could love and snow falls perhaps endeared by skiers, snowmobilers and others of that ilk of which he was not one.

He tingled for a number of reasons, chief amongst them the anticipation that he was soon to extract vengeance on a monstrous man who had nearly (and could have) killed him in the performance of his duty as a union goon but had utterly failed because he had let him (Emile) live.

It wasn't that Emile viewed letting him live as a weakness. In context, there was nothing his antagonist could have done but what he did: tear his (Emile's) shoulder bone out of its socket, kick in his teeth, stomp on his hands and have someone slice off his left hand pinky-finger. There was never a question of killing him. Emile knew that from the get-go. It wasn't a killing operation. Dumping Emile on the front lawn of his (then) employer was exactly appropriate considering that Emile and his boys had brutally beaten up a union organizer on his own front porch then rang his front-door bell so that his wife and kids could find him.

No, it wasn't that at all. What is was was a sense that his adversary had shown undue restraint. The shoulder dislocation was masterful, the tooth displacement predictable, the finger removal a nice touch because he (Emile) had bitten off the end of one of his opponent's fingers, but all in all so much more could have been done to dissuade him (Emile) from re-entering his normal line of business and in that his antagonist had failed; in that, Emile had detected a weakness he could exploit.

And what it was was an overwhelming need, a pathological (Emile would agree) compulsion to confront his assailant and re-claim his rightful position as the number one man in the small world he inhabited, a world of men (no women, yet) whose rank was determined by their ability and willingness to destroy the will of those who opposed their masters.

Emile stepped down the gangplank from the airplane and walked across the tarmac to the airport. The heat stifled him. It seemed to rise from the asphalt. A slight breeze wafted the air and left him almost breathless. He trudged along with his fellow travelers, lined up at customs, presented his passport and declaration form, offered his backpack for inspection, was waived on and stepped out of the airport terminal with an ever-increasing sense of anticipation.

There was no one waiting for him. No one waving a sign with a Canadian flag in the corner and EMILE O'NEAL scrawled with a black-tipped Sharpie.

Everything was going exactly as planned.

EMILE: Brief Bio

Emile O'Neal was born at St Joseph's Hospital in Toronto, Ontario. He was a healthy 7 ½ lb. baby, signed, sealed and delivered back to the room his mama and papa shared in a Portuguese rooming house on Dunn Street in downtown Toronto. It was in this room he lived for the first years of his life; it was two blocks from the school he later attended; it was the centre of the streets he roamed until he turned 12 and everything ended, though nothing on the surface changed.

Emile knew exactly when things started to get different. One day his papa was there and the next day he wasn't. He asked his mama where his papa was and she said, 'He's gone.' Well, he knew that. That's why he was asking where he went, but she wouldn't or couldn't explain it to him. Their life went on without him and though Emile had loved his papa or so he had been told later by those around him, he missed him less and less as Emile settled into a comfortable routine with his mama. Then Ruffino showed up. Emile figured he must have been around 10 at the time.

He hit it off with Ruffino at first. Ruffino was very dark with curly black hair and flashing brown eyes and teeth that seemed to sparkle in his mouth. He was a little bigger than his papa but much much more lively. He would dance his mama around the room and they would sing and laugh out loud. Emile would get excited and dance around them, then they would all join hands and dance in a circle till one or all of them would fall down, laughing and rolling around on the floor.

As time went on, Emile noticed one thing about Ruffino. Unlike his papa, Ruffino never went to work. Emile wasn't exactly sure what 'work' meant but he knew his papa always went to it and that's why he disappeared for most of the daylight. Ruffino never disappeared. He was there when Emile went to school and he was there when he came back again. His mama disappeared, too, during the daylight, but he understood that because he knew that she, too, went to work, like his papa used to, though she sometime came back later than his papa, sometime when it was quite dark.

But Ruffino was always there. He never seemed to go to work at all, unless he went to work when Emile was told to go to bed but he doubted that because at night he would hear them laughing and talking and he wondered how his mother could stay awake so long and still get up in the morning and go to work.

Those days weren't so bad, he would recollect, all in all. He went to school during the day and ran the streets at night. He was of an age when women excited him, all of them, except his mother, of course. He loved the sight of them, the smell of them, not so much the sound of them and never yet the touch and taste of them.

One afternoon during his weekly bath his mother touched his penis with a soapy sponge and he felt an electric impulse course through his body. When she left the bathroom he continued sponging himself until he felt an overwhelming surge of pleasure and settled back in the bathtub amazed and exhausted and resolved to repeat the experience time and time again.

He attended school on a regular basis, plodding through the grades until he reached senior elementary and met Miss Snowdon. Under her tutelage his behaviour was exemplary though his academic standing showed no significant improvement. He sat still at his desk, right hand on the desk top, left hand deep in his pant pocket, drowning himself in fantasies of Miss Snowdon's creamy bosom. At night, hoping to turn fantasy into actuality, he escaped home imprisonment, climbed a tree outside Miss Snowdon's second-story apartment and watched her comb her hair standing in her pygamas before a mirror.

One night, after several un-productive hours perched in the tree outside Miss Snowdon's window, he returned home, slipping through the unlocked front door like a shadow without a body. Tip-toeing his way back to his bedroom, he stopped short at the sight before him. Ruffino had his mother pinned on her hands and knees on the living room floor. She was crying out with pain, crying 'Oh, oh, oh!' as Ruffino thrust against her. Emile charged at Ruffino. "Let her alone," he cried. Ruffino on his knees with both hands grasping Emile's mother's waist turned in time and swatted the boy with his right hand, sending him sprawling.

"Go to bed," Ruffino bellowed.

"Mama?"

"Go to bed, baby," his mother said, her head squashed on a pillow on the floor muffling her words.

"Go to bed, you bastard," Ruffino bellowed again. He stood up, pulling his belt from his pants. As he stepped toward Emile, he exposed Emile's mother's naked buttocks, her underwear wrapped around her knees, her dress draped over her back.

Everything had changed the next day, though everything was the same. His mother was quiet at first at the breakfast table as she served up porridge for Emile and Ruffino, but then she smiled and ruffled Emile's hair. Ruffino even joked with Emile. "Well, you are becoming a man. Or, maybe you are a man already, eh? That's what men do. That's what women do. Forget about the birds and bees, eh? That's how people do it."

Life went on with his mama and Ruffino, and then one day Ruffino wasn't there and he asked his mother what happened to Ruffino and she said, "He's gone" and he thought as he had with his papa, 'Yeah, I know that. That's why I asked what happened'.

When he was fourteen, he started work part-time at a local grocery store. When he was fifteen, he lost his virginity in the attic of a girl he knew from school. She didn't like his love-making technique of doing it doggy-style and wouldn't go out with him again. When he was sixteen, he hired a hooker and masturbated as she knelt naked in front of him touching herself. When he was seventeen he dropped out of school and started to work for a grocery chain. When he was eighteen he was living alone in his own one-bedroom apartment on Dufferin Street between Dundas and Queen, still visiting hookers from time to time.

While still eighteen and gainfully employed stocking shelves at the grocery store, an assistant manager approached him and took him aside in the warehouse. The assistant manager, Allan Johns, had never shown an interest in Emile before this encounter nor had Emile ever shown an interest in him. Emile took his direct orders from the section manager and he liked it that way.

The assistant manager was short, balding, over-weight and pasty-faced. Emile hadn't liked him on sight and liked him even less as the assistant pressed close to him, an odd odour emanating from his body.

"Do you know what's going on?" he asked.

"What's what?" Emile sputtered.

"What's going on? Do you know?"

"Uh, I'm working nights next week. Is that it?"

"No, that is not it. Do you know we are being raided?"

Emile was aghast. "No. Who by?"

"By a union."

"What's that?"

"Jesus Christ, you don't know very much do you?"

"I guess not. Don't spend much time with the others."

"Well, maybe that's good. That's kind of why I'm talking to you."

"Why?"

"'Cause you're not buddies of John and Roger, they're the ones trying to bring in the union."

"John and Roger? They never talk to me. They don't mean shit to me. But what's it mean when you bring in a union?"

"What's it mean to you? You'll lose your job. Hell, we'll probably all lose our job if the union gets in 'cause the company will just shut her down and move on somewhere else."

"Why'd John and Roger want that? That don't make sense."

"Oh don't worry about them. They'll get paid off some way or another. They always do."

"So what do you want from me?"

"What I want from you? Just hang around some. Eat lunch in the staff room. Don't start asking a lot of questions or anything like that but listen to what the rest of them are saying and let me know. Okay?"

Emile hesitated before he asked, "Yeah, okay, I guess, but what's in it for me?"

"For you," the assistant manager said, stepping closer to Emile, "for you things are going to change for the better. You like days?"

Emile nodded.

"You got straight days. You want your own section, like cereals or dairy?"

Emile nodded.

"Take your pick. You want to move up, fast-track, grocery manager, produce manager, meat manager, assistant manager . . ."

Emile gulped.

"I'm telling you kid. Help me break the union and you and me are on the fast-track to suck-cess. You understand my meaning?"

Emile nodded.

"Say it."

"Say what?"

"Say you'll do what I tell you."

"I'll do it."

And so it began.

It was easier than Emile ever thought it would be. He'd sit in the staff room munching on his sandwiches while he listened to the conversations around him. He'd meet with A.J., the assistant manager, at pre-determined spots, like the park at Lindsay and Fair Ave. A.J. would be there throwing peanuts to the squirrels. Emile would sit down on the bench. A.J. would say, "What do you got?" Emile would pretend he was in a movie. He brought a newspaper with him and held it up in front of him, shaking it and folding it while he made his report, never looking to left or right. It was the most exciting time of Emile's life.

One day Emile reported to A.J. that Roger told a colleague in the lunch room that they had signed enough cards to get a vote. Emile had no idea what that meant but he noticed A.J.'s reaction.

A.J. said, "Oh, oh. They're moving fast. Gotta slow them down." Emile stared wordlessly at A.J.s moon face eclipsed by his black horn-rimmed glasses.

Emile watched A.J.'s mouth open and close as he listened to the words A.J. uttered. "Don't know whether you're ready for this or not but this is the time to find out. I'm going to tell you where Roger and John are going to be tonight, the bar they drink at, where they park their car. I'm gonna tell you I want you at work on time tomorrow no matter how long you're on this job, but I don't want Roger and John to show up. It's okay if they show up late not looking too good but it's much better if they can't punch the time-clock for a day or two. This is your chance, mine too. If you succeed in this, we're riding in the fast lane. If you don't, if you let me down or rat me out, you don't got much of a life from now to doomsday, least not in the world I live in."

Emile showed up for work the next morning at 7:00 a.m. Roger and John didn't.

EDDY & JAN: On the Way to Placencia

Charlie Aurilio stood at the perimeter of the exit ramp at the Goldson's International Airport with a large sign reading EDDY&JANET. He had received a call from a friend the night before the pick-up and was glad for the business. Times were tough in Belize what with the price of gas at more than 8 bucks Belize or 4 US a gallon and what with him driving one of the original gas-guzzlers, a 1984 Lincoln Alexandra. He was charging $300usd for the trip to Placencia which sounded like good pay until you factored in gas and depreciation of his beloved Lincoln, and his expenses, which would likely include an overnight in either Placencia or San Bight and maybe even some well-deserved entertainment. He might pocket $80 US for two day's work which wasn't bad but far from great.

He watched the crowd as they stumbled out of the airport after being processed by customs. There was a mix of young, middle-aged and older men, women and children, black, brown, yellow and white, mostly tourists, some he identified as locals returning home from business abroad. As he scanned them he saw a white man in sandals wearing baggy khaki shorts with a bright red short-sleeved shirt break from the crowd and run toward him. He was followed by a younger woman, too old for a daughter, Charlie thought, but younger than a wife.

"Hey, Charlie," the guy cried. "I think you're waiting for us." He wasn't a big man, 5'10, 5'11, a little beefy, but tough looking, not the kind of guy you would want to mess with.

"You Eddy?" Charlie said, extending his hand.

"Yeah, and this here's Janet. Janet, meet Charlie. Charlie's going to take us to Placencia."

"I know, I know, Eddy. Calm down." She extended her hand.

"Hi there, Charlie."

"That all the luggage you got," Charlie said as he shook hands with Janet. She looked to be in her late thirties, good-looking, more than good, real pretty, bright-eyed, well-dressed in a tan-coloured cotton dress. Each of them carried a back-pack and Eddy had a mid-sized suitcase in his grip.

"Don't expect any dress-up occasions, Charlie, and we know we can do our laundry in Placencia."

"Okay, guys, ready to rumble? I've got lots of water, some cold coke, some fried chicken and coleslaw my wife made up for us. It's right up front here. Help yourself. I'm planning to take the Coastal Highway off the Western Highway straight to Dangriga where we can get gas, freshen up, and hit Placencia sometime after sunset."

"Sounds good to us. Let's boogey, brother," Eddy said as he opened the passenger back-seat door for Janet and tumbled in beside her.

Charlie drove with the casual expertise of a man with many years experience. When Eddy asked him a question he didn't take his eyes off the road when he answered, but after he left the airport and swung onto the Northern Highway, he relaxed a little and turned toward Eddy in the back seat.

"Where you folks from?"

"Canada." Eddy replied

"Good place Canada. First time?"

"Second. First time, we went to Caye Caulker, then back to Belize City for a few days." Jan said.

"Yeah, well, you better keep outta Belize City, man."

"No kidding," Eddy said.

EMILE: Meeting with a Rat

Emile liked his room at the Princess Hotel in downtown Belize City. It wasn't low-class; it wasn't high-class; it was just the middle-of-the-road-class where years of experience had taught him he belonged if he wanted to remain undetected.

The same with the room. It was a step up from a regular with a king-size bed but smaller than a suite. It suited him to a T. He made a quick check of the living-room, dropped his bags in the bedroom, made a quick inspection of the bathroom, went back to the living-room and rang room-service. He ordered a club-sandwich and a Caesar salad without bacon and two cans of tonic water. He flipped on the t.v. and put it on mute. He used the hotel phone to contact his friend who now worked security at the Radisson Hotel, the most prestigious hotel in Belize City.

"I'm here," he said. He listened to the voice and said, "Of course you know. I know you know. Let's get down to cases, okay. You've still got a trace on my people? . . . Good. Anything I should know that I don't know now? . . . Good. Meet as planned then? 7:30 at Neries, Queen and Daly? You'll be there? . . . No? Why . . . ? Okay. Okay. But I've got to see you before we close the deal. Face to face, understand? I'll meet Cain and Abel tonight but nothing happens till I meet with you? Clear?" He hung up, swung around and watched the muted t.v. till room-service knocked.

As he bit into the club sandwich, he recalled that he had Eddy Dupuis under surveillance before he (Emile) was out of the hospital. He had a lot of authority on the shady side of the law and he called on certain police contacts as well as others in the union-busting business to prepare a biographical dossier on Eddy while at the same time tailing him wherever he went month after month. Most of the work they did for him was pro-bono, because Emile had the bones to throw to the pros.

He knew where Eddy worked, lived, loved, his favourite restaurants, everything he had to know. He knew that Eddy and his current gal-pal had visited Belize a few years back. He knew but couldn't capitalize on the incident on King Street in Belize City though he had been informed that the kid Eddy had fought died that night and had been dragged by police from a canal by the Belize City bus terminal. He was told that Eddy was planning another trip to Belize and Emile thought, Bingo!

There was a rap at his door. Rap, rap, pause, rap, rap, rap. Emile got up and went to the door. "Bowman?" he asked, pressing his lips on the crack of the door. The person on the other side rapped four times. Emile lifted the chain and opened the door.

"C'mon in, man." Emile said as Dwayne Bowman pushed his way into the room. "Sit down over there," Emile gestured to a chair in the middle of the room and set himself on a chair in front of the picture window with the sun setting behind him.

Bowman hadn't changed much, Emile concluded. A little more beef, a little less hair, but the same rat Emile had worked with for many years back in Canada. He looked like a rat, sniffed like a rat and if he had a tail would have switched his tail like a rat. Emile had counted on him more than once to break a man down and Dwayne Bowman had never failed him.

"So how's Belize, Dwayne," Emile asked. "Everything okay?"

"Better than okay. Let me know when you want to get out of Canada and I'll fix you up real good down here. Money's good. Real good. And the stress level is way down. Got half the cops on our side down here and most of the politicians."

"How does that differ from Canada"?

"Ha ha."

"I'll give it some thought. But let's get down to cases. Tell me about the boys I'm meeting tonight . . . without you."

"Listen, man, can't be helped. I'd love to be there but . . ."

"Okay, okay. Move on. org. Tell me about the boys."

"Couple of hard-cases. Born and bred in Belize City. Raised in crime, street thieves, gangs, syndicate shit, you know, but they earned a rep as guys you don't fuck with no matter what side you're on."

"You called them Creole or something? What's that?"

"Yeah, Creole. That's like black slaves mixed with white trash, way back, you know?"

"No, I don't know and don't really give a shit. What I really want to know is how far can they go, get it? Like I know how far you can go, that's why we are here in this room together, and you know how far I can go, but how far can they go?"

"All the way, Emile," said Dwayne, blocking his eyes from the sun shining through the window, making Emile look like a black silhouette.

"Done time?"

"Some juvenile. A few years hard time in Hattyville."

"How hard is Hattyville?"

"Hard hard."

"Rat anybody out?"

"That's not their style. Have they ever been ratted out? Twice I know of. Those rats are dead."

"Okay, I'll meet them . . . without you. But Dwayne . . ."

"Yes, Emile. I know what you're going to say."

"I'll kill you, or have you killed if . . . ."

"Of course you will."

EMILE: Meeting with the Boys

Emile arrived at Neries on Queen Street a half hour before the meet was to take place and recognized his contacts as soon as he stepped into the restaurant. The place was busy. Belize working-stiffs loved it for the food, cow-foot soup, escabeche, rellano with Ricardo spicing, catch of the day, pork chops and chicken fried, stewed or roasted with rice and beans, rich food that left you stuffed and a little sleepy but ready for the next round of work. There were some travelers who had heard from friends about the place and some who returned time and time again; and there were a few tourists many of whom looked at the menu, blanched, ordered a beer and went back to the Tourist Village.

They were sitting exactly where he would have sat if he had arrived first, at a table off in the corner, facing the entrance. They waved him over before he had a chance to point them out. He wound his way around tables and chairs and sat down on one of the chairs kicked toward him. He smiled to himself as he took his seat. 'Charming bastards', he thought.

"You Emile?"

"I'm Emile. You Cain and Abel??

"Yeah, we Cane and Able, but not as you know it."

"What do you mean?" Emile looked at the men across the table from him. They were both a rich-brown skin colour, natural short-cut African hair, matching deep blue golf shorts, blue jeans and running shoes without socks. They looked to be in their mid to late thirties, a little roughed up but with laugh-lines around their eyes which stared at him intently as he spoke.

"We mean not in the Bible sense, man. Not the Cain and Abel shit you thinking about. My name's Cane, see, 'cause, I'm walking with a cane, and he's able, see, 'cause, unlike me, he don't need a cane to get around. Yunerstan? Cane and Able."

Emile smiled back at them. They were large men with wide shoulders and well-muscled arms from the biceps through the forearms and wrists to meaty sledge-shaped hands. He knew that on a roof top or in an abandoned warehouse he could immobilize them in less than a minute and kill them in seconds but the thought didn't comfort him. All that mattered to Emile was whether or not they were up for the job.

"Okay, let's get down to cases," Emile said.

"Wait a minute," interrupted the one Emile identified as Cane. "Don't you want to know why I'm using a cane?"

"I don't give a fuck, Cane. And I don't care if you call yourselves Toad and Stool or Ass and Hole. Are we here to do business . . ." The man called Able hitched back his chair and started to stand up. "Able," Emile warned, "Don't get all sensitive on me. You're about one second away from making the biggest mistake of your life and I'm not talking about all the money I got for you. Now sit the fuck down."

Cane signaled for Able to sit down. Able sat.

"Look here," Emile said when Able was seated. "Why don't you order me some bottled water, get what you want, food, drink, whatever, and let's get down to cases. Okay? I'm not here to fuck around. I'm here on business."

EMILE: Review of Negotiations

Back in his hotel room sitting in the darkness sucking on a cold diet coke, Emile reconstructed the evening and chuckled. Negotiations had gone well he was pleased to report to himself. He chuckled because both sides had struck a deal that satisfied their respective needs. Chip n Dale or whatever they called themselves thought they were going to get paid better than any other deal they ever made with the possible exception of some slap-happy drug deals which didn't count in the real world; and Emile was as satisfied as he could be that he was going to get value for his money at about half what it would have cost in Canada.

They weren't the brightest lights in the under-world but he had worked with guys a lot dimmer. He had watched them as he talked and he had listened closely when they responded. They had big grins on their faces but their eyes were cold as ice. If words were cards, they played their hand cautiously, holding back trump till it could be used to the best advantage.

He had already paid them $5,000usd to wait for the victim and his gal-pal to arrive in Belize, follow them and ascertain with a certainty where they planned to spend their vacation and for how long. He had paid up-front as a gesture of good faith. Now the bargaining was about to get serious.

"You're certain they're booked for 12 days in Placencia Village?"

"Yeah, we certain, man," Cane said, wiping his lips after he dipped into his cow-foot soup. "Told you that awready."

"No rented car?"

"Thass right."

"And you've booked us into the same place, a cabana on the beach side of Placencia?"

"Yeah, man", Able rumbled. "Let's move on."

"What's your hurry?"

"No hurry, man, but we just goin' over the same shit, man. Tell us what you want so we can figure how much it's going to cost you."

"What I want? You know what I want. I want to kill a man."

"Well, go kill him, man." Cane said. He pushed back his chair and motioned Able to stand up. "Here's the key to the cabana. It's number 2. Hotel name's on the key chain. Placencia Village, 'bout 4 hours south of here as the frigate bird flies. Take a taxi. Your friend's in number 4. Right now there's nobody else there 'cept a night watch man who don't do much watchin' at night. The owner's out of town and won't be back for a couple weeks. You've paid in full. Have yourself a good night."

"Okay, okay," Emile motioned them to sit down. "C'mon, boys, sit down. I'll tell you what I want then we'll get down to the nitty-gritty." Cane and Able sat down and leaned across the table, staring intently at Emile. They saw a middle-aged guy, not quite white but lighter than a Mexican, black curly hair that looked touched up, a face wrinkled by time and scarred over one eye, dressed in a short-sleeved brown shirt and tan slacks, not the usual touristy many-pocketed khaki shorts with brightly coloured short-sleeved shirts. Both of them noticed his hands with one pinky finger cut off at the first knuckle.

"I need some time alone with my 'friend', understand? I need you to gain entrance to his cabana, overpower him and watch out, he's a tough son of a bitch, and remove his gal-pal to our cabana. Bring some kind of hoody you can pull over her head. Duct tape it so she can't shake it off. The less she sees of you the better.

I need about an hour or so to do what I have to do. After that, when I call you, you bring the broad back to my friend's cabana, well taped-up and blind-folded, of course; then soon as we figure the best way to get rid of the bodies we get out of Dodge."

"What's dodge, man?" Able asked

"It's an expression . . ."

"What the fuck, man, speak English."

"It means we leave fast. High tail it back to Belize City. They won't be missed for a day or two and by that time you'll have resumed your life of crime and I'll have returned to Toronto to mine."

"I gotta ask you somethin', man." Cane whispered loudly to be heard over the babble of voices in the restaurant.

"What's that," Emile whispered loudly back.

"You guys from Canada always talk this fast?"

"What, you think we got speedometers in our mouths? Maybe you got slow ears. How the hell . . ."

"You talk too fast and you don't make no sense."

"What do you mean don't make . . ."

"No sense," Cane completed the sentence. "We meet to talk to you about something you want to do. That's cool. You wanna do a dude, thas you're bidness, not ours. You talkin' money, that's cool, we lissning. We neutralize the dude, take the girl away, you kill the dude, we bring back the girl. Is that right? Is that about it so far?"

"Yeah,' Emile replied, "in case some other folks in the other cabanas are out and about, you guys drag her between you, like she's drunk or something and you're laughing and singing and you push open the front door and drag her inside. I'm thinking we kill her right then, bring round the Jeep, Dwayne told me you were driving a Jeep, right, a black Jeep okay? So we load up the bodies and take them to the lagoon place you told me about on the way in and feed them to the fishes. Or maybe we kill her later, depends what you want to do . . ."

"Never mind that shit. It's your plan, man. What's on your mind? What you thinkin'? Where're we goin' with this shit?"

"I'm thinking she's not dead when I'm doing what I gotta do. I don't want her dead right away, okay? Never know, might need her alive, doubt it but you never know. You get the call, you walk her back to her cabana, you know, like between you two, like she's drunk or something, and you're laughing and talking, then you get her inside and shut the door."

Cane: "Yeah, yeah. We already covered that, man. What then?"
Emile: "Well, then we kill her . . ."
Cane: "Wait a sec, Emile. We kill her?"
Emile: "Doesn't matter to me. You don't want to kill her, I'll kill her."
Cane: "And then?"
Emile: "And then we bring the Jeep around and load up the bodies and take them
    to the lagoon where we can drop them off and let the fishes feast on them."
Cane: "My oh my."
Emile: "What's the matter?"
Able: "Cane?"

Cane: "What?"

Able: "This guy's got his head so far up his ass all he smells is his own shit. Let's get outta here."

Cane: "Do you sense my brother's impatience? I'm about out of mine, too, but let's look at it from another angle, okay?"

"Okay," Emile responded, knowing what was coming next, realizing that the Cane who sat across from him was very able.

"We done a recce job for you, paid in advance. Thank you very much, by the way. Bowman tells us you have further needs and we agree to sit down and talk about what those needs are and how much they're going to cost you. Everything's cool. Except a whole bunch of what you talkin' about now ain't anywhere near cool."

"What's the problem?"

"Problem is . . . Able you lissen to this shit! C'mon, man, share my burden. Problem is, recce job? Over and done with, like a P.I. gig paid in full in advance. Find a certain party. Follow a certain party. Ass-or-tain the certain party's whereabouts. Report. No criminal activity there. Startin' to unnnerstan'?

Pick you up and drive you to Placencia? Hey, it's like taxi fare. We drive you from point A to point B, you pay for the trip. No crime there. We rent a cabana at a popular spot in Placencia? Why shouldn't we, I mean me and Able, we Belizean. We can rent a cabana anywhere we like in Belize and long's we pay for it, its okay. It's not against no law I know of.

Entertain a white chick for a few hours on a hot Belizean afternoon? Lotta ladies lookin' for black man's dick. No crime there, neither.

But then you go talking about the man you kilt like that's our business. Then you talkin' about the dead guy's gal like we . . . No, no, don't interrupt me." Cane held out his hand in a 'stop' position. "Don't matter if we do it or you do it, man. If we in that room, it's as good as we done it, including your dead friend. And then you think we gonna pick up the bodies in our Jeep and drive them around the village? You crazy? You believe that bull-shit about feeding bodies to the fishes? That's just an 'expression', man. Means you deep-six the mother-fuckers but you need a boat to get far 'nough out to sink the body. Where you been livin' all your life? What they teach you up there in Canada? Now what we got here is a fuckin' tractor-trailer full a fuckin' criminal actions, Emile. That's hard time in Hattyville. Been there. Done that. Ain't going back. Got that?"

"So you want more money?" Emile asked, stone-faced.

"More money than what?" Cane exclaimed

"More money than what I was prepared to offer you."

"You fuckin wid us, man. How we know how much you gonna offer us?"

"Flat out? First offer, 10 large each, how's that?"

"That not bad, man, till you start talkin' bout bodies and shit like that. Shit like that gonna cost you . . ."

"So you want more money?"

"Yeah we want more money but we don't want dead bodies, neither. There's gotta be more money but, first, we got a dead guy on the floor and a live trussed-up chick to take care of. Let's get that little problem out of the way, know what I mean? So, what are you thinkin' now?"

"I'm thinking you bring her back to my friend's cabana. He's for sure dead. We tie her up real good so she can't move till someone finds her."

"Yeah, awright. That's how I'm thinkin' 'cept for one thing."

"What's that?"

"She seen us when we came in the front door."

"So what? She saw two big black guys for about 5 seconds. C'mon, Cane. She's a white girl from a white country, no disrespect to you but you all look alike to her."

"Yeah, I guess. Seen that before. So, he's dead and she's tied up. What happens when somebody finds them?"

"What happens? What happens is they find two bodies on the kitchen floor. Kitchen's been trashed. Look into the living room, every things been trashed. Looks like a fucked-up robbery. Looks like some home-boys broke in looking for easy cash and everything got fucked up. Then she moves. She makes a sound. They realize she ain't dead. Someone runs for the cops. Cops cut her loose. What happens is she's hysterical. She's spent more time than she wanted lying next to a rotting corpse that used to be her main squeeze. She tells the cops she was abducted from her cabana . . ."

"Say what? She was what?" Able interrupted.

Emile sighed. "She was taken from . . ."

"Why din't you say so then. She was taken . . ."

". . . then brought back, doesn't know what the hell's going on. The cops say, 'Who took you? Who brought you back?' She says, 'Two black guys.' 'What'd they want?' 'I don't know' 'What did they look like?' She says, 'They were big and black'. The cops laugh. 'Well that narrows it down.'"

Cane and Able guffawed.

"The cops check the hotel records. Yours are bull-shit but it will take a little time to figure that out. We'll be long gone. As for my 'friend'? Who cares? He's dead. They can i.d. all they want, ain't gonna bring his speech back.

She'll be babbling about getting in touch with the Canadian Embassy. Embassy don't give a shit; it's just two more Canadians getting themselves in trouble in the Caribbean; cuts into their play time. See what I mean? Time's on our side.

And for that, my friends," Emile continued, "I'm prepared to give you $15,000 usd." He watched as they sat back and then continued, "Each".

Cane looked hard at Emile and shushed Able before he could speak. "You was gonna offer 10 large each if we did all that shit you was talkin' about and now we're not dealin' with no dead bodies, we're walkin' away free and clear, and you gonna give us 5 large more than you were before? What the fuck, man?"

"Whoa down, Cane. Whoa down. Able, sit down, please," Emile pointed to the chair Able had vacated. "Listen up, guys, listen up. Heads together." The three men nearly bumped heads as they leaned across the table. "We just met, right? You don't know who I am and I don't know jack-shit about you. All we got in common is Dwayne Bowman and he'd fuck his own mother out of her last dime. Am I right? So I had to figure out fast if you could do what I wanted you to do, just like you have to figure out fast if you can trust me. I had in mind a number, you understand? It was the number 10. Large. But it was only a number. Numbers can change. When you guys challenged me on how and where we were going to get rid of the bodies, you passed the first test. I wanted to know how far you wanted to go, how much risk you wanted to take. I liked what you said to me. I didn't want to be driving around this dump with two dead bodies in the back seat of the Jeep. And I'm thinking, 'You know what? We're here in Placencia but we gotta get back to Belize City, and I don't get back there without my Cane and Able. You are my exit plan. I'm not gonna get out of here unless you make it happen, and so I'm thinking 15 large each to make it happen in Placencia and 10 large each to get me out of Dodge'."

"Sweet Jesus Christ!" Able splurted.

"Able." Cane spat. "Do not blaspheme. Even criminals like us can be Christians. At least, try to talk like a Christian even if you can't act like one."

Cane motioned a server over to their table. Indicating the plates and bottles, he said, "Clear this shit off a here, man, and bring me and my brother another Belican Premium."

"Yes sir. Three Belican Premium comin' up."

"I said me and my brother, mother-fucker. Ain't you lissning?"

"I'm sorry. I just assumed," the server stammered. He was a young Spanish Belizean who had lived in Belize City long enough to know not to mess with the black brothers who sat menacingly in front of him. Turning to address the white man he said, "Anything for you, sir?"

Emile had smiled at Cane's rebuff. "No, thank you. Maybe later, but make sure those two beers are on his bill. I'll pay for anything up to now." He paused till he had the thugs' attention. "Well, gentlemen?"

"That's an interesting offer, Mr. Emile," Cane replied. "How you plan makin' payment?"

"You want me to talk 'each' or 'total'?"

"Each," Able blurted.

"Total," Cane commanded.

"I'm thinking 30,000 tomorrow when we arrive in Placencia and begin this operation and 20,000 seconds before I leave the airport for Canada."

"What's in between?" Able countered.

"Like I said, in between we high-tail it back to the City. We split up. Pick me up in the morning. Take me to the airport. When my flight's called, I line up and slip you a nice little packet with another 20 large. How's that?"

"No way we splitin' up, man," Able said. "We got a safe-house close by the airport. We stickin' together like glue. We stickin' together like we brothers."

"I'm cool with that," Emile replied, "but I've got to check out of my hotel and you've got to get me back to Belize City early in the morning so I can withdraw the money from the bank. Okay with that?"

Cane and Able exchanged looks and nodded consent.

"So that's that. Can we adjourn now?"

"What?" Able blurted.

'Cab we leave now. Can we stop negotiating?'

"Not yet, man." Able said. "About the airport? No way. We make the hand-off in the men's room and not in the fuckin' line-up for departure. You one dollar short in what you owe us we gonna carve you another asshole and you gonna have the last and biggest shit of your life."

"Anything else," Emile said calmly.

"Why don't we just kill you tomorrow on the way to Placencia", Able said.

"Because if you were going to kill me you wouldn't have said that and because you'd lose 20 large at the end of the job and because if you tried to kill me I'd kill you both and if you did kill me I've already arranged to have you killed if my body shows up dead."

"Okay," Cane snorted. "Be cool, Emile. No need makin' threats. This ain't no competition, this here's a bidness arrangement, but we gotta tighten things up."

"Meaning?"

"There's something else we gotta talk about," Cane continued.

"What's that?"

"You say you gonna fight your 'friend'?"

"That's right."

"In the cabana?"

"That's right?"

"And you gonna kill him?"

"That's right."

"And if you don't?"

Emile was relieved he had been asked that question. If he hadn't he would have suspected skullduggery or, even worse, stupidity. "If I don't, if he kills me, because one of us has to die, we better have a back—up plan. Right?"

"Keep talking, man. Wanna hear what Mr. Emile means by 'back-up plan', Able?"

"Yeah, sure, Cane. My black ass wants to hear what Mr. Emile's got stuffed up his little white behind."

"Manuel," Emile called as the server walked by. "Manuel, would you fix us up with a private room upstairs. I understand there are some rooms like that available."

"Si, senor. Anything else?"

"Fix up my friends here with whatever else they want and bring me a large diet coke with lots of ice. On my tab, por favor."

"Si, senor."

EDDY & JAN: Fun in the Sun

Eddy and Jan bounced in the back seat as Charlie skimmed over smooth boulders on what was euphemistically called the Coastal Highway. Practically speaking, it was a short-cut from the Western Highway to Dangriga, a large town (by Belizean standards) of 9,000 many of whom were descendents of the Garifuna people, a mixture of African slaves and Caribe Indians who landed on the shores of Belize in the 1800's.

Eddy and Jan held hands, felt the hot breeze on their faces, and listened to Charlie as he provided a running commentary on all things Belizean.

"See that there," he said before he turned off the main highway, gesturing toward a road sign with the number 29 marked on it. "That's mile 29 on the Western Highway. Why's that important? 'Cause it marks the Belize Zoo, that's why. Some folks say it's the biggest little Zoo in the whole world. I don't know nothin' 'bout that but I know lotta tourists take the bus outta Belize City and visit the Zoo. A lotta them. Wish more a them took a taxi but it cost $3.00 bze to take the bus and I'd have to charge you $30.00 usd for the same ride. Can't say I blame 'em. There it is there," he pointed to the worn Belize Zoo sign as they whizzed by.

The Coastal Highway was every bit as bad as Charlie had promised. The smooth stones were embedded in hard red clay. Scrabble-bush sprawled on either side of the road and if this was the 'coastal' highway there was no sea to be seen anywhere.

"Sorry, folks," Charlie called out to the back seat. "Tell you what, when you're ready to come back, let me know, we'll go back by the Hummingbird Highway, lot prettier'n you seein' now. Might cost a little extra but it's worth it."

"Okay, Charlie," Eddy shouted back. "Give us your card, man, and we'll let you know when we want to go back to the City."

On first sight, there was nothing about Dangriga that impressed Eddy and Jan as Charlie drove down the main street and turned off to the Chaleanor Hotel.

"Doesn't look like much tourist activity, Charlie," Jan said, watching the people walking on the sidewalk.

"No, ma'am, not much. Dangriga's the place you go to to get to where you wanna be."

"I'm sorry?"

"Don't be sorry, ma'am. Dangriga's got no beach. Folks come here to get out there,' Charlie gestured to the sea that was just coming into view. "Out there there's dozens a cayes where you can swim and snorkel and fish on a little island away from it all. That's what a lotta folks want, ma'am, from where you come from, and if you take it in mind to check it out and have to stay a few days in Dangriga there ain't no better place to stay than right here at the Chaleanor Hotel."

Charlie wheeled his taxi into the parking place in front of the hotel, a faded white, three-story hotel with painted pictures of jaguars, and manatees, and other flora and fauna of Belize.

"Let's take a quick break. Freshen up. Have a bite to eat and move on. Placencia's about 2 hours away, max. Leave your bags, they'll be okay. I'll bring the food in soon as we greet my friend."

Jan and Eddy exited the taxi, rubbing their bums as they stepped outside. "C'mon, c'mon," Charlie urged, leading the way through the open arch that led to the lobby. A bell rang as he stepped inside.

"Manfred, my friend," he cried out. "Hoped we'd find you behind the desk. Whassup, man? You alright?"

"Charlie!" Manfred cried, standing up and pushing back the chair behind his desk. "You old dog, shoulda tole me you'd be dropping by." As Manfred and Charlie embraced, patting one another on the back, Manfred said, "Now who're these fine folk you've brought me."

"Just passin' through, my friend. On our way to Placencia. Want to freshen up, use your facilities, have a bite to eat and move on down the road. This here's Eddy and this here's Jan. Folks, this here's Manfred, owner, manager, desk clerk and chief instigator of the Chaleanor Hotel, only 3-story building in the town of Dangriga."

"You're welcome, here, folks," Manfred said, advancing on Eddy and Jan. "Whatever I can do, let me know. In the meantime, please make yourself comfortable in the lobby, washroom's just around the corner, over there, and there's coffee and fresh bananas right there."

Manfred was a man in his early fifties, Jan guessed. He was wearing tan slacks over sockless sandals, a bright multi-coloured tie-dyed dashiki, and a bright white smile that lit up his brown laugh-lined face which was topped with graying tightly-curled black hair. Jan poked Eddy in the back as if to say if we ever come back this is where we're going to stay. Eddy knew exactly what she meant and pinched her behind.

The Southern Highway was a two-lane, paved road that cut through farm-forests of bananas, grapefruit and orange orchards; every fifteen or so miles a small village whizzed by featuring a church, a school, some ramshackle shops and at least one 'cool spot' where you could stop for Belizean food and a cold beer. Most of the houses were run-down, single-story wooden shacks but between villages they observed set well back of the main highway some very expensive mansions surrounded by manicured lawns, the entrances guarded by wrought-iron gates with guards and cement walls with razor wire rolled on top. Eddy nudged Jan and Jan nudged Eddy back.

"Okay, we're cuttin' off here and headin' for the peninsula, elseways we stay on the highway and you guys gotta take a water-taxi from Independence to Placencia Village. What's it going to be?" he laughed.

The road down the peninsula was newly paved. "Shoulda seen this sucker just last year," Charlie explained. "Real bad at most times and sometimes in the rainy season you couldn't get across. Guv'ment woke up and paved her 'cause Placencia a real hot tourist attraction. That's the Caribbean to the left and the lagoon on the right, lotta rich folks live along here, some Belizean but most rich Americans like Francis Ford Cop-ola, but we headed straight south down the peninsula till we hit the village. That's where you folks goin', and it's a good place to be."

Charlie dropped them off at the end of the road in Placencia Village. "'Member what I said. This here road's the only way in and out. 'Tween the road and the sea what I usta call the 'boardwalk' but now its cement so call it what you want. It divides the village in two. You're straight across this way, past the fisherman co-op, keep goin' till you see the sign 'Golden Sun Cabanas'. Check in at the Office but I hear-tell Sam's away on business but they'll be somebody there to care for you. I'd help with the luggage but you don't have enough to worry about. Have a good time. Phone me when you want to come back and thank you for your generosity. Much appreciated."

Jan and Eddy waved goodbye as Charlie swung his taxi around and headed back north. "Hey, wait, Charlie," Eddy shouted as Charlie drove past them.

Charlie stopped and waited for Eddy to catch up to him. "Whassup, man?" he said as Eddy approached the window.

"You staying in Placencia for any time?"

"Naw, got family in San Bight, gonna crash there, get up and get back to the City. Got a livin' to make, man. Why you askin'? You got my number in the city, I'm only hours away."

"I'm a cautious man, Charlie. I don't go nowhere in my line of work except I have a back-up . . ."

"Thought you was a tourist from Canada," Charlie said, looking up into Eddy's face thrust close to the open window of his taxi.

"I am a tourist from Canada, man, and that's all there is to it, but I make a living up there same as you make a living down here and when I'm out of my country I want to know who I can count on if things go wrong, you understand? Let's not make an issue of this, Charlie. Here's 50usd," Eddy said as he dug a 50 dollar bill out of his wallet and held it out to Charlie. "You give me the name, address in San Bight and phone number of the guy you can most trust, let him know who I am, tell him if I contact him for any reason whatsoever if he helps me I'll fill his hands with gold and anything I give him I'll double for you."

"You ain't kiddin', are you, man. Sure as shit, you ain't kiddin'," Charlie said. He popped open his glove-compartment and shuffled inside. He found a pen and scribbled something on the back of his business card. "Here," he said, handing the card to Eddy. "That's my son. Name, address and phone number. I'm trusting you but you better know if you fuck my son over you gonna wish you was dead before you die."

EDDY & JAN: Fun in the Sun, part 2

Jan stood at the road's end across from the gas station, plugging her nose and squawking to Eddy to hurry up.

"What's the matter, babe?" Eddy cried as he approached her. "Something wrong?"

"Yeah, Eddy, something's wrong. I can still see the sea but I can't smell anything but gasoline. It's like being in a parking garage in Toronto on a hot summer day. C'mon. Let's make tracks."

They followed Charlie's direction, cutting straight across from west to east to the base of the peninsula. The moon was down but streetlights guided them. Jan sniffed the night air and let out a howl. "Yes! I can smell it. I can smell the sea. Do you smell it, Eddy? Like on Caye Caulker? Can you smell the sea?"

"I smell it, babe. Smells good. Got my flashlight there? We gotta find the path to the Golden Sun."

"Oh, Eddy, I'm so glad we're here. Here," she said, thrusting a flashlight into his hand, "show me the way."

Giggling, they ran along the beach. "There, there, Eddy," Jan cried, re-directing Eddy. "See the sign? Office!"

The desk-clerk was dead-drunk when they pushed the well-lit hotel office door open and stepped inside. "Hey, brother," Eddy called, "hello there. We're here, where are you?"

"I'm here, man," the desk-clerk cum grounds-keeper cum security guard replied, sitting bolt upright, white eyes blotched with red veins, fingers reaching for a piece of paper on the desk top as if to assert the appropriateness of his position. "And you are?"

"I are Eddy Dupuis and I are staying here for the next two weeks. Is there anybody else I can talk to?"

"Only me you can talk to, man. Mr. West got called away. Emergency in America, I don't know nothin' about it, man. Wait a minute, wait a minute." His hands crab-walked across the desk and clenched an envelope. "Yeah, that's right, Mr. West said give this to you. I remember now."

Eddy grabbed the envelope out of the desk-clerk's hand, slipped the Swiss army knife out of his pocket and slit open the envelope. Inside he found a letter from the owner and manager of the hotel. Eddy held up the letter and read aloud, "Dear Mr. and Mrs. Dupuis, terribly sorry I cannot be here to greet you. Family emergency in USA demands my immediate attention. No way of contacting you before I had to leave. Edward will give you the keys to your cabana and will assist you in any way he is able. We will do the paper work when I return which, I hope, will be before you leave. In the meantime, please accept my hospitality at no cost to your selves till I return. Thank you for staying at the Golden Sun, yours with great respect, Jeremy West."

"Holy Mackie," Jan exclaimed. "Eddy, what are we going to do? Can we just stay here?"

"Sure we can, and we've got the letter to prove it. Like the man said, Edward here will take care of us, won't you Edward?" Edward struggled to get up, flinging a half salute in Eddy's direction. "So here's what I want you to do, Edward. Listen hard. I want you to walk us to our cabana and open it up. I want you to show us what we have to know. Then, listen hard, Edward, I want you to go into the village and bring us back six beers and two orders of fried chicken, rice and beans and coleslaw. Make that three orders. One for you. Here's $20usd. Keep the change for yourself. Bring everything I've asked for, you listening?, and I'm going to give you $10usd for your trouble and you can buy any kind of booze you want and I sure don't want to see you till sometime tomorrow."

Edward turned and sorted through the boxes behind him until he found the correct keys. He turned to face Jan and Eddy and, stiffening his spine, throwing back his shoulders, he declared, "Mr. and Mrs. Dupuis, I am here to serve you. Please, follow me." Then he stood behind them ushering them out of the office like a sergeant major on a parade ground.

They woke up at 6 a.m. and turned to face one another in the queen-size bed. "Did you set the alarm?" Eddy asked. "No," Jan replied, "I didn't set the alarm but I know we've got about 3 minutes to watch the sun rise." "I'm going to put a pillow over my head." Eddy demurred. "Lazy bum, get up," Jan ordered. "C'mon, let's run down to the beach and watch."

The crown of the sun shone as quickly as Jan said it would, pushing up through lazy grey clouds, illuminating the waves that rolled on shore. In the next moment, it was a golden orb, transcendent above them. "Oh Eddy, isn't it spectacular?"

"Yes, it is. And so are you." Eddy reached for her and grabbed her by the waist lifting her up and walking her into the sea.

"Eddy, I'm in my pyjamas," she cried.

"So, take them off."

"I can't do that!"

"Then I guess they'll have to get wet," Eddy said as he extended his arms and threw her into an incoming wave.

After a full breakfast at Omar's on the Beach, a breakfast that included scrambled eggs, sausages, refried beans, sliced tomato and two orders of fry-jacks for Eddy and toast and fresh fruit for Jan, they perambulated the sidewalk that split the village in two, checking out the restaurants, the tourist shops that featured products from Guatemala, the bakery, the art gallery and the shops that promoted Belizean arts and crafts.

They stopped at a fruit and vegetable stand and picked up some pineapple, oranges, mango and bananas. "Want some veggies?" Jan asked. "Sure," Eddy replied, "what've you got in mind?" "Let's get some potatoes and tomatoes and . . . broccoli?"

"Absolutely broccoli," Eddy exclaimed. "My life is not complete without broccoli, and why not throw in some onions and garlic and celery and what's that stuff no one else likes, okra?" "And then what?" "Let's go back to the bakery and get some bread and buns, track down a grocery store and get us some chicken and pork chops and oil and anything else you think we need and that, my love, should be about enough shopping for the day." "What? No wine, gin, rum, beer? No tonic water? Sparkling champagne? Eddy, my love, you're getting dull in your old age."

"No, baby, I'm just saving the best for the last. Or the next best thing, if you get my drift."

EDDY & JAN: Fun in the Sun/Fun in Bed (part 3)

As the days drifted by, Eddy and Jan fell into a sybaritic routine of self-indulgence. They swam in the sea early in the morning, ate breakfast at Omar's, strolled the beach, picked up odds and ends at the shops, returned to their cabana where they relaxed, Jan reading non-fiction adventure tales while Eddy worked on high-end sudokus. Lunch was prepared in the kitchen, Jan and Eddy taking turns to surprise one another with their inventiveness. Then another swim, another shower to wash off the salt and sand, and another night out at the Passionate Purple Parrot, the restaurant they chose over all the others.

On one shopping excursion, Eddy said he wanted to drop into the Fish n' Bait store. "Why," Jan asked. "'Cause I can and 'cause I want to, my lady."

"Do you fish?"

"Have done a few times on the French River."

"Where's that?"

"A little south of Sudbury. You know where that is, don't you?"

"Of course, silly. Everybody knows the song Sudbury Saturday Night. I'm just surprised you took the time off to fish."

"Not often and not for long but I'm thinking we're here, they can fix me up with everything I need and who knows, maybe I'll go fishing. Even if off the village dock."

"Pretty pricey, my love, but if it's what you want, go for it."

Eddy bought a rod and reel, line, hooks, sinkers, a tackle box and a razor-sharp fillet knife, most of which he stored in the tackle box for easy carrying.

When they reached their cabana Jan stopped Eddy as he bounded up the stairs. "Uh, uh, my friend," she cautioned. "You ain't bringing that stuff in there."

"Why not?"

"Because it doesn't belong inside the cabana, that's why not and that's not negotiatable."

"Well . . ."

"Put it over there," Jan said, pointing to the outside corner of the verandah. "Out of sight, out of mind."

"You're a real cruel woman but I love you," Eddy responded, bounding back down the stairs and stashing the gear out of sight.

One evening after a near-disastrous snorkeling expedition an hour off the tip of the peninsula, they met with two couples with whom they had dined and had drinks with before. Reggie and Marge were from Australia, in their forties, a little loud yet very friendly, but both totally critical of Belizean food which they devoured with gusto after decrying their plight and wishing they were back home in Australia. Maeve and Arnold were in their late fifties, from Calgary, and nouveau-riche, gas having been discovered recently on their farm land which they leased out for a small fortune. "Just think," Arnold said during one of their get-togethers, "I'm nearly 60, farmed all my life and now I'm a millionaire. Don't get me wrong 'cause I'm loving it. I'm living it, but it sure ain't the way it used to be." "And thank the Almighty for that," Maeve chimed in. "I never used to wear real pearls to supper before. Now I can wear them to bed if I want to." "Now there's a sight," Eddy had rejoined, to which Maeve had replied, "In my jammies, of course."

Jan tapped her water glass with a spoon after everyone was seated and a round of drinks delivered. "Excuse me," she said when she had their attention. "I just want to make a toast to my partner, Eddy."

"What's the occasion?" Reggie asked.

"No occasion," Jan replied. "I just want to say how proud I am of him."

"Jan," Eddy remonstrated.

"No, Eddy. I want to do this."

"What's up?" Marge said.

"Well," Jan continued, "we went snorkeling this morning and had the world's worst snorkel guide you could ever imagine. Now, we're not seasoned snorkelers, don't get me wrong, but we went out several times on Caye Caulker and had some fantastic experiences.

This guide might have known what he should be doing but he sure as hell wasn't doing it. First off, he's got 12 snorkelers under his care, that's far too many. Next, after the boat drops us off on the island, he's saying 'Okay we're going in here and we're snorkeling over there and then we're going round the tip of the island and coming out over there'. He's waving his hands all over the place. 'So get on your gear and let's move out.'

That's when Eddy stepped up. 'Excuse me, Mark, it is Mark isn't it?' Mark nodded his head, confused. 'Do you have life-jackets for those who might need one?' 'Well, yeah, in that box over there but . . .' 'But nothing, Mark. Ask us who wants a life-jacket, no, wait a minute, ask us who has never snorkeled before, 'cause they'll need a life-jacket for sure, right?' Mark nodded. 'Uh, who's never snorkeled before?' Four hands went up. 'Uh, okay, go over there and get your life-jackets.' 'Wait a minute there Mark, wait a minute.' Eddy signaled the others to sit down. 'Ask everyone else if he wants a life-jacket.' 'Now wait a minute this is my . . .' 'Ask!' 'Anybody else want a life jacket?' Four more hands went up, including Eddy and me. 'Okay, folks, let's get our life-jackets and meet back here', Eddy said. When we all got back and started to put the jackets on, Mark said, 'Okay, if you're ready, I'll take the lead with the experienced snorkelers and you guys can follow us.' 'Whoa, whoa, Mark,' Eddy interrupted again, walking over to stand beside Mark. 'If these folks want to go off on their own' he indicated the experienced snorkelers, 'that's none of my business. But you are staying with the rest of us. You are a guide, Mark, we paid to have you guide us, now start guiding.'

And the thing of it is when we got in the water the experienced snorkelers stayed with us and helped the inexperienced, Eddy and me helped a little, too, and you know, it wasn't a bad snorkel at all, all said and done."

"Well done, Eddy." "Here's to Eddy." Everyone raised their glass.

Eddy hoped his new tan covered the blush on his face. Jan's story embarrassed him and pleased him at the same time. He had to admit, she was right about one thing. He had shown restraint and turned his rising anger into something more productive, something he had not always, let's face it, rarely, been able to do.

They feasted on salads, fresh vegetables, baked or fried chicken, fish-of-the-day fillets or whole, grilled or barbequed, pork chops grilled or fried, and cakes and ice-cream for dessert. Afterwards, Reggie belched and to cover his embarrassment declared, "Not bad, but not as good as the homeland". And Arnold took Jan aside and said, "There's more to it than that, isn't there?" and Jan nodded and said, "There was a time when Eddy would have torn Mark into little pieces and thrown them to the fishes."

When the couples parted and went their separate ways, Eddy and Jan left the well-lit sidewalk that ran through the village of Placencia. There was a quarter moon. "Oh Eddy," Jan cried. "I left the flashlights back at the Triple P." "Anything else?" "No, just our flashlights. In a cotton bag. Want to go back?" "No, no. Not worth the bother. We'll be okay."

They headed straight for the sea and stumbled along the beach toward their cabana. They had left the porch light on and used it as a beacon in the night. Laughing yet breathless, they turned the key in the front door and burst inside.

Without a word, Jan turned on a light in the sitting room and walked around the cabana pulling the curtains closed while Eddy went into the washroom, relieved himself, and turned on the shower, testing the temperature as the water heated up. Jan stepped inside and closed the door. She sat on the toilet and peed, wiped herself and joined Eddy under the shower water.

They washed one another, head to toe, soaping the hair, the face, the armpits, rinsing as they went along. Eddy soaped Jan's breasts, marveling at their firmness, lightly pinching her nipples while she reached down and lathered his crotch, stroking his tumescent penis, reaching around to soap his bum. He soaped between her legs, then bent her over in front of him and washed her bum, knelt behind her and lathered her thighs and knees and calves, ankles and feet, and when he was done she knelt before him and did the same.

On the bed, side lights glowing, fan whirling above, they positioned themselves across from one another, pillows behind their backs. Jan opened her legs, exposing her vagina. Eddy noted how beautiful she was, her tousled hair, red lips, breasts like ripe fruit, slender white shoulders, lightly tanned arms and long, delicate fingers that opened her vagina revealing the bright pink flower inside. She watched as he stroked himself, fingers playing over his rock-hard helmet-less penis, noting how his body, though heavier than when they had first met, was rock-hard, too, and his face though weathered by time and circumstance still had a roguish aspect with a devil-be-damned glint in his eyes.

Fully aroused, she rose and sat over him, lowering herself on his penis, sliding up and down until her thighs tightened and eyes-closed she arched backwards, gasping. She rolled over and knelt, face down, breasts pressed on the mattress, bum in the air and waited for Eddy to mount her from behind. Eddy entered her slowly, tentatively, pulled out and entered her again, finding a rhythm, feeling himself gather to fullness and explode inside her, breathless.

Afterwards, curtains opened and lights off, they hugged one another as they lay under the sheets. Eddy reached out his hand to stroke her cheek and felt the tears that ran from her eyes.

"Baby, baby, you're crying," he whispered. "Why are you so sad?"

"I'm not sad, Eddy. Believe me I'm not sad."

"Than what . . . ?"

"I'm so happy it scares me."

EMILE: Review of Negotiations Concluded

The back room at Neries was perfect for Emile's purpose. Manuel, the server, set them up and left them. Emile stood up and looked out the second storey window. It was a rough neighbourhood, Emile noted. He had spent many years in Canada's major cities, Toronto, Montreal and Vancouver, and over time had come to recognize certain similarities in the areas of a city that offered little but trouble to the average citizen. He spotted a bling-addled dude on the corner of Queen and Daly and knew a drug drop was going down. A black car cruised by and Emile knew it was not the police. The police tried to enforce the 'law' while the thugs in the black car were interested only in 'order'. It was their turf by right of might and not even cops were allowed to enter.

"Hey, man," Cane called. "You havin' a good time lookin' down there. That there's Shitsville, man. Me and my brother here and our crew, we own Shitsville. You don't get in here or outta here less we say so, so c'mon, man, get your ass over here and let's do some bidness so we can get back and do ours."

"Gentlemen," Emile said as he strolled over to the table and sat down. "Gentlemen, you mentioned downstairs the unlikely possibility that the man I came here to kill might kill me. Right? So the question is how do you get paid off if that happens, right?'

"That's right, man," Cane said. "'Cause if you don't come out of that cabana, we in a shit-hole of trouble. We got a live girl on our hands, some unknown son-of-a-bitch killer on the loose out there, and a dead fuckin' body, yours, in a cabana that ain't ours. Yeah, you gonna hav'ta pay for that circumstance, man. What's on your mind?"

"What I got in mind I want you both to listen to and I don't think Able's listening. Able!"

"What, man?" Able said, startled. "I'm lissnin'. Got a full night ahead of me so get talkin' and quit stallin'"

"We got to fill in a few details before we start looking at my unexpected and unlikely demise. Death. Okay? A few parts of the plan we passed over when we started talking about how much money you guys were going to make. So, let's recap. We go in, neutralize the victim till you guys take the broad back to our room."

"Cabana," Able corrected. "It's Spanish. It means like a 'hut' or a 'cabin'. It's not a room, comprende?"

"Take her back to our cabana," Emile continued, "and keep her there till I contact you by cell phone and tell you that all's well." He held up his hand as Cane was about to interject. "If, I say if a certain amount of time passes by, let's say, on the outside an hour, maybe only 45 minutes and I haven't contacted you, secure the bitch so she can't move anywhere, and get over here quick. You're in the business. Split up . . ."

"Man," Cane interrupted, "he mighta dropped you the minute we left . . ."

"Am I dealing with amateurs here," Emile exploded. "Jesus Christ, boys, you don't know enough when you take the broad back to our cabana that one of you got to be posted outside watch for him if he breaks out?"

Emile pushed back his chair, stood up and yanked his wallet out of his back pocket. He pulled out two 50usd and threw them on the table. "This is for up-to-now. Pay the bill and keep the change. I'm taking a walk alone in Shitsville and you better believe anybody gets in my way . . ."

"Man, oh, man," Cane laughed. "Sit down, man. Sit down. We just testin' you like you test us. Wanna see if you know what's what in this here game. Course we gonna post a spotter and shit like that. We just gotta know if you can walk the walk not just talk the talk, that's all. Shit, man, chill a little. You want something more'n that pussy juice you drinkin'."

Emile sat down, patting his heart as if it were pounding with excitement. As Able reached across the table toward the 50 dollar bills, Emile scooped them up. "Don't get me started," he growled. "And no I don't want anything to drink right now. I only drink when I'm enjoying myself and this ain't one of those moments."

"Okay," Cane said, "continue. And you, Able, pay attention to the man."

"Well, you've already said the negative side of it if he kills me. You got a white-faced hornet named Eddy Dupuis on the attack and the queen bee in your cabana. I'll tell you straight. I can't tell you what you're going to do. You gotta figure that one out yourselves. This is your country, you're not far from home . . . but I'll tell you one thing. I'll be untraceable, no i.d. on me, no record of any kind, nothing that could ever be traced back to you."

"So what's the deal, Emile?" Cane said.

"Let's forget the 5 large in advance, right? That's money paid, not money owed. I've already offered you 15 more, each, if everything goes the way I expect it to go in Belize and 10,000 each if you get me back to Belize City in one piece. Right? That's $50,000 in total. If the unlikely, I'd even say impossible happens and he kills me, I'm prepared to offer you 5 grand more, each, for the clean-up. That's a cool $60,000. Not bad for a couple day's work."

"Then you better be prepared to stick the whole deal up your ass," Cane growled. "You think you gonna leave us knee deep in shit for that chump change? Please, tell me you're kidin', man. Not only that but no matter how we handle all the bodies that have suddenly piled up, we ain't even gonna get our pay off in the City. How fucked is that, man?"

"I got it figured out," Emile replied. "We cancel out the airport pay-off, you guys never liked it anyway, and we make it a one-stop pay-off no matter what the outcome."

"We'll come back to that, mother-fucker. What's the deal if you die?"

"I already told you."

"Well tell me again and don't repeat yourself."

"I'll go an extra 10 total on top of the fifty. That 20,000 makes a total of 60,000, that's as far as I'll go."

"You'll go to hell. $50,000 on top of the $50,000, making an even 100 grand."

"50 extra on top of the 50,000? Stop fucking around. I'm way over my head now. I want the deal done, I'll go 15 on top, totals 65,000 and that's it, ain't no more."

"40," Cane said. "Makes 90. Deal's done."

"You got a hearing problem, Cane. I'm done"

"Yeah," Cane replied. "Like we gonna be done if he kills you. Chances of cleaning up and leaving for home without any complications are zero to none. It's gonna cost to cover our tracks and you gotta pay for it, man. It's that simple. Emile, Emile, what's happening? You all right, man"

Emile rocked back in his chair, head tilted back, eyes opening and closing. He straightened up and looked across the table and Cane and Able. "Yeah, yeah, I'm fine. I'm okay. I'm just doing some mental arithmetic, checking some bank accounts, shifting some money there to someplace here and here's what I come up with, take it or leave it.

Here's where we're at, and I'm talking totals, okay, Cane, that's what you wanted, right? $30,000 to do the job in Placencia. $20,000 to get me back to Belize City and on the plane. That's $50,000 in total if I'm alive to tell the tale, which I'll be.

In the event he kills me I'll offer $20,000 extra, take it or leave it. That means my total pay-out is $70,000 and that, my friends, breaks the bank and I'm not prepared to go bankrupt."

"Tell him to shove it, Cane," Able spit angrily, pushing back his chair and towering over the table. "This job's worth at least a hundred grand and you know it, Mr. Emile from Canada, and it's worth at least that to you. You in the game now, quit bluffin' and place your last bet."

"You got my last bet. It's on the table. Take it or I walk away. And, don't think I can't walk away. Do I want it now? Yes. Am I ready to pay $70,000 for the pleasure. Yes. Am I ready to pay a penny more. No. I'm out 5 large right now. Five large and plane fare. You don't pick it up, I'm on the first flight to Toronto in the morning and on the way back I'm making new plans to kill the son of a bitch somewhere else with somebody else to help me."

"Okay, okay," Cane intervened. "Able, sit down, man. Emile, calm down, man. I'm getting' the notion that the deal ain't as done as you think it's done. You at $70,000 now and you sayin' you're through, Emile. That's it, right? ain't no more. Now, Able here, he's saying, 'Bull shit' the jobs worth more than that, at least a hundred grand, and I'm sayin' 90 gets the job done but 'cause you such a good guy I say let's just split the difference at 75 and Emile I've gotta say the same as you, last offer, $75,000, take it or leave it. What do you say?"

Emile rolled his eyes as if he had been sucker-punched. "Jesus H. . . . Sorry about that," he stammered. "What I meant to say was we're so close, I mean, I'm so close to something I've wanted for so long, thought you guys would be pushovers but okay, okay, I agree, $75,000."

"Okay, done deal," Cane said, "Now let's talk about the money-retrieval problem 'cause without a good plan all the rest is just bull-shit anyway. What you got in mind, Emile. How do we get the money if you dead?"

Emile appeared to calm down. He motioned Able to sit across the table from him. "No disrespect, man," he said. "You're a tough guy and you are both good negotiators. I'm just saying where I'm at, that's all. And I'll tell you straight, I thought we might be having this conversation. I was thinking, they don't bring it up, don't matter to me none if I'm dead. But you guys were smarter than that, so I made a plan. Here's what I'm thinking, boys."

Able tipped the remainder of his Belican beer down his throat and looked around for a re-fill. Cane hunched forward, arms on the table, staring at Emile. Able hunched over, glaring. Both men were enrapt as Emile described his plan.

"Okay, here's where it's at. We meet at the ScotiaBank tomorrow morning. You know where it is, of course."

Cane and Able nodded.

"The manager is expecting us. I withdraw $75,000 in usd, let's say in 100's. I pocket $30,000 which I'll give you when we arrive in Placencia, as agreed . . ."

"Wait a minute," Cane interrupted, "we agreed on the number, we didn't agree on when we got it. We want it tomorrow, before we leave for Placencia. Am I right, Able?"

"No doubt about, Cane. Tomorrow before we leave or forget about it."

"Then forget about it, gentlemen, 'cause if you think I'm going to hand over $30,000 before we even get to our destination, you're crazy. Doesn't work that way where I come from and it's not going to work that way in Belize."

Cane stood up and motioned for Able to join him by the second-story window. After a brief discussion they returned to the table and sat down.

"Okay." Cane said, "here's the deal. We got women, kids to take care of, school fees, shit like that. $15,000 in our hands when we leave the bank, time to drop it off before we head out for Placencia. The other $15,000 when we arrive. Okay?"

Emile nodded and said, "I order a safety-deposit box, which I've already done. You watch me put the remainder of the money in the safety-deposit box."

"45,000," Able muttered.

"That's right, man, $45,000usd. $20,000 if the job goes as expected and as it will, plus 25,000 extra if I'm not around to collect it."

"Let's say thing's go as expected." Cane said. "We come back to the City, go to the ScotiaBank with you and pick up our 20,000 as agreed upon. Right?"

"Right. And if things go the way they won't, tomorrow, in front of the manager of the bank, I will leave instructions that the safety-deposit box will be opened by anyone who shows up with the code name Geronimo."

"Geronimo," Able snorted. "What the fuck's Geronimo?"

"It's the name of an Indian . . ."

"A Mayan?"

"An American Indian," Emile responded.

"Able, shut the fuck up," Cane barked. "Jesus H. Christ can't we stay on topic . . ."

"There," Able cried triumphantly.

"There what?"

"There, I got you, you blasphemed, Cane. Shame on you."

"Can we continue?" Emile broke in, visibly annoyed. "I'm telling you guys, I'm at the breaking point. Are you or are you not 'professional'? If you are, start acting like it. If you're not, let's get the fuck out of here."

"We're pro's, like you, Emile." Cane countered. "Able gets a bit excited sometime, that's all. No big deal. Please, you were saying that we would have the code name 'Geronimo', but we wouldn't have the key. Where's the key going to be?"

"The key's going to be on me."

"I'm almost afraid to ask, but where on you?"

"Rolled up in a serviette . . ."

"Stay still, Able, I'll take care of this. May I ask what is a 'serviette'?"

"Like a napkin," Emile said, realizing his mistake. "Rolled up in a piece of napkin."

"Yes?"

"And stuffed in a condom."

"Yes?"

"And tied off."

"Yes?"

"And shoved up my ass."

"Come on!"

"No way!"

"Show some initiative, lads," Emile grinned. "Buy yourselves some rubber gloves and hope to hell I kill him before he kills me."

Back in his hotel room after being dropped off by Cane and Able, Emile grinned as he reclined in an easy-chair recalling the moment. He paused in his recollection to pour himself another shot of Johnny Walker Blue Label on the rocks. All he had ever planned to do was use the Belizean gangsters to set up the kill and get him back to Belize City at the best possible price and he had achieved his goal. When Eddy was dead and his girl-friend was tied up in the cabana beside him, Emile had already arranged for a squad of Guatemalan banditos to swoop down from the border and take away their bodies, dead or alive, and in the case of the woman better dead than alive. The banditos were one phone call away, poised at the border. As for his Belizean friends, Cane and Able, did they really think Emile would pay two local thugs $75,000usd to set up a kill for him? Dwayne Bowman and his henchmen would be waiting for the call to ambush the Jeep when the brothers returned Emile to his hotel to get a change of clothing before moving into their safe-house. They would 'take care' of Cane and Able, and, as finders-fees keep the $30,000usd hidden in a wheel well and the vehicle itself. The fact that the finders-fee would be ½ what Emile promised was Bowman's problem, not Emile's. "Sometime shit happens," Emile said aloud as he sat alone in the semi-darkness of his hotel room. "You just gotta deal with it." He shuddered with self-satisfaction. All in all, it had been a very entertaining evening.

EMILE: The Boys Arrive In Placencia

"What do you mean we can't take the Jeep to the cabana?" Emile asked. He was irritated that the trip had taken so long. After the meeting with the manager of the Scotia Bank, Cane and Able had a dozen different errands to run before they set off. Cane had to pick up his children, a boy and a girl aged 7 and 8, at a private school in the high-end of Belize City. They sat in the back seat with Able as Cane drove them home for lunch. "Tell your mommy I can't take you back to school. Tell her I'll be back in a couple days. Love you."

Able was somewhat more mysterious. He dropped into a flower shop and bought two bouquets of beautiful tropical flowers and delivered them to two separate addresses in two different neighbourhoods, neither of which could be considered affluent, and then had Cane drive him to an upscale neighbourhood. Cane pulled up in front of an attractive pastel bungalow with a triple garage surrounded by a chain-link fence with Vietnamese barbed-wire circled on top. He came back moments later with a small suitcase and clambered back into the Jeep. "Jesus, is she pissed off," he exclaimed. Cane gave him a look.

On top of that, both Cane and Able felt obliged to provide Emile a running commentary of the countryside as they made the run from Belize City to the Village of Placencia. As they approached an important landmark, Cane said, "Now check this out, on your right. This here's supposed to be one of the best zoos in the world." They whizzed past a zoo the size of a postage stamp and Emile groaned, thinking of the Metro Zoo outside of Toronto.

"And look, and look," Able cried, excited. "See over there, that road, that's the shortcut to Dangriga. From there to Placencia be shorter, but we gonna take you on the scenic route to Belmopan then down the Hummingbird Highway. You gonna love the Hummingbird Highway, man, guarantee you that."

"Thanks, man, appreciate that," Emile said as he settled back in his seat and closed his eyes.

Now he was parked on the side of the road at the end of the Placencia Peninsula in the Village of Placencia being told they had to park there and walk through the village to the resort on the other side by the sea.

"Relax, man," Cane said. "There's only one paved road into Placencia and one paved road out, and they's both the same road. That's the way it is. Chill, man. We travelin' light, let's take a hike."

Edward the desk man was asleep in the office when they trouped in, head slumped on arms on the top of the desk, a half bottle of rum beside him, sans glass.

"Wake up, uncle," Able shouted as he pounded on the desk-top bell. "You got guests to care for."

Edward slowly lifted his head, his hand instinctively reaching for the bottle of rum. "Ain't no one here," he muttered. "Boss-man's gone. Sorry."

Cane pushed through the swing-gate, reached down and hauled Edward up inches off the ground. "Listen to me, old man. We got reservations. Give us the key to number four. We'll sign in later."

Edward clutched his rum bottle, trying to formulate a response. Cane snatched the bottle from him and tossed it to Able. "We hungry, old man, and you gonna get us some food, understand?" Edward nodded, bereft. "You hungry, Emile?"

"No, but get me an order of spaghetti and meat balls."

"Okay, old man. One spaghetti, four orders fry chicken and beans and rice. Got that?"

Edward nodded.

"This here's for the food. We got drinks. We keep this till you get back," Cane brandished the bottle, "and you keep the change and get this". Cane held a twenty usd bill in front of the clerk. "Now vamanos, muy amigo, and get your ass back here in triple time. Comprende?"

Edward scurried out of the office without even thinking about closing the door.

Emile, Cane and Able trudged across the sand to their cabana. "Keep the lights to the minimum," Emile ordered after they gained entrance. "Curtains drawn. One of you check on their cabana and report back to me. Comprende?"

EMILE & EDDY: Clash of the Titans

"Eddy. Eddy." Edward called. He stood outside their cabana waving an empty rum bottle.

Eddy crossed to the front window and peered outside. He flicked on the outside light and looked again.

"Who is it", Jan called from the kitchen area.

"It's Edward. Looks like he's out of rum."

"Oh Eddy, you can't keep giving him money."

"Well, I'll help him out this last time, all right?"

"Yeah, sure, Eddy. Last time," Jan sighed. She turned back to the dishes she was washing.

Eddy opened the door and stepped outside. He hadn't taken a step before Able, pressed against the outside wall, reached out and lightly sapped him behind the ear. Cane caught Eddy in his arms as Able slipped through the front door. He reached Jan before she turned around, one muscled arm around her waist and one hand over her mouth. Cane dragged Eddy inside, dropped him onto a kitchen chair, fumbled into his backpack and tossed a roll of duct tape to Able.

"Mouth, hands, feet." Able nodded. He ripped a long piece of duct tape off the roll and wound it around Jan's mouth, hair and head. When he was finished, he flipped the duct tape back to Cane who followed the same procedure, securing Eddy to the chair so that he could not leap up. Then each man proceeded to search the cabana for weapons, anything that Eddy could use to hurt Emile. Cane dumped all the kitchen utensils into his backpack, then walked into the bathroom, shook the contents of Eddy's kit into the sink, confiscating a throw-away razor and even some needles and thread used for small repairs. Able ransacked the bedroom, pulling back the sheets, emptying the chest of drawers of socks, t-shirts, panties and bras, ripping the blouses and shirts off the hangers and throwing the hangers into his backpack.

Eddy shook his head as he became conscious. He blinked his eyes until they were focused and could not believe the tableau before him: two large black guys on either side of Jan who was bound and gagged. They lifted her a couple inches above the floor. She tried to lash out with her feet but they were wrapped with duct tape. She made mewing noises, snorted through her nose. Her eyes were bright with anger. She saw the man she loved immobilized in front of her and she wanted to kill the intruders who had captured the both of them.

The door opened and clicked shut as Emile stepped into the room. All eyes turned to him. He took a step forward and stopped still, savouring the moment. When he was sure he had their attention, he spoke.

"Hello, my friend."

Eddy struggled in his bonds. He recognized his captor immediately. The guy in Vancouver, years ago. The guy he had shamed. Tarnished his fame. Besmirched his name. Eddy was incandescent with anger and humiliation. He wanted to rise up like some cartoon super-hero and destroy with bare hands the man who stood before him, finish the job he had left undone when he had broken the man's ribs, snipped off his little finger, beaten him senseless and thrown him on the grounds of his employer. But he was powerless. He could only look on helplessly as the two goons manhandled the love of his life because he, Eddy, had become complacent, had relaxed his guard, had allowed this travesty to take place. He should never have come back to Belize. He should never have visited in the first place. He should have kept constant vigil against this attack but he had not. He had failed. And now his life and Jan's life were in dire jeopardy.

"We meet again." Emile said. "You cannot believe how excited I am. I've waited years for this moment. Soon." he inhaled and expelled his breath, "soon vengeance shall be mine. Cut the tape off his face. Let him talk. I'm interested in what he has to say."

Able pulled a stiletto from his jean pocket, pressed the button that shot the blade straight out, slid the blade between Eddy's face and the duct tape, and sliced the tape. He returned the blade to the handle and reached out, grasped the loose flap and ripped it around Eddy's head.

"There," Emile said, grinning. "Now you can talk. You can shout if you want. You can even sing if you can think of a song worth singing."

"What do you want?" Eddy rasped. "Tell me what you want and I'll give it to you but don't hurt her. Let's make this me and you. There's no reason to hurt her."

"Well, there is. There is good reason to hurt her, even kill her . . ." Eddy struggled in his chair. "First, because she has seen us, and second because it would give me infinite pleasure to kill her in front of you, kill her, that is, after 'taking care' of her, but that's not what's going to happen here tonight. You have my word on that, if my word means anything to you. No, tonight is our night. It's my night. Tonight we will relive our fateful encounter years ago, but without your goons to hold me so you could beat me up, dismember me. No, tonight will truly be between you and me. Mano a mano. May the best man win, etc. etc. and then I'm going to kill you."

Wild-eyed, Eddy struggled to respond but could not find the words.

"Okay, guys," Emile said. "You know the drill. Wait for my call. Now get her out of here."

Eddy watched as the two goons dragged Jan past him. He wanted to catch her eyes, let her know from a look that he would somehow save her, but she was gone in an instant and the door slammed shut behind them.

Emile walked over and locked the door. He pulled up a chair and sat on it backwards, arms on the back of the chair, leaning forward, staring at Eddy.

"Oh boy, oh boy, oh boy-o, I've waited for this moment for a long time."

"What moment . . . ?"

"Shut up, Eddy," Emile snapped. "For the moment I avenge myself. I had no idea it was going to be so easy. Hell, I should have done this long time ago. My guys never said a word but I knew what they were thinking. I wasn't number one no more, never would be 'til I took care of you. I'll get my belt back when this here's all over. I'll be the champ again."

"This ain't no prize fight, man."

"Well, it is, isn't it? In our world, until I kill you, I can't be number one. Oh, don't get me wrong, I've fought my way back to the top, but everybody remembers my one defeat. What shall I bring back with me? Pictures, of course. Maybe your ring finger, ring attached? A lock of your hair? Your nose? Your girl friend's fucking eyeballs? Oh, this is too rich for belief, but believe me, my friend, your minutes, not hours, not days, are numbered. Now . . ." Emile stood up and kicked away the chair. "Now we take care of business."

Emile reached out and slapped Eddy across the face, back and forth. "There, that should get your blood up. How does it feel, eh?" He slapped Eddy again. "Pretty good?" He slapped him again.

"Remember when you had your goons hold me while you slapped me around? Remember how you used me as a punching bag? Remember how you twisted back my arm? Remember how you kicked me? Remember how you threw me out of your vehicle in front of my boss's mansion?"

"Yeah, I remember all that," Eddy replied, still bound in his chair. "So what? It was a gig, that's all. You did bad to my people; I did bad back. What's your problem?"

"You shoulda killed me."

"Why? Killing wasn't part of the job, you know that."

"'Cause now I'm going to kill you."

"Yeah, chances are," Eddy laughed. "You've an absolute 99-100 per cent chance you're going to kill me. But why here, why now, why bring the broad into this?"

"Stalling for time, Eddy?" Emile smiled at his captive. He back-handed Eddy across the face. Blood began to drip out of Eddy's nostrils, over his lips, trickling under his chin. "Stalling for time ain't going to work, my friend, and you don't want it to work."

"Why not?"

"'Cause we're both on the clock, old chum, and if we don't settle our business pretty soon, your gal-pal is in very serious trouble. You saw who she's with. They are animals, Eddy. Right out of the jungle. I had to pay them extra not to rape and kill her while we sorted things out here. But they will wait only so long, Eddy, so let's get it on."

"I don't get it. You've got me. I'm helpless. Kill me."

"Kill you? What's your hurry? What about your gal-pal?"

"What about her?"

"Why aren't you begging for her life?"

"You kidding me? She has nothing to do with you and me, man. That's all. Take her back to the City and make her turn tricks, I don't care. What's her life mean to me?"

"Thought she was the love of your life."

"They're all the love of my life, Emile. As long as they last. What's the matter with you? You must know. Bet you've been spying on me long enough. There's been lots before and even some during. Don't you know that? Bring her in here and let your goons do what they want with her. Disembowel her in front of me. It would be like watching a bad movie. I'm just thinking if I gotta die, do it. If you're going to torture me, do it. I'm sitting here trussed up like a fucking turkey, what am I gonna do. Why waste time?"

"Too easy, Eddy. What satisfaction is there in knowing I outsmarted you? Oh, don't worry, the outcome will be the same, but we're going to fight it out, Eddy, mano a mano. Like a cage-fight, only one of us comes out alive."

"Yeah, right. What are you going to do, cut my legs off? Blind me?"

"No, I'm going to cut you loose."

"You're crazy, you know that. Plumb crazy."

"Sure I am. And you're not?" Emile leaned over Eddy and started to loosen his bonds. He unwound the duct tape around the waist first, then the feet, then the wrists tied behind the back of the chair. When he finished, Emile danced back out of reach. Eddy rose unsteadily to his feet. He shook his head in disbelief, astonished at the turn of events.

"What's the deal?"

"No deal, Eddy. C'mon, man. I've been waiting for this for years. You and me. Fight to the death."

They stood facing one another in the centre of the cabana, an open concept room broken by the four foot by six foot bathroom. A futon with a table in front faced one wall. Behind the futon there was a queen size bed with a night-table on each side. Across from the futon and the bed there was a combination breakfast/lunch/supper table with two chairs and behind that a dishwasher, a kitchen counter and a stove. The bathroom was across from the oven.

The two warriors took stock of their adversary. 'He's fat,' Emile thought. 'He hasn't had to fight for at least a couple years. Look at him. He's not the man he used to be. But underneath that fat he's all muscle. He's still strong as an ox. I've got to bring him down as fast as I can and damage him, break him, make him submit and kill him.'

Eddy eyed Emile at close range. He remembered the man he and his enforcers had encountered some years ago when they had all the advantages. He was lighter then, for sure, and the extra weight had gone to his belly, but Eddy knew that Emile was still strong, and still very, very fast. He also had an extreme threshold for pain and was totally unyielding in his defiance. Eddy knew that whatever transpired it would be over quickly. He also knew that Jan would die if he lost this fight and he surrendered to the blood that pounded through his brain.

Each of the men had taken classes in the martial arts, but both still relied on their natural speed or strength and animal ferocity. The men Emile and Eddy employed might watch with some contempt as their bosses went to war; they were old and out of shape, but none of them would have wished to take either of them on, man to man.

Emile lunged forward, feinted a left with his fist, pirouetted and lashed out with his right foot. Eddy saw it coming and shifted his stance but Emile's steel-toed shoe still caught him a glancing blow to his knee-cap and he yelped in pain. As Eddy stumbled backward, Emile stepped in throwing a hay-maker right which Eddy tried to defend leaving him open to Emile's quick chopping elbow to the neck that toppled Eddy unto the bed. Emile seized his advantage and leapt on Eddy, arms stretched out, fingers clenched for Eddy's neck, but Eddy was able to twist his torso and bring a knee up at the same time, connecting with Emile's groin. Emile grunted and fell back, still on his feet but struggling for balance. Eddy snorted as he rose up and lunged at Emile, driving him against the table a few feet away. Eddy pumped his fists against Emile's ribs. Emile reached his hands around Eddy's head and stuck his fingers in Eddy's eyes, trying to gouge them out of their sockets. Eddy had to draw back. Emile lifted himself off the table and coco-bonked Eddy in the forehead. The tight skin on Eddy's forehead split and spewed blood, blinding him, but he continued pummeling Emile with his iron fists, confident he was connecting by the feel of flesh and gasps of his opponent.

Eddy continued to punch until he realized Emile had eluded him. He stood erect, wiping away the blood that poured over his forehead. Emile, realizing that Eddy was blood-blinded, side-stepped Eddy's windmill blows and smashed his fist into Eddy's ear. Eddy went down, dazed, hands on the floor, growling. Emile approached from behind and kicked Eddy between the legs, making contact with Eddy's scrotum. Eddy howled. Emile circled around, wary. He found space between Eddy and the table and raised his foot, connecting with the solar-plexus. Eddy's hands collapsed under him, his breath left him and he could not breathe in fresh air. Emile pounced on him. He grabbed Eddy's hair and banged Eddy's head repeatedly against the floor. "I've got you. I've got you, you bastard, I've got you." He reached behind him, fumbled with something attached to the inside of his belt, and pulled out a three-inch razor with a blade that would slice a falling thread.

Emile cried out in triumph. It was his moment, the moment he had dreamed about, the moment of vindication, and it was as sweet as he had ever hoped, hard fought for but painfully blissful. He held the razor in his right hand and grasped Eddy's hair with his left, pulling Eddy's head off the floor, readying himself to reach across Eddy's neck and draw it slowly across, deeply, slicing Eddy's carotid artery, his windpipe, his jugular vein. As Emile lifted Eddy's head off the floor, Eddy took a deep breath. Oxygen flowed into him. Not knowing where he was or what was happening to him, he strained against the weight that sat on his back, heaving up, pushing it off. Emile, caught off-balance, fell sideways, still clutching his razor. Eddy, regaining consciousness, on all fours, turned and saw Emile trying to get up, a razor in his right hand.

"So that's your ace in the hole," he panted. He crawled over to Emile and grabbed Emile's wrist, twisting it till the razor fell out of Emile's hand, scooting across the floor. Even before Emile registered the pain, Eddy thundered a powerful fist into his face, followed by another, and another, until Emile lay flat on his back, unconscious.

Eddy Dupuis heaved himself into an upright position gasping for breath. He spread his legs apart and doubled over, chest heaving, heart pounding. He straightened up again and looked down on Emile O'Neal sprawled out on his back, still unconscious but coming to, limbs twitching, eyelids flickering. He turned around, carefully placing first one foot then another over O'Neal's body, knowing if he fell now he would never get up. He got a bead on the razor blade. It had ricocheted off the wall under the bed. He took the first step toward it, stumbling, correcting himself, stepping forward again, gaining a little strength as he got closer, breathing a little better, controlling the pain coursing through his body. He knew what he had to do. He knew he would do it.

On hands and knees, he felt under the bed, sweeping his hand across the floor, searching for the razor. He heard Emile groan, another sign of consciousness. He wanted to hurry but he restrained himself. His hand swept up dust but no razor blade. He extended his arm, still sweeping. Then there was contact. Something hard. His fingers surrounded it. His hands encompassed it. His arm withdrew it. His eyes delighted at the sight of it. On hands and knees, he twisted around and crawled back to Emile's still inert body.

Emile O'Neal's eyes opened. Through a cloud of pain he thought he saw the monster who had assaulted him years before loom over him again as he lay half paralyzed on the floor. The monster straddled his midriff, bending over him. He held something in his right hand.

Eddy steadied himself, breathing deeply through his nostrils, expelling the breath from his mouth. He turned the razor blade so that the blade faced downward and lifting Emile's shirt with one hand sliced it from the first button to the last. It fell away exposing Emile's slightly bloated belly.

Emile began to understand what Eddy planned to do to him. He began to think perhaps he had under-estimated Eddy. Maybe Eddy did have what it takes to kill another human being, he thought. Few people come by it naturally. Maybe Eddy was one of them.

Eddy lowered the razor at the centre of Emile's breast bone and sliced through the flesh. Blood bubbled to the surface. He pushed deeper until he was satisfied he had the right depth, then he slid the blade downward over Emile's fleshy belly, not hurried but not stopping until the blade sliced three inches below Emile's belly-button. He inspected his work, made deeper incisions where needed until Emile's flesh parted, exposing his guts.

"Emile?" Eddy asked, placing his mouth on Emile's ear. "Emile, can you hear me?"

Emile nodded.

"Don't nod, Emile," Eddy said. "Speak. Say, 'Yes I can hear you.' Can you hear me, Emile?"

"Yes I can hear you," Emile rasped.

"Clear your throat and say it again."

Emile cleared his throat and repeated, "Yes I can hear you."

"Good. That's better. Now listen to this, Emile, and listen good. I've slit your belly open. If you sit up your guts will pour out and you'll die real ugly. Understand?"

Emile batted his eyes and nodded.

"Say it, man. Do you understand?"

"Yes, I understand."

"Good. Your only hope of survival is to lie still and do exactly what I tell you. I won't pretend your chances of living are very good but I know a guy who had a 5% chance of surviving pancreatic cancer for more than 2 years and that was 20 years ago. Get my drift?"

Emile nodded.

Eddy prodded him gently in the ribs with bare foot. Emile winced with pain. "Use words, Emile. I want you to use words."

"Yes."

"Good work. Now I'm going to get your cell phone and bring it over to you, and you are going to phone your pals and tell them to bring my partner over here, got it?"

"Yes."

"But first, let's do a little show and tell," Eddy said as he began to frisk Emile. There was nothing of significance in the front pockets of Emile's shorts. There was nothing in one of the back pockets. Eddy dipped his fingers into the wallet pocket. As he did so, Emile shat his pants.

"Oh, Christ, Emile," Eddy exclaimed. "That's gross."

Emile looked up as if saddened by his indiscretion.

"Here, let me get your shorts off," Eddy said, undoing Emile's belt and tugging his shorts slowly along his outstretched legs. Emile gasped in pain. "Don't worry, old soldier," Eddy said. "You may die but not from septicemia. I've got some powder in my kit. Funny what we carry around with us, isn't it?"

Eddy grasped each of Emile's wrists in a tight grip, lifted them no more than an inch off the floor, and began, as gently as possible, to pull Emile's body far enough away from his feces to avoid contact with his open wound.

As Eddy straightened up, slowly and painfully, he looked past Emile's feet and exclaimed, "Hello? What's this I spy with my little eye?" He had spotted a small package, a parcel, a rubbery ball left behind when he pulled Emile away. He stepped toward it, bent down, took a close look and backed away. It looked like something wrapped in cloth and stuffed and knotted in a condom. Not wanting to touch it, he moved stiffly to the bathroom and came back with a wet washcloth which he used to hold up the condom. He cut off the top of the condom and dumped out its contents. Something was wrapped in napkin, not cloth. He unwrapped the napkin, exposing what looked like paper folded into a tiny square. Using his bare fingers, he unfolded the paper. It was a note that read: ScotiaBank. See mngr Valaquez. Password Geronimo. Void after 10:30 p.m. Thursday. No i.d. req'd, as agreed.

"Son of a bitch," Eddy exclaimed out loud. As he had slit Emile open he had wondered what kind of back up deal Emile had struck with the Belizeans if Eddy won the fight. It was purely academic, one pro trying to guess what another pro would do under certain circumstances. Now he knew. He knew where to go. He knew how to access the final payment. He knew there was a deadline. What he didn't know was how much was in the kitty. And what he would have to do to get it.

He stuffed the key and the note in his pocket and turned back to the prostrate Emile, stooping over again to pick us Emile's wallet. Flipping it open he counted close to $2,000 USD and quickly identified major credit cards and even Emile's Ontario driver's license. Pretty stupid, Eddy thought as he shoved the wallet into a front pocket. He didn't plan to leave a trace of Emile's i.d. behind, only his live body or his dead corpse.

"Okay, Emile," Eddy said, kneeling beside the prone body of Emile, "it's show time. If you want to live, you'll follow my instructions to a T. What's the number?"

"Cane and Able," Emile whispered.

"Cane and Able in the directory?"

Emile nodded.

"Now remember, your life depends on it. You tell them the deed's done, bring the girl. Got it? The deed's done. Bring the girl."

Emile nodded. Eddy punched the buttons and waited for a dial tone. He heard someone answer. He cued Emile.

"The deed's done. Bring the girl."

"You okay, boss?"

Eddy pushed the off button. He stood up and wobbled over to the bathroom, fumbled in his kit for a zip-lock bag and returned to Emile. Sprinkling a white powder down Emile's sliced body, he said, "That ought to hold you for a while. Best I can do. More'n you would have done for me." He pulled the top blanket off the bed and ripped off the sheet. "Here, wear this for a while," Eddy said as he draped Emile's body with the sheet, "You look like you're dead but you're not, not yet anyways, so keep your effing mouth shut."

JAN & EDDY: The Tables Are Turned

Jan knew as soon as she saw the body draped with a sheet at the end of the room that it was not Eddy. If it was not Eddy, he was still alive. If he was still alive, he was hiding somewhere, ready to strike. She knew she had to create a diversion.

She yanked her hand from Able's grip as he pushed her into Eddy's cabana and flung herself across the floor. Still bound, she tucked herself between the futon and the bed.

Cane and Able looked at her and cursed. As Able moved toward Jan, Eddy stepped from behind the door, saddled Cane's head with his left arm, bending it back, and with his right arm reached across Cane's neck, razor in hand.

"Tell him to stop." Eddy hissed into Cane's ear.

"Able, stop!" Cane commanded. Able swung around and saw the man who was supposed to be dead holding his brother in a death grip. He stepped toward Cane and Eddy, stopped and turned back to Jan huddled on the floor.

"Ahh", Cane cried as the razor cut into the flesh of his neck, "listen to him!"

Eddy's hand was red with blood. He dug the razor deeper into Cane's neck. "Jan," he shouted. "Jan, wiggle back as far as you can get, babe. Okay? Get back against the wall, baby."

"Okay, Eddy. I'm back against the wall."

"Now, Jan, let's not kid ourselves, we're in a pile of trouble here, but I gotta ask you something, baby, so I can figure out what I've gotta do to get us out of this mess and I want you to tell me the truth, okay?"

"Okay, Eddy."

"These guys hurt you, Jan? These guys do anything to you? You know what I mean?"

"I know what you mean, Eddy. I was scared to death, Eddy, but these guys didn't touch me, honest to Christ, Eddy, and I was so scared I probably would've done anything they asked."

"Okay, baby. You just saved a couple lives. You still tied up?"

"Yes."

"Now your fingers are free, reach down and see if you can get the duct tape off your legs. Okay? Work on it. I've gotta talk to my friends here."

Eddy relaxed his grip on Cane's head. "Take a deep breath, man, and listen to me. What I plan is this. I'm gonna tie you guys up, take your Jeep and get outta dodge. Your pal Emile over there isn't dead. You can do what you want with him, but he ain't dead right now. Jan and me are going to drive to Belize City and take the next plane out of town. Don't bother us and we are gone, gone, gone. Come after us and we go to war."

Cane grunted.

"What's that? You say something? You mother fucking son of a bitch." Eddy's hand shook with rage. His fingers on the razor were white with tension.

"Everything's cool, man" Cane stammered, "we just on a job, that's all. Job's done."

"You bet the job's done, you bitch." Eddy took deep breaths to calm himself. "How's it going, Jan?"

"I got the tape off my legs, Eddy. Now what?"

"Come on over here, baby. Wait a minute. Hey, you." Eddy yelled.

"You talking to me?" Able retorted, frozen in the middle of the room.

Eddy re-tightened his grip on Cane's head and slipped the razor a half-inch across his neck. Blood began to pour from the open wound.

"Yeah, I'm talking to you, you low life piece of shit. Take off your sandals. Take them off! Now get on your knees. Now get your belly on the floor and stretch out your legs and your arms. Now just lie there and don't move 'cause I'm a fraction away from killing your buddy. You guys look alike. Are you brothers from the same mother?"

"Okay, man. Chill." Able dropped to his knees and did as Eddy told him.

"Okay, Jan. Go over to the door. Can you open it?"

"It's closed, Eddy. I can't get out. What now?"

"Jan, turn the knob."

"Okay, Eddy, the door's open. What now?"

"Remember that tackle box that guy loaned me?"

"Yeah, it's in the corner beside the porch."

"Open that tackle box, baby, any you'll see a scaling knife. It's long enough, you should be able to cut yourself free, but get a start then unwind the tape. Okay? Then bring the tape and the tackle box and the knife. We're going to need them in here."

Eddy stood his ground and waited for Jan to come back. He was planning ahead as fast as he could. He wouldn't kill the Belizean gangsters but he had to immobilize them. And, as he began to formulate an escape plan, he began to think Emile might be more good to him alive than dead.

"Okay, Jan, let's start with this clown first. Wrap your duct tape around his ankles. Don't worry. If he moves he's dead. I've got a whole roll of duct tape, Made in Canada, in the cupboard. But we've also got this," he kicked the tackle box. "There's a whole spool of 20 lb. fish line inside. These boys aren't going anywhere fast."

EDDY & JAN: Getting Out Of Dodge

Eddy swung the jeep around and headed up the highway, not too fast, not too slow. "Jan," he said, "scope through that bag where we put all their stuff. Find a cell-phone. Looked like there were a few in there when I rifled through it. I don't think it matters what one. I don't think these guys will have call-display and they're probably all stolen anyway."

Jan shuffled through the bag. For all she had experienced in the past few hours, she felt surprisingly calm. Her fingers felt a cell phone and she pulled it out. "Here's one. Don't know whose it is. It's working."

"Okay, here's the number. I'll take it when he answers."

The moon was sliver thin but it threw enough light to sparkle on the waves of the sea as Eddy and Jan headed north up the Placencia Peninsula. Eddy drove through the night, headlights penetrating the road that carried them home. Jan held the phone up so he could hear. The phone rang. And again. "Yeah," a voice said.

"Charlie?" Eddy took the phone from Jan and held it to his ear.

"Yeah."

"Charlie Ariola?"

"Yeah?"

"You took us to Placencia sometime last week, remember?"

"Keep talking."

"What's my name?"

"If you who I think you is, your name's Eddy and your wife's name's Jan."

"Good man. Charlie, I've got some money waiting for you . . ."

"Say what?"

"Charlie, listen to me and listen hard. I've scored big down here, too big for me to handle. I need local help, you understand, that's why I'm phoning you."

"You phonin' from Placencia? Must be a clear night."

"Why?"

"Can't usually get from there to here by cell-phone, atmospherics. But never mind all that. What do you need?"

"First, phone your son in San Bight. I'm not far from there right now. I need to swap cars with him. Believe me, it's a good deal. It's a good deal all round, you me and your son, Richard."

"I'll phone him. Where are you now?"

"Maybe twenty minutes from San Bight."

"Keep drivin'. I'll get back."

Eddy and Jan drove on in silence. Finally, Jan spoke. "Well, what's going on?"

"He's going to contact his son."

"And?"

"Well, we'll meet with his son in San Bight."

"And?"

"Oh, Jan. I'm sorry. I really am. I'm going to have time enough to second guess myself sometime, I hope, but right now we are running for our lives and I'm making up our escape route, literally, as we drive. I've got some thoughts, that's all. So trust me, babe. I'm so pumped right now I could drive this Jeep through a concrete wall and we would both survive."

"Yeah, but would we get back home?"

"That's what I'm working on, baby."

The cell phone rang. Jan answered and passed it to Eddy. "Eddy?" "Yeah." Eddy listened as Charlie spoke: "Everything's cool. Drive slow through San Bight. There's a kid with a flashlight waving drivers down. Just say, 'Charlie' and he'll lead you where you have to go."

They spotted the kid with the flashlight shortly after they reached San Bight, a rustic backwater that fame and fortune had passed over. They followed the kid past shack after shack of rotting wood planks and corrugated roof tops, stopping in front of a pink plaster bungalow that looked as if it belonged in the 21st century.

"Gimme money, mister," the kids said as Eddy and Jan stepped out of the Jeep and slammed shut the doors. Eddy dug through his wallet and passed the kid 10 bze, thinking that was what he should have done a few years back when a strung-out kid on King Street made the same demand.

The kid grabbed the money and ran to the front door. He pushed open the door and shouted, "They here", turned and disappeared.

"C'mon in, folks," Richard Ariola said, motioning Eddy and Jan inside. "Dad says you okay, and that's okay with me. Sit down over there. Make yourself comfortable. We got some talkin' to do."

Jan and Eddy sat on a comfortable sofa, a fan whirring above them. Jan noted the pictures on the walls, mostly of children of different ages. She glanced over at the kitchen and saw that the appliances gleamed, the long wooden kitchen table was empty except for a vase of flowers, slightly wilted after a long, hot day, and the floor was polished, not exactly what she had expected after the ride into San Bight.

Richard Ariola pulled up a chair and sat across the glass-topped table between them. He was in his early thirties, both Eddy and Jan guessed, good looking, very watchful, wary, but calm. He wore a Los Angeles Lakers t-shirt tucked into pressed khaki trousers and was bare foot. "You want her here?" he asked Eddy. "We gonna be talkin' some hard shit."

"Yeah, she stays," Eddy said.

"Okay, but I'm talkin' like she ain't here, so don't take no offense at anything I say or how I say it. Clear?"

Eddy nodded. Jan looked at Eddy, looked over at Richard and nodded, too.

Richard leaned forward and looked straight at Eddy. "What the fuck you doin' here, man? What went down in Placencia?"

Eddy cleared his throat and gave Richard an abridged version of what went down, omitting many factual details and fabricating others. When he was finished, Richard shook his head in disbelief.

"Wow," he exclaimed. "You must think I'm really stupid."

"Sorry, man. There's just some shit I can't talk about, thing's you don't have to know . . ."

"Answer me this: Do I know there are three live bodies, a white bad guy from Canada and two bad black brothers from the city of Belize, in a cabana in Placencia Village that you want me to get rid of?"

"Yes."

"Do I know that you want me to swap my beat up old Toyota for the Jeep you drove here?"

"Yes."

"What else do I know?"

"That you'll get paid well."

"Details, please."

Eddy reached into his back pocket and pulled out a sheaf of bills. He riffled through it and threw a thousand usd on the table. "Starters."

"What about the rest of it," Richard asked, pointing to the money Eddy had returned to his wallet and was stuffing into his back pocket.

"Mine. There's about 900 left and I'm going to need it when I get to Belize City."

"Not sweet enough."

"You got the 1000, you got the money from the Jeep if you deal it or keep it yourself, whatever, it's worth a couple grand or more either way, and you got these," Eddy reached into a side pocket and pulled out Emile's credit cards, throwing down the American Express and MasterCard.

"And this," Eddy said, dropping Emile's passport on the table. The white guy's passport."

Richard picked up the passport and examined it. "Canada, eh?"

Yeah, Canada."

"So what?"

"Richard, you're too smart to act so dumb. That passport's worth its weight in gold. These are both international credit cards. You get someone here in Belize, you get someone in Guatemala City, you know guys like this, some guy to max out these credit cards for a percent and you get at least a thousand more. Don't trifle with me, man."

"Okay, but what we got so far is one guy who's gonna die, right, and two other guys, two black dudes, what's their status? All you said is they's tied up. They alive or dead? Wounded? What?"

"Let's just say they are both Able but one of them might need a Cane," Eddy joked, immediately regretting it.

"Sweet Mary, mother of Jesus," Richard exclaimed. "You tellin' me you got Cane and Able from Belize City tied up in a cabana in Placencia. You know who those mother fuckers are? They's why I'm livin' here in San Bight, you stupid fuck. I never crossed them but, holy shit, look at 'em cross-ways and they'd kill you soon as ask you what you was lookin' at. Never mind, man, deal's off."

"Deal's off?" Eddy retorted. "Deal's off? I'm offering you the deal of your lifetime and you're saying 'deal's off?'"

"What d'ya mean?"

"Think their sorry asses aren't worth something? You lookin' for a big score, start thinkin' big. You get them boys across the border to Guatemala and you're looking at a chest of gold for their return. You listening?"

"Yes, but . . ."

"You looking for the big score, I'm offering it to you. You man enough to take it?"

"Yeah, I'm man enough . . ."

"Then listen to this," Eddy interrupted, "and listen real good. This white guy, this guy from Canada, he's cut real bad. I won't lie to you, but he's not bleeding and he's rich as a thief. You keep him alive you get everything I said plus you set him up in Guatemala and squeeze every dime out of him . . ."

"What's a dime?"

"Richard, are you as smart as your Daddy said you were?"

"Never mind how smart I am. Daddy know all this 'bout Cane and Able? What you and my Daddy got brewin'?"

"'Course we got something brewing. Why do you think I'm given you all this opportunity? But my deal with you ends right here. If you want to know more, ask your father. And if you want a better cut, you're getting it out of Charlie's piece of the pie. Now, we gonna deal or not?"

Richard sat upright and puffed out his chest. He realized this was the chance he had been waiting for since Cane and Able forced him out of Belize City and made him eke out a thief's living in out-of-the-way San Bight far from the bright lights and big scores of the City. Now this stranger had offered him the keys to the Kingdom of Thieves and he knew he could not turn them down.

He extended his hand. Eddy, suppressing any sign of relief, swept up the credit cards and handed them to Richard. "Don't go all sentimental on me. Make sure your Toyota's full of gas . . ."

"My Toyota's a shit-box, man."

"Yeah, sure it is, least ways it looks like it is, but you don't work out of this backwater 'less you got a full-time mechanic to make it run like new. I know, I know," Eddy said, holding up his hands to stop a protest. "C'mon, man, you can't kid a kidder. You keep it ugly so even the thieves won't steal it. Just make sure it's full of gas, man."

Richard stood up and extended his hand to Jan who rose to the occasion and shook it. As they reached the door, Eddy waved a salute to Richard and ushered Jan outside.

Jan paused for a moment, took a deep breath and whispered,

"Mother Fucker", flashing a smile at Eddy as he gave her a quick look.

EMILE: Cane and Able break their Chains

"Hey, Mr. Eddy. Hey, Miss Jan. Seen the lights on. Can I come in?" Edward, the desk-clerk/night-watchman stood outside the cabana, broke and desperate for a drink, wondering why the lights were on after Mr. Eddy and Miss Jan had left the hotel.

He poked open the door and stepped inside, calling out again, "Hey, anybody there?" knowing nobody was. But why were the lights on and the door not locked? It occurred to him that it did not matter, actually made it easier for him. Who could lay blame on him if a thief had slipped in and cleared the place out before he had a chance to check it?

It took him a moment to adjust to the light and focus. When he did, he saw two men on the bed attached leg to leg by duct tape, their toes touching, their heads cheek to cheek. His gaze followed up one set of legs to a torso to a face. He blinked and followed the other set of legs to a torso to a face. The eyes and mouth of each face was wrapped with duct tape but he recognized the men immediately. He thought maybe he had the wrong cabana and snorted as he shook his head. It was definitely the hard cases from Belize and this was definitely not their cabana.

"Desk-clerk?"

He swung around. His eyes followed where his ears had heard the voice. He saw a corpse lying on the floor wrapped in a shroud. The corpse spoke again.

"Desk-clerk?"

"Yes?"

"I'm Mr. Emile," the corpse said. "Remember me? Go to my cabana and bring back some scissors or a knife. Understand? Cut these men loose." The corpse fell silent. The shroud rose and fell as the corpse breathed short hard breaths. "I'll give you 20usd and a large bottle of rum."

"Whatever you say, boss," the desk-clerk said. He scooted out the door and scurried to Mr. Emile's cabana. Fumbling through the utensil drawer in the kitchen he grabbed something that would do the job and returned to Mr. Eddy's and Miss Jan's cabana with a butcher knife. He was breathing hard. His head pounded and he felt sick to his stomach. He needed something quick to straighten himself out. He cut through the duct tape and sawed at the fish line until he freed Able's hands. Able grabbed the butcher knife from him and cut his bonds, then freed Cane. They sat on the edge of the bed rubbing their limbs.

"Can I have my money now, sir," the desk clerk said, addressing the corpse.

"Wait a minute, mother fucker," Cane spoke. "What were you doing here? You knew they weren't here, dint you, but you came a'callin' just the same. Gonna steal some booze? Gonna clean them out? You knew they not comin' back, dint you?"

"I, I was comin' to clean up. Guests check out, I come in an clean up."

"They checked out?" Able asked, dubious that they would stop to check out when they were on the run.

"No, not checked out. They never checked in . . ."

"What the fuck!" Cane and Able spoke in unison.

"They said you gave them your Jeep," the desk clerk's teeth rattled, "and did you have a safety deposit box."

Cane and Able sat still as marble as they listened to the desk-clerk's tale.

"They said you said to open the box and give them everything what's inside and I . . ."

"You gave them the package in the safety deposit box?" Cane murmured. "You . . ."

"You gave him that bag we left with you?" Able shook with fury.

"He had a knife, a big fish knife. Said he'd kill me," the desk-clerk improvised, "said you guys gone fishin', that's what he tole me. I was afraid, man," the desk-clerk fell to his knees, "he tole me I'm gonna die, man, he's gonna cut . . ."

"You asshole," Able shouted. "That's our up-front money. 15 thousand American dollars. Jesus fucking Christ!"

"Able!" Cane cried in rebuke. "That's blasphemy . . ."

"Shut up, Cane," Able rejoined, clutching the butcher knife in his hand, drawing back his arm and driving the point of the knife through the desk clerk's neck. "And this here's just retribution!"

The desk-clerk staggered backwards, blowing blood from his windpipe, exhaling his last few breaths before he tottered and fell across Emile's legs.

"What the fuck!" Emile cried. "What's going on?"

"You deaf, mother fucker", Cane said. "We got no Jeep, we got no money, we got no fuck-all."

"You guys leaving me?"

"Quit feelin' sorry for yourself, Emile. No we ain't leavin' you. We just gotta get our Jeep back . . ."

"And our money," Able added.

"And kill the mother-fucker that done this to us . . ." Cane continued.

"Yeah, like if you done your job we all be back in the city havin' a party, bitch." Able said.

Cane and Able walked over to the doorway turned for one last look. Able snarled, "Leastways you got some company. You got Mr. Dead Desk-clerk cross your legs. Right now, we ain't got jack-shit." He flipped off the light as he left the cabana.

CANE & ABLE: Searching for Eddy and Jan

Though they conducted most of their criminal activity from Belize City, Cane and Able were not unfamiliar with Placencia Village as a pleasure spot where they could relax from time to time and somewhere they could take the family for holidays. They knew where the closest taxi driver lived and barged into his house unannounced.

Silas Bergeron having just minutes before mounted his Garifuna wife, Mary, for the evening romp, was in the home stretch headed for the finish line when Cane and Able burst into the bedroom at the back of the two-room house. He rolled off the bed and grabbed for his pants on the floor. Able stepped on his outstretched hand.

"You don't wanta be goin' for no gun, mother fucker. Or we gonna be killin' you and your loved one here. Now, where is your gun, 'cause we know you got one."

"Over there," Silas stammered. "In that desk drawer by the window."

Cane opened the drawer and pulled out Silas' handgun. "My, my, nice piece. Where'd you get this?"

"Cops give it to me."

"Why's that?"

"Saw 'em kill a kid up the peninsula a way. Kill him and throw him into the lagoon. They give me that '44 automatic."

"Well, that's real nice, Silas. And if everything goes good, I'm gonna bring this piece back to you. Now, where's your cell-phone?"

"Ain't got no cell-phone, man." Silas heard the click as Cane released the safety. "It's over, over there, over on the kitchen table."

Cane flicked the '44 to Able and sat down at the kitchen table. He waited for someone to pick up the phone on the other end. "Marvin? . . . Good . . . Shut up and lissen, man. That's right. Me and Able down here in the village. We gotta situation, unnerstan'? Silas the taxi-man's lettin' us use his taxi, got it? We'll be at your place in ½ hour, max. Okay? . . . Gonna need wheels. What you driving . . . No way, that's a shit-box. We got serious business in the city. Still got the Esplanade? . . . That'll do fine. Get it gassed up. Now lissen up, Marvin, you know we in a dead zone here in the village. No way we can get through to the city, so contact Leon and Devon. Put them on full alert. Tell 'em to get a crew ready for action in the morning. Tell 'em I'll contact 'em when we get to San Bight. Tell 'em we takin' the short cut on the Coastal Highway so if they drunk or stoned they only got a few hours to get right."

Cane walked back to the bed where Silas sat shivering. Silas's wife Mary had not moved or made a sound since the intrusion. She remained ass in the air, head pressed into a pillow. "Lookin' good, baby," Cane said, tapping her buttocks with the barrel of the '44. She flinched. "Make sure Silas here do his duty when we gone."

Cane looked down at Silas. "Bet he ain't got much dick left to satisfy a gal like you. Me? I'd be spreading some real nice icing on that puddin' pie if I had the time.

Now, Silas, we gonna go, unnerstan'? We taken your 44 and your cell phone so's you don't phone no one. We taken your taxi, too, man, 'cause we got bidness t'end to. Pick it up at Marvin's in the morning. You wanta know the good news, Silas?"

Silas nodded his head. "Yessir. What's the good news?"

"Good news is we ain't taken your life. You can thank the good Lord for that mercy. C'mon, Able, we got work to do."

JAN & EDDY: A Reluctant Return to Belize City

"You know where we're going, Eddy?" Jan said.

"Yeah, Jan. Pretty sure."

"Pretty sure? That's not much relief."

"Jan, when I'm on assignment, and you're getting to know more about that than I ever wanted you to know, I get driven through back streets of big cities, and I learned fast I'd better know where I was going if I wanted to get back on my own."

Jan was silent for awhile. Then she said, "Well, where are we going now. No, wait, I know we're going back to Belize City, right, but if you think you know how we got here from there, what's 'pretty sure' all about?"

"Remember Charlie took a short cut to Dangriga? We cut down south from the zoo and saved a lot of time. Remember that?"

"Yeah, Eddy, so what?"

"So I don't want to go back that way."

"Why not?"

"First, 'cause that's more of a rock bed than a road and there aren't any lights from start to finish and this moon's not bright enough to light the way."

"And second?"

"Second is that that road's got to be robbers' paradise. You're travelling on that road under those conditions at night there's a fairly good chance you got some contraband on you . . ."

"But there'd be cops,' Jan sputtered.

"You got it, baby. Cops vying with crooks to make the score. Not much different back home. But never mind that. My only problem is when we get to Dangriga we get on the Hummingbird Highway. That takes us through the Mayan Mountains and puts us on course for Belize City. I'm just not too sure where we pick us that road. Don't worry, baby, we'll make it, and when we get there I'm going to track down our friend Sergeant-Major Thadeaus Wright."

Oh, Eddy, that's a great idea. But what about Charlie the taxi-driver, don't you trust him"

"Up to a point, we're going to have to, Jan, but first off I'd rather fall on the mercy of Thadeaus Wright. He's already saved us once. He's like a knight in shining armour."

"Well I hope he's not tilting at windmills."

"Huh," Eddy said without taking his eyes off the road.

EDDY & JAN: Re-Union with The King

Thadeaus Wright, King of King Street, ex-Sergeant-Major in both the British and the Belizean Army, sat slumped against the inside wall of an abandoned warehouse one half a block from his regular digs in a one bedroom apartment with a private bathroom over a restaurant on Albert Street. He had had thoughts of getting up and tottering off to bed but those thoughts kept drifting away. He sipped on his One Barrel rum and ruminated on days gone by, cherishing memories of his life as a soldier. He chuckled softly and raised a glass in a mock toast to more recent experiences with his merry band of old men, school kids, grandmas and single moms, all dispossessed and all fighting for survival in the nasty environs of downtown Belize City, his birth place and designated place of death.

"King! King!" Someone stood in the doorway whose door had become unhinged and stolen years before. "King! They's some folks here to see you."

Thadeaus stared at the silhouette and ordered it to step inside. As he had thought, it was the Bradshaw boy, though what he would be doing out this late at night when he had school in the morning Thadeaus made a note to himself to find out.

"What folks, boy?"

"White folks, King. Man 'n woman."

"Well don't keep them waiting. Show them in. Up lads," he commanded his troop, a dozen or more of whom had assumed positions of repose and lay strewn on the floor in front of him. "On your feet and stand steady."

Thadeaus hauled himself up and approached the open door. As he got closer his eyes widened and the hand on his billy slackened. "Well, well," he said, "if it isn't Mr. Eddy and Miss Jan. Last time we met was three years ago, March 16, a Thursday I believe, around 7:30 p.m. An altercation with a young lad who, I regret to tell you, was murdered, most likely by the police, that very same evening. Been in another fight, Mr. Eddy?"

Eddy, usually never at a loss for words, tripped over his own tongue. "Ah, well, hello, Mr. Wright. Was the boy killed? I had no idea. I, uh, that is, no, I haven't been in another fight, not exactly, but we're in a bit of a jam and have come to you for your assistance once again."

"Please, call me Thadeaus, or King, if you prefer. It appears that our destinies are entwined, wouldn't you say? Please, come over here and sit down." Thadeaus directed them to an old table, barely discernable in the darkness, with old wooden chairs scattered around it. "Pick a chair and sit upon it, my Canadian friends. Tomy, bring us some candles, or better yet, a kerosene lamp, before we commence our conversation. Now then, what are your immediate needs, Mr. Eddy and Miss Jan. Would you like a drink? Some water? Some food?"

"Oh Thadeaus, what I need most is a bathroom," Jan cried out. "A bathroom, more than anything, please."

"I could go to the can, too," Eddy admitted.

"You go over there." Thadeaus instructed Eddy, pointing to the darkest end of the warehouse. "And you, my dear, will be escorted to my apartment a few steps up the street where you will have the comfort and privacy you deserve. Then and only then will we get down to business. Tomy, make sure Miss Jan has a safe journey and bring her back asap. And Mr. Eddy," Thadeaus called as Eddy stepped away from the table. "How did you get here?"

"By car." Eddy turned around and called back. "It's parked outside, but don't worry about it, King. It's not worth anything to anybody."

"Down here, Mr. Eddy, everything's worth something to somebody. Tomy, send two men, no, make it three, to watch the car. Knives and cudgels only, but use them if necessary."

When Tomy left to carry out King's instructions, King followed Eddy into the darkness. As Eddy relieved himself, he half-turned toward King and whispered, "That beat-up old car's a well-oiled machine. It's loaded. It's yours. Next point, when we get together I'm going to be asking for your help and you're going to be asking me what it is worth. Anything I say, think double that. You do what you want with the overage but I reckon you can distribute the money better on your own."

"Anything else," King whispered behind him.

"I'm gonna need a reliable phone to make contact in Canada, no trace, immediately. And, we'll need a safe place to stay tonight, okay? And take these," Eddy reached into side pocket and pulled out the remaining two of Emile's international credit cards. "Max them out fast and chop them up. And, good to see you again."

"Good to see you, too, Eddy," King said.

KING: The Sergeant-Major Plans an Attack

Sergeant-Major Thadeaus Wright listened to Eddy and Jan describe the events that had lead them out of Placencia Village to the King of King Street in Belize City.

When they finished, he exclaimed with a faux British accent, "By Jove, Mr. Eddy and Miss Jan, that story is extraordinary. You mean to tell me that he came all the way from Canada with the sole purpose of killing you? To avenge himself? To rub off the one black mark on his escutcheon? Remarkable! But the lad seems somewhat unfit for duty now, wouldn't you say? Somewhat worse for wear, what?

But what I'd like you to explain, if you would be so kind: why would you deny that you had been in another fight?" Thadeaus held up his hand for silence as Eddy began to speak. "You'll have your turn, but really, old chap, wouldn't you admit that denying you were in a fight was a little bit, a wee wee little bit misleading?"

"May I explain," Eddy asked, looking across at the man seated opposite him. In the flickering kerosene light, Thadeaus looked like a general anticipating a battle by a camp fire from the time of Rome to the present. His eyes sparkled. His white hair and beard shone. He sat erect, shoulders pinned against the back of the chair. He nodded approval for Eddy to continue.

"It wasn't exactly a 'fight', as I know it. A 'fight' is between two people who, for whatever reason, agree to engage. When me and the kid fought on the corner of Albert and King Street, that was a fight. We both agreed. With Emile, I never agreed. It was an assault and I did what I had to do to defend myself."

"Ah, you're a crafty one, aren't you," Thadeaus crooned, momentarily lost in the bliss of past battles, especially on the Guatamelan front where his manhood had been sorely tested. He had passed the test with flying colours and had always longed to carry the flag again. "But enough of this. I said I would stand by you and stand by you I shall, me and my soldiers. But we must have some assurance of success and some coin of the realm to get the troops together, armed and willing to do battle."

Eddy stood up, his crotch not two feet from King's face, prepared to make his case.

"Sit down, lad, or back up a foot or two," Thadeaus said. "All I can see with my weakened eyes is the bulge in your pants, if you'll pardon me, ma'm. Time and place, lad. Time and place. And this is neither."

Eddy sat down. Jan snickered and poked him in the side.

"Well I agree that this is neither the time nor the place but I'm glad you both find me amusing . . ."

"Oh, get on with it, lad. We've had our laugh, now let us get on with business. First off, you have not mentioned anyone that we do not know. Cane and Able are bad men, hard-coré criminals to be sure, and they and their gangsters have hurt many of my people and beaten and almost killed some of my men. They are bullies, all of them. Oh, we do a little bit of this and that down here to make ends meet, but even that they object to and want a cut of the action.

Charlie Aurilio, your taxi driver, I'd trust him with my life. Known him since we were both kids. Went to school together. Charlie's son, Richard, don't know him so well. Left the city shortly after he gained manhood, got involved in the rackets but ran afoul of Cane and Able. An honest thief in a corrupt world full of villains still has to make a living without so he moved down to San Bight to take care of business. My take: if he's Charlie's son, I would be inclined to trust him, too. So here's my question, Eddy. If you have Charlie's son cleaning up the mess you left in the village, and Charlie himself to pick you up in the morning and drive you around, what in the name of sweet Jesus you need me and my men for?"

"Here's why," Eddy replied, leaning across the table to face the King. "We left three men back there, one maybe dying, two tied up and very much alive. It's the two tied up I'm worried about right now. You said it yourself: they are bad-ass killer guys. They aren't going to just lie down and give up. They are going to try every which way they can to get loose. They get loose, they are going to steal a car and head straight to Belize City.

And to be honest, I'm not so sure about Richard. Maybe he's not up to the task of taking them out of action long enough for us to grab the money and run. And listen, King, they know what I know. They will stake out the bank and soon's I walk out with the money they'll be on us, like flies on shit. What's Charlie going to do? He's going to back up his cab and drive straight home and have an early morning nap. If asked, he don't know nothin' 'bout nothin' and I don't blame him a bit. But if that happens, me and Jan, if we are lucky, are dead before they decide to have some fun with us. And you know exactly what I mean."

"You make a good point, Eddy," the King said. "Don't seem likely but could happen, that's for sure."

"And, how about this, King. I've thought about this, too. You said yourself that you don't know what Charlie's son is really like. He knows Cane and Able. Christ, he's got their Jeep. He's got them in his power but he thinks, this is my big break. He may be thinking, 'I cut them loose. They are going to owe me big time. We go back to the city and make sure that white dude and his gal disappear before they can get away and I'm solid gold'. In either scenario, we've got Cane and Able sitting outside the bank waiting for us to bring the money to them and if we manage to slip away they have the airport covered like a blanket."

"So you need King's army?"

"Exactly."

"And what are you prepared to pay for it?"

"I've got three thousand in my pocket. It's yours."

Eddy heard the rustle of men moving closer. "What I want to know is what do we get for it?"

"Get back, boys," the King commanded without looking around. "I'll take care of business. Well, let's see," he peered across the table, the orange kerosene light illuminating Eddy. "You'll get 4 units of men, there's 4 in a unit, armed and on duty as early in the morning as you want. They will be instructed to mingle with the folks on the street, keeping an eye on Cane's thugs, most of who they will know on sight. They will disable as many vehicles as possible by whatever means are open to them, but their first priority will be to watch for you when you exit the front of the bank. In other words, don't try something cute like slipping out the back door. When they see you, they'll move in around you. When the thugs move in, my army will take action. Let me make it clear. My lads and ladies will be risking their lives to save you. They will be armed with cudgels and knives only but they should be able to kick up enough fuss for you to reach Charlie's taxi . . ."

"Charlie won't be there."

"What?"

"We are going to be driving ourselves."

"What happened to Charlie? He would never chicken out. There's something you are not telling me."

"Yeah," Eddy said. "I'm not telling you I can't put Charlie in so much danger. His family would be in danger. Do you know he's had four more children in the past 10 years and he's over 60. So I carved out another role for him, but don't worry, he's still in the game."

"Does he know?"

"Not yet, but he will soon enough."

"Okay. That is good enough for me. But the Toyota?"

"It may be plug ugly, but I tell you we'll make it to the airport in no time."

"No, you will not."

"What?"

"I like the idea of you taking the wreck, but I don't want you to drive it. You are too conspicuous. No, I have a driver, Razor, he will take you to the airport and you and Jan will hide in the back seat."

"But . . ."

"But, Eddy, you are in Belize City and I am the King of King Street. You came to me. You want my help. You will do what I say. I don't mind you making suggestions, providing me with information, but if we do this thing, I've gotta be in charge. Is that clear?"

"Yes, King, it is. Jan, it is, isn't it?"

"Yes, King, it is clear. Let's move on."

"We'll move on, Miss Jan, when we finish the business part of this here discussion."

CANE & ABLE: Back in the City

Cane and Able, showered and shaved and wearing clean bright red Caribbean shirts and dark blue slacks, sat at a table of a safe-house situated near the cemetery in the toughest part of Belize City. Though surrounded by shacks built from corrugated tin atop wobbly docks over mosquito-infested swamp water, their stand-alone bungalow was high and dry and comfortable with electricity and hot and cold running water and enough satellite power to keep them in touch with the rest of the world.

Cane looked at Leon and Devon the two men standing half at attention, waiting to be de-briefed and dismissed. They were both pimped up, wearing Havana fedoras, pastel coloured long-sleeved silk shirts, and beige slacks with Kobe Bryant basketball shoes on their sockless feet. Despite their cool appearance, they were tightly wired, fearful that their bosses would take out their anger on them. Leon shifted his stance and Able barked, "You gotta piss?" "No, boss." "Then quit jumpin' around, you hear?" "Yeah, boss."

"So you're sayin' Dwayne Bowman text'd you that Eddy Dupuis and his bitch are in the City, that right?" Cane looked up at Leon.

"That's right, boss." Leon nodded.

"And they hooked up with that old fool King. What's that about?"

"Somethin' few years back," Devon offered. "Somethin' bout a fight with a punk kid, you mighta knowed him, momma lived over on Plues, pulled a knife on that white dude you after an' King chased the kid off. Broke his wrist, hear tell. Kid got drowned that same night. So they go back a little, they two."

"Yeah, okay. That 'splains it. He holed up with King till mornin', then he gonna take a run at the bank, use the 'scrip he stole from Emile, grab the money and get the first plane outa Belize."

Able smashed the table with his fist. "Goddamn, Cane, we gotta move in and take him out. He's got the 'scrip, our 15 thou Placencia money and our Goddamn Jeep. That son of a bitch gotta be taught a lesson he never forget."

Cane reached across the table and covered Able's closed fist with his hand. "Able, I want you to lissen to me and lissen real good." He patted Able's fist, then covered it again. "Now, they's no doubt we gotta get the money back, we gotta get the Jeep back, we gotta get the money from the bank. No doubt about it. But lissen to me, my brother. We ain't gonna kill that mother-fucker. We ain't gonna kill or even hurt his bitch. We want them both on that plane 'cause if we kill them or even hurt them we gonna have a shit-storm descend on us 'cause one thing our own people cannot tolerate, you hear me, cannot tolerate, is any suspicion that white folk down here are gonna get killed. If they get a smell, a little sniff, that we be involved in any of this shit, our asses are gonna get dragged back to Hattie and we cain't let that happen.

Let's be clear on this, Able. We want the money that's ours and we want the Jeep that's ours and we're gonna get them. Those folks that Emile wanted to kill, that give us so much grief, forget about it. You unnerstan that? That shit's done. We want what's ours, that's all . . ." Cane paused to catch his breath. "But they's one more thing I gotta say, my brother, and you better lissen up. Stop with this blasphemy shit, this 'Goddamn' this and 'Christ' that. I ain't gonna put up with that shit no more."

"You ain't my daddy!"

"No, I ain't your daddy, but daddy hear you talk this shit he take you out back and whack your black ass blue. You right about that, daddy ain't here, so I gotta do it for daddy, and momma, too."

Able flipped Cane's hand off his curled up fist. "Okay, okay, I won't take the Lord's name in vain no more. But I want my money back and I want our Jeep back . . ."

"Leon, what's the status of the Jeep?"

"Don't know, Cane. Bowman said them white folks came back with a wrecked-up Toyota. It's parked on King Street by King's apartment and it's being swarmed by King's people, kids, grammas, old men, shit like that . . ."

"I get the picture. That means two things. One, we can't take a run at them tonight. Two, King gets the Jeep and gots it hid already and they get the junk piece of shit Toyota to drive them to the airport. That's a nice pay-off right there."

"No fuckin' way," Able shouted, standing up.

"Able, relax," Cane commanded. "Let's get the cash first, come back day after and track down the Jeep. Okay? Time we put that old man King down anyway. He be a pain in the ass for a long, long time. Leon, get six men on the street before 8. That be enough to face down King and his Army. Bank opens at 9. Set two men out back case he tries to slip out the back way. Get one man on the car where they park it. You and the rest watch for him to come out. Use what force you have to but get that money from him . . ."

"How much force?"

"'Nuff to get the money. No killin'. No blood neither. Bruise 'em up. Break bones they make you do it. That's all. You, Devon, take 4 men up to the airport case we can't close the deal down town. Pay off the security cops if you gotta. Don't let them white folks check in, you hear that. Take 'em back of the building or into the washroom and do what you have to do to get the money but when you got it make sure they got their passports and can walk to the plane. Got that? When we got the money, we want them gone. Make them submit but don't break 'em into pieces, yunnerstan? Maybe even help 'em with their luggage, just get'em gone.

Able, you and me stay back in the alley with the Caddy. Good sight lines on the bank and car. Everything go good, you, Leon, grab the money and bring it to us. Everything don't go so good we follow their car to the airport and you get your asses up their fast. Let Devon know they comin'. Might even grab 'em in the parking lot. Same thing about the money. When you get it, bring it to us and disappear. Anybody got anything to say? Okay then. Me and Able gonna get a little shut-eye. Make sure we're up by 6.

Eddy& Jan: Getting Ready For Bed

King's one bedroom apartment surprised Jan and Eddy, not because it was so Spartan nor because it was so clean and neat but because its walls were hung with the original works of well-known Belizean artists and its table tops adorned with wood carvings and decorative pottery from Belize, Guatemala and Mexico.

King emerged from the bedroom with some clothing and blankets. "Bedroom's yours. I'll kip on the couch. Sorry about the cots, folks. Might be a little uncomfortable, 'specially for you, Eddy, but it's only overnight and there ain't much left of that, is there?"

"You've nothing to be sorry about, King. Appreciate everything you've done for us. Let me tuck Jan in, okay, and we'll have a little chat. C'mon, Jan, gotta get some sleep. Big day tomorrow."

Jan stood up and hugged King. "Thank you so very much. You don't know how relieved I am that we tracked you down and you took us in. I've been put through a wringer but I'm feeling better now."

"No problem, Miss Jan. I know good people when I meet 'em and you two are the best."

The bedroom was small with two parallel cots against each wall and a clothes rack and chest of drawers against the other. Eddy watched as Jan slipped off her shirt and slacks. There was no shower in the bathroom and no time for a bath but she had scrubbed herself as well as she could before she came to bed. As she stepped into the pyjamas King had loaned her, Eddy had to stifle a groan and fight back the tears that filled his eyes. That she seemed to love him as much as he loved her was a phenomenon of staggering proportions equaled only by the careless stupidity he had shown by putting her in such harm's way that he had endangered her life. She was so beautiful, bright and bubbly that he had forgotten he had spent most of his adult life in subterranean darkness where men measured their success in terms of blood and broken bones. No wonder Emile had come after him. He could only vindicate himself by an act of such violence he could once again claim to be a champion of the underworld. Eddy should have known it, watched for it, and when it came, been ready for it.

Dressed for bed, Jan sat across from Eddy, reached out and took his hands in hers. She saw his pain and knew what caused it, and yet she was more sanguine than she had ever been before. After the incident on King Street years ago, she had caught a glimpse of the hidden life he lived, and now, strangely, after she had become a part of it, she understood how it worked, and, stripped of morality, what Eddy had to do to survive. Like King, she thought, Eddy is a soldier in a never-ending battle that pits men against each other. Full stop. And she was a woman who loved the man who came back from the battle fields always wounded but always able to reach out, touch, and love as passionately as he was loved. She lifted up her hand and stroked his cheek.

"Eddy? That boy you fought on King Street, did you hear what they said, that he died that same night?"

"Yes, Jan, but it wasn't because of our confrontation. I'm sure of that. So's King. That kid was alive when King ran him off."

"And Eddy? Do you think Emile will live, Eddy?"

"He's got a chance, more than he was prepared to give me. We may never know. I had a chance to kill him but I didn't."

"For me, Eddy?"

"Yeah, for you, babe. But for me, too. I'm not a natural born killer. If I had to, yes, I would. But when there's an option to killing a man, I'll take it."

"You should get some sleep, my love," she said.

"Tomorrow. Tomorrow we'll get all the sleep we need. And the day after tomorrow and the next and the next, but tonight King and I have to make a plan."

"Thought you had a plan."

"Jan, right now, we only know what we want to achieve. Now, we have to figure out how to achieve it. King's a career soldier. I've had my share of battles, too. We'll work it out."

He leaned across the space that separated them and half-way across their lips touched in a tender kiss.

CANE & ABLE: Early Morning in the City

After an early morning breakfast of bacon, sausage, refried beans, scrambled eggs and two portions each of fry-jacks, Cane and Able drove up one-way on Albert Street, past the ScotiaBank. Most of the stores were still closed but Belizeans on their way to work had started to fill the street and vendors were setting up on intersections, already seeking shelter from the heat of the early morning sun under their multi-coloured umbrellas.

"Cane, check this out," Able shouted from his passenger seat. "Look, look, that car right there. That beat-up Toyota. That's gotta be their car. They musta moved it, man."

"Okay, okay, calm down, bro. So they moved it. So what? Doesn't change nothin'. I'm just gonna back into the alley and we gonna wait till they walk to the bank. Shit, man, it's only a block. They gonna go in, get the money, step out the front door and our guys are gonna grab 'em. Nothin's changed, man. They just moved the car closer. Better for us, too."

As they shifted in their seats to get comfortable, anticipating a long wait, Cane's cell phone rang. "Yo," he said, cradling the phone to his ear. "Whassup?" . . . "When?" . . . "What? The back door?" . . . "Okay, okay. Pull a man from the front to the back case they come out that way. Don't see anything on the street now's going to bother us. Don't think old King's got his mojo going. We're good, we're good. Wait for 'em to come out and we got 'em, front or back."

"What the fuck," Able exclaimed as Cane snapped shut his cell phone.

"Leon says they came outa King's apartment little while ago, maybe twenty minutes, got in the car, musta circled 'round and come back on Albert Street, parked the car and walked straight to the bank . . ."

"But it's not open, Cane."

"Leon say they walked direct to the back entrance and went inside, like someone inside waitin' for 'em."

"What the . . ."

"Don't know what's goin' on, man. All I know is we gotta sit tight and play this thing out. No other choice. I'm gonna call Leon and tell him to chill . . ."

"Wait a minute, wait a minute, Cane. That's them, isn't it? That's them comin' out the front door of the bank, see, see. Bank door's closin' behind them. He's got a briefcase in his hand. See that. That's our money he's got."

Able began to open the door separating him from the money the white folks were carrying out of the bank. Cane restrained him, grabbing Able's shirt collar and hauling him back into the Cadillac.

"Wait, wait, what's this," he exclaimed. They watched through the windshield as a phalanx of King's rag-tag army emerged from the basement stair-wells and the doorways leading to the upstairs apartments. Old men and women in tattered clothing, young women, some pregnant, pre-school children, school age kids in school uniforms, marched in a shuffling manner and surrounded Eddy and Jane as they half-ran to their vehicle. Eddy clutching desperately to the briefcase. The goon assigned by Cane to keep watch on the beat-up Toyota moved toward Eddy and Jan, pounding his sap in his hand in anticipation of a slaughter. Two of the older students stepped in front of him and held up their hands. "Stop right there, mister," they cried. Puzzled, the goon stopped as the crowd in front of him drew closer. At that same moment, another student crawled behind him. The two kids charged at his chest and pushed him, flipping him over backwards. Before he could twist around and gain his feet a gnarled old man stepped up behind him and smacked him hard on the head with a cudgel he had concealed under his shirt.

Cane and Able were out of the Cadillac, hanging on the open doors, transfixed at the sight across the road from them. They watched one man go down, then turned their attention toward two more of their goons who were pushing their way through the throng that surrounded Eddy and Jan. "Get them!" Cane yelled to his underlings. "Get the money!" "Kill the bastards!" Able screamed, frothing. As Jan and Eddy approached the car, the group around them, as if on command, turned and formed a wall of protection, some of the students fumbling in their pockets and back-packs as they retrieved cans of soda that they shook, aimed, pulled the tabs off, and shot pressurized streams of coke, pepsi, orange crush and 7-up into the faces and the eyes of their assailants. The goons stumbled, flustered, flailed their arms wildly, held their hands in front of their eyes and lost their momentum. Eddy and Jan jumped into the Toyota and made their get-away.

"Leon, Leon," Cane shouted into the cell phone. "They got away. Take the short-cut and get to the airport before them. We'll follow 'em from behind. Out!"

EDDY & JAN: On the Way to the Airport

Eddy pounded his foot on the gas pedal and shifted gears fast, careening down Albert Street.

"Slow down, man," a voice spoke from the backseat.

Jan turned to look behind her. "What the hell? Who're you?"

"That's Razor, baby," Eddy explained. "He's going to give me directions to the airport. Right, Razor?"

"That's right, boss. That's what Mr. King tole me, almost."

Jan stared into the eyes of Razor, a young Mayan with a vivid scar across his face from his forehead over his nose to his cheek. She turned back to Eddy and exclaimed, "Isn't he the one King said would drive? What's he mean, 'almost'? What's going on, Eddy?"

"Had to change plans." Eddy geared down as he reached the end of Albert Street.

"See this here hairpin comin' up, take it on the right, then straight ahead over the canal. Take it easy, boss. This ain't no race. Mind the stop streets. We don't wanna hurt nobody."

Eddy geared down again and touched his foot on the brake.

"Change plans? Like at the bank?" Jan shouted. "What was that all about? What's happening?"

"Gotta trust me, babe."

"Oh, I trust you, Eddy, I'm just thinking what the . . . ?"

"Can't explain everything to you every time, Jan. Told you that. Gotta make plans on the run. Don't worry, everything's going to work out, then you can get mad at me, but right now do what I tell you, okay?"

Jan sat back and stared out the front windshield. Taking a deep breath she brushed the hair off her forehead with her hand and said, "Okay, Eddy. Okay. I'm not mad at you. This isn't a deal breaker."

CANE & ABLE: Hot Pursuit

Cane and Able watched from a distance as Eddy took every turn they expected him to take. "Look at that," Cane said, "it's like someone drawed him a map."

"Someone?" Able snorted. "Someone? King drawed him that map, bro, that's who. 'Drive up here and drive down there and round about and left and right and lookee lookee you's at the airport and you catch the plane and steal the money that ain't yours by no stretch of nobody's imagination."

Cane stole a glance over at his brother. "You okay, bro?"

"Nuffin' wrong wit me. I wanna kill the son of a bitch, that be all."

"What son of a bitch? King? The guy? How 'bout the gal?"

"Kill 'em all, mother fucker, 'cept save the gal to last and have some fun with her before I slit her throat."

"Sounds like a plan to me, Able, 'cept for one thing."

"I know, I know, we gotta let the white folks go, but not with the money."

"Not with the money, brother. I promise you that. They's not leavin' here with our money."

Cane slowed down to maintain a distance between him and the Toyota. When they passed the city limits, the Toyota sped up and Cane nudged the gas. "You know, brother, I gotta ask you one thing."

"Yeah."

"Back there in the village when you pig-stuck that old drunk, why'd you do that?"

"Huh? 'Cause he fucked us up, bro. He give 'em our money. He give 'em our shit, man. What's the problem?'

"'Cause sometime it ain't smart to go killin' people, Able."

"Now you tell me," Able laughed. "Kinda late, ain't it? Maybe you shoulda learned me better."

"Yeah, you right about that, kinda late . . ." Cane watched as the Toyota slowed down and made an unexpected left into the Best Western Hotel on the Northern Highway 6 miles before the turn off to the airport. "What the hell?"

"Slow down," Able advised. "Pull over on the shoulder. Let 'em get to the hotel before you pull in."

JAN & EDDY: Change of Plans

"Eddy, Eddy, what are you doing?" Jan exclaimed as Eddy turned left into the Best Western.

"Part of the new plan."

"Oh, great. Part of the new plan."

Eddy pulled the Toyota in front of the hotel, turned off the key and waited.

"Okay, boss," Razor said peering out the back window. "They turned in, they see you, they slowin' down."

"C'mon, Jan," Eddy said quietly. "Show time. Get out of the car and we'll walk to the main entrance. I've got the briefcase. Walk a little bit fast, but not a run, okay. I'll set the pace. Thanks, Razor." Eddy reached back and patted Razor on the back. "Now keep way down. You know what to do."

"See you on the other side," Razor mumbled, head pressed on the hump of the back seat floor.

As Eddy and Jan approached the front entrance, Eddy took a quick glance and saw the Cadillac that had been following them out of Belize City pull up behind their abandoned Toyota.

CANE & ABLE: Trip the Trap

"What they up to, Cane?"

"Dunno, but hang back, bro. Give 'em a minute then we go in after 'em. Maybe we close the deal right now."

"Gonna phone Leon?"

"We go in first, then we phone Leon."

Cane and Able stepped out of the Caddy, adjusted themselves, and walked up to the entrance of the hotel. Inside, they took off their shades and approached the desk-clerk, a young man in his late teens, probably right out of Form 6.

"Good morning, sirs," the desk-clerk said. "Are you checking in?"

"No, not today," Cane said. "We are looking for a couple of tourists, an older white gentleman and his . . . shall we say, 'companion'. We've been trying to catch up with them. They left a parcel at the restaurant. We were about to pull them over when they turned in here. Have you seen them?"

"Oh, yes, sir. They were here a moment ago."

"Checking in?"

"No, sir. They said they had something for a guest in room 317 . . ."

Able growled.

"But I informed them there was no guest in room 317."

"Let's go. Able you take the stairs. I'll take the elevator. Quick now!"

"But, sirs," the desk-clerk implored, "there is no one in room 317."

"Keep an eye open," Cane ordered the desk-clerk.

The desk-clerk watched the elevator inch upwards past the 2nd floor, stop at the 3rd floor, pause for a few moments, then descend slowly past the second floor, stop at the main floor, open the doors and discharge Cane who hurtled toward him. "I shoulda got a key . . ."

"But there is no key, sir. Only key cards. No guest, no key card."

Able pounded down the stairs and ran panting to the desk. "No one there, Goddamit!"

Before Cane could remonstrate, the desk-clerk cried, "Look, isn't that them. Outside there," he pointed a finger at the front entrance, "getting into a car!"

Cane and Able rushed to the front door, bumping into one another as they stumbled outside. They saw the Toyota burn rubber away from the hotel, race toward the highway and without hesitation cut across traffic heading north toward the airport.

"Son of a bitch. They musta made us," Cane yelled. "Get Leon on the phone. Tell 'im they're coming in and we're right behind 'em. Tell 'im not to block the entrance. They gonna drive that car close as they can get it and make a run for inside. Tell 'im to close in soon's they leave the car."

Cane burned rubber as he swung the Cadillac around and followed the Toyota in hot pursuit. Razor looked in the rear end mirror and smiled. Hook, line and sinker, he thought, not quite sure what the words meant but liking them. He fumbled in his shirt pocket and pulled out his cell phone. Driving one-handed at 90 miles an hour up the Northern Highway, he said, "King! Razor! Ten minutes max!"

JAN & EDDY: Eddy and Charlie Tell All

Jan sat alone in the backseat as Charlie Aurilio's '84 Lincoln propelled them north/east toward the Mexican border. The sun was shimmering hot in the bright blue sky and a few white clouds drifted by like sail boats on the Caribbean sea. Although scorching hot outside, inside the Lincoln the air-conditioner purred, lapping up gallons of gasoline but keeping the occupants comfortable.

Leaning forward with her head between the two front seats her voice dripping with sarcasm, Jan addressed Charlie and Eddy. "Not that I'm not having the best time of my life and not that I am not praying this fun will never end, but will someone, anyone, please tell me what the fuck is going on!"

Eddy and Charlie exchanged looks. "We being followed?" Eddy said.

"Uh uh." Charlie grunted.

"Think we shook them off?"

"Yep."

"Time to tell?"

"Yep."

Eddy swung around in his seat and kissed Jan's forehead. "Jan, you've been incredible. Thank you, thank you, thank you."

"Enough with the sugar, Eddy. Give me some spice."

"Okay, babe, here it is, chapter and verse." Eddy looked at her and smiled before he continued. "Remember when I told King I'd be driving the Toyota and he said, no, Razor drives. Well, I didn't know how much I could trust King then. Didn't want him to know my get-away plan, such as it was, but as we talked I realized that King and Charley here were buddies, not just friends, and if I was going to trust them I had to go all the way, and when King realized I was all-in, after you went to bed I went back to the living room and helped King put together a battle plan that left me speechless."

"King's one smart cookie, Miss Jan," Charlie added, "known him all my life and he's one smart cookie."

"So King phones Charley and sets up the Best Western trap. We walk in the front entrance and out the back door and take off in Charley's taxi. Razor waits in the Toyota and watches for Cane and Able. When he sees that they see him he takes off. They think we're driving the Toyota and take off after us."

"Wasn't that kind of dangerous, Eddy? What about the desk-clerk, couldn't he . . ."

"Desk-clerk was ours, Jan, a nephew of Charlie's. He knew what to do and what to say . . ."

"Okay, but we're not headed for the airport. Where're we going?"

"Mexico."

"Mexico?"

"Cancun."

"Cancun?"

"Air Canada."

"You mean . . ."

"We're flying out tonight."

"But how . . ."

"Got a friend in the Government, Miss Jan, Ministry of Tourism," Charlie explained, one hand on the steering wheel, looking back at Jan. "Told him what we wanted and he said he'd get on it in the morning and I said it's worth a 1,000usd, split it any way you want but do it now, and he phoned back in ½ hour and said 'What flight you want?'"

"Oh my God, Eddy . . ." Jan sat back in her seat processing the information she was receiving. She leaned forward. "What about the border, any trouble there?

"Covered," Eddy said.

"Both sides," Charlie added. "They'll be very happy to see you, believe me. Very happy indeed."

"Then what about the money, won't that be a problem? I mean, maybe not at the border, but on the plane, when we land in Toronto, aren't there laws . . ."

"What money?" Eddy asked.

"The money, Eddy, the money in the briefcase sitting on the seat next to me. That money."

"Oh, that money," Eddy said starting to laugh. "That briefcase's full of stacks of Belizean one dollar bills. Charley can use that to buy gas for the trip back, right, Charley?"

"And maybe a tire or two."

"C'mon, Eddy, quit clowning around. Where's the money Emile owed Cane and Able?"

"In the bank," Eddy put a finger to his lips and shushed Jan. "You see, King started asking questions about my background, what I did for a living, things like that, and when I told him he asked if I was well connected and I said, yes, and he said how high connected and I said the president of the biggest national union in Canada and he said, good, get him on the phone right now, and I phoned the prez last night about 2 o'clock."

"You phoned Jim Douglas at 2 o'clock?"

"Well, it was 3 o'clock in Ontario, but you know, Jim doesn't sleep much . . . ."

"And . . . ?"

"And I told him what was going on and what King thought he could do to help. Then King talked to him and then Jimmy phoned Neville," Eddy turned to Charley to explain. "Neville's the treasurer of our national union. After that, I don't know who phoned who. All I know is that Jimmy phoned back and told me to be at the back door of the ScotiaBank before 8 this morning, Belize time, and we were."

"Yeah, we were, but once we got inside I couldn't follow what you were doing. I kind of stepped back, you know."

"Yeah, I know. I was in the same boat, didn't have a clue. Remember the manager saying that he had received a call early in the morning and he was very pleased to oblige us. After that he whispered that he had put Belizean dollars in the briefcase instead of bundles of $100 usd and that he had opened a joint account in our names for the cool sum of $45,000usd. We didn't even have to sign. And more than that we can access it any time we want from wherever we are to wherever we want it sent. You heard him, when we were leaving, he was exuberant, couldn't stop wishing us good luck. Knew something was going down and was definitely on our side."

"Okay, okay, wow, I get it, I think, but Eddy," Jan said, "a couple more things, sorry, I'm starting to sound like a gangster's moll, but what happened to the 15 thousand we took at the hotel?"

"Charley gets some, King gets some, and we're each taking some back with us to Ontario, less than we are allowed. We sure as hell don't want any trouble getting back into Canada. Don't think Charlie or even King can help us that far away. But you said two questions."

"Right, next question: what's going to happen at the Belize airport?"

"Seems like King's got a big surprise for them," Charlie replied.

"What's that mean, 'King's got a big surprise for them'?"

"We don't know what it means, Miss Jan. He just said he had a big surprise, and knowing the King like I do, it's goin' to be a doozey."

"Eddy? What'd he say last night?"

"He just smiled and said, 'I got an idea for a big surprise for Mr. Cane and Mr. Able'. I said, 'What is it?' and he laughed out loud and said, 'Well, now, that's for me to know and you to find out' and he reached over and smacked me on the knee and said, 'Oh, my, I'm liking it more the more I think on it' and then he said, 'You get some shut-eye, Mr. Eddy, I got some work to do'."

"That's fantastic, utterly fantastic," Jan exclaimed, making herself as comfortable as she could in the backseat before she fell asleep, snoring softly as Charley headed for the border.

KING'S BIG SURPRISE

Goldson's International Airport, named after a prominent politician who helped Belize gain independence in 1983, was an un-prepossessing two-story structure 20 miles northwest of Belize City. International aircraft took off and landed on the runways on the east side of the airport. The main entrances for arrivals and departures faced west. Access to the main entrances was along a one-way two-lane paved road that looped off Airport Road, ran in front of the airport and exited back on Airport Road. Across the road directly in front of the entrances was a large parking lot for the public.

Razor took the turn off Airport Road on two wheels whooping with excitement. Cane followed not far behind, both hands on the steering wheel, swerving as he made the turn, narrowly avoiding driving the Cadillac into the ditch on the side of the road.

Razor roared past the arrivals entrance and slammed on his brakes, skidding in front of the entrance for departures. He immediately slumped down in the driver's seat, quickly adjusting the rear-view mirror of the Toyota so he could see as Cane and Able careened into view and stopped with a jolt 10 feet behind him.

Cane's men under Leon's command stepped out from the overhang shading the entrance doors and approached the Toyota cautiously. They had been ordered to wait till the driver and his passenger exited the car but there was no movement, not even a sign of the occupants. Cane and Able sat in the Cadillac tensed for action, hands on the door handles.

Across the road in the parking lot, four pickup trucks in the front row, windshields faced directly across from the airport, simultaneously backed up and as if on command executed a maneuver that brought them into the space next to the one they had vacated with the pay-load facing the arrival entrance where the Toyota, the Cadillac and Cane's men were frozen in a dramatic tableaux, a stasis of uncertainty.

Directly across the road from them, three men jumped out of each of the pickup trucks. Two clambered into the back of the truck and the third raced around and slammed open the back gate. In the sudden silence as the men in the back of the truck fumbled with explosives, King's voice could be heard barking, "Ready. Set. Fire!" The men in the back of the trucks raised their BBQ lighters and lit the fuses of the first salvo.

At the same time, Cane and Able, unable to restrain themselves any longer and oblivious to the activity in the parking lot across from them, exited their vehicle; on that cue, Cane's men, equally oblivious, surged forward toward the Toyota; and Razor with perfect timing sat up and blasted the Toyota back on the road toward the exit.

As the first round of fireworks whizzed over the heads of Cane and his men exploding in brilliant Technicolor upon contact with the airport façade, a second column of King's troops made up of school kids, women, widows and old-timers emerged from behind parked cars armed with fire-crackers which they lit and lobbed across the road at Cane and his cronies.

"Fire!" King ordered and again the fireworks propelled through the air, some slanting upwards and exploding high above the airport in bizarre bursts of stars, pompons and banners while all the time the squibs and giant noise-makers deafened Cane's men and filled their lungs with acrid smoke.

"Aim low and fire!" King commanded and his men lowered their sights, lit their fireworks and watched as the final barrage whooshed across the road aimed directly at the enemy.

"Okay, troop, head for the bus," King shouted as a min-school bus rolled toward them.

Razor slowed down as he turned the Toyota left on Airport Road and pulled over. He watched as a stream of police cars and ambulances, top-lights twirling, sirens blaring, made the turn to the airport, closely followed by another dozen cars and jeeps and T.V. trucks from the media. When all the vehicles had made the turn, he shot back onto the road and headed for Belize City, not realizing that two trucks loaded with heavily-armed Belize soldiers had made the turn on the exit side and were fast approaching the airport.

Cane and Able and their thugs, pistols drawn and knives unsheathed, stared through the smoke and pink-tinged mist aghast with disbelief as they faced Inspector O'Brien and his police and Captain Furlough and his soldiers all of whom had their firearms out and pointed directly at them. Behind the police and the army, they noted a large gathering of men and women with microphones and cameras in hand.

"Drop your weapons, now," Inspector O'Brien bellowed through his bull-horn.

"You don't need that thing, Manfred," Cane replied, recovering his cool, relieved that the officer facing him was none other than Inspector O'Brien, familiarly known to Cane by his first name, Manfred.

"Do what I say, Cane," the Inspector ordered, "I'm not kidding."

"Drop your guns," Cane turned around and ordered his men as he bent over and laid his '44 Special on the asphalt.

"What the fuck!" Able yelled at him.

"It's gonna be okay, boys. Trust me," Cane replied.

"Put your hands on your heads," the Inspector bellowed.

"Do as he says," Cane said.

"Now line up against that wall over there and spread your legs," the Inspector commanded. He switched off his bull-horn and turned to Captain Furlough. "They're all yours, Captain. Make sure they're clean and we'll take 'em downtown."

"Sorry, Inspector, but I've got orders to take them directly to Hattyville."

"Orders from?"

"My commanding officer, Inspector, who got his orders from the Prime Minister. And, furthermore, Inspector, I'm impounding that Cadillac. Same chain of command."

"Stand down, men," the Inspector ordered his men. "Have a smoke, whatever, this matter's out of our hands. But, Captain, one favour? I want to talk to one of the prisoners. That one," he pointed out Cane, "right there."

"Okay, talk to him."

"What the hell's going on, Cane?" Inspector Manfred O'Brien demanded in a hushed voice when they stood alone.

"Don't know, Manfred, honest I don't. We had some business here, that's all. No big deal. Then all hell broke loose."

"Yeah, we know. Somebody phoned dispatch, said you and your brother was gonna blow up the airport. You dealin' with a full deck here, Cane? We arrive on the scene and all we see is you and your boys with guns drawn standing in a pile of shot-off fireworks. Not to mention that we are both surrounded by a pack of reporters with note books, cameras and film crews. You better make up a story real fast, Cane, 'cause the jackals are coming to eat you up."

Cane stared, incredulous, slowly realizing that he had been set up, suddenly understanding the implications of his defeat. "Oh, Jesus fucking Christ! I get it now. When you comin' down the road, I look up and seen a school mini-bus leavin' the parking lot. That was them!"

"Who is 'them', man? C'mon, give me something to tell the press, give me something to take back to the Chief."

"That was King and his crew, that who."

"King and his crew?"

"Yeah, man, look across there."

The Inspector turned and looked at the backed-up pick-up trucks, their payloads heaped with two feet of sand and remnants of fireworks.

"So?"

"It was the King, Manfred. Thought I recognized his voice. Then they took off in that school bus. You gotta get those bastards before they get back home."

"You talkin' 'bout King of King Street? You shittin' me, man. King don't have much step left in his walk. Think he organized all this? That ain't gonna fly nowhere."

"Tell the Chief . . ."

"Know what, Chief's not gonna help, Cane. Right now, he don't even know your name."

"Oh, Goddamn. I done wet-work for that mother-fucker. Helped you, too, man. Alibi'd you for that kid from Plues Street's so-called drowning. 'Member that?"

Inspector Andy O'Brien looked at Cane, not with pity but disgust. "Now, why'd you want to piss off the one guy who might've helped you? Let me put you on notice, Cane. You mention any of that shit today or any other day, you'll be dead before tomorrow and your family, too." He turned around, motioning to one of his men. "Sargeant, take this piece of shit back over there to his buddies. The Army'll take good care of them. And if he tries anything, shoot the ignorant son if a bitch."

JAN & EDDY: Flying Home

Air Canada flight 901 lifted off the tarmac in Cancun at ten minutes past midnight with an eta in Toronto of 06:00 est. Eddy and Jan sat in aisle seats across from one another, holding hands across the aisle as the plane gained altitude. Later, half-asleep, Eddy reached again across the aisle for Jan's hand, just as a steward pushed her cart of food and drinks between them, bumping his hand. Without thought, Eddy jumped up, hands clenched into fists, ready to strike out.

"Take it easy, soldier," the server, a petite brunette with a mischievous smile, said. "I'm a friend, not a foe. What'd you like to drink?"

Flustered, Eddy took a deep breath and smiled back at the server. "Sorry, musta dozed off. No harm meant. Coffee, black, please."

As the steward pushed her cart further down the aisle, Eddy looked sheepishly over at Jan. "Sorry, babe. What's that expression, 'the more things change the more they remain the same?'"

"Yes, only I don't think it applies here, Eddy. I think it should be the more things change, the better they get."

When the steward returned with her cart, she was stopped by the locked hands of Eddy and Jan stretched across the aisle, both fast asleep.

"Beep, beep," she said, gently nudging their fingers.

THE END

ARMED AND DANGEROUS

SCENE 1 (The Bust)

Rory Valquez, aka Mike Tyson, was smoking weed with his auntie in their shack on the leeside of Caye Santana[2], an island off the coast of Belize in Central America when the Santana cops broke down the door and assaulted them.

"What the fuck?" his aunt shouted.

Rory was going to say something like, "Hey, man, whass happenin'?" but a cop rousted him off the couch and slammed him against the wall.

From his vantage point slammed against the wall, Rory counted 2 or 3 cops in the room, guns drawn, maybe 4, shouting at him.

One of them held him by the throat while another frisked him.

"What's this?" the cop frisking him said, holding up a baggie with a small amount of marijuana in it.

"What's this?" another cop shouted coming out of the bedroom with a larger amount of cocaine in it.

"That's . . ."

"Shut up, Rory," his aunt screamed. "Don't say nothin'". She was squirming in the grasp of a big bald-headed cop with sweat pouring from his eyebrows. "These pigs don't got no right to ask you nothin'!"

The boss cop stepped up to Rory and snarled, "Got you, kid. Think you can come to our island and fuck us up? Fuck you. Where you goin' you gonna need a new asshole every week. Cuff the mother fucker."

The cop with his hand on Rory's throat stepped back and Rory took the only chance he knew he would get. He pushed off the cop who was trying to cuff him, ducked low and swung around boss cop, pushed his auntie into the cop who was trying to block his path to the doorway, raced outside and flew over the porch railing, landing on his feet. He took off, running fast, then faster, then faster still, headed for the sea-side of the island with no plan, no idea even what he was doing, just running faster than he had ever run in his life.

---

[2] Caye Santana is an imaginary island off the coast of Belize in the Caribbean Sea

BACK-FLASH (Rory Valquez in San Bight)

Rory Valquez was 16 years old when the cops broke into his shack on Santana.

The police later described him as approximately 5' 4" tall, 110 lbs, black hair, brown eyes, medium-brown skin colour, prominent scars on the cheekbones.

He was born and raised in San Bight,[3] a downtrodden village in the south of Belize, 10 miles north of the village of Hermanosa[4] at the tip of a peninsula which boasted a sand-swept beach, wooden walkways, handicraft shops and a plethora of restaurants and pastel-painted cabanas on the sea shore for tourists with a taste for adventure and a yen for creature comfort. Hermanosa faced the challenges of tourism, survived its impact and thrived.

San Bight turned its back on the influx of foreigners and sulked.

San Bight became a gateway, not a destination, and made no effort to attract the tourists who drove past over bumpy sometimes almost un-passable roads with no encouragement to stop and stay awhile.

Rory Valquez was the seventh of ten children. His mother worked hard to make ends meet and keep the kids healthy and the shanty clean but with no electricity she laundered by hand and cooked on a coal pot and without a refrigerator she relied on catch-of-the-day and the occasional gibnut or iguana friends brought to her. Other than that it was canned food from the local Chinese grocery store and fresh vegetables from the Mennonite community 50 miles away and the costs were more prohibitive than other parts of mainland Belize.

Rory was unique in the village in one way only. He had no grandparents. His mother's mother and father had come to San Bight to settle years before, convinced they had found their homeland, but after years of frustration and the theft of their only daughter, Rory's mother, by her husband, Rory's father, they had reluctantly returned to Honduras, severing all connection with Rory's family.

Nothing was known about Rory's father's family. But there were rumours.

Rory's father was a fisherman who seldom fished though in his day was heralded as one of the best in the area. At first he turned his catch over to his wife who took what the family needed and sold the rest. As time passed, he turned his catch over to his wife minus the fish he sold at the seashore to buy rum. At a certain point in his life he quit fishing.

Drugs had arrived in San Bight as a point of entry into Belize from South America and then on to Belize City, an up-and-coming distribution centre and then into Mexico and then north into the U.S. and Canada.

---

[3] San Bight is an imaginary hamlet on the coast of the Placencia Peninsula

[4] Hermanosa is an imaginary village at the tip of the Placencia Peninsula

His father joined a local gang whose job it was to ensure the drugs flowed through without interference from police, politicians or gangs from outside the area who wanted to share the plunder.

It was during this time that his father nick-named him Mike Tyson, a black boxer from the USA of legendary savagery whom his father had never seen but whose myth of impregnable superiority made him a worthy man for his father's son to emulate. His father did not know much but he knew you had to be hard to survive and he pounded that lesson into his son on a regular basis, boxing Rory aka Mike Tyson bare-fisted on the wet seashore as the tide went out and the sun sunk below the horizon.

Although forced to attend the local 7th Day Adventist School for five years, Rory managed to achieve the lowest possible standard of education in Belize where education is mandatory until the age of 16.

Mandatory, but not cost-free. Though most schools were religion-based, there was little Christian mercy shown and if poverty-stricken parents could not pay for the books, school uniform and tuition of the child, like Rory Valquez, after a short period of grace the child's name was no longer called in the homeroom and soon after expunged from the school records

There was no record of Rory Valquez in the Ministry of Education files in the capital city of Belmopan. For all intents and purposes, Rory had officially never dropped out because had never dropped in.

For the better part of his childhood in San Bight on the shores of the Caribbean Sea, Rory Valquez ran wild and free.

At age 11, when his father sent him to live in Belize City, he could neither read nor write nor speak English. He could speak Garifuna, the native tongue of his parents and some Creole, the patios of the country. He had a brain and he could think, but his thoughts were limited by circumstance and his communication skills by language.

Neighbours in San Bight generally agreed that Rory Valdez left the village as a child and came back from the City from time to time in his teens with a bad attitude and a streak of mean.

SCENE 2 (The Chase,)

Rory Valquez criss-crossed the streets of Santana headed towards the sea. He had only lived on the island for a few months but the island was small and though most of his explorations of it took place at night he knew where he was headed. As he raced along he formulated a get-away plan that might at the least break him loose from the police and give him time to think things through.

He felt the presence of police pursuit, noting the startled look on the faces of tourists and villagers as he dashed by. He heard muffled shouts behind him. Glancing right as he crossed an intersection on the sand-packed road, he spotted a police golf-cart a block over crossing seconds ahead of him. Without hesitation he swung right and pounded down the street, hoping to cross over two blocks and reach the sea on the other side of the cops.

Ahead of him he saw an old tourist with a red bandana wrapped around his head about to mount his bike in front of the First Caribbean Bank. Rory lowered his shoulder and sent the old man sprawling in the dust, jumped on the old man's bike and pedaled furiously away, careening wildly till he brought the bike under control, then twisted and turned to avoid the golf carts that plied the road and the pedestrians who wandered up, down and across it.

Behind him, one of the policemen on foot made the 90 degree turn in hot pursuit but tripped over his own feet and fell to the ground exhausted, managing only to get on his hands and knees and desperately try to catch his breath.

Another policeman who made the turn passed his fallen comrade and came upon the fallen old man with the red bandana struggling to stay on his feet. The cop watched the kid disappear into the distance and stopped briefly to contact by cell phone police headquarters to inform dispatch that the kid had assaulted a tourist, stolen the tourist's bike and was headed south.

Two more policemen arrived at the intersection and ran straight through, not realizing that the kid had changed direction.

Rory Valquez glanced over his shoulder and saw no one in pursuit. It occurred to him in that instant that he might elude the cops and buy himself a little freedom. He pumped the pedals hard, exhilarated.

At the police station, the Chief, informed of the assault on the tourist and the bike theft, ordered his dispatcher to contact Constable Donald Usher on bike patrol in New Town, a small community recently developed on the northern fringe of the mostly unsettled southern part of the island.

"I've got him on his cell phone, sir," the dispatcher said. "What should I tell him?"

"Tell him there's an escaped felon on a bike headed south."

"Constable Usher wants to know his status, sir."

"What the hell!" the Chief exploded. "He's a cop. Apprehend and arrest the . . ."

"Not Usher, sir," the dispatcher said patiently, "the status of the kid on the bike, sir, like is he armed, is he a danger?"

"Well, he escaped arrest didn't he? He's already knocked a guy down and stole his bike. You bet he's a danger.

Is he armed? How the hell should I know? All I know I'm not sending any one of my men into a situation where their lives may be at stake, so tell Usher the kid's armed and dangerous. And tell him to intercept the kid on the path along the coast. That kid can't go straight south on the street he's on now, he's gotta turn right back into town or left to the sea. My bet's on the sea."

Constable Usher listened to his instructions and snapped shut his cell phone. He reached his right hand down to the holster strapped on his hip and released the catch that secured the 38 calibre police-issue revolver inside. An escaped felon on the run. Armed and dangerous. His heart beat fast as the adrenaline clicked in. Intercept. Apprehend. Arrest. He pushed off with his left foot and began pedaling quickly to the path by the sea that led to the south of the island.

Rory Valquez had made the left turn where the street t-boned. In minutes he reached the sea and picked up the path that would take him to the south of the island. There was no sight or sound of pursuit. He stood up on his bike and pedaled as hard as he could, grunting with every stroke.

Constable Usher felt his thighs burn as he pedaled his bike hard east to the sea.

Rory Valquez and Constable Usher were going full-tilt when they collided.

BACK-FLASH (The Red Bandana Tourist)

Larry Duval, a sixty-seven year old ex-welder from Brantford, Ontario, woke up as usual around six a.m. that day, made coffee as his wife, Betty, slept a little longer, took the coffee out to the verandah of his cabana and watched the locals pass quietly by on foot, by bike or driving battery-powered golf-carts as they went about their business.

It was a serene time of day. The sun was up but not so bright it glared off the white sand-packed roads. Red and pink bougainvilleas shone with a soft brilliance. The vegetation had a luster it lost beneath the unremitting rays of the mid-day sun. Black-sheened grackles perched on overhead wires and orioles splashed orange on the leathery green leaves of the zericote trees, jumping from branch to branch, blending in with the orange zericote flowers they fed on.

Afterwards, he showered while Betty washed and dried their breakfast dishes, and dressed for an early trip downtown to pick up some odds and ends and to visit the ATM at the local bank. He wore sandals, khaki shorts, a bright short-sleeved shirt with *Belize* emblazoned on it and wrapped around his head a bright red bandana which he thought contrasted nicely with his long white hair and, more practically, stopped the perspiration from trickling into his eyes and clouding his glasses.

Larry felt good as he pedaled downtown. He rode one-handed to wave to friends and said "Good morning' or 'Beautiful day' to pedestrians who walked toward him. He and Betty had been visiting Belize off and on for years but now, in retirement, they spent a full month on Santana at the Oasi Apartments.

Many Belizeans described their country as Paradise. Larry would not go that far, not if Belize City was included, but if you were just talking about Santana you were not far off the mark.

He skipped down the step from the bank after withdrawing some money and was about to mount his bike when he suddenly felt himself thrown hard to the ground. Stunned and disoriented, he struggled to get up, lost his balance and fell back to the ground.

"You okay, Pops," a cop asked, hauling him to his feet and holding him upright.

"No, I don't think so," Larry replied, slightly winded, somewhat in pain in parts of his body, and oddly embarrassed. "What the hell happened?"

"Some punk kid knocked you down and stole your bike, sir."

"A kid?"

"Yes, sir. Some kid we after for drugs, he knocked you down and took your bike. But don't worry, we gonna get him. Get back your bike too."

After supper that night, Betty said, "How do you feel, love. I mean, I know you're stiff and sore, but, you know, how do you feel?"

"Not so great. Kind of embarrassed, but I'll get over that. Bike's pretty banged up but I can get it fixed when the cops release it, doesn't really mean much in the scheme of things, does it? No, it's not that, it's what with the kid? Cops say he's only fifteen or sixteen. What's that all about? Then he shoots a cop and almost kills him and now he's got the cop's gun and the cops are beating the swamp for him. What the hell? What was he running from?"

Betty sat next to him on the couch and took his hand. "It's hard to understand, Larry, I'm struggling with it, too."

"Yeah, I mean I, we, wanted a safe place to vacation, right, and we thought we'd found that place, and now I'm not so sure, know what I mean? Now I'm not so sure at all."

BACK-FLASH (Rory Valquez in Belize City)

If anything, life for Rory Valquez got worse instead of better when he was shipped to his auntie in Belize City.

Belize City had one of the worst records in North, Central and South America for murders per population. The media overlooked this fact because Belize City was inhabited by only 80,000 census-identified citizens, therefore, its total numbers looked puny when compared to its immediate neighbors Guatemala City and Mexico City, both of which had millions of inhabitants. Compared to these and other cities, Belize City numbers were small, but proportionately Belize City was right up there with the champions.

His auntie lived in the worst shack on stilts above a canal in the worst enclave in the worst section of Belize City. Her friends and associates were amongst the worst citizens of Belize City and she was probably the worst auntie in the world.

Rory Valquez had no idea in any language what 'auntie' meant. He certainly did not know whether she was the sister of his mother or his father or neither. He only knew that when he was dumped off at her shanty above the canal waters as an 11 year old he would rather have been back in San Bight pretending he was Mike Tyson boxing with his father on the beach than curled up on the floor at night in his aunties' shanty, covered by a worn-out blanket, shivering with fever and suffering from home-sickness.

Over the next five years, Rory Valquez attended what his auntie described as the 'School of Hard-Knocks', not the school proscribed by the government of Belize. People say an education opens doors", she laughed. "The only door your education will ever open is the prison door."

Realizing that Rory spoke no English, she ordered all around him, including those who spoke Spanish as their first language, to speak to her nephew in nothing but English.

While Rory was learning English, his auntie, on orders from Cane, the most prominent drug-lord in Belize City, dressed Rory up to make him presentable as a uniformed student with a back-pack. She put him out on the street across from schools and churches and later in the day in play-clothes with a little lunch bucket in his grasp at designated street corners under designated street lights. He was dropped off, most often by a guy on a bicycle, picked up, sometime in a car, taken to a drop-off spot where grown men would take his backpack or bucket and empty it. Then, he would be returned home where his auntie, if she had not passed out from whatever it was she took, would scream at him, often in Garifuna, which he understood, slap him a few times and return to whatever it was she had been doing.

Not satisfied with his progress in English and cursing his mangled Spanglish mixed with Garifuna, Creole with a little Mayan thrown in, she identified Rory to her friends and fellow-addicts as an idiot child from San Bight, home of the human stupid people.

At first he did not realize why all the grown-ups laughed at him, but as time went by and his English improved he began to understand.

Cane, in particular, a man they all cowered in front of and bowed down before, called him 'tard' and 'stupe', and made him dance around the room, cracking his cane on the floor, trying to hit the kid's feet, making him jump up and down while everybody laughed.

Cane paid regular visits to the stink-holes of the inner city to let it be known that without him their corpses would be thrown into the canals that surrounded Belize City and washed out to the Caribbean Sea.

Cane was born and raised in Belize City but had his roots in the Garifuna communities of San Bight and Dangriga, roots he did not cherish but took advantage of.

Gang-connected from boyhood, Cane was himself a graduate of the 'School of Hard Knocks' where he was an over-achiever with straight A's in theft, assault and battery, prostitution and later armed robbery and drug-trafficking. After a three year stretch in Hattyville Prison, he was granted a post-graduate degree in Criminal Proficiency.

By the time that Rory arrived on the scene, Cane, after another five year stretch in Hattyville and a murderous overthrow of the old gang leadership, was firmly ensconced as the gang's war-lord.

One of his first initiatives as war-lord was to implement the practice of talent-searches in the most impoverished of the Garifuna communities, whereby some of his most trusted lieutenants were sent out to discover potential gang-members, buy them from their parents, and bring them back to the City for training.

Rory Valquez was such a discovery, but he did not know it then.

All he knew then was that he both feared and hated Cane in about equal amounts of fervour.

Rory Valquez' life was not all fear and hatred. Like anyone else, he responded to the people he met day-to-day with a variety of emotions from interest to apathy to envy and disgust.

He liked Marcos, a Spanish-speaking soldier in Cane's army of thugs. Marcos was bright and lively with long black hair and gold-flashing teeth. He talked Spanish and Creole in his auntie's shanty till his auntie shushed him and made him speak English, then he laughed and said, "My liddle brother, let me tell you 'bout Hinglish. You gotta learn it, si, but it stupid language. Don't try unnerstan it, comprende? Go with it, man. Someone say, 'Yes or NO' lissen what he say, *how* he say it. Someone say, 'Do you KNOW?' sound the same, eh amigo, but lissen the way I tell you, lissen *how* he say it, think wha'choo bin talkin 'bout, that make the difference, man'.

Rory Valquez liked Anthony Boner, a kid from someplace else but similar to San Bight. They played when they had time off. Ran the streets pell-mell, bumping into strangers on purpose, begging from the tourists, stealing from the china-men by pretending to shop in their super-stores and stuffing their pockets with cans and candy, anything small they could shove in their pockets and dash outside and disappear around the corner, laughing like crazy.

Anthony was a year older and had been on the streets as an apprentice gang-member a year longer than Rory but somehow he seemed much smarter and wiser. Once, after ripping off the collection box in a church, they ran all the way to Bird's Isle and hid behind the basketball court where no one would ever look for them. Still panting, Anthony said, "You gotta be careful, man."

"'Bout what?" Rory replied.

"They watchin' you, and me too."

"Who?"

"Cane and the gang, thass who."

"Why? What we done wrong. We juss thievin' thass all."

"No, it's not that, man. We gotta pass the test, man, or we doan go nowhere."

"Whaddya talkin"bout, man? Wha' test?"

"You doan know, do you? You doan know why you here, do you?"

"Sure, 'cause I come to stay with auntie, thass why."

"Yeah, but you know why you come stay with auntie? Thass what you doan know, man. You come stay with auntie 'cause you in trainin' . . ."

"Trainin' fer what, man?"

"Trainin' to b'long to the gang, man. Thass what. An if they doan like what you doin' in trainin', they gonna kick out your ass, maybe worse. An' if they like what you doin', they gonna give you a test. And that test be that you gotta kill someone, man. You gotta kill sommen Cane tells you to kill, man, even a friend, doan matter. You gotta prove you can kill for Cane. You kill for Cane, you in. You doan, you dead."

"Wow, man," Rory responded. "You sure auntie know 'bout all this?"

"Auntie know 'bout all this, man. An' she ain't even you auntie. She just a bitch Cane lets hang around 'cause they go way back, but she nothin' now, man, just do Cane's biddin' to keep her high, thass all. She do anythin' he want, juss keep her high."

"My mommy and daddy know this?"

"Your mommy and your daddy sol' you to Cane, man. Juss like my mommy and daddy sol' me."

Rory shook his head with disbelief. He could not, he would not accept that he had been sold and shipped off to Cane in the City, but deep down he had doubts, deep down he knew it might be true.

Another time, sitting side by side next to over-filled garbage cans in a narrow one-way alley after a night on the streets doing drug-deals, Rory and Anthony passed a bottle of One Barrel rum back and forth and slowly numbed themselves. "Gotta question, man," Rory said to Anthony.

"Whass that?"

"Boner doan soun' like a Belizean name, know what I mean? Where'd 'Boner' come from?"

"Boner ain't my name, man. It's what they call me, my gang name. You know what is 'boner' in English? In English, 'boner' mean 'hard-on', mean you ready to fuck. One time I'm runnin' round naked right where you livin' now, and one a the guys say, "Look at that liddle kid, he got a boner, and thass what they called me since that time. Boner."

"Why'd they do that, man?"

"'Cause it make you feel bad, make you feel 'shamed. They wanna break you down, man. Wanna train you and break you down at the same time, then wanna stan' you up and say look a what we got here, we got a little man gonna do whatever we tell 'im to do. Doan you know they doin' you the same way, man, callin' you retard and stupid and when they finish, when they grind you down, what's left a Rory?"

One early morning several months later, Rory checked into a bar where everybody carried a gun, handed over the money for the drugs he had delivered, and said to anyone who could hear him, "Where's Anthony?"

Marcos the Spaniard called through the smell and the smoke and the noise of the bar, "My little friend, c'mon over here. C'mon, amigo, por favor."

Rory approached the table where the men were sitting. "Seen Anthony?"

A cane smashed on the table, upsetting drinks and sending bottles flying.

"Boner took a dive into the canal," Cane, the drug-lord said. "Wanted to wash his clothes in the filthy canal water, got flushed out to sea like a piece of shit from an open toilet. If shit can swim he's out there with the fishes on the barrier reef."

Cane reached across the table and gripped Rory's neck, thumb pressed on Rory's adam's apple. "Boner made a little boner. And you, my little man, you had better behave yourself or you will be swimming with him. You understand?"

"Yes, boss, I understand," Rory said obediently. And he did. He knew that Anthony had betrayed them. And he knew why. What he did not know was what to do about it. When would it be his time to decide? He knew he was being trained and would soon have to pledge his loyalty to the gang by killing someone that Cane wanted dead. It was not the killing that bothered him, not as much as it bothered Anthony. Human life, other than his own, meant very little to Rory. It was the realization that if he did not pledge his loyalty to the gang it would be himself who would be killed. You were in or you were dead and Rory did not like either option.

Rory Valquez also liked Rachel Shaw, a pretty Creole girl who worked at a restaurant serving traditional Belizean food and beer, the gang's favourite 'hot spot' and hang-out.

Rachel flirted with Rory when he came in and sat down and waited for her to take his order, though she quickly learned that he was a young man of habit. If the special was cow-foot soup or rellano he would order it. If not he would order two eggs over with re-fried beans, a double order of breakfast sausage and fry jacks. Now and then, for variety, he would order a hamburger with cheese and bacon with a side of fries.

She liked his shyness, the way he mumbled when she talked to him, looking away from her, though she noticed how his eyes followed her when she was serving at another table. She smiled at him and said nice words and the guys laughed and said, 'She like you, hombre. She some nice puta, you gotta get some a that.'

But Rory did not know how to flirt back. He liked the way she looked, shining brown eyes, bright straight teeth, soft red lips that looked like candy. But he did not understand his feelings toward her. She was just a puta, after all. Like his father always said, women were born for two reasons only, citing his own wife, Rory's mother, as proof of his observation. According to his father, his mother only lived to serve her husband's sexual and domestic needs and bear children for him. Other than that, she served no purpose whatsoever, except cooking and cleaning and raising the kids.

His father also said, 'Don't stick it down there', gesturing to the crotch, 'less the bitch you wife an' you wanna have a baby. Stick it down there and shoot you juice into some bitch ain't you wife, that bitch gonna make you pay every time. How you s'posed to know that kid for you or some-other? No, you stick it inna mouth, shoot you juice, let some-other make a baby'.

Rory did not want to stick it anywhere in Rachel. He got serviced all he wanted by the drug-addled bitches that would do anything for a fix as he made his drop-offs and pick-ups around the city. He wanted something else but he did not know what it was.

SCENE 3 (Confrontation with a Cop)

Rory Valquez hurled sideways from the impact of the bicycles, landing on his left shoulder on a tuft of vegetation.

Constable Usher flipped over the handle bars and landed on his back on the hard-packed path.

Valquez crab-crawled back a few feet clutching his shoulder, simultaneously assessing the damage to his bike and his current situation vis a vis the cops in pursuit.

Usher, winded, looked up at the deep blue Belizean sky and wondered whether he would ever breathe again.

Valquez noted that the front wheel of his bike was twisted, not likely ride-able. The cop's bike didn't look much better, not a good get-away option.

The cop looked like he was glued to the ground, maybe even dead. There was no other sound except birds squawking in the bush beside them, the bush that had blind-sided them. He struggled upright, a little dazed, still clutching his shoulder, and approached the cop on the ground.

Usher looked up and saw a kid leaning over him, the kid's face magnified as he bent over Usher's face, big nose and large brown eyes getting closer like in a bad dream. Suddenly, the air expelled from his lungs and he began to breathe again, fresh almost orgasmic breaths, filling his brain with oxygen so he could think and respond.

Valquez stepped back and kicked Usher in the head. "Fuck you," he cried out. "Leave me alone, you fuck. Leave me alone."

Usher caught Valquez' foot as he tried to kick him again, twisted it and sent Valquez tumbling to the ground. Before Usher could roll over and get on his feet, Valquez sprung up and caught Usher with a boot to the ribs. Valquez followed Usher as he crawled on his hands and knees and kicked upwards into his stomach, another kick to his ribs and as Usher deflated on the ground Valquez stomped on his back.

Upright and triumphant, gasping for breath, Valquez looked at his opponent flattened in front of him and noticed for the first time the butt of Usher's revolver peeking out from the holster strapped to his hip.

"Holy fuck," Valquez muttered as he bent down and plucked the revolver from the holster. "Jesus fucking Christ".

"Don't do it, kid," Usher pleaded as he rolled over, watching as the kid stepped back, clicked off the safety, walked over and lowered the gun to his face.

"Why not?"

"'Cause you kill me, you dead, man. Hear me? Pull that trigger, you dead as me."

"I be dead from day I born, man. Doan you know that?"

Usher made one last desperate attempt to defend himself before the revolver exploded.

SCENE 4 (The Strange Fate of Officer Usher)

The only motorized police car on the island skidded to a halt when the driver saw Constable Usher's body spread-eagled on the path, Usher's bicycle and another bicycle stretched twisted on either side of the road. The driver and his partner leapt out of the car and ran to the fallen body of their comrade.

Constable Usher lay on his back, blood staining the khaki sleeve of his left shoulder, blood forming a pool beneath him.

The driver ran back to the police car to call for help while his partner performed emergency first aid on Usher.

Usher was in pain but conscious. "Where's the kid," he asked his fellow cop.

"Kid's gone."

"Where?"

"Down south. Down to the mangrove swamps. Don't worry. We'll get him. We'll get the son of a bitch. You gonna be okay?"

"Yeah, seems like. Lost some blood, but why ain't I dead?"

"'Cause he shot you in the arm, man, that's why."

"Kid had me dead-to-rights. Had my gun. Had me flat on my back. Knew how to take off the safety. Stood over me super cool. Aimed straight at my heart. And missed?"

"You need some rest, mi amigo. But don't worry. He won't get off this island alive."

SCENE 5 (The Hidey-Hole)

Rory Valquez was exhausted by the time he reached his hidey-hole deep in the south-end of the island amidst mangrove trees leeching on swamp water.

Rory had discovered the hidey-hole on one of his many visits to the south-end.

Once, bending over to pick up what he thought was a gold coin but turned out to be the golden top of a rum bottle, he noticed an indentation between the ground and a mound of garbage covering it. He reached down and pulled on the opening and it gave way. He pulled again and it opened up more and then again and it creaked open a few more inches and then again and it yawned open maybe a whole foot.

'It' was a bent, rolled-over sheet of corrugated metal, the kind used as roofs and sides for shacks on the island. It was maybe 2 and ½ feet wide and the earth-end had become imbedded, except for the opening Rory had discovered. The rest of it had snuggled between the tarantula-like roots of a black mangrove tree, bent downward at a 15 degree angle.

He could not tell how deep it was but later that night when he returned with a flashlight he had stolen from a back-packer he saw that it dipped down maybe 3 or 3 and ½ feet and was pinched tight and dry at the bottom. Immediately he tugged on the opening at the front and crouched in front of it, slowly inserting his legs through the opening, slowly lowering himself down.

It was a perfect fit. He was not a big boy at 16. About 5'4, maybe 110 pounds. He had to bend his legs and huddle up and his bare arms and legs scraped the corrugated metal, but it felt good, it felt safe, it felt secure. It felt like a cocoon.

It felt like his hidey-hole. A home away from home.

SCENE 6 (The Speech)

Superintendent Roberto Reyes the Third blinked his eyes and sipped some water before he addressed his troops, which, at that time, numbered eight, the full complement on Santana.

"Lissen up, and lissen good. We got a officer down and that mean we gotta get the son of a bitch that done it.

Now lissen and lissen hard what I gotta say. I'm sayin' we gotta bring this son of a bitch that shot and nearly killed our fellow-officer to Justice. That mean we gotta catch him, not kill him, hear what I'm sayin'. Bring him in and let 'im stand trial. Let 'im have his day in court. Let 'im do his time.

But thing is, you go out there lookin' for 'im, you riskin' you lifes and you got wifes and chil'ren to think about. That punk-kid got a police-issue revolver and he know how to use it. That makes him armed and dangerous. He showed he can use it, but you gotta serve a higher power, you gotta serve Justice, you hear that? Justice.

That kid come outa hidin', hands in the air, surrendering, doan shoot him dead. Unarmed kid shot dead doan look so good, so doan do it and doan worry, we'll make him pay down the road.

Now, somethin' else could happen. He could come out shootin' with that gun and then you gotta defend yourselfs. Doan hesitate, I am right now tellin' you to shoot to kill if he comes at you wavin' a gun. Don't kill yourselfs in the cross-fire, but in the case he come out shootin', kill 'im. Hear what I'm sayin'? Shoot 'im dead.

There's somethin' else I'm thinkin'. Maybe he disappear. Never hear a him again. Friends get him off the island. They in the City laughing at us, you unnerstan'?

Well, let the cops in the City track him down and bring 'im to Justice, not our job no more.

Or maybe that poor son of a bitch drowns or maybe digs himself so deep in a hole he gets turned upside down and dies with his mouth full of his own shit."

The cops laughed appreciatively at the Superintendent's wit.

'Think about it. Jus' . . . gone. No body. No arrest, no charges, no conviction, no sentence to a life of getting ass-fucked forever at Hattyville. Save a lotta money and keep the kid from a life-time of abuse, but would that serve Justice? Some would say yes and some would say no but you guys on the front-line know what you gotta do. If you be lissenin' you know what you gotta do.

We got officers comin' over from San Pedro, Belize City and Orange Walk. We thank 'em for comin' to help us, but whatever happens, *whatever happens,* we gotta be the ones that make it happen. Is that clear!"

The Superintendent looked at his men and saw them nod their heads and mutter assent.

"Force, dismissed," he barked.

Superintendent Ronaldo Reyes the Third turned and marched back to his office, slamming the door behind him. He staggered over to the chair behind his desk and collapsed, head on his arms on the top of the desk.

"Sir," his dispatcher exclaimed as he followed the Superintendent into his office. "You okay?"

"I'm okay, Pierce. I'm okay," the Superintendent replied, peeking up, eyeing his dispatcher over his forearms. "Think I'd make a good politician?"

"Sure. Why you askin'?"

"Thinkin' a runnin' for council next year. Changes comin' too fast on Santana. Gotta slow her down or next thing you know the tourists gonna pour in with their pockets full of credit cards and cash and the bad guys only half a step behind them. Then what're we gonna do?"

Meanwhile, in the meeting room, the constables milled about, talking amongst themselves. A newly-arrived constable, a 'newbie' as they were called, approached a veteran on the Santana Police Force.

"Hey, Tomy, gotta question."

"Yeah?"

"What the fuck the Soup want us to do, man? We gonna serve Justice, we gonna take 'im alive, we gonna kill 'im dead."

"Soup don't make good speeches, man. All over the map. He's a cop, notta politician."

"Yeah, man, but he's tryin' tell us somethin'"

"Okay. Some things he gotta say, like about Justice, like about doan shoot unarmed man. Forget all that, man. Only one thing Soup's sayin', he's sayin' that kids gotta be killed by us, man, by the Santana police force, else we look real bad in the eyes of others . . ."

"But he say if the kid come out hands up, doan shoot 'im."

"No, man. He's sayin' the kid comes out hands up, no gun, shoot 'im dead. The kid'll have a gun in his hand long as one a us kill 'im and get to the body first."

"Oh," the newbie said, "I get it. Wow."

SCENE 7 (Life in the Hidey-Hole)

Rory Valquez was panting heavily as he pulled down on the corrugated sheet and stuffed it six inches deep beneath the surface.

The hidey-hole was hot and dark and it was hard to breathe but it was secure. Gradually he caught his breath, calmed down, listening for sounds of pursuit, knowing it would take time to organize a search of the south end but not wanting to get careless.

As soon as he was able to compose himself, he reached down with his right hand and scratched until he found the water-proof purse he had stolen weeks ago. Sightless, he pulled it up to his face and un-zipped it. His fingers probed and pulled out a stack of American bills, more than 500 dollars worth. He curled them up and stuffed them in his pocket. The rings and necklaces he left inside the purse and shoved it back behind him.

The money was meant to get him away from Cane and Belize City but it looked more likely it was his ticket back to Cane and the City, unless he could use it to get a plane to Guatemala or Honduras. At least four planes, sometime more, touched down on Caye Santana from Mexico or Belize City every day and he was sure some of them flew straight to neighbouring countries. He knew he might have to wait a long time before he could stroll into the ticket-booth at the ricky-dicky airport and buy a ticket, one-way any-where but out-of-here.

With his nose at an air-vent he had created at the corners of the opening, he took deep breaths, still listening for sounds of pursuit, but more relaxed, more able now to reflect on what had happened no more than an hour ago.

It was obvious someone had ratted him out. Who? Why? His mind flicked by a number of scenarios but none of them fit.

Then there was the matter of the cops chasing him after he bolted out of the shack, lept off the verandah and took off. It was difficult to second-guess himself but he had to ask why had he run?

At any time in his escape and flight through the streets of Santana he could have given up, not really surrendered, just given up, just said, 'Okay guys, you got me, I give it my best shot. What now?' They did not have that much against him, just a little weed, and he could say the coke belonged to his auntie. And then, in the background, there was Cane, his nemesis and saviour who could intervene and save him.

Most likely they would have taken him back to the police station and smacked him around, maybe even beat him bad and thrown him in jail for a few days because he knocked over that stupid old tourist and stole his bike; then they might have shipped him back to Belize City with a warning not to come back ever again.

But no, the more they pursued, the faster he fled.

Even when the cop smashed into him with his bicycle, when they both sprawled on the ground from the impact, it could have easily ended.

But it had not.

He attacked the cop and kicked him into submission.

He took the cop's gun out of the holster. He released the safety the way Marcos had taught him. He stood over the cop who lay powerless beneath him. And he pulled the trigger.

Cane his drug-lord boss would say, 'Hey, kid, you got big cajones. You passed the test. Now you full-time member of the gang.'

Marcos his one-time mentor would say, 'You gotta do what you gotta do. If you doan do it to them, they gonna do it to you.'

Anthony Boner his one-and-only real friend would say, 'See what I tried to tell you, man? You trapped no matter what you do. Me, I tried to rat Cane out to the cops and one a them ratted me out to Cane. Can't win."

Rachel Shaw the girl he worshipped from afar would say something to comfort him, he didn't know what. She was so clean and so pure she would never understand why men acted like they did but she would always forgive him.

His daddy would say, 'You shot 'im. He dead? Why'nt you pump another cap in his head? You some kind a 'puta? Whass a matter wid you?'

His mommy would say nothing but open her arms and wrap them around his little body and nurture him but she was no where near enough to help him now.

Rory Valquez pulled the revolver from where he had tucked it behind his belt over his underwear.

It felt cold even in his hot-box. It felt hard. He sniffed the barrel and smelt cordite.

It smelt like death.

But it wasn't.

Rory Valquez knew the cop he shot could die from loss of blood or shock but he did not shoot to kill. He shot to miss.

Only he and the cop knew the truth.

BACK-FLASH (Rory's Ticket to Santana)

"Okay, kid, this here's the deal," Cane said as he accosted Rory Valquez on Plues Street in one of the death-zones in Belize City one sun-hot morning.

Cane's driver braced Rory, hands on the hood of Cane's Cadillac Esplanade, looking for drugs he shouldn't have or firearms that might pose a clear and present danger.

"You gonna get your auntie outta here first thing t'morra. She drunk, she high, she so wired think she can fly. You gonna take a little trip to Santana Caye and chill her out. You unnerstan?

Here's start-up money, my little man, but this ain't no holiday. I got you a place, ain't no Radisson Hotel neither, know what I'm sayin', but it's safe and it's a chance to get your shit together what with your friend's drownin' and all. Broke my heart about your friend, got my boys out lookin' for who done it. We get the mofer you got first dibs to off 'im, unnerstan?

We doan have much bidness on Santana, usta be too small to bother, but it's growin' real fast, so you take care a your auntie and sniff around, make some friends, start doin' some bidness. Freddy be your contact, 'kay? Once a week. Doan go lookin' for 'im. He find you. You get all the weed you need for you and your auntie but check out the market for coke and meth and shit like that, unnerstan? Jus' tell Freddy. This you chance, my little man. This here's your opportunity to succeed."

The next day Rory got his auntie on the first water-taxi from Belize City to Santana Caye. She was un-responsive for the most part but burst into profanities from time to time as the water-taxi skied over the waves of the Caribbean Sea.

There was a taxi golf-cart waiting for them when they disembarked. The taxi skimmed over the hard-packed sand roads, thudding when the driver could not avoid one of the many pot-holes scooped out by heavy rains.

Ronny Rubio was there to greet them when they arrived.

Ronnie was a two-bit hustler in his fifties making a dollar whichever way he could.

Born in Belize on the island, he entered the USA in his teens as an illegal immigrant, joined the first gang that would have him, did whatever it was they told him, served a four year stretch in the penitentiary, was deported, picked up by Cane in the City, served a three year stretch in Hattyville where, upon his release, Cane thanked him for being a stand-up gang-member by banishing him to Santana for life. It was better than being dead, but Rubio harbored ill-feelings.

"Got you a place all to yourselfs. Right over there" Ronny Rubio pointed to a shanty.

"Cane said take care a yous and I do what Cane tell me to do. This one got a propane fridge, kitchen and bedroom. There's a couch in the kitchen. Cane say you takin' care a yourselfs but you want anythin' I'll get one a the kids fetch it for you. He bring change back on what you order or I beat him good. You wanna tip 'im, thass you bidness.

So, ev'rything all right? All right." Ronnie Rubio flipped a key over to Rory. "They's a lock on the door that a monkey could open with one paw. Other'n that, I doan wanna know what you do or how you do it."

The shack was one of five shacks on stilts side by each on the lee-side of the island on Crown land that the Crown was not at that time claiming. Each shack had a staircase leading up to the front door. Rory's shack had a small verandah with two chairs sitting on it.

Rory did not notice the smell of garbage in the air or the accumulation of detritus surrounding the shacks. There was no municipal garbage pick-up on Crown property inhabited by squatters, but his Belize City neighbourhood stunk just as bad and looked even worse.

Big difference was, in Belize City, Rory was another slum-kid in a crowded room. On Santana, he had the key to his own shack.

In the City, Rory risked his life every day with nobody anymore to watch his back.

On Santana, looked like all he had to care about was his auntie. Cane had his back.

"Hey, Rubio." Rory called over his shoulder as he helped his auntie up the stairs. "Get that taxi back here, man, I wanna check Santana out."

Santana awakened hope in Rory. It was the closest he had come to feeling he had found a home other than San Bight.

SANTANA AND RORY

Santana was an hour by water-taxi off the coast of Belize from Belize City and a half-mile before the Belize Barrier Reef. A caye was a low-lying island and the word was pronounced 'key' as in the Florida keys. It was 9 miles long from point to point and 4 miles wide at its centre. Approximately one and a half miles at either end was uninhabitable, covered by mangrove swamps that anchored the caye on the sea-bed. Man-made paths cross-hatched these extremities and when the weather permitted were traversed by hikers and back-packers and bikers on beach-tires from the tourist world and natives of Santana.

The island was populated originally by Mestizos, native Indians from the Yucatan Peninsula, pushed off their land by Spanish Conquistadors and forced into exile. Their diaspora swept them south and many of them landed on the island later known as Santana Caye. Early settlers begat a second generation which begat another and so on and so on until the island was cleared and built upon and over time most of the mangrove trees were uprooted to allow docks to be built to allow fishermen to ply their trade.

Santana was re-claimed and designated a part of colonial Spanish Honduras. More wars ensued, more treaties signed and Spanish Honduras became British Honduras. As world-views changed and colonialism became a bad word, Britain, having sucked the life blood out of the mahogany trade, surrendered its claim and granted Belize independence in 1983.

The Brits never forgot Belize and stationed their troops there for another twenty years. The soldiers, on rotation, went back to the British country of their choice and told remarkable tales of a tropical country called Belize and a wonderful island called Santana Caye.

Soon American troops were training Belizean troops, the Americans happy to have a military-base only miles away from Cuba with sight-lines on the fractious Central American countries which ended at Panama, the gate-way to South America.

By word of mouth, the Americans identified Belize as a tropical country worth looking at and San Pedro on Ambergris Caye the place to go for a Caribbean holiday. Travelers and then tourists began to check it out and thousands of vacationers descended on San Pedro, leaving Santana Caye as a second choice.

None of this was conveyed to Rory as Charlie, his taxi-driver, took him on a tour of the island. What Rory saw, and what excited him, was a small, self-contained island with pastel-painted buildings no more than two stories high, clean hard-sand streets, electric golf-carts, dozens of bicyclists weaving in and out of golf-carts and slow-paced pedestrians wearing bright shirts and shorts and looking like they came from all around the world and mixed well with the dark brown, light brown, copper brown people of the island who wore bright shirts and shorts.

On the main drag he saw several hotels, snorkel, scuba and wind-surfing shops, restaurants advertising catch-of-the-day, retail shops and grocery stores but not like it was in Belize City where nearly every store on Albert Street and its side streets up to the canal and beyond was owned and operated by Indians, Pakistans and Taiwan and main-land Chinese all of whom had their own gangs and tried their best to keep Cane and his crew off their turf. They would whole-sale drugs off Cane but they wanted the retail business for themselves.

He saw one Rastafarian on the main drag, and he knew where there was one there would be others. He mind-checked the location.

Off the main drag there were two streets with restaurants and retail stores, a bakery and a couple Chinese take-outs.

On the lee side he saw the wharf where the goods were brought in and behind that the harbor where anchored yachts of adventurers from around the world bobbed up and down while those on board went ashore, spent a few days or more and moved on to the next stop on their Caribbean adventure.

A little past the wharf, Rory heard loud machine-noises he had heard before in some of the industrial areas of the City where he made many of his drug-related pick-ups and drop-offs.

When they broke through the sound barrier, Rory clutched Charlie's arm and asked him what made all that noise and Charlie told him it was the generator that provided Santana with all its electricity. And what would happen if the generator blew up, Rory wanted to know. Charlie said there are a few hotels on the island that have their own generators but for the rest of the island it would be a major fuck-up.

Two blocks south of the generators, Rory spotted his shanty and waved to auntie who maybe but not likely would be sitting on the verandah smoking some weed and generally enjoying herself, as he was.

Past that, Charlie the taxi-driver drove him south where some rich Belizeans lived and where some North-Americans and Europeans had bought property and had built or were building their retirement dream houses, and past that to New Town, a newly-developed residential area where many of the workers who served the owners of the downtown establishments and who had built and were building the houses of the new-comers could afford to live.

Past that, Charlie could not go. Rory wanted to know why not and Charlie told him that there were no roads, the whole southern end and the whole northern end of the island were mangrove swamps and there were no roads passable by golf-carts but there were man-made paths you could hike or bike in good weather.

Rory mind-checked that information.

Rory asked Charlie to take him around the coast again. He took a second look, marveling at the colours of the Caribbean Sea, the same sea he had been born beside, brought up with, swam in and fished. Somehow this sea looked bigger and brighter and better.

Charlie continued his guided tour and stopped when Rory told him to. Rory wanted to know what the building across the road was though it was clearly marked Police Station and Charlie told him that it was the Police Station. Rory asked him if that was the only Police Station on the island and Charlie told him that it was. Rory asked Charlie how many cops were stationed on the island and Charlie said eight or ten, depended on the shifts and the time-offs and Rory said something like Holy Cow.

The next day, Rory met with the Rasta guys in their cabana on the seaside in the inhabited north end of the island. They lounged on beach chairs on the verandah, smoking weed, laughing and talking amongst themselves. They were big men, dark complexioned, dreadlocks covered by long bright-coloured cotton hats. The older one, the Rasta he had seen on the street, had a straggly white beard. The other two were seasoned, not old, and clean shaven.

Rory easily picked up on the Jamaican intonation of their English because he had done business with Rastas in the city. When they had done talking, the old one said, "You look like a school-kid, man, sure you can get the shit we want?"

"Young. Old. Whass the diff? I get what you want cheaper'n you payin' now, man, who gives a shit. We gotta deal?"

They high-fived when the deal went down, the Rastas wondering whether one day they would have to kill the kid.

Rory sat back and sucked on a joint, holding it till he had to exhale or explode.

SCENE 8 (Meanwhile Back at the . . .)

The Superintendent opened his office door at the first knock and let Constable Emory Aguilar slip inside. The Superintendent motioned for Aguilar to sit down and waited till he sat, then took his place in the big chair in the middle of the expansive desk.

The Superintendent was wearing civvies, yellow t-shirt, well-worn blue jeans, old adida sneakers. His hair was still mostly black and curly, but the two-day growth on his face showed many white whiskers. Though overweight, he still conveyed strength, and in his presence one still felt his power. His eyes were dark and piercing but his lips were often pursed in thoughtful repose and laugh-lines spread over his cheeks when he laughed or smiled.

The Superintendent was at the cross-roads of his life and he knew it. He was at the threshold of fame and fortune, and if forced to pick between the two would take the money any time.

"So, amigo, we have something to discuss, you and me."

"Sir."

"You may call me by my first name, Emory, or should I call you Em as your friends do."

"Em's good. Roberto?"

"Robert's good, Em." The Superintendent looked across the desk at Emory Aguilar. Short in stature, Aguilar had the appearance of Mayan mixed with native Indian and old-world Spanish.

Aguilar had been in charge of the first search party, which had been split in two to approach the southern mangrove swamp from east and west. There was no known trail leading north out of the swamp, but Aguilar still plied on his 125 Honda motorcycle from one group of policemen to another.

Fatigue showed on his face and in the way he sat slumped on the chair but the Superintendent knew by his record and his 6 month experience working with him that Aguilar was a good cop, and, he hoped, an ambitious cop worthy of his trust.

"It's been a big day, Em," the Superintendent continued. "One of ours almost murdered. Kid on the lam. Armed and dangerous. Can't get much worse than that. All our officers at risk, and the public, too. Can't underestimate what a kid with a cop's service-revolver can do. What's going on between his brain and his trigger finger? So time's of the essence, Em."

Emory Aguilar nodded.

"You've noticed I'm in my civvies, no doubt. What I mean by that is I want this meeting off the record. Comprende?"

Aguilar nodded again.

"I'm going to say things to you that I never planned to say to anyone, but everything's changed since that kid went nuts today." The Superintendent paused then continued. "I know you had the kid in your cross-hairs from the time he landed on this island. Good police work, Em. I know that he made a drug deal the day after he landed because you reported it to me and I know he started thieving about a week later and I have a pretty good idea who he thieved and what he got. Right? So you were waiting and watching and when you thought it was time to bust him you busted him. Right? Then things went wrong, wasn't any of your fault or your men. Things just got fucked up. Right?"

"That's right, Robert. Things got all fucked up and David almost got killed. Now we gotta take care a that . . ."

"Okay, Em, I'm with you all the way. You heard what I said today before you went out?"

"Yes, sir."

"Did you understand?"

"Yes, sir, you didn't say it but you said it best he disappear. Best the kid just not be there no more. Got away to the City, maybe drowned, who knows?"

"You agree with that?"

"Yes, sir," Em replied, leaning forward, raising his voice a little.

"Well, we'll come back to that, Em. In a minute. First let me tell you what I've learned today 'cause it's changed things even more." The Superintendent held up his hand to stop Aguilar from speaking. "Hold on. Let me tell you what I've learned.

First of all, gotta phone-call from Queen Street Division in the City. Chief's a friend of mine. When they got the description of the kid they knew right away who he was. Name's Rory Valquez, not Mike Tyson like he called hisself here. Dragooned by Cane, the drug-lord. You know Cane?"

Yes, sir. Ev'ry cop in Belize know Cane. He one bad dude that one."

"You know 'dragoon'?"

"No, sir."

"Means taken away from home and forced to work for Cane and his gang. That means the kid works for Cane. That means that punk-kid whatever you call 'im is here for one reason only. An' that's why you couldn't find out who fronts the kid, right? They work for Cane, they pros, that's why. Know all the ins and outs . . ."

"That's right, sir. Never could figure who was bringin' the stuff in, where they met, all of a sudden the kid's dealin' and we doan know what happened. Thass why I said bring 'im in. Thought we could beat some answers outa him . . ."

"Bad news, Em. Really bad new," the Superintendent interrupted, "'cause that means Cane's got Santana targeted and that means he's planning to take over the drug bidness on Santana and that means we be in deep shit 'cause we can't handle the trouble Cane'd bring here, comprende?

We got our Rasta guys and our local boys but Cane come here we got nothin' but trouble and I mean capital T, comprende?

"No, sir. Not capital T."

"I mean Cane wants this place he can take it any time he likes. He got machine-gun totin' nigger mother-fuckin' killers on his payroll. Only reason he's not here now 'cause he figured it's not worthwhile, risk not worth the profit. But he sent his kid here to do bidness and like you said now you know where the kid got the drugs from."

"Yes, sir. Now I see what you gettin' at. Cane come here, ain't just David Usher gets shot dead. He's gotta clean the island up, get ridda old arrangement, start fresh with his own men, an' that doan 'clude the likes of me and you."

"You got it. We can't let Cane come dancin' in here bringin' big city crime to our island. The kid can't get caught 'cause he gets caught Cane's got the money and connections to let him walk and Cane's just sittin' back smilin' and waitin' to send the big boys in. Then the shit hits the fan . . ."

"And hits our faces," Aguilar added.

"Yes, Em, yes. And more than that. Just when Santana startin' to grow, Cane moves in an' scoops the profits. Them's our profits, Em. We earned 'em. We deserve them. We gotta drag Santana into the real world but we gotta do it gradual, step by step, and keep control, that's the key, Em. We gotta keep control.

And thievin's same as drugs, Em. You know that. You gotta have thieves so we can say we doin' our job but you gotta pick and choose and make sure you get your per-cent. And look at that kid when he get here. Goes wild. Thievin' every day like he din't have to pay to thieve on Santana. That's why we brung him in, right, put a little beatin' on him and wise him up to the ways of Santana. Now if he goes free he's laughin' at us, little prick.

So, I got a proposition for you, Em. Take it or leave it. Leave it, no problem. No penalty. Just walk away.

Here's what I'm thinkin': the kid can't just disappear the way I say it to the guys, okay? Not the way I tole it today. 'Disappear' the way I say it today mean beaten up till the kid's dead, okay, but no one knows what blow killed the kid, right, so no one has to feel guilt he killed the kid, right, but three or four guys know the kid was killed, right, and that's okay long as no one's askin' any questions, but say someone like Cane wants to know who killed the kid or who ordered the killin' of the kid, any one of our guys can be made to talk, right, and we're back in the shit again, Cane's gonna start gunnin' for us.

No. We need one guy, one guy alone, can kill the kid.

Can that guy be you?"

Aguilar turned his neck around, hearing the bones crack. With his fists half closed, he faked blows to an imaginary torso, twisting his shoulders for maximum impact. He shut his eyes and opened them again.

He was stunned at what the Superintendent was telling him. He had no idea except by rumour and innuendo that the Super was on the take, and now he was being offered a share of the profits. It was like the sea-lottery his people gambled on. It was like the pot of gold at the end of the rainbow the old folks believed in.

"Tell me what you got for me, Robert. I like what you say, answer's yes."

"You can do it? No group beatin', jus' you, mano a mano?"

Aguilar looked at Superintendent Reyes and nodded.

"You done it before?"

Aguilar nodded.

"Gun or knife?"

"Knife."

"Front or back?"

"Both."

"What's the difference?"

"Front. Better lookin' in his eyes."

"When was this?"

"Guatemala. You know I born Guatemalan. It's in records. On the guerilla side, 'gainst the guvment. Sometime hand to hand with bayonets. Sometime from behind slit the throat. Sometime mano a mano, so close you smell his shit. Yeah, I done it."

"Need help?"

Aguilar shrugged. "Just a satchel."

"Satchel for?"

"The parts."

"Parts?"

"A the body. Gotta get rid a the body."

"Okay," the Superintendent said, taking a sharp breath. "Here's my info. When you guys were out looking, I got a call . . ."

"Rubio?" Aguilar guessed. Rubio was a well-known low-life slum-lord, detested by the cops on the island and even the friends he hung with but an important source of information.

"Yes, Rubio."

"What that rat's ass want?"

"Told me where the kid's hiding. Told me 'xactly where's he hidin' in the mangroves."

"You believe Rubio?"

"Not much. Not often. But this time, yeah, I believe 'im.

Rubio's the kid's landlord. Said Tyson or Rory, whatever, hung out with one kid special, a kid his own age, went fishin' with 'im, thieved at night with 'im, smoked weed with 'im, done some girls with 'im. So Rubio brought the kid in for a little talk. Hadda cut two pinky fingers off before the kid ratted out his buddy. And . . ."

"What knuckle?"

"What knuckle of the pinky fingers? Think he said first knuckle. Why?"

Aguilar made a snorting sound as if he were about to spit. "Not vera good friend, first knuckle. Good friend take two knuckles before he squeals. Really good friend lose the pinky on each hand before he spills everything. Best friend dies.

So where's the kid's friend now?"

"At the doc's office havin' his pinky fingers re-attached."

"Okay. I'gree. We know where he's hidin'. What now?"

SCENE 9 (Slow Cooking)

Rory Valquez spent the rest of the morning and the afternoon cuddled in a fetal position in his hidey-hole, parched, panting and sweat-hot.

He had been out with his new buddy, Ryan, who made him think of his old buddy, Anthony. He had been drinking rum and coconut milk and smoking weed till late at night, then smoking weed with his auntie before he even peed, then being rousted out of his shack and chased into his hidey-hole in the mangrove swamp.

Although very hot, he shivered in his shelter, wishing he had prepared for this occasion the way he had planned with a reserve of water bottles and dried fruits and a plastic hose for better breathing.

As morning turned to afternoon and noon to dusk and dusk to night, Rory crouched in his hidey-hole, crimped in all sides by corrugated metal getting hotter by the minute and giving off a corrosive smell not unlike baked flesh sprinkled with sizzling battery acid.

Minutes and hours tick-tocked away.

Thoughts and images boiled in his brain bubbling up snap-shots and memories, thoughts and dreams that tumbled about in his mind like a crazy kaleidoscope:

Stomach rumbling, he sniffed fried chicken and cow-foot soup and rellano, licking his lips like he licked them in the hot-spot, Rachel serving, leaning over to ask him if he was satisfied;

Sleeping on the floor in his aunties' apartment, shivering in the cold, contagious air rising from the filthy canal water where Anthony leapt into the dirty water and swam out to the Caribbean sea;

Coal-pot flickering in his shanty by the sea watching his daddy beat his mommy while he huddled in a corner with his brothers and sisters;

Running naked on the beach, breathless with excitement, pursued by his brothers and sisters who laughed and hooted as they ran after him;

Creepy crawling with Ryan on Santana, scooping wallets and jewelry, i-pods, cameras, blackberries, throwing most of it into the water by their Crown land shanties;

Crying as Marcos threw him into the truck of a car and sped away to the City;

Standing in front of schools and churches, crack houses and whore houses, waiting for the contact to arrive, drugs for cash;

Running with Anthony, rolling drunks, snatching purses, drinking rum in back alleys;

Fighting his daddy with bare fists, wondering why his daddy liked to hurt him, crying with fear, crying with frustration, crying with anger as his father taunted, "C'mon, Mike, gimmee your best shot, what d'ya got, Mike? That all you got?";

Listening to Anthony talking, telling him about Cane, about the gang, about getting out;

Jumping back as Cane crashed his cane on the table, sending bottles and glasses crashing to the floor;

Sharing weed and chicks with his Rasta brothers on Santana; laughing at the cops; checking out the island;

Going to visit Rachel in the City, flush with money—"Rachel ain't here no more, man, gone back to school in America";

"Rachel ain't here no more, man, takin' care a her mother in Santa Elena";

"Rachel ain't here no more, man, got pimped up and moved to Mexico";

"She some sweet pussy, man, you gotta get you some a that."

Running back to the water-taxi; running back to his shack; running, running, always running . . .

SCENE 10

By six p.m., the Superintendent had 12 more men added to his search-force, making a total of 20 under his command, and had been advised that Captain Raphael Louis from the Lady Ville detachment in Belize City would be arriving first thing in the morning to take charge of the operation.

The Superintendent walked to the door where the entire force was waiting for him to address them, opened it a crack and called out, "Constable Aguilar, a word, please."

When Aguilar stepped into his office, the Superintendent said, "Shut the door and sit down, Em."

Emory Aguilar shut the door, crossed the room and sat down.

"We got one chance, Em. One chance only. Captain Louis is coming in early tomorrow. Means we gotta get it done tonight. You okay with that?"

"Tole you I was okay."

The Superintendent noted the attitude and filed it away.

"Okay. At 2200 hours under your command you will deploy 15 men down the southern pathway past where we know the kid is hiding. Keep them on the path for at least a hundred yards, then turn 'em over to Constable MacKenzie with orders to intensify the search as per routine search procedures. Then drop back and position yourself as close as possible to the kid's hide-out. If the kid breaks out, you know what to do. If he doesn't, the men will re-convene by the airport, take a break, and repeat the maneuver at midnight.

In the meantime, for appearances, I'll post two men at the west end of the mangroves and two men mid-way to prevent the kid from breaking through the middle. It will be assumed that you will be watching for a break-through at the east end, which you will.

If the kid doesn't make a break the second time, you will initiate contact. Is that clear?"

"Yes, sir."

"Okay, let's ride this horse to the finish line," the Superintendent said.

SCENE 11

Rory Valquez pissed his pants a few hours after he found refuge in his hidey-hole and sometime in the afternoon defecated in his blue jeans, struggled out of them, turned them upside down and let the feces drop in a corner.

The smell made him vomit.

By night-fall, dehydrated and prostrate from the blazing sun that heated his hidey hole like an oven, he hallucinated, convinced that cannibals were after him, wanting to tear him apart and eat him alive; his mother had warned him that he was marked by the devil and the devil would seek him out.

In turns lucid and watchful, delirious and crazed, he began to scratch at his arms and his chest and his neck till the flesh bled, then he began to pull at his hair till his fingers yanked tufts from his scalp and his head pounded with pain.

At this time, he began talking to himself, sometime admonishing himself for past crimes and misdemeanors, chuckling at recollections of Arnold and Ryan, crying like a little baby when his daddy struck him, sending him skidding across the floor.

He made-up rhymes like, 'Ryan, Ryan, why're you cryin'' 'Look a me, man, Mike Tyson's dyin'' and 'Rory, Rory, thass the story, Rory, Rory, you'll be sorry'.

Rory Valquez felt the tremors in the ground from the pounding of the search-party's boots and snapped into consciousness again, fumbling for his revolver, grasping it tightly, resolved this time to kill or be killed but then, as the cops passed by, slipping back into psychosis. He began babbling incoherently, snorting and yelping as images presented themselves to him.

Outside in the darkness, wearing his camouflage fatigues, face blackened, Emory Aguilar heard the sounds resume after the second march-by.

The kid made no effort to escape.

Aguilar had no time to lose.

He crept up to the entrance of the hidey-hole and initiated contact.

"Rory Valquez, that you?" he hissed into the opening of the hidey-hole.

"Stay back, stay back, doan move a crack," Rory answered.

"Rory, that you?"

"Rory, Rory, thass the story."

"C'mon out, man. We wanna help you."

"Wanna help me, go way. Leave me 'lone."

"Can't leave you 'lone. You know that, Rory. C'mon out. I'll take care of you."

"You take care a me? Take care a Rory?"

"Yeah, man. I take real good care a you. But first, you gotta give up the gun."

"Doan got no gun, man. Promise you that. Lost that gun, man, runnin' away. That cop okay?"

"That cop's okay, Rory. Said you coulda killed him, but dint. That's good, man. That's why we wanna help you."

"Okay, I'm comin' out. Don't shoot."

"No shootin', man. Promise."

Rory eased his way out of his hidey-hole, pistol clutched in his right hand, ready to kill the intruder, the man who had pursued him from the day he was born. With his head and shoulders outside, he said, "Doan got no pants on, man."

"That's okay, man. C'mon out." Aguilar was crouched three feet away from the opening.

"First, show me your gun and throw it away."

"You promise you lost the cop's gun?"

"Promise."

"Okay, then." Aguilar knelt on his knees and unbuckled his gun belt. "I believe you, man. You watchin' me? Look." He flung the gun belt with the gun in the holster as far away as he could. "Now. c'mon out, kid."

Overhead the clouds drifted by and let the moon illuminate the mangroves.

Rory inched further out of his hidey-hole, lifting his eyes skyward, marveling at the beauty of the night.

Emory watched as Rory emerged from his hiding place, noting that Rory had David Usher's service revolver clutched closely to his thigh.

Rory wobbled to his feet, head spinning, trying to focus on the man he planned to kill.

Emory stood up and embraced Rory, pinning Rory's right arm to his side, his hand still clenched on the butt of the revolver.

Emory drew the 8" bayonet from its scabbard strapped on his waist.

Pulling Rory closer till they were face to face, nose to nose, lips almost touching in a kiss, he thrust the blade of the bayonet into Rory's intestines, sliced upward through his stomach and with a grunt jabbed under the rib-cage cutting through vital organs.

Rory died hugging Emory, blood flowing from his eyes, ears and mouth.

It was the hug Rory had been waiting for all his life.

The revolver fell from his hand.

SCENE 12 (Preparing the Body for Burial)

Emory Aguilar dragged Rory Valquez' dead body five feet to the swamp water, quickly stripping off Rory's clothes, frisking the clothing, especially the jeans which he had scooped out of the hidey-hole, discovering a lump in one pocket, pulling it out to find a wad of American money in his hand. He stuffed the roll into his own pocket and jammed the clothes into one of the satchels

Next, he shoved Rory head-first into the swamp until Rory's back and shoulders floated on the water. He pulled his ivory-handled switch-blade from his side pocket, pushed the release button that flipped open the well-whetted six inch blade and locked it in place, straddled the body and with one steady motion slit Rory from crotch to sternum.

Cutting and scooping out Rory's entrails into the swamp water, satisfied that the guts would be gone by morning, Aguilar hauled the body back from the water to dry land and butchered it.

He severed the calves from the knee-bone on both legs and sliced the arms from the shoulders. He snapped the fore-arm from the upper-arm by putting the arm-elbow down on his bended knee and leaning on it till it cracked. He used the switch-blade to cut away the tendons.

He had to roll the body over to cut the skin and flesh away between the thighs and the waist; then used his bayonet to hack through the pelvis, finishing the job with his switch-blade and brute strength, cracking bones with his bare hands.

He chopped off the head with his bayonet, yanked it up by the hair and spit in Rory's face, whispering, "You shoot my friend, puta. Go back where you belong. Go to Hell."

He stomped on the rib-cage, smashing it into skin-covered fragments and severed the back-bone so it could fold over the ribs.

It took two trips carrying his satchel to the near-by garbage dump where he threw its contents into the garbage dump's burn-pit.

SCENE 13 (Wrap Up)

The Superintendent and Constable Aguilar conspired in the shadows behind the police station.

"Good work, Emory. You more than met my hopes for you, mi amigo. Now get home and get some rest.

I've called for a patrol boat to pick up the kid's aunt. She's a handful. Strung out like a tight wire. Gonna have 'er escorted to Cane's turf in the City. There's gotta be a connection between her and Cane. Family, who knows? No sense pokin' the hornet's nest."

Aguilar waited while the Superintendent reached into a pant pocket and pulled out a packet of chew-tobacco. He watched as the Superintendent rubbed his gums and left a plug between his front lip and bottom teeth.

"We'll announce tomorrow we've been unsuccessful and have reason to believe the kid got off the island and has found sanctuary in the City. We'll keep that other kid, what's his name, Ryan, as a material witness or obstructing justice, something. Like a red heron, know what I mean? When we finish with him that kid ain't gonna talk to nobody about nothin'

When Rory don't show up in the City, Cane'll know what we done. He'll know we're serious. I'm countin' on him to back-off for a spell, forget about Santana as a new market. I'm not sayin' we'll scare him off. You and me both know how hard he is. I'm jus' sayin' it'll buy us a little time to solidify our position on the island.

You gettin' all this?"

"Got it, Sir," Aguillar said curtly.

Superintendent Reyes the Third narrowed his eyes, staring through the shadows at the man who had killed for him.

"Sure you do," he said.

SCENE 14 (Wrap Up)

Before dawn the next morning, Cane was awakened by a persistent tapping on the front door of his apartment. Cane lived on the second floor of the three-unit apartment building he owned in the Quinto Harbour area. He slipped out of the bed in the guest room and quietly made his way to the door, gun in hand.

"Talk," he whispered hoarsely.

"Boss, it's me. Marcos. Gotta talk, right now."

Cane padded over to the door of the master bedroom, knocked and went inside.

"Okay, baby. Time to get up." He waited for a moment before he pulled the sheet off the woman curled up and sound asleep in bed. He shook her by the shoulder, waking her.

"Whassup, baby," she said.

"You're up, thass whassup," he answered. "Get your things and get out, right now. I'll phone later."

"C'mon in, Marcos," he gestured for Marcos to enter as he gave the woman a little shove in the behind to move her along.

"Sorry to bother you, boss," Marcos said, getting right to the point. "Cops dropped off Esmeralda in front here 'bout half a hour ago. Tried to get her calmed down a bit but she strung out, man. What'dya want me to do?"

"'Bout Esmeralda?"

"Yeah, well, that too."

"Get 'er fixed up, then send someone with her to one a my apartments over on King St. Keep her happy for a few days. Keep her away from me till I figure what I'm goin' do."

Cane opened the refrigerator door and pulled out a couple bottles of Belican Premium beer. Tossing one to Marcos, they both sat down at the kitchen table.

"So, Santana's on your mind. Whaddya think?"

"Think them cops over at Santana snuffed Rory is what I think."

"Why'd they do that?"

"Little thing like shootin' a cop, boss," Marcos laughed, "and somethin' else, I'm thinkin'".

"An' what'd that be," Cane rumbled.

"I be thinkin' they wasn't too happy 'bout him cuttin' in on local trade. He was a very active boy over there, boss. Said so yourself."

"'s right."

"So they be watchin' 'im, tryin' to figure out how come this kid's gettin' such good shit at them prices."

"And?"

"And they run out of time and patience. Freddy said the kid was outta control. So they busted 'im. Dint know he was gonna shoot a cop."

"One question I got: they know that boy's workin' for Cane before they snuff 'im or after he dead?"

"Thass a good question, boss. I'm thinkin' no way they's gonna kill that kid if they knowin' that kid's workin' for you, see what I'm sayin'. No, I'm thinkin' they find out after they kill 'im . . ."

"How?"

"Rubio, most likely, boss. Like Rubio hears what went down and he's like, Hey, Soup, you any idea what you just done? And when he finds out Soup says, Holy Shit and the first thing he thinks of is that kid's aunt may be Cane's kin, get her outta here, send her back home to Cane before he gets really pissed, yunnerstan what I'm sayin'?"

"Okay. We're goin' to play it like that, play it like Esmeralda's a peace offering. We'll step back a bit, maybe they'll relax, but there's gonna be a war, Marcos. You know that."

"I know that for sure."

"He wasn't kin, but he was my boy."

"That's right boss. Nobody fucks with them that's yours."

"He was a good boy, better than that other kid, Bonehead. That kid ratted us out."

"No doubt about that. Easy killin' that rat's-ass."

"Yeah, he was one crazy fucker wasn't he? Our boy I mean. Rory. 'Nother year I woulda made 'im a full gang member.

And thinkin' a that, you get on down to San Bight and bring me up another boy. Shop around. Bring me a good one. Like the one the cops just killed."

THE END

Paradise

She arrived at the airport at 7:00 a.m., one hour and 35 minutes before the flight, mindful that the ticket information had advised her to be at the airport at least two hours before the scheduled departure.

She'd wanted to arrive earlier (i.e. on time) but her mother, a seasoned traveler, insisted that it didn't really matter, and her mother had turned out to be correct.

She waited her turn in line, showed her ticket and passport at the airline check-in, had a medium-sized suitcase weighed and taken away, keeping a back-pack with all her toiletries in case anything went wrong at the end of the flight.

Her mother said she had packed far too much but she was determined to wear clean clothes and there was no way she knew to wash, dry and iron them herself.

She filled out the required forms for leaving the country, handed them in and cleared customs.

At security, she took off her shoes, emptied her pockets, and placed her backpack on the conveyer belt so it could be scanned and stepped through the x-ray arch without setting off any alarms.

There was an uncomfortable moment when the security woman asked her to open her backpack for inspection. She tensed up as the officer fumbled through her belongings, thankful that she hadn't packed anything of a 'personal' nature, relieved when the officer withdrew her hand from the bottom of the backpack with a mending-kit, acquiescing when told that the needles in the kit had to be removed if she were to be allowed to proceed.

She wanted very much to proceed, wondering at the same time what harm she could do with a couple of sewing needles, except, of course, to attempt to sew clothes, which she had never done before but thought it might be time to learn if she were every to become independent.

On board the airplane, she tracked down her row and seat number, sat, and waited patiently for take-off. The flight to Cancun was uneventful. A large, rumpled man sat in the aisle seat in her row but there was no one in between the rumpled man and her window seat so there was ample room for both of them. Neither seemed inclined to converse. She was grateful she did not have to answer such questions as, 'Where are you going?' followed up by, 'What are you going to do when you get there?'

The plane arrived in Cancun on schedule. She shuffled off the plane in her turn and went through customs like a robot, offering her passport and customs declaration sacrificially, pleased when they were accepted.

She stood at the carousel watching for her luggage, noting the similarities in the suitcases that whirled around the carousel, retrieving her medium-sized piece of luggage, adjusting her backpack before she walked through the cavernous but crowded airport exit.

Her mother had warned her what to expect when she arrived, and a website she had visited described the scene to a "T", but it was nothing short of overwhelming when the shills for taxis, shuttle buses, tours, hotels and time-share condominiums descended upon her.

She spotted a booth against the far wall identifying itself in English as Shuttle Bus Tickets/Tourist Information. She honed in on the booth, cutting diagonally across the traffic, leaving the shills in her wake casting for other tourists.

She knew exactly where she wanted to go and thrust the 3x5 inch index card with the hotel's address and section number clearly written. The clerk in the booth punched in her ticket and pointed to the waiting area for the shuttle service. When he turned his bright smile on her and began to explain the deal he could offer on new condominiums, she held up her hand to stop him and moved on. The last thing she wanted was a time-share in Cancun.

True to her expectations, Cancun was big, fast and entirely uninviting. Her little downtown hotel was an oasis where she took her meals and rested, venturing out only to locate the bus terminal and purchase her ticket to Chetemal the day after her arrival.

She enjoyed the 5 ½ hour trip from Cancun to Chetemal, partly because the bus was big and spacious with a toilet at the rear which she hoped she would not have to use but was comforted by, and partly because it got her moving again, out of Cancun toward Belize, her ultimate destination.

The bus stopped briefly in Playa del Carmen, again in Tulum, and then headed south until four lanes gave way to two lanes as the traffic thinned.

At the border town of Chetemal, the bus driver advised the passengers in Spanish and English to disembark. She claimed her luggage from the bus and stepped back, momentarily unsure what would happen next. She knew what she thought should happen but it hadn't happened yet and she was at a loss.

A thin, dark-skinned man called out in English that the bus for Belize City with stops at Corozal and Orange Walk was leaving in 45 minutes. She bought a ticket and filled out the customs' declaration for entry to Belize.

The bus, a dilapidated old Blue Bird school bus that she recognized from her hometown in Brantford, Ontario, rattled a few miles till it stopped at Mexican Customs.

After clearing customs, the passengers filed back on the bus and were driven a few more miles to Belizean Customs. Four passengers were denied entry because they did not have the proper paper work. She wondered how people could travel without the proper papers.

Several hours later she arrived at the Bus Terminal in Belize City.

She was prepared for this part of the journey. She hired a taxi to take her directly to the Caye Caulker Water Taxi Terminal. Once there, she bought a ticket, waited in line and boarded a forty-five passenger open boat called Serendippity.

The 45—minute boat ride was the most fun she'd had since leaving Toronto. The sun burned in a bright blue Belizean sky and the boat manufactured a strong breeze, riffling through her hair and spraying her face with foamy salt water.

It was late afternoon when she scrambled out of the boat, retrieved her bags and walked down the dock to the shoreline, her bags going clickity-clack as the wheels bounced over the wooden slats.

She had realized by then that she had brought too much stuff with her, a back pack would have been sufficient for such a short stay, but she refused the offer of a taxi-driver who gestured toward his golf cart, and when a young man approached her with a cart attached to his bicycle she shook her head. She dragged her bag along the path parallel to the shoreline. It was hard work but she knew exactly where she was going.

The path was not too busy, though bicycles and golf carts whispered by. Young tourists with backpacks passed her and men, women and children whom she assumed were Caye Caulkerans walked this way and that, some light brown, some dark, some almost a yellowish colour whom she surmised where Mestitzos, the original inhabitants of Caye Caulker.

She checked into her hotel and was directed to her cabana, fifteen meters from the sea. It was what she had expected and would do fine.

She showered and changed into clean clothes, then made her way up to the patio restaurant-bar and ordered a rum and pineapple. Her waitress, a dark brown woman with large buttocks, round belly and large breasts, smiled as she delivered two rum drinks, declaring that it was happy hour and drinks were two for one.

Ice cubes jingled in the glass as she lifted the drink to her lips, watching the condensation form and run down the glass when she placed the drink back on the table. The sun settled fast and before she was ready for it, night fell. Lights twinkled on the patio.

Bob Marley tunes played in the background. The waitress returned to check on her and chatted about Caye Caulker, a gold-plated tooth flashing in the semi-darkness.

A tanned white man with white hair and a bushy white beard sat two tables across from her. He seemed to know everyone and engaged the waitresses and other customers in easy-going, bantering conversation. She wondered whether or not she should speak to him and decided not. He would only ask her who she was and what was she doing there, and these were questions even she could not answer with any forthrightness.

She ordered another round of rum and pineapple, sipping slowly as she settled back in her chair, closing her eyes for a moment, inhaling the clean air, feeling the sea breeze tickle the hair on her arms.

Then, on a whim or a fancy or a wish, she picked up a drink and stepped from the patio and settled herself on a deck chair on the beach, illuminated by an outside hotel light, darkness around her, full moon behind clouds.

She listened to the water tinkling on the shore line and heard in the distance the muted crash of waves breaking on the barrier reef.

Suddenly, startling her, a little man stepped in front of her, only feet away. He had a large, buffalo-sized head on a body probably two inches shorter than her 5'6". He wore his hair in dreadlocks that looked all—the—world like a buffalo in molt. His skin was chestnut brown in the lamp light, the colour emphasized by the white t-shirt hung loosely on his slight frame. He wore baggy blue shorts and stood before her barefoot.

He addressed her in a language she at first did not understand, although she recognized some English words. Then, he shifted into straight English, telling her how pretty she was and how much he wanted to know her.

There was no one else around. The lights of the patio twinkled behind her. He moved toward her in a shuffling movement, backed up, lifting his arms at the same time as if trying to fly, all the time talking to her, repeating how much he would like to know her.

She didn't know what to think. Didn't want to think. Watched the little man with the big head shuffling toward her, then back up, then shuffle forward again, arms raised level with her shoulders, flapping.

He continued talking to her, now in English, then in a language she began to recognize as Creole, a mixture of English and Spanish and African dialects she had read about before her journey. She adjusted quickly to the lilt and cadence of his voice though she would not admit that she understood what he wanted.

She didn't know why when he reached out his hand she arose from the beach chair and accepted it. She felt the strength in his arm as he pulled her, slightly unsteady, to her feet.

He took her by the elbow and walked her beyond the circle of light and she let him lead her, stepping alongside him. They moved in tune with one another, past the hotels that ranged the road a short distance from the shoreline and the lapping water. They stepped off the road into a deeper darkness punctuated by kerosene lights and burn pits and an orange glow emanating from the windows of the houses on the lagoon side of the island.

In his shanty by the water, he undressed her in the darkness, chanting softly, soothing her with his now familiar language, touching her as she stood there still as her own silence. And then he wrapped his arms around her, lifted her and carried her to a corner where he lay her gently down. And then, in the pitch darkness, she felt him on her, in her, all around her.

Very early in the morning, moments before the sun rose shimmering across the dark sea water, he returned her to the deck chair on the beach in front of the hotel. She sat motionless, looking seaward, caressed by a slight breeze, startled only by the voice behind her.

"Everything all right?"

Turning slightly, she recognized the man she had seen on the patio the evening before, the friendly man with white hair and a bushy white beard.

"All right?"

"Yes, you know, you disappeared, you've been . . ."

"Everything's fine," she interrupted. "Don't worry about me. That's why I'm here. That's why mother sent me."

She turned away, closing her eyes to the blinding sun that warmed the breeze that touched her.

THE END

ACKNOWLEDGEMENTS

Many friends encouraged me in this endeavour but no one helped me more than
Shirley Howarth, the desk-top publisher of my travelogue
Think Belize!

CPSIA information can be obtained at www.ICGtesting.com
Printed in the USA
LVOW132048190213

320808LV00009B/966/P